I0662771

# WAKING OLYMPUS

## Book One of The Singers of the Dark

ISBN-13: 978-0-9944514-0-8

Dedicated to Rachel, Tristan, and Gavin. You inspire my efforts in all things.

# one

There had been no word or signal for so long, but he, for 'he' still thought of himself as flesh and blood at times, he would continue his duty. He took the usual daily readings, made any necessary slight course corrections, or repairs, then listened for a few minutes. There was nothing; across radio, laser, neutrino, or a dozen other modes, electromagnetic or exotic, the voices he sought still slept. He saw the terminator receding from the Western Sea on the world below. A new dawn was coming, a quiet dawn, like many before.

Once more he shut down his non-essential systems and drifted off to sleep waiting, perhaps in vain, for the world beneath to awaken, and, even though he was now just a machine, a ship, he still missed the wind and sky and the sound of human speech.

Far below on the cloud strewn world the sun was rising.

# two

Day 6, the month of Regin, in the year 635 of the Center.

He looked up, straight into a gust of wind whipping his face with the sharp sting of sea spray. It made him want to yell with joy for no reason. In his heart, there was a reason; this brief trip would make him a Wizard.

The bucking of the sea and ship and the waves all seemed a greeting, a joyous celebration of his life. Even against the mockingly sacred laws of Murphy, he felt nothing could go wrong now. Even with his infamous curiosity? He stopped a moment, just for an eye blink, squeezing out the saltwater. He'd be fine.

The last time he was at sea, he didn't quite remember. It was as if it happened to someone else. In a tale, he had no connection to it. It was just a story he told himself, that he came to the island as a refugee rescued from slavery, to study as a Wizard. A fairy tale. Literally *a fairy tale*, his mother told him stories like this, about children taken by the Wizards to learn the great secrets. He didn't remember her; he didn't want to, for now there was only the rise and fall of the ship, the spray, the joy of living.

He tried to hide the almost hyperactive need to rush from one side of the ship to the other like a small boy, in case he missed anything. His hands closed on the coarse wooden railing, slick with ocean spray, reddish yellow wood glistening in sunlight, on what he was told was the starboard side; such an odd term, no one knew its origin. In the distance the horizon pitched, the ship bucked, the sea like a vast creature was trying to shake the minor annoyance off.

He was standing on the deck of what was quite a small ship. The vessel was one of the biggest in Lind, which was the biggest of the islands in the Farrel Archipelago. That meant they didn't really come much bigger than this. His thoughts stopped as the ship came over a cresting wave and, for a moment, it seemed they were airborne. He saw deep blue sky over the bow. He became almost weightless. Then the crash, splash, surge, and heave as they hit the wave trough. Sea turned to white foam, suspended in mid-air, then thrown in his face. Wind and salt spray. Pure exhilaration!

The other passengers didn't share his enthusiasm. Most were ill below decks. He was perhaps the only passenger enjoying the experience. The sails overhead flapped noticeably, possibly because of improper trimming. The trade winds at this latitude normally drove towards the continent from the west instead of from the north like this wind.

The sea calmed a little. Enough time for him to look back at the drenched and dripping caravel. Its usual cargo safely stowed below. *Usual* for Lind was not the same as elsewhere; clocks, mechanisms, medicines, specialized tools, and so forth. Merely a fraction of what his people truly excelled at, the rest often embargoed.

The dolphins no longer shadowed the vessel. They had given up mocking the wooden hull with their effortless grace and speed. Now the ship only had the companionship of a few flying fish; sometimes one would dart out of the water, fins flapping, sounding like a cicada in flight, as if the sea wanted to remind them it was alive. Only a few of the fish flew high enough to land on the deck as it dipped and flew over the waves, casting spray over everything. He would rush to where one had fallen, like a stricken, slick bird. Pick it up, a quick examination, forming an indelible image to think about later, then throw it overboard; returning it home. Life aiding life.

The entire ship was built from an amber-red colored timber, which he realized with a blush he didn't know the name of. There was a rough hewn impression here and there, like an experiment, a giant carpenter's first effort. They still knew so little about sailing, so that each new ship seemed like a step into the unknown.

Should he ask the captain some details about the ship, including the name of the wood? He was supposed to know these things. He should start behaving professionally. Though, he wondered, was being professional an act, or did it come from maturity? How was he going to manage this new magician's trick? He wondered about too many things. It was time to find out. He was almost a Wizard. He had completed his studies, although normally he was supposed to spend a year of apprenticeship to one of the Majors — Wizards of acknowledged skill and achievement. So close, it was almost impossible to suppress an elation greater than the thrill of riding the waves. When he finally became a Wizard, he could undertake more of his own projects, and there were so many things he wanted to explore. However, even then his vows would always tie him to the higher aims of the Center, especially direct orders, such as the ones he was now tasked to complete.

Once he was a Wizard he could decide to work his way up to becoming a sea captain if he wished. Since captains were also navigators, he could use his skills to make money or make discoveries for the Center. Mikel enjoyed learning new things, or rather it was an obsession, beyond mere liking, and the world was full of so many things to learn, discover, and record. They said he was *promising* back in Lind. His Mentor, Master Samuel, had said he was a fine empiricist but a better theorist, *creative* was the word he had used. His undergraduate work was worthy of a full Wizard. He wasn't supposed to hear that conversation, but he was testing a directional hearing trumpet he had made and...

"Just an accident," he said aloud.

But he was getting ahead of himself. *Don't be so impatient, you can't do everything.* The intersection of all of his mentors' wisdom distilled right there.

About him, he saw an almost universal seascape. It could have been anywhere. But this was the Western Sea of Neti. Waves cresting in a fresh wind below a deep blue sky, isolated ragged patches of cloud fleeing at right angles to their course. He judged that the wind must be faster at the altitude of the clouds. He remembered the kite experiments back in Lind when he was just twelve; it had been fun inventing techniques to measure the wind speed at the kite altitude. Finding out something new like that, it was a feeling nothing else could ever promise or deliver, such good times.

"So, boy! Got your sea legs yet?"

Mikel jumped. Caught daydreaming, again.

Captain Woran was a couple of centimeters taller than Mikel. Suntanned, he looked lean, cured like a piece of leather tailored to a purpose. He wore an earring in his right ear. Sailors wore one on their left ear when they first went to sea. Switching when they took their first command. He seemed about 45 years, black hair creeping down the side of his face, a touch of graying at the temples. A decent black beard rounded him out, white streaked and now flecked by salt. Sun blemishes beneath his clear blue eyes betrayed his age and experience. The total effect made him seem a pagan god of the sea.

"Yes, sir," he said.

"I remember when I was just out of training. Marvelous time, but you know when the sea gets into your blood you just can't stay away. Many of our captains were Wizards you know." He was distracted, but had to keep the customers happy in this rougher than usual weather.

"So I have been told. But I'm not sure I understand it"

"Well, Mikel. You learn astronomy and mathematics. Chemistry, biology, geology. I must confess I balked a bit at the quantum mechanics lectures. But most importantly…," he didn't finish it.

The great secret, secret lest it be polluted. The Method itself. More than a method, more than an art. As they say.

"And then, well, many want to — test the ideas, make their own observations. Contribute. *Explore*." He said the last word with emphasis and drama. There was blue fire in his eyes. Mikel's own skin tingled in sympathy. The captain turned to check on his men and women, which gave Mikel a chance to see the man rather than the 'force of the sea'. He wore a brown shirt, sleeves rolled up to the elbows, with red stitching crisscrossing and occasionally making intricate Celtic-like designs, as if either of them had ever heard of the Celts. His face was partly in shadow from the faded, salt crusted sky blue captain's beret, a style which had been fashionable a generation ago. Mikel could see on the captain's left forearm, partly visible, a stylized dragon. A symbol of the Center: a Wizard. Not all Wizards identified themselves that way or at all.

The captain noted his gaze. "And where are you off to, young one? What is your *grand* quest?"

"I have been instructed to research the trade routes east of Bethor."

Not for the first time, this mission made him lie to a colleague. He was told he would learn a great deal. This was not what he had imagined. His first accomplishment apparently was learning how to lie. He calmed his unease, remembering that he had not really lied, since it was true or half true. He had only told half the truth, the unimportant half. Seems he had also learned to lie to himself.

"I'm not actually a Wizard yet, still an Apprentice."

The captain nodded, aware that the missions were simply exercises to test the candidate's ability to think and not get lost. He muttered something about how Mikel should work hard and it being a valuable thing. Then he must have remembered his duties and lost interest in this youngster, wished him well, and wandered off yelling commands to his sailors.

What was his quest, anyway? Mikel pondered. It all seemed so vague. He had been called to the Center's ancient Main Hall eight days ago. The building that always suggested momentous actions and ideas to him and now he was heading to Bethor, of all places. It filled him with dread, and he was afraid to know why.

# three

It had only been three days since Mikel's advancement when Master Samuel came for him, about an hour after sunrise. He had just finished some physical exercises; yoga, then running, pushups. He didn't even regard the dawn swim as exercise, rather it was simply pure delight.

The hut that he rented from the Center for a pittance was at the top of the small green hill overlooking the deserted beach. No one else wanted it, too far to walk, too remote and alone. Perfect. The southern coast of the island here was divided up into small beaches separated by low sandstone headlands. It somehow felt homely and comforting.

He had planned to meet Mai and Dmytri at the old abandoned pier just a few hundred meters to the west. They would go fishing and later build a fire, or get distracted by something interesting. That was the "noplan" as he liked to call it. Mikel had made a clever fire-starting kit just for today. He thought he could even sell the idea to some merchants, or perhaps make them himself and export them. It could give him a supply of coin for his projects.

Master Samuel sometimes visited, but he had never come this early before. There was usually a period of grace after the apprentice had left mentoring and before beginning work on a small project, under the watchful eye of a Major. He had expected to have a month off. He guessed the visit was social and was very glad to see his teacher so soon. There were so many things to talk about.

"Master Samuel. How are you? What brings you out here?"

"Hello, Mikel. I am fine. How are you, young *Wizard*?" He smiled as he emphasized that last word with his resonant voice.

"But I'm not..."

"Pah! The apprenticeship is a formality. You've already turned in work that would have earned your medallion several times over and just call me Samuel from now on. You know those formalities get in the way." He grinned.

"I'm going out today with some friends. But I've got so many things to talk to you about. Theory and some experiments. I have had some great ideas..."

Samuel interrupted him, "Sorry Mikel, it will have to wait. I'm sure they are good ideas and normally I would like to hear them, however I have come on official business." He stood up as if to impress on the boy the seriousness of the message. "I have come to bring you to a meeting with the Council. They have some urgent things to discuss with you."

He saw the worried look on Mikel's face. The lad probably thought they were going to take away his advancement and bust him down to year one or even kick him out of the College.

"Don't worry, they just have an important task they would like you to do. We must go to the Center Main Hall by eleven this morning. If you do this well, and I know you will, then I think they will promote you directly to Wizard. But I don't think it is urgent enough for you to miss breakfast." He smiled reassuringly.

They sat and talked, shared some roasted shellfish that Mikel had cooked. He wanted to talk about ideas, theories, technological applications, and friends, but there was no time. Samuel looked up at the sun. "Ah, Mellis is getting high. Must be almost nine. We have to get going."

Mikel didn't have a clock, well he made an improved water clock, but lost interest after he saw some of the newer clockwork mechanisms. Some Wizards were using them to do computations. That possibility fascinated him. Next to that, the water clock looked uninspiring. About nine? The position of the sun seemed about right.

They traveled northwest over grassy hills to meet Dmytri and inform him of the change of plans before heading east into town.

Lind is the largest island of the Farrel Archipelago. Other islands stretch out to the northwest with decreasing size. The geology is odd, since the island chain is not volcanic and appears to be made of continental rocks. The archipelago is thought to be the remains of a small sunken continent that was subjected to sea level change. Supporting the idea is the fact that the surrounding seas are shallow. These seas are a rich source of fish. Dried fish was a vital food source and export in the hard, early years of the islands. These days, manufactured goods got most of the interest, but fishing was still important.

*Rainforest once covered the islands. The main island of Lind suffered extensive deforestation in the past, which only now was being restored. There are farms and settlements on all the major islands with certain islands specializing in produce and manufacture. Lind itself has the Center and the Larc.*

*Lind's administrative, political and academic capital is the Center. The Larc, to those who dig deeper, is the Lind Advanced Research Center, and that is about all that anyone will admit to knowing about it. The name "Lind" is commonly associated with the political capital, the Center, but it actually refers to all the inhabited islands in the archipelago. Many people use Center and Lind interchangeably. Even locals do it, adding to the confusion.*

*To the west lie the islands of Gowss, Laplas and Newton, with other much smaller islands named Alpha, Beta and so on. Beyond Epsilon Island is the Unknown Sea, believed impassable.*

This was Mikel's Unofficial Lind Tourist Guide; unofficial because he would get into enormous trouble if he mentioned the Larc in any document, so it existed solely in his head.

Mikel knew all this, having absorbed it at a ferocious speed since he had come to the island as a frightened, heartbroken orphan. He had been to Gowss and Laplas, but they didn't count for seagoing experience, as the water was shallow and usually calm. There were some islands that were off limits. You needed special permission to go to Newton, but he didn't know why.

When they finally reached the Hall, he saw an ancient building constructed out of a strange gray stone. He had seen it so many times since he came to his new home, yet it had never lost its mystery. Rescued from slavers, he had been so very lucky; sometimes he had flashes from those times before, sad and painful memories that he could never quite hold on to, like a dream that offends our sense of real so much that we banish it.

He had never set foot inside the Main Hall. The tough guards on the outside were the reason for that, though now they didn't seem as big or tough as they once did; especially when you knew them by their first names. Still, it was such a strange building, even after all the times he had seen it from the outside, and it was old. You could see that it was crumbling in places, yet it remained sturdy.

Samuel and Mikel stood before the building while Mikel built up his nerve.

"Mikel, I cannot come in with you. You must go alone. Chin up. I will talk to you after." Samuel left, ambling down the road, every step making Mikel feel more alone.

He approached the nearest of the two uniformed guards, who sat under a shaded canopy. A slight breeze blew the faded blue tassels, with rippling sine waves traveling along the canopy edge, enticing him into a comforting world of mathematics.

"Apprentice Mikel Peres to see the Council". He almost stuttered. He had met no one from the Council.

The guard was an old friend, Nils, a kindly aging fellow who always radiated good cheer. Though he tried to act stern, it was probably the reason they selected him for the job. He wore a very uninspiring blue uniform and hat with ragged gold trim. He looked Mikel up and down from his chair as if he had never seen him before.

"All right, Mikel. Wil can escort you inside. None of your usual shenanigans either. This is one place where curiosity really will kill the cat. Understand?"

Wil was always cheerful enough, but Mikel could never get away with anything with him. He had eyes like a hawk and seemed to sense the mischief in the students before they knew it themselves.

The guards knew him when he was a young college student wandering through empty, dusty streets after class. Always on the way to some adventure; usually ending up getting back to the dorms late.

Inside the building it was dark as night despite it being lit by the most sophisticated lamp technology and perhaps more. He thought he had made out some devices using the new gas lighting; he so wanted to investigate, but he had to behave himself here. Wil handed him over to a guard he did not know.

"Follow me." The guard said in an unfamiliar, deep voice.

They did not give his eyes time to adapt; he had to follow immediately.

"Why didn't they angle more external light inwards?" he said to no-one in particular. His guide would not answer, as expected. He was just analyzing to distract himself.

He thought if they had shafts that could let in light, they wouldn't have to light it artificially, or at least as much. Master Torrens had built perfect mirrors years ago, so the technology wasn't new, only expensive. They would only work at certain times of the day, so that wouldn't solve the problem. Then he remembered when he and Alice found an outcrop of mica and played with it. He thought if he could insert small flakes of it into a paint, then he could paint a tunnel to conduct light which would bounce off the reflecting mica flakes. That got him thinking. A light pipe? That would have interesting properties and uses. What would it look like with mirrors? What would be its limitations? How small could it be? Could it be a solid rod of glass using total internal reflection? He took every opportunity to look down side-corridors, hoping to glimpse one of the rumored miracles. He didn't see any of the experimental electric lighting that some whispered about, so perhaps it was still in R & D at the Larc.

Walking down the dim halls, he still felt an irrational desire to explore. Who knew what lay in some of the dark corners of this place? But he was being led now by the guard from just inside the door. This guide wasn't day-blinded and therefore had a great deal of control over Mikel and where he went. By the time his eyes had adjusted, he had entered a somewhat semi-circular room with tiers of seating. Like the contoured maps Master Marnath had devised, he vividly remembered her presentation of them. Here the contours formed a half of a descending cone, narrowing to where a speaker dais stood. Once there had been attachments for seating through the room, but now it was just rock and cushions. Someone had designed the room for acoustical reasons. He looked about to see how the echoing in the chamber was being controlled. Above, natural lighting came in through a bank of windows which seemed to use the latest in glass technology.

"Young Wizard! Come and sit."

"I'm not..." He said.

Mikel turned toward the voice and saw a gray-haired man standing by the dais. His voice had sounded far more powerful than he looked. The room was almost empty except about a dozen men and women seated in the front row. Then he saw the purple cloaks clearly. Elder Wizards.

They patiently waited while he walked the short distance to a chair placed before them. Sitting down, he was now face to face with the Elder Wizards. Close up, their robes didn't seem so fancy, and they didn't seem so lordly, but they had control over his future, and therefore deserved respect.

Master Sorgi was the one who had spoken, and Mikel knew Sorgi did not like sitting. He thought better when walking. It was common knowledge that in public ceremonies, Master Sorgi would not stay seated. But he was the Master Wizard, not just *a* Master but *the* Master, so no one was about to tell him to sit down. Meeting the Master Wizard was like meeting Zeus.

Why was he, of all people, talking to Mikel?

"Apprentice Mikel Peres. I know this is not normal procedure. I beg your indulgence. Although you are not scheduled to continue your work as an apprentice until a full-month has elapsed, an urgent matter has come up. Unfortunately, we need your services immediately. However, to make up for that, upon successful completion of this task, you will advance to Wizard ranking. We will also arrange for an extended period of supported research after your mission as compensation."

"I serve the Truth and the Way," he responded, mostly by instinct.

"Yes, yes. We know that." The Master said. "No need for those first year platitudes now," he said, annoyed.

He continued. "Right now, we need your perceptive and insightful view of things. We need you to be a seemingly casual observer. You have a knack for seeing things others don't. We need that. Ah, I'm getting ahead of myself. You know the Traders of the Plains? The plains that stretch east from Bethor into unknown territory in the east of Arva?"

"Yes, I know of them, but not really much about either the Traders or the Plains."

"Exactly our situation. We have only ancient records of them. The Traders could be valuable — trading partners. We often have occasional contact with them, but we don't have any substantial information. We need some preliminary information before we send a trade mission. I have a contact name amongst the Traders. It is a simple task though we need someone guileless who won't appear a threat. We want background information about their culture and trade routes. Be careful, we don't want to upset them. There has been a fair amount of foolish mistrust by both sides in the past that we are only now overcoming. Do as they ask and it should be trivial."

He shifted in his seat, then looked directly in Mikel's eyes.

"Now, about your primary goal, which must remain secret. During the last month, we have lost two of our agents while stationed in Bethor. We do not know what has happened to them or why. We don't want you to be an agent. You are simply to listen to rumors and ask about anything interesting you come across. Naturally, if you find anything of personal interest, record it and bring it back as well for our archives. We hope that as an apprentice no one will consider you worth troubling. Finding information about the Plains is your cover story, but still important. Finding out about what is happening in Bethor is critical. Just be eyes and ears and report back."

Mikel thought about it for a moment. "My inexperience probably counts against me since I am not familiar with the customs of the Traders, or even Bethor."

"True. But we don't want a seasoned traveller, we want someone who can see the situation in Bethor without bias. We also want you to evaluate what you hear around Bethor and to verify it. As a mere Apprentice people will understand your curiosity and incessant questions. Someone older and more seasoned will look like a spy."

That spoilt any sense of adventure he might have had. He hadn't considered that possibility.

"What kind of *information* do you want me to gather?" He was getting worried that this entire venture seemed ad hoc. No planning. So unlike the Wizards. Was he being chosen because he was so expendable?

"Just *eyes and ears*. Report what you see and hear. The cover mission, your meeting with the Traders about trade routes, is less important but is also required. We need that information. We have a contact who can quickly supply you with that information. Do you agree to this? Once committed, you cannot back out."

"Sure," Mikel said. Though his voice was very uncertain.

"Good, you will leave in a week. Before that, we will fully brief you. I will give you money, some standard supplies, and a choice of additional items. Remember, you can't take everything you want. You will be on foot. Pack light. That is all for now. Master Samuel will take on your preparation. Please make regular reports via our Trade Mission in Bethor if you can. Goodbye."

A deep raspy voice spoke in his ear. "Follow me, son." The guard.

The preparations for his mission took up Mikel's entire time for the next week.

He selected a set of instruments. A mini-sextant, oiled leather wraps to protect things from rain. Compass, abacus, string, rope, a measured piece of string with a small weight (used for precise timing and length), a sling, a small sword. He had practiced with the sword but knew that although he still had some skill with it; he had forgotten too much. Various cloths, chemicals, a few herbs, and medicinals, which with his understanding of their use would serve him well as a healer. A well-made pair of boots and a protective set of clothing. One small code book; a onetime pad. Also, a small telescope which he had made a couple of years before. Then essentials: a bedroll, basic cooking items, his fire-starting kit, a piece of waterproof canvas that could shelter him and fold to become his backpack, and a tent or bundle on his staff if easier. Some dried food. Finally, a small journal with ink and pen for recording his journey. Mai had offered him one of her bows, but he was a lousy shot with them. He preferred his sling, which he was — against all expectations — quite good at. Also, carrying a bow on his back, even unstrung, was not being inconspicuous.

The pack and outfit felt comfortable, but after a day's walk, he might think otherwise. He knew he was likely forgetting some important things and taking unnecessary items.

He had gone over the list of items several times. There were so many things he could add, but he could only carry so much and most of what he wanted was unnecessary. Master Samuel cast his eye over the pack, gave him a stern look, and removed some things and suggested others.

Mikel's greatest concern was that he was so out of practice with a sword that he would be easy game. Because of his concern, he practiced with a weapons master and added a small shield to his collection on her advice.

Master Samuel sent him off to the armorer who fitted him out with a set of light leather armor, with hidden thin stiff inserts of some material. They looked like cuttlebones. To prevent being easily stabbed in the back, he was told; he didn't ask about the *easy* qualification. He knew that protection could limit damage but not prevent it, the hope being that it would limit any damage to the merely *uncomfortable*. It looked great when the armorer's junior assistant put it on, though he knew he wouldn't look as good as her; she was familiar with it and confident. When he tried it on, the reddish brown leather squeaked, and it felt awkward and unnatural. The squeaks when he moved made him sound like a mouse. They oiled it, which helped, but the impression lingered.

"Wear some loose clothing over it." Suggested the balding armorer, speaking earnestly, his words seemed to be strengthened from a permanent ruddy glow in his face, looking as if he had just come from the forge and would pound him with a hammer if Mikel wasted his time.

"Remember, deception is a strength," the assistant added.

Hardly necessary, Wizards learned many magic tricks both to dazzle the ignorant and to train in manipulating human perception. After all, they weren't warriors.

By week's end, he thought he was ready — it wasn't true, of course.

Looking back on his preparations made Mikel feel cold and alone. He came back to the present with a start and saw that night was falling. The sea was much calmer, and the wind had eased. A member of the crew was making his way around the deck, lighting some strategically placed lamps. The stars were coming out. He examined the familiar constellations and the bearing of the ship and realized that the wind must have returned to its normal westerly direction. It was a smooth run downwind with a good sea. He brushed his chin with his left hand unconsciously and discovered a layer of salt and the beginnings of a beard. Being on the sea was like surfing, but without the feeling of being preternaturally clean or being in control. No golden seaborne inner glow here. He couldn't wait until they got to port and he could wash.

The Captain approached him again. He had been taking some measurements with a sextant. Not a straightforward thing while the deck still pitched from the trailing end of the rough sea.

"We are pretty much on course, about a day out of Bethor, by my estimate. I will know more accurately when I plot it," he said.

"Can you determine our longitude easily using Thaytan?" Mikel asked.

Thaytan, the Constant Star, was only a magnitude three star but maintained the same position in the sky always; it was hard to single it out for the untrained eye so it was essential to have an excellent knowledge of the night sky to see the star that didn't belong among the constellations. Stellar magnitudes follow a logarithmic scale, which meant that magnitude three stars were about 2.5 times dimmer in real terms than magnitude two, with the brightest being magnitude one. That meant that the Constant Star was two magnitudes, which meant 2.5 times 2.5, or 6.25 times dimmer than the bright magnitude one stars, roughly, and just as well human eyes were logarithmic so they could see and not be overwhelmed. Though it was probably the case that human logarithmic eyes were responsible for the logarithmic magnitude scale.

Astronomers determined the length of the year using the Constant Star, easier than using the sun or the planets. Using a modified sextant to measure the position of Thaytan and one or more other stars, it was straightforward to determine the latitude and longitude of any place on the Western Sea. It was said, many Captains could just look at the sky and tell you precisely how long it would take to make landfall and the true heading. All of this was second nature to Mikel and the Captain.

"Easy to determine the longitude and latitude, but there are winds and currents. But still not hard."

"What if Thaytan didn't exist? Or, for example, if Lind was on the other side of Neti?" Mikel was genuinely curious. He wondered if other cultures were stymied by their inability to determine longitude.

"Well lad, it is speculative. I would say it would be almost impossible to measure longitude without Thaytan. How would you tell? One could use the phases and movements of the moon to measure longitude, but it would be fiendishly complicated. The moon isn't always visible, even on clear nights. We should be thankful that Thaytan is in a geostationary orbit." Mikel nodded and had to agree. He pitied anyone on the far side of Neti.

The Captain touched his beret, to be polite, and then bid Mikel a good night as he retreated to his cabin to record the values from the 'chip log'.

# four

The morning was bright and clear. The wind behind them was warmer today, perhaps a sign that winter was truly gone. With luck, there would be no more cold snaps. It was one week into the month of Regin, mid-Spring, the month of Greening was already gone. It should be warmer by now. Many in Lind said the weather had been changing over the years, but he had seen no change over his lifetime. He was nineteen. Maybe it was too short a time to notice, or to fool yourself. The clouds to the east that morning heralded the approach of land, then came the comforting but soon annoying sound of seagulls wanting a feed. Later, the low, dim outline of a mountain range darkened the horizon. Soon they were a smudge of white tops with a green base. There were white seagulls poised in mid-air as if free from the world of sea and land, never having known the touch of gravity; dolphins raced ahead like a marine honor guard, and a white-green horizon. It was beautiful.

Some time after they passed the heads of the bay, he could see in the distance the slowly emerging shapes of ships, masts, squat buildings, temples, and a few spires. Bethor was the trading hub of the known world, which meant the western part of the continent of Arva. No one knew if there were people in the east beyond the Great Desert. Center ships visited the other known continent of Werrin, but found either it barren or semi-arid, and uninhabited. Lind now concentrated on setting up trading posts on the southern coasts of Arva. But everything still seemed to end up going through Bethor.

Bethor had riches and knowledge, and Mikel was eager to see the fabled Library and the Museum.

The city straddled a river called the Inda, which emptied into the Bay of Pennit. The Inda formed a delta on the eastern side of the bay with several tributaries throughout the delta. Bethor was known as the Blind Spot because the bay and river resembled an eye with Bethor on the optic nerve, as wryly noted by Wizards. Beyond the city was an imposing mountain range running north-south, snow capped — the Cantas.

The ship had already started maneuvering to head to the northern port, so he still couldn't see much of the city. He popped out his collapsible spyglass, but it couldn't resolve anything very well. Too far away; the scope was small, and the optics were probably not the best. The port itself was some distance to the north of the delta area, near the northeast part of the bay, which was about eight to ten kilometers in diameter and circular, but eroded and missing a western arc that opened into the Western Sea. Locals called the shape a *crater*, though none knew why. The delta area of the city, called only "The Delta," wasn't big, about half a kilometer wide by a kilometer long, but it had become the center of the commercial district.

When the ship docked at the northern port, he wasn't sure of his next step. He approached the Captain who was relaxing now that the heavy cargo was on shore. His first mate, a woman of loud voice and quick wit, was organizing the loading onto wagons below on the dock, her black hair just poking out under her cap.

"My first mate, Dana, will take the cargo via the wagons. She is very capable. I'm surprised she hasn't applied for her own command by now. Be that as it may. We won't be following her. We will take a small boat over to the Delta."

"So, is it just passengers to the Delta port, then?"

"Transport to the Delta port is much more expensive and it would require extra handling for the cargo. So, more complicated and more expensive, and probably slower to take the cargo with us."

"Then why are there two ports?"

"This one, the Northern Port, is deep water, but as you can see, there isn't a lot of hinterland to develop a sizable town. It's squeezed right up against the cliffs of the Rim. The Delta has a lot of flat ground with rich soils, suitable for a city and farms, but the river is very shallow, with shifting sandbanks, nasty to navigate."

Mikel and the Captain crossed over to a smaller boat with a single sail. Dana waved at them and yelled, "See you later, Dad." The Captain waved back and gave Mikel an almost embarrassed look.

To the North there rose an escarpment 50 to 100 meters above the bay, forming the rim of the crater. The area was simply called the Rim. Compared to the imposing snowy Cantas far to the east, the Rim was insignificant, though still an impediment. Despite the difficulties, the Northern Port had houses built all the way up the Rim with the best ones at the top. He knew there were roads that crossed the northern and southern rim to communities up and down the coast, but he couldn't see them. He was originally from the North, somewhere. It gave him a strange tingling feeling.

East, beyond the city of Bethor, there was a sizeable gap in the mountain range, the Bethor

Valley, visible from anywhere in the Bay. It was a wide pass that split the Cantas in two and linked Bethor to the inland regions of Arva. North of the Bethor Valley and the Bethor Pass were the Northern Cantas, and to the south the Southern Cantas. Both mountain ranges showing white tipped peaks that towered above the bay. East of the Bethor Pass, the countryside opened up into the famous Great Plains. In the center of the Plains was Lake Baikal, and around it was the ancient and legendary Cities of the Plains. To the East beyond the Lake, somewhere in the Great Desert, it was told, was the half-mythical Trader city of Tanten.

When he finally arrived in Bethor, Mikel's doubts about this mission just got stronger. Did the Center really know what they were doing? He was stunned by the masses of busy people. Too many to note, analyze, and observe. Too many to get to know. Lind, including the Artist's Enclave, was just too small. He felt like a country hick. The docks were full of life and activity. There were horses and other animals of burden and people working to take goods off some boats and load onto others. There was constant noise, strange smells, and colors that he had not seen or experienced in such profusion before.

He saw a team of men naked to the waist, sweating, carrying things on their back off another vessel to the right as he walked up the gangplank.

He could think of ways to save them some effort, and he thought about having a talk with them when they stopped for a break. Then he noticed the well-dressed man looking at them and the heavy set overseer beside him with a whip at his side. Slave owners and slaves. Ugly memories mixed in with sweet. This was best forgotten. He had a mission; he took a deep breath and moved on.

He walked with Captain Woran through the crowd at the docks. So many people with different clothes and styles, different smells, unknown lives. He felt very plain.

The Council and Enclave often recruited promising candidates from Bethor and smaller towns, including himself. They must have intimate knowledge of the mainland cities. He wondered if relatives were passing him on the street without his knowing. This gave him strange uncomfortable feelings, yet there was simply no way to know who his family was, even if they were still alive, which he doubted, or maybe the doubting was just convenient denial. He dismissed the train of thought. It just wasn't helping him.

He got a lift with Captain Woran into the city. The good captain had left the cargo handling to his first mate, his daughter. When the cargo wagons arrived, he had business in the city. Huge black animals called horses pulled their open air carriage. Mikel had never seen such creatures before, though he had heard stories that The Center was trying to breed them on one island. The carriage started with a jolt and the horses leaped forward. He had ridden on some bullock carts, but this was wonderful. The vitality and power together revealed new possibilities. The carriage slowed down once away from the docks and made its way through the crowded, muddy streets, narrowly avoiding low overhanging drapes of various colors, and balconies decked by faces peeking over, looking at them with curious but impenetrable expressions. They let him off at a street corner.

"Be careful, Mikel. There are many pickpockets in Bethor. We don't have them in the Farrel, but we have little wealth to steal. Just take care, even if you look pretty poor."

He looked about at the crowds, many in exotic clothes of different hues.

"By their standards, I suppose I am poor." In Lind, he and his fellow students thought themselves special. White knights of knowledge who would free the world. Now it seemed more like an adolescent fantasy.

Captain Woran pointed down the nearby street and rattled off some directions that went over Mikel's head. Then he was gone and Mikel was by himself, surrounded by Bethor.

Eventually, after all the hustle and bustle, and he seeming to not know where he was going, with his incessant questions, he now stood by himself before a strange wooden building three stories tall. The external structure of the outside was painted dark brown and black in places, the walls in a fading white that he recognised as lime, with the bottom of the building edged in green by algae. A sign outside announced that this was "Ted's Haven and Inn - Finest in Bethor". Mikel was sure the building had a lean to the right. Didn't these people know anything about statics? No, of course they didn't. But they should at least have decent eyes.

He didn't quite regard them as barbarians. The Center was scrupulous about that. "We serve the people by improving their life and their future." He mouthed the words, deeply ingrained into his thinking and habits.

He hefted his backpack to reposition it on his shoulders. Set his staff in what he thought was a confident pose and walked through the door. The building was wooden, but had a large front window that let in the light. Although it was common in Lind, window glass of this quality seemed quite rare in Bethor. Inside, he could see reasonably well despite having just come in out of the sun. To his left was a polished bench like fixture which he had been told was a *bar*.

*"On your left will be a bar. Talk to the owner Ted. He's usually doing barman duties."* Master Samuel had advised him.

The bar seemed to be where alcohol was served. He knew about alcohol because the Islands exported wine and spirits, and almost every kid brews beer at some stage because they can. Eventually, they try their hand at a still, at first to make alcohol, and later to make more interesting things. A man behind the bar was pouring a beer from a keg that was against the wall. He turned and saw Mikel. The man looked to be over 50, loose wild gray hair, sunspots on his face and freckles, dark brown skin. He obviously did a lot more than stay in this place.

"What will it be?" He asked, with as much carelessness as if good manners had to be paid for, in advance.

"I was told I could get a room here," Mikel said.

"That is correct. The rate is two silver dollars per night, in advance."

Mikel realized his uncertainty was obvious. But he didn't know if he was supposed to haggle or not.

"New from the College?" The barman asked.

Might as well be honest, he thought, "Yes. Just here to see Bethor and learn about the trade routes."

"Well, the standard rate is two silver a night. The Center knows me, and they know I look after my charges."

"Charges?"

"Yes, young Mikel. My charges. I was told of your visit in advance. The Center and I have an —

arrangement — which I honor."

He didn't know what to make of this. The man knew his name. Was this innkeeper privy to the workings of the Center and its plans or did he get wind of some details from the Port somehow, and now using it as a ruse to get more information? His head filled with multiplying possibilities, bizarre and contradictory. He decided a bit of caution would be wise.

"Thank you. Yes, my name is Mikel, and I am from the Center. Just landed from the *Wavesprite*. Here to get to know Bethor and the Plains."

The innkeeper turned to get a key and gave a momentary glance upwards, which Mikel understood as adding a touch of mockery to his action. He had seen the caution many times before.

The Inda River opens onto the Eastern side of the Bay of Pennit. The official population of the city is 50,000, which is an old joke since it changes seasonally as the various caravans bring trade riches to the city and take other riches to remote places; at its smallest it is much larger than 50,000. Bethor Island, the main island of the Delta and the city, was chosen for defense. It is now the site for many of the public buildings of the city, easily distinguished because they are built of stone rather than wood. The city has grown and spilled out onto the floodplain to the north and south of the river. A series of wooden bridges link the Delta islands to the mainland and the southern bank to the north, just east of the Delta.

This much, a crude map, and not much else, was in the brief pamphlet they gave him in Lind.

As soon as he had secured his things in his room, he quickly washed and left the inn to explore. He started wandering around the Island looking for sights, not even sure which direction he was walking, and he still felt strange walking on a surface that was not continually pitching, but more walking would surely fix that. He was particularly interested in the Library and Museum. A few minutes after he started walking east, he found the Museum. He stood still, looking at it, trying to guess or deduce things from the outside. He soon saw that he had become a small stationary island in a river of people. A sea of browns, black, gray and here and there bursts of color... reds and yellows and blues. He wondered what kinds of dyes they used, what ideas they had, what their lives were like. The mix of people did not surprise him, since many people came to Lind to train. The clothes and fashions were unexpected, but it was the large numbers of people that surprised him most. People everywhere.

From the outside, the Museum was not as impressive as the Center on Lind. But it was completely unknown to him, and that made it an adventure. His heart even raced. He walked past the entrance guards and gave the seated official a silver dollar as required. Inside there was more natural light and some lamps of Lind design brightening up the hidden corners. He saw many things, some from the early history of Bethor and some things that were just strange. Objects of odd gleaming metals or perfect glass, but the plaque said it was not glass. The Ancients had "made these things" the text went on. Which meant nothing, since all that meant was that someone older than the historical records made these things.

As an apprentice he understood the language of the artifacts, in fact it festooned the Main Hall in Lind. But the words here made no sense. What could you make of: "F3N CRYO Rack"; "Comm Crypto Unit 5"; "Library Neural Cortex"? They took most of these items from the Cities of the Plains during the time of the Fall of the Cities, when a very young Bethor sacked the Cities. He looked about and understood. The museum was popular and well funded because it celebrated conquest, not knowledge.

The next day he located the Library which was on the southern side of the Delta, just by the riverbank. The path there meant he passed by both spectacular opulence and heartbreaking squalor. He had never seen either before. It was depressing, the contrast between the two enhancing the emotions. He noted it but postponed judgement. He would write about it later, after he had time to evaluate what he had seen.

The Library was a stone building less well executed than the Museum. It was also in a fairly run down sidestreet. Grass grew between the stone slabs of the entrance, and the sign was faded. The area seemed almost deserted. Few people were in the streets, giving an impression that the Library was neglected and depressed, and would soon fall into ruin. Entry was free. There were books in Bethorese, a dialect of the common tongue, which, like all dialects, was based on Ancient. The books seemed to mostly be about heroic adventures and deeds. There were some very basic books from the Center. There were also some old crumbling texts in open boxes with lids. He presumed at night the boxes were closed. Their titles were strange, but he could understand them. Some of them were definitely unknown to the Center. In Lind, these books would be priceless. Here they weren't even worth the effort to lock up. He looked at the case plaque to see if there were more details. There was no translation because no one knew the language, yet he could read it and one of the loose pages that was pinned right beside it. So close. He looked at the bored official who was sitting nearby, leaning against a column, as if sitting wasn't relaxing enough, listlessly picking lint off his mock-military uniform.

"Is there a translation of this?" He asked in good Bethorese. He remembered the accent from childhood.

"No," the guard said, in a way that also said, "and I don't care."

Mikel persisted. "I've heard that the Wizards at the Center can translate this. We could then read it."

He sneered. "Wizards! Hah! No, we won't take any notice of that scum."

He stood up, excited, glad to share this one idea in his humdrum life, shaking his finger at Mikel.

"You watch. One day, Bethor will take them down a notch. We'll burn their *Center* and string them all up. Watch them twist in the wind. Maybe the two of us will be there to hold the ropes." He laughed. Then sat down chuckling to himself.

Mikel gave a nervous smile and excused himself. Outside he stood in the sun, he had never experienced such raw, irrational hatred towards an entire people. His people. It was scary and somehow familiar.

Now, as he walked through Bethor, it didn't seem so interesting or colorful. He saw the unusual numbers of armed soldiers; dressed in their red uniforms with black trim. They looked impressive, but there were so many of them. The colorful banners he first admired, he now saw, had highly stylized phrases written along their sides; proclaiming the superiority of Bethor. "Retake the Cities". "Bethor, Born to Rule". This city was a terrible place for someone like him to be in. It was just waiting to explode. It was drunk with pride and arrogance. He knew those were the reasons, but not why he knew. He now could guess why the agents had died. When they came here, the signs would probably have been much less obvious and the agents would have triggered too many alarms with their questions. Now Bethor was intent on war. Bethor wanted to rule all of Neti, and probably kill all they didn't like. Their navy, if it could be called that, was pitiful, but they didn't have to take Lind. All they had to do was shutout all trade routes and ports. Soon, Lind would have to negotiate.

By the time he got out of the district containing the Library he was hungry and the sun was low in the west. He stopped by a roadside merchant who had a stall selling food. He just followed everyone else and ordered something that seemed popular, thinking, "*well, if it's poisoned then I'll have company in the hospital*," only later bothering to wonder if Bethor had such a thing as a hospital. It looked like meat wrapped in a pale cloth that was, on examination, a kind of bread. Anyway, it tasted pretty good. Different, but good.

Now, with a new appreciation of the city, wherever he looked, he saw the slaves. It wasn't like the poor, or the people of Lind, who were never rich. There was a look of dejection that made him shake inside. He thought at first that what he was seeing was fear, but he knew pretty soon that it was frustrated anger, as much in himself as the others. The Bethor dialect, an accent so strong as to be almost an unfamiliar language with its own meanings for familiar words, surrounded him. The more he heard it, the stranger he felt.

He sought refuge in a small park by the water, looking out on the bay, and tried to calm himself leaning against a waist high weathered gray stone seawall. The sound of waves lapping the rock like lifeless clapping. He felt as if he was going to panic. Breathing the clean salt air deeply to calm himself. It all went back to when he was a kid. No doubt about it.

He had forgotten it all, pushed it out of the way, making a new life by denying the old. Now immersed in this all too familiar culture and accent, it came back in a flood. There were tears in his eyes and he struggled to know why.

He remembered he had been playing with Aleis and Tomi, his older sister and brother. They had all just had a wonderful morning with their older cousin Ayo before she left on one of her trips. The children idolized her and thought of her as so grown up, even though she was just out of her teens. She went on long trips with her father to mysterious places; he wasn't a fisherman like his father and Mikel didn't know what that meant; to Mikel, being a fishing was everything — and exploring, always exploring, or thinking, or making things. It was the exploring and thinking that saved him yet again. Ayo had left, and they played a game. Mikel had thought of some new rules. There were many places amongst the rocks to hide. It was his turn. He gave them cryptic clues where he would hide, then they would turn, hide their faces and count up to twenty. All of his family could count. His mother had insisted on teaching him much of the 'old knowing'. She said that the Wizards knew of the knowing and had special magic and could do things like the stories she sometimes told him. They were to be respected and feared and maybe one day her children could be like the Wizards, and meet them face to face, though they said that if they looked at you straight, then you would die or at the least lose your soul. Others said that the Wizards moved about us invisible, observing and acting without our understanding.

While Tomi and Aleis were counting, he darted over the rocks, barefoot and agile, impervious to the jagged edges clothed in faded brown rough-knit. He hid in a crevice, covering himself in very smelly kelp. It was near a rock shaped like a pelican. The clue was "big hard bird." He was sure they'd get it quickly and wouldn't just look everywhere at random. Their voices were approaching, talking, working it out. He could also hear little crawlies scuttling in the dried kelp. He had to hold his nerve.

Outside, there were the cries of seagulls. He hoped they would not give him away. He must have uncovered some morsels for them, but the sounds weren't that close. Then he knew it wasn't seagulls he could hear. They were screams. People screaming. Fear paralyzed him. The screams stopped. He still hid. But he had to know.

He came out of his little crevice, like a small crab. Then made his way over the rocks to the beach. His brother and sister weren't there. This beach was hidden from where his village was, so he would have to round the small headland to see. He walked up, past the few rocks, the waves carelessly rushing around his legs, splashing up. Then he heard talking, strangers. There was the smell of smoke as he walked towards the village. As he got closer, he saw that some huts weren't there anymore, just translucent columns of smoke. It was past midday, and there should be so many people here. Who were these people he could hear?

As he approached the village, he saw shapes on the beach sand. Dark shapes like mounds of kelp with red color running over them and off them in little rivulets into the receiving waves. There were two small piles of seaweed getting closer. Every step made them clearer, every step, and he knew more clearly that it wasn't kelp. It was his brother and sister. He ran up to them, laying there dead like cold fish washed up by the waves, lifeless eyes staring out. There were more voices, clearer and closer. He couldn't breathe. There was a rising tide in him, a wave of feelings, that he had lost everything. He was near panic. There was movement just over a low dune, close to him, then voices.

"You were supposed to get prisoners. Lots of prisoners. How are we supposed to make money out of this, sell shells in Bethor? I should feed you to the sharks. You've always been trouble. I've a good mind to make you walk back."

"Ha, you, against me? You're no match. What's the problem, anyway? There's plenty more villages up the coast."

A scream. Then the first voice again.

"Thanks Dale. He ripped us all off. Hey, who's that? Looks like it isn't a complete loss."

He turned and ran, but one of them cut him off before the headland. He glimpsed him coming from the right side; tall, black ragged armor, a frozen grim, indistinct face in his mind.

They rammed him face first into the wet sand. A bag thrown over his head while someone tied his hands behind him. He remembered the fear, and the pounding of his heart, salt water around and in his mouth and nose mixed with sand, bright pinpoints of yellow light through the coarse weave of the bag, the stale smell of the bag mixing with the sharp tang of the sea. He saw no more of his village and never knew if his parents or other kin escaped. There was a time huddled in the bottom of a rocking boat, too exhausted to fear anymore, too helpless to do anything but let fate take him.

Much later, he would find himself in Bethor at the slave market. His hands tied and a rope around his neck, then paraded onto a small stage. They, those anonymous faces that he tried to purge from his mind had given him some extra food so he wouldn't faint on stage. Masked the odd casual whip mark with a smudge of dirt. Bruises even easier. The buyers had all gawked at him, but one in particular. The others had merely grabbed his arms and legs, roughly testing his strength, making sure he wouldn't die within a day of purchase. This one had come up to him, face covered in a cowl, as if he had come in from a rainstorm or he was a monk. He asked Mikel about the games he played, what interested him, how he had got caught. It was a moment of warmth, as if the stranger cared. There was a small flurry of bidding. He didn't hear what the final price was, a child didn't have a high value, they were often killed outright since they were more of a nuisance.

His new owner came to him, lifted his cowl, gazed at him with his clear brown eyes. He was in his late twenties, had not shaven for several days, black hair, pale skin. Not like anyone in his village. He stooped down to look at Mikel at eye level, put his soft hands on Mikel's shoulders. "Don't worry, little one. You are going to be all right. What is your name?"

"Mikel." He had not spoken his own name since he was taken. They had taken away his identity, and with a simple question, his world changed.

"Well, Mikel. How would you like to be a Wizard?"

He nodded to the man, who smiled, took him by his hand and led him out of the building and down to the sun-drenched docks.

But that was not right. He remembered the first day he set foot in Lind, the day his new life started. He was at least a year older than when he was captured. It surprised him that even now, when he thought he was being most honest with himself, there was still something hidden. What was it?

So long ago. Around his neck still hung a tiny leather pouch. In it was a fragment of the clothes he had worn and a stray piece of kelp from his hiding place that he always kept even though he banished the memories they represented. The only physical remnants he had left from the time before his other life ended.

He bowed his head, trying to breathe deeply and soothe those old unfinished aches.

"Son. Are you all right? You don't look so well?" The speaker was a middle-aged Bethorese gentleman, well dressed, out to take the air, it seemed. Lower Upper Class, he would guess. Speaking in a refined accent.

"I will be fine. In just a moment. Thank you." He spoke naturally.

"Oh. You're from Lind." The voice suddenly hard. "You better be off before the police come by. They don't take kindly to your type. Best to be away from Bethor if you get my meaning."

It was a remarkable transformation. The man looked at him in a rigid stance, as if possessed. He knew that demon. He had seen it in the slave market. It was still alive, and now stronger.

He made his way back to his room. Noticing everything: the uniforms, the slogans, an unnatural orderliness in manner in a haphazard town. This place was dangerous. The less time he spent here, the better. He had to find out about the trade routes and get out of the city, return home.

Next morning he devoured breakfast and proceeded east towards the Caravanserai: a combination of market, exchange, social gathering, and festival. He crossed the bridge from the eastern end of the Island to the southern side of the river. The Caravanserai was a large flat area, a riot of color, sound, music, smells of food, and animals. It was like a huge fair, except it was far more serious. Here was a rich selection of things for sale, barter, deals to be done, people to meet. That was his aim. He was looking for a Trader to question about trade routes. Simple. Then he could go home. They had given him a name of someone who was knowledgeable and trustworthy. He had to get to the Exchange.

The Exchange turned out to be a curious 'U' shaped stadium like structure. A central stage area was for food, drink and other amenities. The "audience" was the true highlight. As he looked up from the stage area near the entrance, he saw tiers of small tables and stalls and people talking and doing business. The higher the position, the more respected. Areas of the stands had a colored flag here and there. He was looking for a yellow flag with a blue wheel symbol on it: the mark of one particular family of Traders. The Trader section, marked by square flags rather than pennants, was in fact very large, taking up most of the space; soon he saw his target, high up.

Walking up the stairway near the yellow section of the crowd, he saw hard inscrutable faces looking him up and down. He had read about arenas and amphitheaters, but this was nothing like that; these people were not passive observers. He was the observed. They were evaluating him, catching the slightest clues as to who he was, how wealthy and vulnerable he supposed. He looked up to see where he was going and was confronted by a wall of leather. He was about to collide with a young Trader standing on a higher step. The chest armor had two interesting bumps at eye level. He looked up, embarrassed.

"I'm sorry," he said as he stepped around her.

"Mikel Peres, of the Center?" she said with an odd accent. She spoke almost in the manner of Lind, and she knew who he was. The questions were rhetorical. Everyone seemed to know his name, and he knew nothing about them. He was way out of his depth.

Her name was Tei. A young Trader of about 20, though, she came highly recommended. She had shoulder length auburn hair tied behind. Startling blue eyes and slightly dark skin, though it was hard to tell if it was just the typical deep suntan of the Traders or if she was naturally brown. When she walked down onto the same step as Mikel, he saw she stood a few centimeters shorter than him, dressed in well-fitted leather armor with straps and a loose white cloak. She looked dangerous even before he noticed the sword on her left hip and a remarkably small crossbow hanging from her other hip. The wind was picking up, now and then blowing her cloak back, revealing the weapons and armor like the warning display of a wild animal. Her forearms were bare, showing her wiry muscles rippling a few tattoos. She looked tough, formidable.

# five

Tei Lin Valis had been a Trader for as long as she could remember. Her father taking her on the safer routes when she was a small child, learning to hunt and survive, negotiate or fight, and how to read people and places. She would return to Tanten, showing off her new prizes to the rest of the family, or bringing news and letters from extended family in remote encampments and towns. When she was thirteen, she was taken on a special journey, as is the custom, and saw the Eternal Citadel. Seeing that changed her life, as it does to every Trader who has the chance to witness it. Once a Trader sees that, then the world of men and the attraction of cities fades away like the chill of the desert night. She was twenty Neti years old now, the same in standard years. Her father had always referred to her as his golden princess; referring to her auburn hair. Nowadays she pulled the shoulder length hair back severely, trying to get rid of the curls and waves in her hair. She wanted men and women to remember her for her leadership, not for her looks, but deep down she still longed to be the golden princess saving the world. Her travels had tanned her skin more easily than expected. Somewhere in the past, she had a relative who gave her some welcome resistance to the sun. Now her skin and her hair were golden, but reality never matches the dream.

Her discipline could never waver, she still had to earn respect, but she had a slight build; a caravan leader must be able to lead her people into battle if needed. She had the courage; she trained daily to get the strength, yet at times it seemed like a hopeless quest and she wondered how her team regarded her.

She wore typical Trader garb. Well-used leather armor, though not so much as to slow her down in a fight. A sheathed curved sword at her left side, made from many-folded steel, the sheath beautifully crafted in red leather and some silver. A small pale yellow crossbow and quiver at her side. There were light clothes under the armor and a flowing white cloak on her back. The cloak was a desert thing, not usually used here, but it protected from the wind and dust.

She was in front of a strange creature who seemed

the antithesis of her aspirations. He was perhaps two years younger than her. But he was as helpless as a child. He couldn't track or fight, she suspected, yet the word was that he was special. The Traders and the Wizards had an unspoken alliance. They both had deep secrets and wished to keep them, and each wanted to know the secrets of the other, but they also shared a common hope for the future. Amid these subtle interplays, this lad obviously did not know what was really going on, which made his reputation even more of a mystery. Perhaps something else was intended. She might as well play the tough guy and see if she could shake something out of him.

She casually evaluated the boy. Not strong and wiry as a Trader should be. No poise that spoke of horse riding. His leather armor, what there was of it, was new. New? What was he thinking being out here? A lamb to the slaughter. Yet there was something in his gaze.

"Well, are you Mikel Peres?" She said, climbing a step and using the added height from the stairs to project an aura of haughtiness. She was curious to see how he reacted. If he didn't react, her suspicions would escalate.

"Yes, my name is Mikel, from the Center in Lind." There was no reaction from the woman, so he decided to just continue and hoped things improved. "I was looking for a Trader by the name of Tei Valis. Is — is that you?"

Duty called. She was just getting started and now she couldn't play with him any longer. She had a job to do.

She visually softened, stood more at ease.

"Yes. I am Tei Lin Valis, Trader of the Plains. Left Hand of the Mark of Valis of Tanten."

Mikel translated from what he had learned about the Traders. Tanten was their major city or town. Details on it were scarce and contradictory. The Mark was a clan head. To be the "Left Hand" meant that she was a talented and stealthy troubleshooter for the Mark, whereas "Right Hand" would mean she was more of a soldier. She was an agent. She must be fearsome to have earned such a title at her age.

"I am..." He awkwardly repeated.

"Yes, I know who you are, Mikel."

"Oh. Yes, what now?" The easterly wind was drying out his lips and face, making it that much harder to talk to this amazon. She looked like she had lived in the desert, as if she regarded this as a gentle breeze.

"Mikel. We can talk in my tent. It isn't far from here, just beyond the stadium. I know you islanders have delicate skin."

Had she read his mind? Or more likely noticed him licking his cracked lips.

The tent was a surprise. He had expected a two-man tent or similar. Instead, he was in a much more elaborate and larger structure. Calling it a tent seemed wrong. Yes, it was made of cloth and leather, but the blue and gold embroidery, the hanging tapestries, and the carpets were the trappings of royalty. It was also big, big enough for parties for several dozen people to gather.

As they entered, she proclaimed, seemingly as a matter of protocol. "Here in this hexayurt, I sit as the representative of the Mark of Valis and the Council of Tanten."

Not royalty, rather — Ambassador.

"Do you know why you are here, Wizard?"

"I am not a Wizard, I am merely an Apprentice. I don't know why I am here exactly. I was told to find out information about trading networks in the Plains."

She sat on a chair that was not quite a throne, but not quite a chair. It suggested that she was the focus. It was made of dark carved wood, and looked ornate and very uncomfortable. Perhaps the hardness of the wood matched her nature.

Now she had a cold, steely look in her eyes as she examined him, deciding her next words.

"Some think you are a spy sent by Lind. Others say that you are a token of continuing friendship. Others that your Master sees a common use for you by both parties that will be — profitable."

"And what do you think?" he said.

"Perhaps you are one masquerading as another. It is too early to say. But know this trail companion. If you are here for the ill of my people, The Center will never see you again."

"*Trail companion?*"

"Yes. You are going to join me on the Plains. I am your guide, am I not? And I am going to guide you into Arva until we resolve just what is going on here. Meet me here the day after tomorrow, after morning prayers. I will conclude my business in Bethor tomorrow."

"All I need are some words from you about trade routes. Less than an hour of your time. No need to waste any time taking me with you. I assure you I would be hopeless."

"Then think of this as a wonderful opportunity. You are coming with me. Only then will you find out what you want to know and so will I."

He walked back to the inn, feeling alone and uncertain. Was he going to his death, letting this woman take over his plans? He felt abandoned and an idiot. He dropped into the Lind Embassy on the way to his rented room and encoded a quick report, warning of his findings in Bethor and his trip to the Plains, then sealed it with wax.

It would be on the next return ship, back to Lind and the Master Wizard. He handed it to the Wizard at the counter who was looking down, hooded, busy writing what looked like a report.

"Official courier to The Center."

The man took it, noticed who it was addressed to and instantly put it into a large pouch below the counter.

"Do not fear, it will leave on the morning tide."

Suddenly, the sound of a Lind accent was very comforting. He wanted the man to speak some more.

"How long have you been stationed in Bethor?"

"About five months. I will be returning in another month."

"I guess you would be eager to see home again," Mikel said.

"Of course." He audibly sighed.

"It isn't a very friendly place, is it?"

The man only nodded, head still facing down, only the top of his hood visible.

It occurred to Mikel that the staff at the Embassy should have seen the warning signs he had seen. Why had it been necessary to send him?

"I've seen a lot of signs in the streets. Bethor seems to be getting quite aggressive and restless."

The man looked up and pushed his cowl back, revealing his face. Mikel almost gasped. The same face, almost unchanged, that had changed his life.

"What is your name?" Mikel asked, returning that question asked long before.

"Alberto Elrick. Yours?"

"Mikel. Mikel Peres."

Alberto looked at him. His eyes widened for a moment, then they both smiled.

"Glad to see you did so well." Alberto said.

"I really can't express how much I owe you. Why have I never seen you before?"

"I spend most of my time here, only spending one or two months each year back in Lind or one of the islands. It's pretty unlikely our paths would cross."

"I know you are busy, but I've been wondering, is there something wrong with Bethor? It seems really aggressive and intolerant."

Alberto smiled. "It is always like that. It just varies in intensity from year to year. You get used to it, but I find I need a break now and then."

Mikel concluded that Wizards in Bethor were just too close, too acclimatized to the danger, and could no longer see the signs becoming urgent.

It seemed the hard task was done, but the straightforward task was going to get him into a lot of hot water. He dallied there for some time, reluctant to leave. The place radiated safety and felt like home. He wanted to stay until morning, then take that letter back personally to the Master Wizard and beg for forgiveness. Even if the Master forgave him, deep inside, he knew he would have failed at his very first mission. It would be humiliating. Perhaps, if he was older and more seasoned, he may have thought differently, but now, right now, he was compelled to go along with circumstance. Yet deep down, it gave him a chill. It felt irreversible, and final.

He had a day to spare in Bethor with no idea what to do. He could fake a Bethorese accent pretty well, but he didn't want to push his luck. Briefly, a temptation flashed into his mind to travel north and find his home, but there was no time and he didn't know if his village was a day's ride north or a week's ride, and he didn't know how to ride, anyway. It would be better to stay in the city, besides he wasn't ready yet to find the graves of his family. He took a random walk through the Delta. Explore the places that he had no official need to visit.

Most of the streets led to more and more merchant premises. But one street on the southern side of the Delta ended in a large circular area fronting an imposing yellow stone building, sandstone probably by the delicate shading and grain. He had never appreciated until now how beautiful it could be, especially with the sun low in the sky and the mellowing light. There were six armed guards standing watch at a large gate made of iron bars and wrought iron mesh that looked like a black rose garden. Great workmanship mixed with memory flashes, momentary feelings. He took a deep breath and took a step backwards. The building was clearly a government structure, but it was very ornate. He was raised in a deeply egalitarian society and had no familiarity with the concepts of aristocracy or opulence, so he did not immediately associate the building with an individual with great power and wealth and therefore did not know that it was not public or open or safe.

He walked around the arc of the cul-de-sac. The rut marks showed it was for carriages and such. He just wanted to get a better look at the building and the workmanship.

"You. If you don't have any business here, leave," said the guard.

"Certainly, my apologies. I'm just a visitor from — a village to the north. Pardon."

He turned to walk away up the road when he saw a carriage approaching rapidly. He turned and jumped to the right, out of the way, back onto the footpath. The carriage pulled up. The front horse was a huge, black, beautiful creature, uncomfortably close and snorting in his direction while the bridle and other horse's tack jostled and clinked from the sudden stop. A woman stepped out of the carriage dressed in some kind of simple but well made gray military uniform. Brown hair plaited and braided, forming a crown around her head. She looked at him.

"You there! Who are you?"

"Just a visitor to Bethor. Name's Mikel. I was

admiring the workmanship of the building. We have nothing like it in my village."

Her deep blue eyes narrowed. Judging. She had a light skin, no makeup or jewelry. There was something cold and familiar about her look, a disdain and matter-of-fact attitude toward stepping on others. He recognized it from the slavers. But this woman had more than that. She was very familiar indeed, and that voice.

"You don't belong here, citizen. If you feel pride in the work of Bethor, then enlist. Be a patriot and join the national will to greatness."

He didn't understand what these words meant. They were gibberish, but he knew he had better act like one of the faithful.

"Yes, yes, majesty." He bit his lip. He knew nothing of protocols for royal or imperial courts.

The woman's eyes narrowed, and she smiled crookedly, as if acknowledging an in-joke only she understood.

He started walking away briskly. Behind him, he heard the guard say, "Welcome back, Ms Markham."

He picked up the pace, eager to get as far away from her as possible. His jaws tensing in fear. A strange thought occurred to him. Perhaps it wasn't that we remember the past, but rather the past often remembers us and was all the more dangerous for that.

Finally, the bartering was concluded for the major goods. Letters of credit and arrangements with the Trader bank completed, but the biggest hurdle was yet to come. Traders really don't enjoy socializing with aristocracy. They can do it, but it is almost an affront to their beliefs, which they conveniently keep secret, spreading the lie that they are unsophisticated, which is starkly at odds with the fact that they trade information and technology, and run the banking network.

Now she had a party to go to. She had to meet the evil family at the magic castle, like one story her Nan used to tell her.

It was typical Trader formal wear for a woman. Yellow and pink silk pantaloons, a formal deep blue jacket, yellow silk sleeves; the colours of morning. And a ceremonial dagger. The dagger had no edge, otherwise the guards would never let it in. It did not have jewels or gold but was made from materials sacred to the Traders. Ancient wood from the pines of northern Xan, trees that no longer existed; steel reforged from weapons of the Ancients. There was no reason for overly strict or corrupt guards to keep it.

She hired an enclosed carriage to the castle. It was strange to ride without the wind in her face, or able to see everything around her at a glance. She couldn't anticipate the bumps and lurches. It was horrendous.

"The things I do for duty," she murmured to

no one. She went alone. A party of one woman looks forlorn and harmless, at least with the odd perceptions that Bethor was noted for.

The castle was everything she expected from the old fairytales. A great black gate reminding her of a story about a castle surrounded by a cursed forest of thorns. She gritted her teeth and pulled her mouth into something superficially resembling an insipid smile greeting the guards.

Inside, she was introduced formally to the room and started mingling.

On the far right of the room were three merchants that Tei recognized. They all seemed to wear well-tailored coats of some reddish brown material. She should ask what it was. It might be worth sourcing a supply if the fashion spread eastward.

First among the little gathering was Terrance Alistero, he was a balding, portly middle-aged merchant who had once ventured out to all the Cities, but had been getting rich and fat staying in Bethor the last few years. He, like most merchants, was friendly with the Traders but unlike most, he actually meant it. Tei knew him but thought she should get to know him more. He could be a useful ally in easing some of Bethor's dangerous tendencies. The other two were Gilda Wosheska, a woman in her forties, and Adrian Finn, both of them Tei barely knew.

"Hello Tei. I'm surprised to see you here,"

Terry said, smiling.

"Good evening, friends. I'm just here wearing my ambassador hat for tonight. Keeping up good relations."

The other two merchants chuckled at the "good relations."

Gilda was a dark-haired, dark-skinned woman who was no longer young, with streaks of gray in her hair and the start of wrinkles on the sides of her face; the intensity in her eyes overrode the trappings of age. She spoke up, getting back on topic, which meant *goods*.

"Have you seen the new clocks from Lind? Mechanical, with gears. By the stars, it makes you wonder if those old stories of the Ancients are true. Pricey, but there are so many willing takers. I have a contact in Lind. If you wish to purchase from me, I can be extremely reasonable."

Adrian sneered and spoke. "Just how many clocks do you expect to sell? I too have contacts in Lind and I have the rights to sell a new water purification system."

That got Tei's attention.

"How complex is it? Are you selling parts or the plans? And how much?" She said.

He smiled. "It requires kilns to produce charcoal. But once you have the basic components, I am told it is very easy to use and very effective. Cost, open to negotiation, of course," he said.

"Charcoal? How is black soot going to make

clean water?" Gilda said.

"We would have to see a working demonstration first. I cannot stay much longer in Bethor, but I will pass on the details, to my relief," Tei said. He passed her a small note with his name and contact details.

Terry leaned in, whispering. "Good that you are going, Tei. I honestly don't feel comfortable here anymore." He looked up, startled. He gave her a quick wave. They all backed away, frightened like wild animals.

Before she could turn, a woman sidled up to her left, a drink in a beautiful green glass cup in her right hand. She wore a stark gray uniform. It stood out in this refined atmosphere like a bloody sword at a wedding.

"Excuse me, Ambassador. My name is Liz Markham." They shook hands awkwardly while Liz transferred the drink to her other hand.

"Markham? Now there's a name that invites some questions. My name is Tei Lin Valis. Call me Tei."

"Pleased to meet you, Tei. Hah, yes. Many people have the name Markham, doesn't mean much these days. So what interesting insights can you give us for the latest fashions in goods, Tei?"

"I just look for what people want now and try to give them that. Too hard for me to anticipate fashion, I'm afraid."

She passed Tei another drink. Tei did not

know where she got it from. She didn't have it a moment ago.

"I have heard so many interesting things about Traders. Is it true you travel all the way east, past the Eastern Desert? That you worship Zeus?" She took a sip, held the pose, waiting for Tei to take a sip. It looked like a white wine, it had the taste of sweet wine with extra alcohol. What was the bet dear Liz was drinking colored water?

"No, we haven't been beyond the Eastern Desert. We know what was once on the other side, but no one has returned from expeditions to the East. As for Zeus, we respect Zeus, but we don't worship him."

Liz looked quizzically at her. "Does that mean he is real but not a god? Or just another god who you don't bother worshipping?"

She laughed suddenly, then caught herself. The typical laugh Bethorese use when they dismiss outsider ideas as primitive and superstitious.

"And you have a city in the desert, Tanten, I believe?"

"Yes. Our capital is Tanten in the Eastern Desert."

"Must be small. A desert can't support many people. So, Tei, how big is it compared to say the village of Fairmeadow, which you pass by in the Gap? Smaller? Same size?"

"It is big enough for us, Lady Markham."

"Don't be so formal. We are all friends here. I

just want to get to know our friends from the East."
She smiled. Tei gritted her teeth and smiled back.

"I must introduce you to some friends of
mine, Tei." She waved her arm at someone across
the crowded room.

Two young men in ornate, formal Bethor
uniforms made their way across the room, each a
full head above everyone else, a blur of red, black,
and gold.

Liz, conspiratorially, whispered in Tei's ear,
hand on her shoulder. "They're brothers. Can't you
tell? They are magnificent, but don't tell them that.
You know what men are like."

It was a setup and Tei knew it. She just had
to ride this dust storm out to the end. And smile all
the way.

There was some typical small talk as the two
men introduced themselves. They were Brian and
Roberto Hammersli, Bethor aristocracy, officers by
appointment and welcome in the Royal Court of the
High Emperor of Bethor.

"Ah yes, we were talking about Tanten. I
would like to visit it sometime. But I don't know
how to get there. What is the best route, Tei?" Liz
said. An obvious invitation for them to add pressure
on her.

Roberto added his voice. "Oh, Tanten. I've
heard of it. A friend said he visited it. Just headed
southeast from the Eastern Caravanserai."

Tei smiled. "Don't believe everything you are

told. I cannot tell you the way to Tanten. It is just a place in the desert, no valuable land."

Liz leaned in to her, her smile vanished for an instant then returned, "but you see my dear, there are stories of treasures and knowledge. There are so many who would like to visit to see it. You have a library, don't you?"

"I thought Bethor had the best library in Arva?" Her irritation was showing. Those words were unwise.

"It does. But you know it would benefit us all if our scholars could safely visit other libraries and museums, especially those of the Traders. Perhaps we could arrange a cultural exchange to strengthen our friendship?"

"I don't think that will be possible, I fear. Only the council can authorize visitors to the Library. They are strict and do not listen to a mere ambassador such as myself."

It was getting too much. Three against one. Time to leave.

"Pardon me. I must be going now. Have to make arrangements to take a caravan tomorrow morning. I will have to be up early. Good night, Brian, Roberto, Ms Markham. Thank you for the party. It was most interesting."

She got out the door. Took a deep breath of the sour town night air. Briskly down the steps and through the gate. Night, dim yellow street lights, lamplight through distant windows, acrid smoke rising above the city from hundreds of small home fires. Some stars above showing through the murk, always the stars watch us, she thought. She got into the nearest carriage and headed back to the Caravanserai.

The Emperor of Bethor, Karl Maximilian Pederson, was young. Liz regarded him as a rather foolish, immature, distracted man of 23, or a boy pretending to be a man. Her own family's history no doubt darkened her view of him. She didn't care. Many women in the court praised his dark hair and green eyes. Their fawning almost made her gag. He claimed an interest in the arts, could paint, write a decent sonnet. She thought him a decadent who did not understand the forces at work in his own realm.

Now he wanted to meet her. She had never met him for any serious discussions. She was always in the background. *Better for me to spy on you.* She thought.

However, she needed to curry favor with him, especially when his advisors were about. His advisors: the Secretary Kahl Enoos, Treasurer Vinnis Ortens, Securitor (Head of the Ministry of Order, secret police and propaganda) Tovan Frisch. Frisch was an ally and seemed not to share his emperor's hopes for peace, or else he was duping her. Stories of his excesses with female prisoners were legendary and likely true. She suspected he was waiting until he could have her body all to himself on a rack in the dungeon, away from prying eyes, when she was no longer of use in his plans. They were all a pack of jackals. One day, they would get an appropriate reward.

Frisch had been pushing the recent propaganda messages, designed the banners himself, so he said, arguing to the Emperor that a new program of "greater understanding for our brothers on Neti" would follow. *True enough, there will be greater understanding when we are in control, after a lot of blood is shed*, she thought, suddenly grateful that the Ancient mind reading tech of legend no longer existed.

"*Lady* Markham, I have heard you have been raising the readiness of our troops near Lindin. Is this true?" The Emperor asked, as if he was discussing the flowers in the Imperial Gardens. The way he pronounced "Lady," mocking and questioning, was a reminder that her family had a question mark over it, that her demonstrated loyalty was paramount no matter how talented she was as a general.

He went on, converting the question to a rhetorical one and this meeting into something more sinister.

"Remember who your Emperor is. I know you want to recapture old glory or something. But there is nothing out there. The Cities are poor. What could you possibly gain from them? The climate is so variable lately we can't even rely on their grain shipments. Good heavens, they have become a liability, not an asset."

"I am maintaining my army's readiness. Regular drills and so on."

"Don't lie to me, Lady Markham. I know you are up to more than that. What are you doing?"

"As I said, drills, because I do not trust the Cities. Also, there may still be knowledge left in the Cities. If we look properly instead of just sacking them like we did last time."

"That was centuries ago. I doubt there is anything left in the ruins."

"Maybe, but if we don't look, we won't know. They are also a stepping stone."

"To what?" he said.

"If we control all the Cities, including Sanfran, we can control the Eastern Caravanserai whenever we want. Choke or tax the Traders into submission. Find out where their damnable Tanten is located, then lay siege to it or subvert it. They must have lots of secrets." She flushed with anger. Then a few calming breaths while he rambled on.

"And what are you going to do even if you succeed, after you have wasted all these resources? Do you think Tanten knows where to find vast metal deposits? Or hydrocarbon reserves? Do you think they have stashed away warehouses of intact Ancient photovoltaics?"

Composed again, she continued. "By

controlling trade, we will also bring The Center to heel. Then we can access their knowledge and skills."

"Without energy and resources, what do you think will be achieved by that?"

"It's better than slowly going downhill! This situation enslaves us all. We are running out of options. We will all end up paupers," she said.

"By *why* do you include the commoners? There is no need to share knowledge with them. The more ignorant they are, the more compliant they will be. I would not be surprised if that is the Center's rationale for its aloofness. There will always be the rulers, and the ruled. Just remember your place. You must cease this little project of yours, yes I know of it. Let it die. Go now, you have your orders."

She bowed and walked out, smiling. He clearly knew nothing about her "project," otherwise she would be dead by now. *I know my place, boy. Don't get too used to that throne.*

She laughed.

# six

Morning prayers are a traditional Bethor practice which takes place when the sun is at fifteen degrees above the horizon. The Traders also follow a version of the ritual, praying to the gods usually at sunrise but sometimes when the sun is at the thirty degree mark. The Bethorese had water clocks and other more precise mechanisms purchased from Lind to work out these important times on overcast days, but the Wizards themselves only used them for more practical tasks.

There was a brisk morning breeze kicking up a little dust, blowing from behind as he faced the rising sun, probably a sea breeze. The sun was rising through the Gap; at a few degrees above the horizon, the effect deserved worship, beautiful, almost divine. He had been here early enough to see it, but for some reason, that was not the time when most of the worship occurred. To the west, he faced the gateway to the Caravanserai. He was wary about entering, mostly because he didn't know if there were some customs that forbade Wizards and their minions intruding on periods of worship; there were rumors about wizards told to him by his mother and the darker ones from his uncle. He had almost laughed at the mention of minions, just as well he had some sense. The tales about Wizards seemed so bizarre, thinking of them as a wizard himself. Such legends affected the attitudes of others and the taboos that they would impose. Best to keep his identity secret. He smiled inwardly, as he acted just like some legends. Going 'hidden amongst the ordinary folk', however not because of power but because of vulnerability.

He started walking and entered the Caravanserai. He noticed that there were groups clustered here and there, offering prayers to different deities, represented by figurines on the tops of poles. There were Neochristians and similar, Buddhists, and inevitably prayers to Zeus. There were the familiar Pantheists of Lind and Tanten, hence the sunrise worship. Mikel himself had tasted various religions while growing up, but had concluded that any real god would be more impressed by him acting as a decent human being than mumbling formulaic words at the local patch of sky.

The Caravanserai itself was an odd

arrangement, it was a rough wooden palisade on the outside, more of a formal border marker than anything else, and inside were tents, wooden huts, some larger wooden structures, all looked temporary as if it could disappear overnight and leave nothing but a dusty field by next morning.

When time had just passed for the morning prayers, he proceeded toward the hexayurt. He had never seen the design before and thought it must be a Trader invention, though Tei would later tell him it was an ancient design from Earth.

Approaching the yurt, he noticed unfamiliar Traders inside. He was about to enter, there was nowhere to knock, when he heard Tei behind him.

"Psst. Mikel. Over here." She was about ten meters behind him.

"I am only the Ambassador when meeting you for the first time. Now my mission requires me to be merely a Trader. Others now have the role of Ambassador. We meet and transfer the role. You should probably write that down. This is the first day of your lessons about the trade routes and Traders."

He supposed that perhaps a Trader Ambassador was only concerned with Trade. Or maybe he could just admit he had no clue and should ask when he had the chance.

The rest of the day, he followed Tei listening in as she negotiated horses and camels. He had never seen either creature before coming to

Bethor. Now they were everywhere. It was fascinating and appalling, as it usually is when you discover a profound ignorance in yourself. Apparently, there was a complex ritual of handing over horses or camels when the caravans arrived at a destination. The creatures would be fed and rested, taking weeks or even months to recover from the longer journeys. Then when a return caravan of the same clan was leaving, a payment would be made for the agistment and the animals would once again come under the control of the family. This way, a family could build up a network of stocks of beasts to maintain the trade routes and survive dry or difficult times. Dealing with Traders was highly ethical since anyone who wanted to live would never double-cross a Trader, and in response Traders also were highly ethical since they applied the same strict standards to each other. It was a case of mutually assured trust.

That night he did not return to the inn but stayed in the Caravanserai. He had thought they would have left today, but this was also part of the leaving, and Tei wanted him to experience it. The camp was like a very large tent city with lots of things going on. Noises of people laughing, arguing, drinking, lovemaking, carousing, but mostly singing. Smells of smoke and cooking and animals. It was pure transience and yet the Caravanserai endured, a shimmering entity of campfires that was more than the present occupants.

Above him were the stars. It was quiet now. The various fires were barely more than embers. There was no tent. Just stars above and a bedroll. Tei was a couple of meters away. He presumed she was awake. He had seen the reflection of the dying fire in her eyes. She, too, was looking at the stars.

"I should take some measurements of the Constant Star."

She rolled over, facing him, her body a silhouette of mystery. All he experienced was her disembodied voice.

"Do you mean Raytans?"

"Thaytan. Yes. I have estimated the distance I travelled by ship to Bethor, so by measuring the change in the background stars I should be able to determine the distance to Raytans, as you call it. After I correct for the latitude and longitude, change in the angular position due to parallax, and factor in motion of the background as part of the astronomical year, of course. Then I can confirm our estimates." He said, slipping now into his normal thinking even in this strange place.

"The *Raymond Tans* is in geostationary orbit. Not that far away, as those things are measured. I presume that is what you mean by 'estimates', but we only have the hard figures, not the calculation. It is about 34,000 kilometers above us."

He said nothing for a moment. What was going on here? He knew about geostationary orbits.

It was secret knowledge. But not only did she know about them, she also knew the computed distance to Thaytan, and she seemed to know things that the Center itself did not know.

"The 'Raymond Tans'?"

"The *Raymond Tans* is a starship. Your Master Wizard knows this. He also knows what a starship is and should have told you. I can tell you no more. Go to sleep, young Wizard."

"I'm not a Wizard," he said softly and rather pathetically.

"Oh yes, you are. Now I know why they sent you. I'm sure you'll figure it out yourself." She gave a wry laugh, then rolled over.

Seven other Traders would accompany Tei with the caravan. The usual pattern was for each Trader to take charge of a file of camels. There would be eight files this time, and each file would be a linked line of twelve to fifteen camels. Mikel and the Traders would ride horses as far as the Eastern Caravanserai. There, instead of a chaotic mix of tents, there would be a defensible fort with space for many camels, places to sleep, feed, bathe, buy necessities and do some bartering. There could be no true Western Caravanserai because Bethor would not tolerate any permanent structure that challenged their cultural authority. Tei knew because the Traders had been continually trying to get permits to build. The most they could ever get was the open piece of land, as long as there were no permanent structures, not even in wood. So it had become a tent city. Even the stadium was regularly dismantled, as it was just a series of elevated platforms. It looked more imposing when full, but when deserted, the pretense was obvious.

Her team had arranged previously and boxed the trade goods while she had been "wasting" her time with Mikel. Though now the whelp was becoming interesting. Annoyingly inept, but interesting. He must have clearly stood out within the Center. Perhaps the Traders could use his talents and naivety to their advantage.

The caravan would head out across the relatively lush regions of western Arva. Some rivers from the mountains to the north and south of Bethor flowed inland, forming a network of smaller rivers that ended in a large lake. The entire area was a fertile food basket for the known world and produced many highly tradable items. Beyond the lake, the country went rapidly from lush grassland to semi-arid and then to desert. They would then be in true camel country. Then the Trader's renowned skills would dominate.

Normally, a caravan would visit as many of the Cities of the Plains as possible but recently there was a sense of trouble brewing. No one knew exactly what was coming, but if Bethor seemed crazy at the moment, it was nothing compared to the Cities. Even if they headed east as directly as possible, they would come dangerously close to Lindin on the northern shore of Lake Baikal. They would have to divert further north. The added revenue from visiting the Cities was just not worth the very high risk. But she was curious.

He was dreaming of a gentler time, soothing voices, bright sun and waves gently rushing up over the damp sand to sweep around his ankles. There were voices behind him, calling to him, but he started running away. Soon he stopped and turned around, but there was nothing behind him. There was no way back to the soothing voices.

He woke with a start. A dark hooded figure against the pre-dawn sky was shaking his arm.

A woman's voice. "Come on Mikel. Time to get up and get packed. Dawn will be here soon."

He didn't remember what he had been dreaming about, just that it somehow left him with a feeling of incompleteness, like giving up on a puzzle you couldn't solve.

The camels were quickly loaded. They had prepared everything the previous day, so this morning was just a matter of putting the last pieces together. It seemed like they were ready to go. The reality was different. Some camels were more than reluctant, while many seemed good tempered others were nasty and loud; he was warned that they could bite. Everyone else took this in their stride, even joked about it as if this was just good natured banter by the animals before the journey.

Finally, he would have to ride a horse. The day before, one of the older Traders, Tarvis, had led him around on a horse like a child, giving him a quick introduction to riding.

Tarvis was a man in his mid forties. He was resourceful, smart, an excellent scout. His graying plaited blond hair against his sun-browned skin made Mikel think of a wise guru or hermit, and he had beads to match. He was no hermit, but he kept to himself a bit. He was leery of outsiders, but trusted Tei implicitly.

Mikel blocked out the laughs when he was on the horse, but noticed that none of them came from his own caravan. He felt like a fool out of his depth. He didn't have the physical attributes, knowledge, or skills. This was going to be a nightmare, but as they say, when you jump off the end of the pier, you either remember your swimming lessons or you drown. He would have to do a lot of learning and remembering. If he survived, this was going to be the most incredible adventure. He caught his breath, reached into the bag on his left hip. His journal and writing tools were still there; he must record all of this later.

By midday there was no city in sight, only trees, a few clouds in the sky, the grass in the surrounding hills and farms so intensely green it seemed like a chemical stain. The sound of rustling leaves as the light easterly breeze fanned the roadside poplars, their leaves shimmering and rustling, birds calling, the buzz of insects some droning close. It was day 12 of the month of Regin; the second month of Spring, just after the month of Greening, second month of the year 635. The islands were always lush, so there wasn't the eruption of life that Spring produced on the mainland. Now he could appreciate why some still worshipped this season.

To the north and south rose the Cantas, the mountain range running roughly north to south, and into the distance with dazzling snow-capped peaks, giving the view a crystal-like clarity. He had first seen them when entering the Bay of Pennit, but the closer he got, the more amazing they became. There was no sense of familiarity.

They attached him to Tarvis's file. He explained the general dynamics of the caravan.

"You see, a Trader has to be independent. That is the most important thing. When we join a caravan, it is for mutual protection and also for mutual gain. Tei runs this caravan so makes quite a large profit. We also get payment for our duties. But we get to include some of our own camels in our file, so we also make a much greater profit on those. Because there is an acknowledgement that we assist each other, young Traders are often loaned a camel or two by the caravan leader, but aren't paid for their services. The extra camel or two is much greater value."

"Services?"

"The Plains can be dangerous. We sometimes need to defend ourselves, and everyone helps. Everyone also helps to get the caravan to the Caravanserai in the East."

"Is there no Caravanserai on the Plains?"

"That would offend the Cities," he said. "And they show their displeasure by arriving in the middle of the night and burning your buildings and confiscating your goods. Worse, if you aren't lucky."

"Really?"

"We had two caravanserais on the Plains once. You can't even tell where the buildings stood now, and that was in my lifetime. We have excellent reason to be wary of the Cities."

"What are the Cities like?"

"Ruined cities of the Ancients. Not all of them survived, some were obliterated in the forgotten times, marked now only by odd glass in the dirt. Most survived, after a fashion, only to fall to Bethor a few centuries ago. Barbarian invasion, but don't ever, ever say that in front of any Bethorese."

"Don't worry, I won't *unintentionally* insult anyone from Bethor."

Tarvis then spent the next hour lecturing Mikel on Duty, which seemed completely at odds with the talk on being independent. He had to admit that even if it appeared contradictory, it all seemed to work. This seemed deep, perhaps a little too deep, because he still didn't understand it all.

# seven

The route was now taking them to the beginning of the Great Plains. Even 80 kilometers east of Bethor, the countryside had changed remarkably. There were no more wooded areas or patches of swamp from ox-bow lakes. The meanders of the Inda River, the outflow of Lake Baikal, dominated all of it. The road cut across and around the obstacles. Mikel pitied the builders of the road and bridges; off the road it might look pretty, but would be a nightmare to cross.

Increasingly, the road now wound through low undulating country covered with grass. They were entering the Plains on the northern side of the Inda River; soon to become the Great Plains. A place of legend and history. Even in Lind and through the Islands, it was told how once the Cities had been great centers of learning and knowledge, how much of what he learned came originally from those places. This journey for a Wizard was almost like a pilgrimage. The Master Wizards spoke little about where such knowledge came from. They just insisted that the student master it and how they should all test it and challenge it, do experiments and publish, always question, and seek to improve or exceed; a relentless quest.

The Cantas still towered to the north and south as they proceeded through the Gap, clouds forming on their upper snow-covered eastern flanks. This would be their camp before entering the Plains. The air had a lush humidity, complementing the vibrant green hills and trees. Few farms here. He expected there to be more people. Bethor had been hit by the plague a dozen years ago, but the Center histories described its effect as much milder than previous years.

In the morning, just before sunrise, Mikel grabbed something to eat while the camp was being struck. The first morning sunlight was lighting up the horizon, and the air was full of birdsong. He walked to the top of a nearby hillock with his piece of bread and unidentified meat and stood on a small mound maybe three meters above the camp. It was enough. He saw the horizon clear, unhazed. The sun, Mellis, was not in sight but was lighting up the few clouds with violets and pinks. There in the distance was the food-bowl of the known world, the Great Plains of Arva. Once it had been the center of a great civilization before Bethor; he hoped he would find out more about it. Mikel heard footsteps behind him crunching the gravel.

"The Great Plains," Tei said with a smile. "We will not be visiting the major towns. It is too risky. Even for us. They have no kindness for strangers, even Traders."

"Why?" Mikel was puzzled. The Traders delivered a valuable service, did not involve themselves in local politics (as far as anyone could tell) and were an important source of information.

"Since the fall of the Cities of the Terrans, rebellions and hatred have troubled the area. The Bethorese conquered the Cities over three centuries ago and so much was lost in the destruction." She paused, the smile gone, replaced now by a look of resignation.

"Most of the people in the towns now are descended from Bethorese immigrants, whereas the farmers are Terrans. As I said, we will avoid the towns. Lately, they have become very dangerous. The Caravanserai lies on the other side of Lake Baikal at the end of the Plains. We will pass to the north of the lake, avoiding the more populated regions."

Tei was quiet. Not finished but also not talking. Then she said, almost whispered, "Lest one good custom should corrupt the world."

"I beg your pardon?" He had no idea what

was meant, though he was surprised that she had spoken in the language that preceded the Ancients. He knew a little of it, it was enough like Ancient to be understood though not the same.

"An old poet of the Terrans, and us all, named Tennyson. You know, things change, even good things pass away and that isn't necessarily bad because sometimes there has to be renewal."

Still looking to the East, she continued, this time louder so he could hear.

"The old order changeth, yielding place to new,
And God fulfills Himself in many ways,
Lest one good custom should corrupt the world."

He still did not understand what she was talking about, but figured this was a time to suspend curiosity and just go along. They looked at the sunrise, silent for minutes, the cool living breeze in their faces, the sound of green grass rustling all about, the fading dawn chorus. Finally, he spoke gently. "When do we head out?"

Tei snapped out of whatever state she was in, perhaps embarrassed, and looked at him hard. She was blushing. "We move NOW Wizard. Get ready, fast!"

He rushed down the hill to gather his things,

gulping down the last mouthful of food. He glanced back. Tei still stood on the hill looking to the east as if there was something out there that she had lost.

They had been in the Plains for two days. Mikel was incredibly sore from the horse riding and trying to do his part to help manage the new file of camels he was part of. Perhaps Tei thought camels would be easier for him. They weren't. Rijart, who managed the file, was an endlessly friendly older man. When he should have become annoyed at the questions, he simply got funnier. He was a renowned negotiator, about forty years old, with reddish hair and a short beard. Mikel had learned a great deal of useful information from him about maintaining the horses and camels, writing the details dutifully into his notebook, Rijart sometimes critically examining what he wrote and correcting him. Mikel was sure Rijart had saved his life by warning him about the less friendly behavior of the camels. He knew all of his camels by name, but they still deserved respect and caution.

Rijart was from Tanfel, far to the south on the Zanda River. It had started as a trading post and now it was booming. So many new trade goods and new spices there. They would bring wagons up from Tanfel to the Eastern Caravarserai. Apparently, the southern road was in reasonable condition, much better than the main road across the Plains. On one trade journey, he met a woman at the Caravanserai. They fell in love and married. She lived in Tanten and he followed her there, thinking it was an opportunity. He had three children, a boy and girl in their teens, both of whom he was so proud of and a toddler whom he missed and loved terribly.

Each day they moved deeper into the Plains. Rolling green hills, with surprising pockets of stream fed pools with fish. Each, the land equivalent of a tidal rock pool. Although all of this was interesting, it was also intellectually deadening. He was traveling through one of the most historically significant areas of the world and it might as well be a walk to the college. Even Tei wasn't speaking much. So he was very glad when the path brought them to a collection of farms fed by some of the natural streams that crisscrossed the Plains. It would be a chance to walk around, talk, buy fresh food and observe. He was literally aching to just lie down.

Ahead, through the lazy rolling green, lay a few widely spaced, meagre houses. The insect sounds of late spring gave them an air of abandonment. Reeds and grass for thatching with a few sticks as supports, mud and grass walls all merging to dull brown amongst the vivid green. There were trees here and there near the village. In the distance on the hill lay a cluster of trees, with abnormal spacing, likely coppiced. In Lind they gave excellent curved wood for ships, but there were no ships here. Now and then the light shone through them in patterns, reminding Mikel of a diffraction grating as the trees seemed to momentarily line up to let light through.

The hamlet was nestled in a gentle hollow, the surrounding hillocks rising several meters above the roofs of the half a dozen huts, yet there were still fields here since the hills rose gently enough. One hut was bigger than the others and from the chairs and tables outside, he got the impression that it was some kind of tavern, big for just these houses that he could see, suggesting there were other farms nearby. Some of the surrounding mounds had jagged edges that protruded out of the soft grass, probably ruins of some kind, while some huts had sturdier walls that looked like they contained masonry; material from the ruins. He wondered what the ruins were like before they were plundered for building material. The village was at a crossroads of rough tracks, the other tracks running haphazardly northwest to southeast, but the amount of grass over the tracks showed it was not a busy place.

The fields that he could see had young but good crops growing. By summer, they would have a good harvest. Recent years had been plagued by drought, heavy rains, and erratic rainfall, Rijart told him. Apparently, the farmer's lot was never easy.

After the villagers spotted the caravan, a small market appeared out of nowhere at the crossroad. Both caravan and settlement knew each other, a symbiotic relationship. The caravan came to a stop less than a hundred meters from the village. Here they would make camp, just a little way out, giving the locals some space. The campsite had the remains of past fires suggesting that this was a regularly accepted event. A meeting of friends. A few Traders left the campsite and headed into the town, though calling it a 'town' or even a 'village' seemed to be an exaggeration. But it was good to walk around and talk to people. They wore simple work clothes that he remembered seeing and wearing, though he couldn't say when. They spoke in a dialect that was familiar to Mikel. It reminded him of the formal language of the Center. He couldn't see any hewn or finished timber. Even the small set of rickety fences surrounding the houses were only made of sticks as thick as his thumb, just poking out of the ground, as if no one cared. A few substantial fences here and there made of rocks, laid on top of one another, no mortar. Again, a feeling of despair and surrender. The place was called Penrith, an old name, the locals said.

People were coming out of the huts, rapidly setting up crude stalls with great speed and skill. Their approach must have been signalled because he could see some people walking over the tops of nearby hills, with large bundles on their backs, pieces of wood poking out. More stalls and goods. Trade goods, he reminded himself. He might not be interested in what they had to sell, but the Traders regarded these people highly.

When he looked back at the nearby stalls, he thought he must have been daydreaming. They were up and ready for business already; a few last second rearrangements of the displayed items. Smiling, eager, perhaps slightly desperate faces. The nearest sold pendants, some of which he noticed, made of pieces of ancient tech items, and a few rare ones made of bright pieces of metal with illegible arcane script written on them. The pieces looked different to the items he saw in the museum in Bethor, and the script was nothing like any language he had seen. In the next stall were beads of semi-precious stones, closer to his budget. He moved on; some amazingly vivid and artistic colored cloth. Many items. Looking back, he saw his companions were not looking casually, they were in active — but he sensed fair — negotiations. Both sides were friendly. This was why Bethor still reluctantly needed the Traders. The Traders were interested in ideas, workmanship, beauty, utility, not in prejudice or ideology; so Traders found and appreciated things the Bethorese wouldn't even bother to look for.

Nearby Kay had bought some of the tech jewelry. He was curious about why she selected those pieces.

"Very interesting items here. I wonder where they find the old tech stuff. Do they have to dig it up or are there old ruins? I was wondering, is there something special about those items you selected?"

Kay looked at him, a cold hard gaze sizing him up; it was not pleasant. He decided he must have been too brusque or violated some custom.

"My apologies if I said something wrong. I'm just curious. Maybe if I start over again. My name is Mikel …" He extended his hand to shake hers. No reaction.

When she spoke, her words were short, clipped, filled with a tense, painful venom.

"I know who you are. And what you are. You can act like everyone's friend, but your voice tells the truth. Stay away from me or I swear I'll gut you. Don't think Tei will come to your aid in time, either."

She moved on.

Mikel stood completely still. He was in a heightened state of consciousness, as if his mind thought he must be in a dream and was trying to wake up. That just made the strangeness more intense. One of the others walked up to him, Rijart.

"Ahem. You intend to act like a pole all day? Farmers will confiscate you as a scarecrow, you know. How will we explain that to Tei? 'No, Tei, don't know where he is, but I'm sure he is being useful'."

He looked at Rijart, not even hearing the lame joke. "Rijart, I — I just had the strangest talk with Kay."

"Leave her be. She'll take a while to trust you. She's a good person. Been through a lot, but that's for her to say, not me. Word of advice, try to lose that Bethor accent. I know it is mild, but it won't win friends where we are going."

He bought a few pieces of food and some small, simple items. On impulse, he bought a bandana for Tei. He didn't even know how he could have thought about giving this to her. What was he thinking? He didn't want to argue too much with the man behind the rough stall when he bought it. There was little opportunity to wheel and deal out here like his Bethor cousins might. It just seemed wrong. He bought the headband. But Mikel was curious.

The man at the stand had thinning gray hair, face vertically lined by age, like jail bars; he stooped slightly over the rickety table of wares. He would often sit down on a stool behind the table and rub his lower back. Nearby there was a rough walking stick and an empty stool.

He coughed slightly to get the man's attention. "I am a scholar." The old man did not react. "I was wondering if there was someone who could tell me any stories of the old Cities?"

The man's eyes lit up. He smiled, a jagged

smile as much a ruin as the cities.

"You want to know the stories of the Cities? Hey, Leif!" He shouted at an equally old man behind another counter.

The man had suddenly become ten years younger. The other man joined them and they introduced themselves to him. Zhu and Leif explained they were finding it very hard to maintain the stories that they had once known. Stories about the origin of the world, and tales of the Cities. They were childishly eager to allow Mikel to preserve some of it. Zhu's face was lined in a criss-cross of age lines with dark brown skin and sun blemishes from working too long in the fields. Leif seemed younger at first sight, but there were telltale signs he was about the same age. But it looked like he had taken better care of himself, probably because of the crude straw hat he wore everywhere. Leif was about five centimeters taller than Zhu. Physically very different people, yet they spoke and interacted like close brothers.

The stories were disappearing, they said, all the triumphs and pain would be lost. The few stories they knew were told to them as bedtime stories when they were children. No one knew if they were true, but it was all they had of their heritage. They wanted it preserved before it was destroyed by the Bethorese. They were the remnants of an old culture, receiving no respect except from the Traders, their culture was about to be snuffed out and they wanted to save their wisdom and dreams, so that others would understand even as more and more of their young people were attracted to the Cities or Bethor. For a moment he remembered his own village, the people, just like these. For that moment the emotions came strong and sudden, as if a giant's hand had grabbed him and squeezed him tightly so he could not breathe. There was an attachment he had to these people. Perhaps he would never understand it, but he couldn't ignore it.

Mikel wrote down some of the shorter stories. Some were straightforward legends and fables. Others were so fanciful he couldn't even follow them. One of his literary friends from the Artist Enclave would probably do better. Still others sounded like they preserved older knowledge that was now misunderstood.

That night around the campfire some farmers came over, everyone shared food and drink. There was a young lad among the villagers who recited an ancient poem, or rather a fragment. He didn't know how old it was. One small piece caught Mikel's attention.

> Stone-faced it rises
> A God's throne fire-barbed baited.
> Waiting.

What are we
that godlike force hand-
offered
pleads our help?

Who are we
who fight eternity with
questions?
With no answers.

Non-answers that gave us
stars
godlike, mortal, flawed,
questions cannot now save
us.

The poem, or whatever it was, perplexed him. He could understand why they were despondent now, but this piece was from before the Fall, when humans built the Cities. Why would they say, "questions cannot now save us"? Questioning was the only way to learn about the world.

The villagers told of their sorrows and the stories told to them since they were children. Strangest were the stories of the Dark. It seemed to involve astronomy, but from the point of view of navigators. There were no stories of the Fall of the Cities, but there were stories that hinted at how they had declined considerably by the time Bethor had delivered the coup de grâce.

Later that night, as Mikel was about to get into his bedroll, Tei came over. She stood unnaturally stiff in the fire's light, flickering on her face, perhaps even vulnerable; looking over him and not at him.

"Thank you for treating them well. Traders remember the *true* greatness of the Cities. And we preserve some of their knowledge, but we don't understand it. Perhaps you can help. Maybe ..." She stopped herself and realized she was going beyond some self imposed boundary. She clenched her fists, hesitated, and then walked away into the night. An enigma. He put his head down, a deep sense of unease in his mind ... this woman was latching herself into some deep part of him. Some part of him was becoming very fond of her, despite any argument or logic he could muster. This was not a good idea. It wasn't even an idea; that was the point and the problem.

# eight

Before the world was made as it is, the Gods ruled the heavenly realm. In heaven, the Gods were ruled by wise Zeus, and in great ages past, he had beaten his great foe the Demon Lord. He then imprisoned and sealed him in a cave. All knew where the cave was and that there were no guards. One day, his mortal assistant, Amaris, whose curiosity was great, ventured into the cave and found the enchanted urn that imprisoned the Demon Lord. Amaris looked into the secret runes written on the urn and she saw great beauty in them. But in her curiosity, she mishandled the urn. It slipped from her grasp and with a loud bang hit the floor of the cave. She picked it up but saw that the urn now had a crack in it. She was afraid of what this meant. Zeus would be angry, but he must be told of this.

She ran from the cave and told wise Zeus. Zeus now understood his folly in not guarding the cave and forgave young Amaris, whom he still favored.

When Zeus arrived at the cave, there were grave rumbling sounds from within and he could just make out dark things flying in the air at the mouth of the cave. In a great voice, Zeus roared, "You cannot come back. I will not permit it."

The Demon Lord laughed in great gusts, like far off thunder. The darkness in the cave trembled at his voice. "We lived before the Gods and we still endure. We will take back Heaven and make it ours again. All that is not of our creation we will sweep aside and burn."

With these words, the Demon Lord strode from the cave tall and mighty, dressed in a golden cape and followed by a thousand small dark shapes of his servants. He threw lightning bolts at Zeus, but Zeus was prepared. He struck his staff into the ground and a hail of burning spears and arrows rained down on the Demon Lord and his minions. Zeus struck the ground again and now the Sun itself concentrated its gaze on the Demon Lord and burned his servants. So great was the light that the Demon Lord himself was forced back into the cave.

Zeus uttered a spell. An incantation that made the mouth of the cave close and knit like hard rock. But he knew his enemy would dig his way out.

"The Demon Lord will not rest. The cave must be guarded."

Zeus struck the ground once more with his staff. The ground rose, grass and soil fell away, leaving raw rock. It kept towering up, up, beyond the clouds, and storms played around its flanks. Now that risen rock was revealed to all as the throne of Zeus.

"I will cast this place from Heaven, and this throne will contain my Spirit and will guard the cave. If ever the Demon Lord returns, I will be waiting for him. To help me I will create a new people who will guard this new world. The world shall be called Neti."

He then called across the space between Neti and Heaven and called that sky boats should come, bringing his new people.

# nine

The Citadel lies to the North where the icy winds flow head-on to the traveller. The dry, frigid air is a test for all but the strongest and the purest of Spirit. Those who reach the Citadel will find a mountain like no other. Towering before you is a work of the Gods, built when the world was made, Throne of Lord Zeus, King of the Gods and Keeper of the Law. From his high mountain, often called Olympus, he watches the world and protects all. He keeps the demon gods at bay lest they afflict the world again.

The way to the Citadel is barred now. North of the poisoned land of Xan the way is guarded by a fearsome dragon. Even those who flee from the dragon and the cursed land return only to sicken and die.

Back in the days when the Gods favored

humanity, the path to the Citadel was clear. In those times there lived a boy, David.

Young David lived in the city of Nu Londin of the Plains. Once he set off with his father, Wulf, to go to the Citadel. Wulf had a magical carriage that would take them there.

David was afraid and said to his father, "Father! The Gods will punish us for approaching them without sacrifices."

"Never mind, little one. They know the carriage and its maker. They bless us and keep us. Zeus himself has blessed our pilgrimage."

They climbed into the carriage, which shut itself around them. Many lights, like jewels, blessed them within and the carriage was lifted into the air as if by the will of Zeus. Soon the carriage was rushing through the clouds and far below they could see the Plains and the Cities and the Lake of Baikal.

In a time shorter than it takes to run from the center of Nu Londin to the Library, they beheld before them a great mountain. Clearly, the home of the Gods: Olympus, The Eternal Citadel.

Of their time in the Citadel, we know no more for all who enter accept a vow of secrecy.

David and his father returned to Nu Londin and told about their journey, but not what was discussed. But all remarked that from that day onwards, David had a long, far look in his eyes. He would grow to become a wise mayor of Nu Londin but would never divulge his message beyond the Circle.

# ten

Before the cities were built, men came down from Heaven in great boats, unlike those that fish the Great Lake.

One of these boats was steered by a great fisherman. He was Ray Tans. It was said he found a sunken boat once, laden with treasure, that no-one else could lift but he. That he knew the ways of the Gods and could gain their Grace for his acts.

Now, Ray Tans had gone on many great journeys, so when he was getting old, the Gods gave him the honor of bringing people to our world. He left them on the Plains where the air was good and there were many wild animals, grains and other foods. But the people forgot who they should thank. They didn't pay homage to the Gods and so fell into conflict and strife. When Ray Tans saw how they acted, he was sad and felt great pain. He said:

"They are young, and need to learn wisdom. They have forgotten the path."

Zeus then struck the Plains with his anger and brought hunger and suffering, and the Cities withered and burned in those times.

All powerful Zeus appeared to him and spoke. "You worry you will not live to see them overcome their folly. You do not need to fear, you have served me well and for this I will grant you a splendid gift. I will set this boat in the sky, motionless, to look down upon the Plains until the day comes when their folly is at an end. You will remain ageless, a light to guide them back onto the path."

# eleven

It is often said that once the Cities were fair and beautiful. Many-colored, their spires rose into the sky far higher than the trees that were then common around the Lake. Strange tales come down to us of those days of magic and power, but the hardest to figure are those of the Dark. The Space between. The ships, you have heard, brought people to Neti. They were not like the fishing boats you may see on the lake. These were gleaming shapes, slender and silvery like a great fish of the air. They would float down to the cities, and from them would come men and women from the sacred places in the sky. This is one story told by the old ones of those who travelled the Dark, the realm of eternal night.

Long ago, a great people built cities and had great thoughts. But their time came and went.

When the People of the Cities flew in their sky ships through the Dark, beyond the stars, their arts were so great they could persuade the gods to grant them passage between the worlds in the blinking of an eye. Their ships of the air sailed to strange places in the Dark, where even words like 'now' and 'then' no longer had the same meaning. So it was that Ancients of the Cities found the world whose time had come and gone. Their cities turned to dust. A few grander things remained impervious to time, just as the Citadel of Holy Zeus resists time itself. Two worlds close by they found, one they called Term and the other Fortress, and the air was good. The plants did not poison them. They saw it was blessed and made it their home. They raised great cities of their own, greater even than those on the Plain.

There was a young woman named Tahani. She took her ship from the world of Term and sailed far into the unknown Dark. There it is said she found a great mystery. She returned to tell of another people, the Others, far greater and more skilled than her own in the art of the Science, the highest and darkest Magic. They told her many things, some were secrets which she never revealed. She told her tale and showed a magical augury containing histories and events unknown to the Ancients. But she couldn't remember the course she steered, and the Others had removed this knowledge from her magical ship. Term prospered and explored but never found the Others. It is said the Others predicted that they would not parley until the people changed their ways. Term and Fortress boldly said that they would never change, that they were the seed of a new endless age and a new empire. They would endure.

But to all things there comes an end.

# twelve

In the morning Mikel awoke, and took half an hour to get his aching muscles moving, then slowly and without thinking started packing his stuff. The daily ritual of pain. There should be more commotion. In fact, someone should have been annoyed that he wasn't up earlier. It looked like he was the only one packing, the others were still unpacked.

He walked over to Rijart who was busy trimming his red beard with an evil looking knife, more weapon than anything else, staring at his reflection in a bowl of water.

"Rijart, what is going on? Or not going on? Why aren't we moving?"

"Talk to Tei. She has a surprise for you. I know you will be thrilled." He burst out laughing hilariously, bumped over the bowl of water, which made him laugh harder.

Tei was packing, but dressed in odd clothes. He did not understand their customs, so it was probably best if he assumed everything was normal; except for them staying here.

"Good morning, Tei. How are you?"

She turned and smiled. It was not reassuring.

"Mikel, I have a great surprise for you. You and I are going to make a secret visit to Lindin."

That sounded intriguing until he remembered what Tei had told him.

"Didn't you tell me just two days ago that the Cities of the Plains were in a highly unstable state and were too dangerous to do any trading? I think you even said something about 'blood thirsty psychopaths'."

"You are right. It would be too dangerous to go in as a Trader, but if Mikel the Merchant were to go in with his wife, that would be very different. It has to be wife. Bethorese don't trust low born women in positions of power — no breeding — so I cannot be your business partner or your boss. Besides, I've heard you fake a Bethorese accent. It is damn near perfect. We need that. They'd recognize my accent in a second, so I will be quiet and demure."

This was not supposed to happen. He just wished he could cancel this trip and make his way back to Bethor. Surely he knew enough. But this apparently crazy woman was explicitly to be his guide. He didn't want to offend the Traders, and therefore the Center, however this woman was going to get him killed.

"I really don't think this is a good idea. Look, why can't I just go back to Bethor by myself?"

"No. You'd get robbed and likely murdered before you got 10 k."

"I could pay one of you to take me back."

She laughed. "No one is going to accept your pitiful allowance for a share in a caravan's profit or their own sales. You come with me. Was that not what you were ordered to do?"

"Fuck! Sure." He gave a growl of frustration.

He was powerless. "When is all of this going to happen then?"

"Take some essentials. Your clothes are fine. Can you act like you are a haughty, I-don't-give-a-crap-about-anyone, sleazy bastard? Good. Wow, you should have been an actor."

"Or a slave," he mumbled, wondering if he was again.

"Whenever you are ready, we will leave. I am taking some Center items as trade goods. I'm sure you are familiar with them. You should have no trouble working up a convincing sales pitch."

They followed a track south, then southwest through lush green grassland and farms. Then he lost his bearings. Looking at the sun didn't help. He couldn't remember where it was last time he looked. Finally, they came to a rough road. This, unbelievably, was the main 'highway' connecting the Cities. From here he could even see the beautiful blue lake in the distance, a slight shimmer over it.

They followed the road. Eventually, a town came into view. He spoke to Tei, in Bethorese, "I'm surprised we are so close to Lindin. I would have thought we would have gone further north."

"It would have taken too much time. This is the best route I could think of."

"Did you also factor in a trip to Lindin as part of that?" he said. A possibility that made him angry.

"We do what we have to."

The walls of Lindin were a palisade of upright rocks, masonry, old wooden beams and sticks. Almost like a giant had mashed a town and piled the debris up as a wall. Inside the gates there were hovels lining each side of the wide road, so many people in rags, interspersed by some in fine clothes. The soldiers at the gates let them in without question once Mikel spoke to them, almost magical: speak and enter, he only said his fake name, in pure Bethorese. There was a great deal of activity, some shops in poorly built wooden structures. Here and there an old stone or cement building, aged but with an old glory. In the distance towered some of the old skyscrapers, the few still standing were little more than shells. Tei whispered they were too old for anyone important to risk their necks in, just for the poor. They seemed immensely impractical, hard to climb, hard to bring water and food up, and waste down. It didn't make sense. He would have to think why the Ancients would even think of building something like that.

The roads were once wide, but the edges were now taken over by stalls and tents of families and hucksters. Noise and bustling. Not the colors of Bethor, but overwhelming grays, browns and dirt. An oppressive, almost ominous heat complemented the pressing eyes and hunger. It was drab and dirty; it was wretched.

"Tei, why are the fields so lush but everyone looks like they are hungry? Don't they farm?"

"Unreliable growing seasons. The attitude that farmers are rebels. Previous reliance on other sources of food, now exhausted. Hmm, yes, it shouldn't be this bad. They have their own farms."

Despite that, it was busy. He saw lots of bartering, the glint of silver coins.

"Lots of activity here," he said.

"A very profitable place. But money is no good if you get your throat cut."

"There also seem to be a lot of soldiers here. Is this normal?"

"Not at all. We should investigate."

"Damn. Why did I say that?"

They brought their horses up to an inn that Tei knew facing a large square where a market was in progress. Inside, it looked cosy enough, or maybe dingy enough to hide them. He had trouble concentrating. He was sore and still not used to riding a horse for so long. His body was aching, he just wanted somewhere to fall into a bed. The innkeeper greeted them. Tei still kept the hood over her head, hiding her face.

"I would like a room for me and my wife. The name is Mark Oconnor, and my wife…"

"Tei," the innkeeper said, and smiled. "You and your *wife* are welcome here. I hope your business goes well. Standard rate is five silver."

Later in their room.

"He knows you?"

"Shhh. These walls are thin, whisper. Yes, he knows me. We are old friends. Traders trade and make friends. Not all in Bethor are swept along in this craziness."

"But — can you really trust him? A casual word from him and…" An old memory, hideous, flashed in his mind and was gone. He took a deep breath. He couldn't remember it, but his shaking body did.

"Mikel. I mean, Mark, you look terrible. How about you lie down on the bed for a quarter of an hour, dear?"

He sat down on the edge of the bed without thinking. His mind clouded over instantly.

"Huh? Doesn't make sense. An hour is 63 minutes can't divide by four."

"The homeworld of the Ancients had a 24 hour day that had 60 minutes in an hour. On Neti they just changed the minutes in the hour to 63."

He was sitting on the edge of the bed. Growing weary. He heard Tei. It should be fascinating, but he was having a hard time thinking. How long was a year on the Ancient's home? Did they also have a leap year every second year, except for the 72nd? No, that would vary from world to world. He couldn't work it out. He toppled over. Tei came to him and pulled his shoes off. Vaguely, he heard an angelic woman's voice.

"Sleep, my prince. I'll protect you." Maybe a kiss on the forehead. That was surely a dream, perhaps.

He came to, then snapped wide awake as a single memory came back. He was in Lindin, and wanted to jump out of bed, but his whole body ached so much he couldn't move. Slowly, he swung his legs off the bed and pushed himself up with one hand. There was pain everywhere.

"Ah. You're awake! Good. How are you feeling? Don't worry, I think you only slept for about an hour."

He groaned.

"I'm sore all over. Can't move."

"Ready to go? Come on, once you get moving you'll feel better."

The sun was noticeably lower in the sky. It was a

pleasantly warm day. But the smells of the city were atrocious. There was poor sanitation, and everywhere the signs of disease in the people he saw. Many of the problems he knew were curable, even avoidable with sewers. They didn't even know about antibiotics or aspirin, much less the new vaccination. Although many diseases had returned, they had saved some practices from the time of the Ancients, less so in Bethor and not at all in Lindin. This was a city that suffered unnecessarily. Its only painkillers were nationalism and jingoism. He didn't know the history of such things, but guessed it would not be good. Tei told him that the Traders knew the histories and that he was mostly right, it would not end well. They would unleash a wave of terror, eventually that terror would be directed internally, first at traitors, then finally it would be self-justifying and perpetuating. It would consume the society that gave it birth, it would cause endless suffering for the innocent.

They walked south out of the market area into an area that looked very different. Here, the old city had decayed or been obliterated. Now flat and replaced by row upon row of army tents. A pall of smoke was rising from campfires. Men in the distance were practicing drills. It was highly suspicious, and he knew they were too close already. A guard — no, an officer — approached them. He was beefy, heavyset but with the air of someone who was fit despite that. He was dressed in the red and black of the army, his face had a red blush, more from health than overindulgence of anything, and a great mustache that flowed off his upper lips like a curl of reddish brown smoke across and up both sides of the face. The man stopped, put both hands in his lower vest pockets, chin up, announcing confidence but betraying a complete lack of animosity or guile — not a professional soldier. He spoke in a boisterous, barely disguised, friendly voice. A broad southern Canta accent. Not the picture of the Bethor war machine he expected.

"Citizen! What is your business here?"

"Good afternoon, sir. I was merely walking with my wife to see the city. I have never been to Lindin before. Most of my business is in Bethor. Come to think of it, is there anything that our troops miss from Bethor or the Cantas?"

He smiled. "Well, yes, quite a bit. For instance..." He gave Mikel an almost shy look, embarrassed to be talking about trivial things at a time like this. "You know that salami they make in Grahamville, south of Bethor? You can get it in Bethor, at Fenth's deli on Steel Street. It always reminds me of home and my Beth. A lot of us miss things like that. I know you think that is silly. There are lots of things we need, but we miss home most of all. That and such like that would be a welcome relief."

"Sure. I'll see what I can do."

"Look forward to it, sir. The name is Miley,

Miley Aarons, sergeant first class. At your service."
He saluted.

They smiled and left, walking to the south.
Mikel wanted to see the Lake close up.

After a few blocks, they were out of sight of
the camp. There were fewer people here.

"Tei, there were thousands of troops there. I
think we know why everyone else looks hungry, all
those extra mouths to feed, and guess who gets
preference. Surely, they don't need that many to
defend Lindin?"

"Correct. They are preparing for war. But
against whom?"

"We can figure that out later."

They continued to walk south towards the
lake. Some of the old buildings he noticed were in
reasonable condition and inhabited, others were
just rubble.

The histories of the Cities and their fall were
complex and confusing with sizeable gaps and
inconsistencies. No one understood it. Much of the
damage was done long before Bethor conquered
them, but for some reason, they didn't repair it.
The sun was setting, the reddening light mellowing
out the harshness, giving a false friendliness to the
faces that passed him. They would not get to the
Lake in time, and he didn't want to be on these
streets in the dark.

In the middle distance to the left were the
ruins of a once large old building, a few walls

poking out of the dirt, some blackened by an age old fire. There were soldiers guarding it and a team of people in rags working, digging, carrying loads of debris. Overseers walked among them dressed in the latest fashions with whips in hand lashing out, seemingly at random at the workers who were dressed in shredded rags. In his mind he saw blood dripping from the shreds of cloth, as if it was ragged flesh. They had leather collars.

"Slaves."

He remembered. This whole depressing, decayed atmosphere. The death of hope and humanity. It all flooded back.

He was perhaps nine. There was a family that needed a few children for a special occasion. His owner had given him as a loan to the refined household, just for the event. The Lady of the House had come to his owner's villa one afternoon. There was muffled talk, all in private, in a locked room. But adults forget how well they could hear as a child. He heard it all; he understood he was to perform a role and nothing else. The matron of the house wanted children to serve at formal parties. She thought it would be a sensation, a new trend. He should look cute.

Next day they delivered him like a package to the servants' quarters of the household. He was washed and dressed in fancy clothes. Do this, do that. Don't do this, don't do that. The staff were paid servants. He was only a slave. Property. The scars from the whips hidden under the fine clothes. It was a soirée. He held an elegant plate of small bite-sized pieces of food with outlandish adornments, none of which he was allowed to eat, of course.

There was a discussion on the tides in the bay and wave patterns. How they would affect the shipping.

He walked up to them and let them take one of his offerings. As he listened in, a sudden urge to connect overcame him. He spoke.

"Which way do the waves bend when they enter the bay? I've noticed that waves change direction when the depth changes."

They looked at him strangely. As if the teapot had just spoken.

A maid whisked him away to an adjoining room, who was about to scold him when a young woman in a red party dress approached. The maid addressed her as "mistress".

"So little one. You want to talk to adults as an equal? Not just as a free child. But as an adult. Most curious. Come with me."

"I only wanted to talk about what I had seen and what it means?" he said.

"*What it means?* How about you consider what your situation *means*?"

She grabbed him by the arm and led him to a room at the back of the mansion. There was a man sitting there. Big, bearded, dressed in leathers and skins, as if he had just come from a hunt. Several elaborate knives were tucked into his belt and a sword in a leather scabbard on his left side.

"Henry. Take him." She said.

The man casually walked up to him and grabbed him. Pushed him down onto the floor on his back and pinned him there.

The woman walked over to him in her so elegant dress and pulled out a dagger with a wavy blade. He had never seen such a thing, but it spoke of pain and terror.

"It is called a *kris*, beautiful and deadly. Remember this and remember me."

He pleaded. He didn't remember what he said, he just pleaded like the child he was.

He didn't see what she did, but he felt it. There was a nightmarishly sharp, blinding pain in his left kneecap. She dug the point of the dagger into his patella, making sure she didn't damage the *property*. Just piercing the bone a bit. She removed the blade, leaned close to him.

"Little one. Let this be a lesson. Learn as I did. If you don't want to be stepped on, then become the one who steps on others. I'm doing you a favor."

When she got up, he saw she was shivering. The look on her face was strange, as if she was distressed and excited at the same time. It was more frightening than the blade.

She looked at Henry. "Tell Alfonse that he isn't suitable for tonight, but I will want him again. Take him back and tell him I don't want him damaged."

"Yes, m'lady."

"I've told you before, don't use that archaic feudal address around me. Address me properly."

"Certainly, Ms Markham."


Alfonse was not happy. He got out a whip and raked it across Mikel's back a few times until he saw some blood. He strode about dressed in an unseasonably thick leather coat. Perhaps it hid weapons and armor so he could deal with his business associates.

"I've had another who's been giving me problems. Even more so. Can't sell him. Can't even put him on the streets. He'd bolt just as you would."

Mikel could tell he was getting angry, and he had been drinking. He couldn't do much himself, locked as he was in one of the bamboo cages, hunched down. Sometimes other children were here, but the others must have been sold. Mikel hadn't been sold, maybe he didn't look compliant enough, perhaps a touch rebellious or independent.

Alfonse came back into the room dragging a boy, his hands bound behind him. His name was Paul. He was slightly older than Mikel and had blond hair and brown eyes; he was only dressed in ragged short pants. Paul had a tender nature, or so Mikel thought, based on the little he saw of him.

Then, in front of Mikel, Alfonse slowly cut him into pieces as he screamed. Every time he tried to look away, Alfonse would yell, "Look! Or I'll do this to you next."

He wondered why guards, or neighbors, or any passerby who had any decency didn't burst in through the door. There was so much blood, he prayed for little Paul to die quickly or faint. But the screams just went on and on.

He watched as Paul was cut into pieces, screaming. Endless screaming. Then it did end. Then Alfonse fed Paul to his dogs, bit by bit, in front of Mikel. He was shivering in terror and numb at the same time; deep inside, there was a white furious rage growing. He wanted to rip the cage apart, but he knew he couldn't. He wasn't strong enough, and if he tried, he would get a dagger in the throat, or worse.

That night Mikel had shut his eyes and tried so hard to forget what he had seen and heard and felt. But it went round and round, always there.

The same household as last time had requested him. So he went along, dressed in smart clothes, but not too smart. He was only a slave acting as a servant.

The woman with the knife met him at the entrance to the ballroom. She saw the hollow look in his eyes.

"I see your master has instructed you in the ways of the world. Obey and live, and maybe someday you will be the master."

It was a mindless party. He did what he had to do. Always there were flashes of Paul, screaming.

Back at the dingy slave dwelling that night, Alfonse had been drinking again.

"You know, you little piece of crap, I get favors, financial ones, from that damn Markham family. Resting on their laurels. *Almighty conquerors* — in their imagination. They have coin, but I don't get enough."

He staggered over, casually picked up his favorite big stick, and whacked the cage for no apparent reason. Then he smiled, pointing the stick at him and jabbed him through the bars and straight into his ribs. Mikel doubled up in pain.

"Damn that lot. Maybe they like toying with you, but I need some cash. I'm selling you tomorrow. If you aren't sold then you'll be meeting your friend." Alfonse said.

Mikel didn't feel any fear. His emotions had hit some saturation point. That capacity was exhausted.

The next day at the slave market, horrors were still floating in front of him whenever he closed his eyes. It didn't look like he would be sold. Then a softly spoken man, hooded in a plain brown cloak, came up and talked to him. Alfonse stepped up to intervene, but the man flashed something at him. Alfonse's eyes went wide, there was a look of fear in his eyes. It thrilled Mikel.

He talked some more to Alfonse then to Mikel and then took him by the hand to his new life.

He was back in the here and now. A warm night was falling, faint putrid smells, acrid smoke but a fading of activity, as if the earth was preparing for sleep. They were in great danger. He was in Lindin and this was a dangerous place to remember. Tei had moved him behind a half fallen, carbon scored, gray wall. He was shaking with fear and rage and pain. So much pain. For his family butchered, for other slaves casually murdered or mentally scarred. There were tears running down his face. He knew it was bad, but he couldn't stop.

Tei said, "Mikel! What is it? Oh gods! What was I thinking coming here?"

He remembered now. Remembered the relaxation mantras they had taught him, the practice that had saved him after he came to Lind. The breathing exercises. He took a deep breath and clenched his fists, breathed out and relaxed his fists. He repeated the process, again and again. Repeated the mantras, again and again. Felt the wave of relaxing muscles flow from the top of his head to his toes, and finally within his mind. At last, he looked at Tei, who was breathing too deeply and quickly.

"I will be fine, Tei. I — I just remembered a lot of things, all at once."

He told her. Not all of it, just a summary. A bloody, chilling summary.

"Gods! Damn! Here I thought you were some clueless child shielded from the real world. This was a mistake. I've got us into danger. I wasn't thinking."

"I am fine. Really. We'll get out of here. Tonight. I really don't want to stay any longer. Too many memories here."

"It will be too dark to leave. It will also look very suspicious. We can leave first thing tomorrow. You've been here before?"

"No. Just the slaves and the attitude. Makes me very uncomfortable."

They got back onto the main thoroughfare, heading back the way they came. Some others were on the same path. They were the overseers from the excavation.

Mikel approached one. Tei reached out to stop him. Too late.

"Hello sir, Mark Oconnor, a merchant from Bethor. Recently set up my business. I thought I'd visit the Plains to see what the Cities needed." He offered his hand. The other fellow accepted it.

He was dressed in a dark waistcoat, with light colored britches. He couldn't tell the colors in the fading light.

"See our quartermaster, he should be able to

supply you with a list. It would be very welcome."

"Looks like you're digging. Foundations for a new building? Or perhaps a metal mining venture?"

"Those would be boring but more useful. Lindin is pretty much mined out these days. My family got rich stripping the skyscrapers way back. Nothing profitable about this, however. I have to babysit a group of academics from the College of Bethor. Some archeological 'dig'. Looking for surviving parts of the Lindin Library." He ended it with a conspiratorial sneer.

They talked about the weather, the opportunity for hunting in the area, fishing. All poor, it seemed. Then they farewelled him.

"Mikel? How did you do that? How could you just shut that off?" Tei looked worried.

"When I was young, I had to block it out. So I used the hope of a new life, a new way of looking at the world. It turned my old world into a bad, evil dream, irrelevant and best forgotten. Now I not only have hope, but anger. I can reject everything they stand for with glee; deceiving them is a joy."

Tei put her arm in his, holding on to him. Not just an act now. Even in the fading light, she could see the tears in his eyes.

At daybreak the next morning, they left.

There had been some rain in the area they were going through. The grass was bright green, glistening with raindrops like diamonds, bright starlike points sparkling from individual drops, the clouds rapidly breaking up and disappearing to the west, the sun low in the east. Insects were buzzing, and the world looked too clear and perfect to be real.

"Mikel? Are you all right?"

Mikel was in the lead, which was unusual, and hadn't said a word in more than an hour.

"Not really. Still so many terrible things in my head. Let's talk about something else. Hey, what was that fellow talking about? An 'archeological dig'? Since when was Bethor interested in broadening their minds? I smell a rat, or a lot of rats."

The hardness in his tone was new. Whatever he had remembered had changed him. Tei wasn't sure if this would make him a liability. She had seen others blinded by hate leading their team into certain death, ignoring all reason and strategy. It only ended in slaughter. Fortunately, Mikel was still a novice and not in command of anything. This admission made her wonder why he was still on this trail with her. Why didn't she just send him back?

"Hmm. Can't say. You are right, it is very unusual. Who would fund it and why?"

"Why excavate a library? Surely, all the papyrus would have long since decayed?" he said.

Tei almost stopped, as if startled. "That's it! I was so busy trying not to get noticed it didn't occur to me before. The Cities when they were in decline, transferred a lot of their knowledge to paper and papyrus, but they also converted some of it into a permanent form. There were stories that the Cities made some books of thin sheets of nickel with information printed onto it. Lindin had the greatest library. They must be after designs of weapons. They would only do that ..."

"If they were going to start a war. A big war."

Tei didn't speak anymore because she was afraid of sharing her suspicions about what would come next.

Mikel did not speak because the memory of his last message to the Center was fresh in his mind, and now there was a vision of an army of enslavers on the march. It hurt so much he wanted to physically scream, instead he picked up the pace. He knew he would be part of this war one way or another, and any fear had gone. He welcomed it.

When they got back to the camp, Tei gathered everyone around and recounted what had happened, leaving out anything that would embarrass Mikel.

Mikel sat away from everyone, just staring at the dirt, or admiring a grass stalk he constantly twiddled with his fingers. He wasn't even listening. He didn't see the occasional glances towards him.

Tarvis came over and sat by his side.

"Tei says that you had some problems in Lindin. Didn't say what exactly. You know…"

Mikel could feel Tarvis coiling like a snake about to strike.

"I'll be straight with you. Your Bethor accent is too good. I heard you practicing it before you went to Lindin. By Zeus, son, if you try to hurt or betray Tei, or us, I will slit your throat myself. You got it?"

"That's bullshit, Tarvis! You know how I spent my time in Bethor? I was a slave. Someone I knew was murdered in front of me, legally, because he was a slave. I've been in Lind since I was ten years old, when the Wizards rescued me."

"Tarvis!" Tei's voice, slow and edged with anger. "Leave him alone. He's okay. He has even more reason to hate Bethor than we do."

Tei gently grabbed Tarvis by the arm and pulled him away. Tarvis, looking back at Mikel slowly understanding.

Later, Travis came over and sat next to him. There was only the sound of insects; chirps, clicks, the breeze in the grass, darkness had fallen, a slight rushing sound from the darkness beyond as if the night had a voice. Mikel still felt dangerous, like a booby trap waiting to wreak harm over all those nearby.

"I'm sorry about what I said earlier. I didn't know. How are you holding up?" Tarvis said.

"I've been worse."

"Yeah, so I heard. You know, you're not alone in that, son. You see, everyone here has had to deal with tragedy in their lives. It seems we live in hard times. So they understand. Tei, 'boss lady' herself, do not tell her I said that, lost her twin brother to a bandit attack when she was young. Blames herself. Don't tell her I said that either."

He paused, looked at Mikel, then looked away into the dark. "My wife, love of my life, died in childbirth, lost them both."

Mikel looked at him. A focused stare, lasting maybe three seconds, the stare you sometimes see, or receive, when someone re-evaluates another, seeing them truly for the first time.

"I'm sorry."

"We all have our own unique pain. But sharing eases it better than anything else. Don't hide away Mikel."

Tarvis got up and lit the fire; built in such a way that almost no smoke rose from it. He had dug a small pit and placed the fire inside it to reduce the chance of anyone else seeing it, unnecessary here, but it was a habit he couldn't break. He used Mikel's fire-starter kit, which he had taken a liking to. Then they sat together, silent, occupying a cocoon of yellow, flickering light. Cozy, familiar, with friends.

He didn't know what Tei thought of him now. Did she think him useless for his breakdown in Lindin?

Was he a burden she would quickly dispense with, dispatching him back to Lind with an attached note: "rejected, please don't insult me?" He would just have to push through this. Usually, when this feeling would come over him, he would surrender to his curiosity — or was it embrace? It had saved not just his life and sanity but his spirit, it had helped make him a better person. He was curious and interested in all things and all people, and found a deep human bond with almost all of them. The hatred in Bethor was an aberration, a wall to keep the truth and companionship out. Or perhaps he was simply naïve; no, it felt right.

Tei came down the files, checking on everyone and scanning the horizon, the animals, the riders. And Mikel. She matched pace with him.

"How are you?" She sounded concerned, even gentle. "I was anxious back in Lindin. You're a good man, Mikel, a credit to the Wizards. Don't worry, you'll do fine. We're all here to back you up. Any questions?" She smiled.

"Well. There are some things that I have wondered about. No one in Lind could answer them for me. For example, why is Bethor so different? I mean, there is the Center, and also the Traders. They both respect knowledge and learning. Even tolerance."

"And the original Cities. They were the same. You want to know what made Bethor so crazy?" She said.

"Yes."

He had never understood this. More than anyone, he knew what the people of Bethor were capable of, and yet they shared the same origins and culture.

"Long ago, after the calamity that overcame our world, there was a small fishing port called Benthic. Many refugees flooded there. It was where Benthic Corp had established a fishing fleet, one of the few remaining sources of food. Over the years, the name mutated to Bethor. There were petty revolutions, but at least in Bethor they didn't fight with Ancient weapons, as they did in the Cities. But they had too many revolutions. Too much history was lost. They forgot who they were and became different. They thought they were special, that they had a 'Destiny'. Among the revolutions, some people returned to the Cities. But most stayed. Eventually, Bethor took on the Cities, who no longer had any functioning weapons and had lost the ability or will to rebuild. It was a terrible and sad time, so the histories tell us. Does that answer your question?"

"I guess so. I hadn't realized how traumatic their history was. Before you go, I have another question, a little one this time?" He smiled at her. To his surprise, she smiled back.

"What was that unusual tech the farmers were selling as jewelry?"

"Good question. Maybe someday you'll find

the answer to it, in short — I don't know. No one knows. It is very old, older than the Ancients, but we don't know what it is. It is hard to find, and usually you have to chip it out of solid rock. I do not know where the farmers got it. But they are pretty, aren't they?"

"Indeed, and the mystery makes them even more alluring."

"And about that 'calamity'."

"No. That's enough. And no one knows much about that, anyway." She moved her knees and the horse leapt forward. She was back on duty.

# thirteen

From atop the South Tower of the Palace, she looked toward the Lake and southern Lindin. There was a low blue haze over the city, shading to a brown smear as she looked to the horizon. Brown floating above the shimmering lake. She thought about Tanten to the East and Lind far to the West. Once they had access to such great knowledge, then her own wizards would rise in power, and all that power and knowledge would find her at the nexus. As it should be. She looked down at the people of Lindin going to and fro like mindless ants.

"Look at them all scurrying about. An ignorant mob, unthinking, ignorant of their past, clueless about the present, muddled about the future. I will fix that. Under me, they will be educated and learn their own history, they will forget Earth, make their own way in the Universe.

The knowledge of the Wizards and Traders comes with strings attached. We will forget the past and its failed morality." She looked about. Her entourage smiled knowingly. She had picked them well. They agreed with her completely and would obey without question.

"Ellis, Mirren, are you clear on your goal?"

"Yes sir, General Markham." Both replied on cue.

One day, she would change how they addressed her. But it was too soon to call her Empress.

"A boat to Pareth is waiting for you. I repeat, make it known to Lord Atkins that he will be well rewarded for his efforts. He will know what I mean."

She waved them off; they saluted and her two lieutenants departed briskly. All of her people had a sense of purpose missing from the rest of the world. It always gave her a thrill to look at them and think of their destiny. All obstacles seemed to fall before her now, now that she had understood what was required, the selfless devotion to the Cause, the sacrifices, the deaths, even those at her hands would be honored one day.

She stood, considering the view for another twenty minutes. Thinking how she would rebuild the Cities, educate the Bethor people, and with so many new slaves at their beck and call.

She also considered her revenge, how she

would imprison, then torture, so slowly, so creatively, those she despised, and the list was so long, even before she thought outside of Bethor. It almost made her flush with excitement and anticipation, but not yet. Soon. *Be patient*, she told herself. She did this occasionally, her own private pep-talk, to bolster her resolve, especially when she had to do something 'distasteful' which, by her definition, was to practice her revenge on those she knew were innocent.

She left the tower and proceeded down endless stairs to the dungeon. Only the light of a brazier and a few oil lamps lit the room as she entered. There, strapped to a table, with the odd bruise, spatter of blood, and burn mark, was the subject of her inquiry. The man's name was Marius, he was the owner of the Horse's Whistle Inn, which catered to merchants on the Eastern Road, but now he was of interest because someone noticed him talking to a man and woman, but the woman was overheard later to have a Trader accent. The informant claimed to have heard from an adjoining room. Liz thought this spurious, but they might as well see what this innkeeper knew. A pity he was just an ordinary man, still there needed to be sacrifices if the future she planned was to be achieved.

She didn't bother letting him have his name in her mind, which made it easier to ignore his suffering.

"What did you find?"

"He has paid less on the Tax than he should have, about 130 silver. Also, he has been watering down his beer. He welcomed a Trader and allowed her and her male companion to stay the night. He ..."

"That last one. What are the details?"

The Master of Inquiry, a learned man who 'assisted' the palace torturer, consulted a rough parchment with his notes.

"He took in a Trader who he referred to as 'Tei', and her companion who identified himself as Mark Oconnor." He read out in his reedy voice, which mocked the black ominous clothes he always wore in failing compensation.

"Tei? Tei Lin Valis? One of the camel-herders-acting-as-ambassadors they have, because they don't have the wit to have real ones," she said, smirking at the assistants. They all laughed.

"What about this companion? Anything more on him?"

"He had a Bethor accent, he also had clothes that had a Lind style," the Master of Inquiry read without emphasis.

"What?"

She held up her hand as he was about to repeat his account.

"And ...?" Her icy look pressed him, making him aware of the price of a lack of diligence.

"That is it, Ms Markham. Perhaps a merchant

who visited Lind or who likes their clothes?" he responded instantly, his hands shaking slightly.

"No. Bethorese people dislike Lind styles. Our merchants do not visit Lind, and in fact are forbidden to. Gentlemen, we have an ambassadorial Trader traveling with a Wizard, probably of some skill if he can fake an accent that well. What does that tell you?" Not a glimmer of understanding in her *select* audience. "I'll tell you …" She looked at their consternation. Waste of time explaining, she decided.

"Never mind." She turned to a soldier behind her, took his short sword out of the sheath, looking at it glint so beautifully in the light of the oil lamps, as if liquid gold was pouring down the blade. She turned to the table. The man strapped onto it looked exhausted, as if some vital aspect of his life had drained from him and could never be replenished. The orange light hid most of the insults to his body, while his exhaustion almost gave him a look of peace. She walked up to the table, sword held up like a torch.

"Don't worry, friend. I am here to set you free."

He smiled, thankful, then in a moment of horror he understood. She lowered the sword and thrust it horizontally, the vertical edge of the blade passing easily through the ribs. She pierced his left lung, arcing down, and felt it slice into his heart. A satisfying feeling. The man shuddered, his eyes went glassy, as if looking at her from a great distance.

She pulled the blade out. In part, it was still touched by that liquid gold, now also tainted by fading lifeblood oozing downwards. She handed the sword back to its young owner and thanked him, disregarding the look of shock on his face.

She called her assistants. There was much to do.

*A Trader ambassador with a Wizard. This could only mean trouble. Lind and Tanten forming an alliance? Damn, this changes the timing of everything. They would have to move sooner than planned.*

"Tori, tell General Chen I need to see him. We will have to speed up our plans. And Boris, tell me you have found something in the Library dig site."

"Yes, my Lady. I mean Ms Markham. My apologies." He was embarrassed. But she understood it was hard to fit into their current culture while maintaining a different one in her presence. Still, she had to bring him into line for his own good.

"Do you want to work for me and the Cause? If you do, then address me correctly. Continue."

"Y — yes, the dig — the dig has been confirmed as the site of the Lindin library. We have already found some intact old books, very fragile. The conservators are stabilizing them so they can be transferred for analysis. We are still in the outer sections, all collapsed. But there is evidence that the lower sections may still be intact. The site foreman estimates we will reach the lower sections in three days."

She considered this news. It was too slow; there was a Trader and a Wizard together out there. If such an alliance was made, then it would complicate things considerably. Who knew what Lind or Tanten had up their collective sleeves? They were secretive and possessed Ancient knowledge. Individually, they were dangerous, but together they might be invincible. Too many unknowns, though it was clear her war must use 'divide and conquer', which meant she had to move quickly.

"Proceed, but dig around the clock. This has the highest priority. Report any new discoveries to me immediately. I will want an update at sunset."

# fourteen

They had been moving east, heading towards the rising sun, visiting the few small farming settlements along the way. The stories they told were strikingly similar. The Ancients, according to the stories, were not from this world. Zeus was real. The northern land of Xan was desolate and guarded by a monster. Thaytan, or Raytans as the Traders called it, was a ship of some kind. None of it made sense to the Bethorese, who dismissed it all as primitive superstition.

Apart from the day excursion to Lindin, it had been a week of easy travel since they had entered the Plains. They had seen only farmers and had only used the almost forgotten paths through the grass and rolling hills. From the distance they were almost invisible. Eventually, they reached a river that was a true river and not an easily forded creek. The Euphray came from the north and the only crossing was a bridge to the south. This made everyone nervous. But in the end, crossing the river was uneventful. There were no guards or much of any traffic at the bridge. The caravan now turned southeast as far as he could tell. Mikel noticed the grasses were losing the vibrant green color, and they had seen no farms since yesterday. Tei was riding near him, probably managing the files. He guessed someone, probably Rijart, was doing double duty and minding her file.

"Tei! No farms. Are we leaving the Plains?" He spoke louder than he should. She wasn't that far away.

"Not quite. 'The Plains' is a misnomer. The term originally described very large ecosystems, but these plains are not 'Great'. We have just passed to the northeast of the center of the Plains and Lake Baikal. Now we go into drier country as we head southeast towards the Caravanserai." She gave him a nod and a smile. Then she rode off towards the front of the caravan. After she had gone only 20 meters, she abruptly stopped, wheeled around and came back to him.

"Ah. I have something for you, my Wizard."

"My name is Mikel."

"Of course, but it sounds so good having a Wizard in my team. Anyway, I have something for you." She was close enough to hand something over to him, easily synchronizing her hand to the

147

bobbing of the two horses. She dropped it into his hand. It was a bracelet of brown beads.

"Tigers-eye beads. Brings *good luck and insight*. Not that you need the insight part."

"I have something for you as well," he said.

He pulled out the bandana, blue and yellow, that he had bought from the first farmer's market they had visited and handed it to her. She smiled at it, then clutched it to her chest and whispered something he couldn't quite hear.

"Thank you, Mikel. You know, in some parts, the exchange of gifts is considered to be a courtship ritual. Even a marriage proposal." She laughed.

He felt uncomfortable, perhaps because this was getting too close to feelings he was having to fight. The Center does not forbid love for its wizards, but on missions it is a risky idea.

"Wait, you started the *giving* with the bracelet. In which case ..." he said, smiling. Perhaps he just should have said nothing.

She wasn't listening. Tei was looking towards the head of the caravan. There was another caravan coming towards them. It took only a few more seconds before he knew it was not a caravan. Riders on horses with weapons. He could see the glint of metal just above them, likely from the tips of spears. Tei was galloping immediately to meet the band at the head of her caravan.

It was a large patrol; he supposed out of

Sanfran, the nearest and most easterly of the Cities of the Plains. The Traders said that the Cities often tested the borders with each other, and also liked to put down the local peasantry just in case they decided to recover their birthright. So patrols could turn up anywhere at anytime.

He hung back and tried to look like a Trader. Wizards rarely wore distinctive clothing. They did carry a unique medallion, which each wizard made himself, but it was rarely visible. Wizards preferred to quietly observe and ask questions. People who knew wizards could identify one, if he or she was young. The older ones learned to blend in, seem ordinary and boring and occasionally intervene if needed. It was an ethos he admired: to act and do good without expecting recognition, even avoiding it. He was not an experienced Wizard who could blend in. He could only do that in Bethor and Lindin because he remembered the accent and attitude so well. Mikel felt very exposed, so he would have to fake being a Trader, a Bethor merchant with Traders just would not be believed.

The Captain, that is what he called himself, quickly rode past the column of freight camels. He stopped for a moment near Mikel, to his right, then looked at the camels that stood patiently as if waiting for the journey to continue. Mikel couldn't resist a quick look at this Master of the Plains. The Captain was slightly taller in the saddle and looked to be about 30 years of age. He had dark skin, a small scar on his right cheek, and hadn't shaved for several days by the look. He had the beginnings of a black beard on his face. His armor was made of chain mail over leather. The Center knew about chain mail but had already devised countermeasures. No-one dared attack the Center. It was not an ivory tower. Against the Center, any arms race was already lost. He was impressed, but not awed. On the Captain's head, he wore a bright metal helmet made from a silvery metal. Probably silver itself since Bethor lagged far behind in metallurgy, in which case was that burnished look of the chain mail, copper? At the front of the helmet was a crest or insignia, but he couldn't make it out.

The Captain barked an order in Bethorese, ordering his men to escort the caravan. It seemed they were now to become the guests of the Court of Sanfran.

They travelled south to Sanfran along an old but serviceable road raised slightly above the surrounding land. Now Mikel could finally get a glimpse of the farms. Not as productive as those to the west, he presumed, noticing the distinct telltale lack of deep green around the fields, but more than further east, which by the looks was harsh. To the north of Sanfran, farms stretched along the coast. Tei explained to him that there were once farms further inland, but since the Drying of the East and the silting of the irrigation systems, the farms had increasingly hugged the lake shores. Some new irrigation works had been constructed, but they did not extend far inland. There were no plans at present to connect the new system to the old, as far as Traders knew, because there wasn't the labor force to get the old system working again.

"They can farm here through all seasons. If they got their irrigation system sorted out, they would be in a much better position." Tei said, with some implied sarcasm or perhaps irritation.

"From what I see, they are at least doing something. Not like Lindin, which is a mess." He said.

"The big problem with Sanfran is that they do not have enough storage capacity for the grain they produce. If they could store more, they could increase exports, they could expand their farming. We could help, but they are an insular society. They usually ignore overtures from us, even though they despise the other cities and Bethor. It is very unusual for them to grab one of our caravans. We will see soon enough what this is all about."

Contrary to what he had seen in Lindin, the farmers looked healthy, and although they were not dressed well, they seemed better off, happier, and there were no whips here. Some of them even waved as they passed. Mikel couldn't help but wave back. He had small town habits and saw no reason to abandon them.

The city was not what he expected. Bethor had been bustling with many new buildings, some rough, some impressive, but a city with a future. Sanfran was an occupied ruin. He had not really seen Lindin in the daylight, but he thought it was better than this.

He looked about the small dirt-gray, sun-bleached market square they had entered. It was hot, and the glare was oppressive. The soldiers wandered a distance ahead, confident that their guests wouldn't be slinking away. Mikel turned his head and saw why. A brace of guards on horseback now remained behind them. Further down the street was a roadblock where they checked those entering the area.

The square itself was not designed to be a market. Bordering it were ruins and across the square, in the dirt the imprint of some of the ruined walls. The market contained about a dozen rickety stalls draped in brown leather and cloth. Business was not brisk. In the distance above the low ruins were the more distant and greater ruins, skyscrapers.

He knew what skyscrapers were. He had seen them in Lindin. Well, that wasn't quite true. He knew what they looked like. He just didn't know their purpose. When he was twelve years old he was taken, with the other twelve-year-olds, to see the Celebration Mural. It was a reminder of What Was Lost. Some aspects of the mural were explained, but mostly the experience was of being face to face with a mystery. It showed a city with great, gleaming towers and floating vessels. One ship had landed in the mural's foreground and people were coming out on a walkway, showing the huge size of these floating craft. Beside the city was a lake with floating buildings and boats leaving wakes in the water, the background forests and farmland stretched into the distance, with the occasional tower showing another more distant city. He now understood, for the first time, that the mural was of the Cities of the Plains including Lake Baikal. He mentioned none of this to Tei in case he was overheard.

The soldiers in front of him were talking to the merchants. He could see the fear in the merchants' faces, the excessive smiles, and the threatening stance of the Captain. In short order, the square was cleared, and the merchants streamed back out of the square past the roadblock.

The Captain rode up to Tei. They spoke quietly for some seconds, but Tei was getting agitated and loud. The Captain was implacable, yet more restrained than he expected.

"This is where you will stay until we make our decision about you."

"What about food for my people and animals?

We will need water? How long will we have to stay here?" She said.

The Captain ignored her and just rode off on his horse and continued on past the roadblock.

They all dismounted. Tei sighed, took a deep breath and called everyone over for a talk. They stood around in a circle with Tei at the center.

She said, "Screw it! He says we have to wait until they decide what 'tax' to impose on us, or whether we are spies."

There were murmurs, and Arel expressed what others thought. "Maybe we should just fight our way out."

Tarvis rolled his eyes. "Arel, that is crazy, even for you. We are grossly outnumbered, in *their* city, effectively in a prison environment, and would escape to flat, open country."

Mikel interjected, "So, what can we do?"

Tei smiled, "Parley."

"I don't know if you have noticed Tei, but I don't think we have a lot to bargain with." There was a look in her eyes and a slight smile.

"What exactly do you have in mind?"

The queen of Sanfran, Queen Elena Andreiv, had summoned Tei to a meeting. Tei didn't know whether the Queen would accept her request for an audience, but it was important to act with confidence, so she insisted she needed her scribe, Mikel, and one of her trusted aides to attend as well. For her aide, she chose Tarvis. Maybe being older and wiser-looking would make the group also seem older and wiser as well. Then pretend that being imprisoned was not a first impression.

The three of them were escorted to the Palace.

The Palace stood at the end of a large empty square flanked by the gray ruins of buildings now one or two stories tall, just jagged walls and rubble. It must have been the true heart of the city. The Palace was a magnificent building six stories high, with towers at each corner. The three of them, unarmed, with their armed guard of ten soldiers, walked toward the grand entrance, which was two stories tall, and made them feel as if they were entering the home of giants. Mikel looked to the left and the right. Two towers stood like minarets, fifty meters away in opposite directions and four stories higher than the rest of the building. The one on the left was in almost pristine condition, whereas the right-hand tower was a blackened shell. The whole structure of the palace looked tarnished with signs of battle and age, the various gaps in view made the building look slightly pock-marked, even more so close up with dozens if not hundreds of small random holes in the building's face, as if it was afflicted by some kind of stone weevil. But here and there flashed some of the original color of the building; pale yellow and light blues. Altogether the building looked like the decayed remains of some gigantic many eyed creature, once magnificent but now only a dry, weathered husk. Yet, incredibly, in some places there were glass windows. They appeared to be original, and he was at a loss to understand how they could survive from human and natural forces.

The door they approached was clearly not the original. The doorway itself was four meters high by about three meters wide, made of granite, a stone he had first seen in Bethor; this was black with dark flecks, probably from hornblende with sparkling flecks of biotite, exquisite. He wished he could stop and examine it. Even a quick glance showed this stone was polished to perfection. Once there had been statues on either side of the doorway, but they had been smashed and now only pink crystalline stubs remained embedded in the black granite floor. The door was made of thick beams of reddish-brown wood, braced together with iron clasps and great nails. The wood looked as if it was originally roughly cut but had been later sanded down. It didn't sit square on the hinges. The crudity of it against the rest of the building was jarring. Mikel thought that before he left the Center, it would not have been that odd. It was only after seeing some buildings in Bethor that his standards had been raised. He wondered if that was why the newer buildings at the Center were so much better because, like him, they had seen Ancient examples. He didn't think that idea would fly. The Main Hall on Lind itself was an Ancient structure, so familiar that everyone had forgotten its history, and now he had seen many buildings made of the same material, *concrete* they called it.

They were led down a short, dark passage. He had a moment of déjà vu, then remembered that similar walk into the heart of the Center's Main Hall to see the Master Wizard, on*ly a month ago.*

Tei emphasized, several times, to Mikel that Sanfran was not like Lindin. It had always been more independent, perhaps because it was so remote from Bethor and so close to the Caravanserai. They didn't even have slaves, and that was a problem for them. Since the end of the machines, when humans wanted something done, it was easier just to enslave people and have others do it for them. So Sanfran's stand on this was highly regarded. He wanted to like them already, unless he had to fight them.

Two soldiers escorted them into a beautiful garden courtyard where there were fountains (original by the looks) and plants and flowers he had never seen before. He was delighted at the treasure of this new knowledge before him. A woman in fine bright yellow and red clothes seated on a great yellow chair was positioned at the center of the garden, flanked by guards and surrounded by flowers. Everywhere, the scent of herbs, the perfumes changing in the mix as they walked towards the throne. It was so pleasant that it almost warped reality. He wondered how he could document it, how he could duplicate it. Surely, Lind needed something like this.

The woman they were approaching was Queen Elena, and she was talking to a high-ranking soldier. Tei moved forward to greet the Queen. Mikel was further away and fascinated by some plants. As usual, he faded into the background as he tried to make some drawings and descriptions of them. Maybe even press a few leaves into his journal.

The Queen now turned towards Tei. "I welcome a caravan and ambassador of the Traders."

Tei gave a nod and a smile to show she accepted the welcome. Clearly, the reference to 'Ambassador' meant that more was going on here than merely a border policing action.

Tei now spoke with that same sense of authority he remembered from the hexayurt. "Thank you, Your Highness. The Trader Alliance has always held the Cities in high regard, none more so than Sanfran."

The Queen was dressed in yellow and red flowing cloth that he could almost see through. He had never seen a woman dressed like that. She was quite attractive, early thirties, he would guess. But his curiosity about the garden was too great. Mikel was oblivious to the conversation between the woman and Tei since he was too engrossed in taking copious notes about the plants, statues, and anything he could jot down within the time allotted to him in that place..

"Mikel!" Tei's voice. Sharp like a warning.

He looked up and saw a large suspicious guard next to him eyeing him and the notebook. This guard wasn't like the friendly ones at the Center. This man was tough, with armor and carrying weapons that had seen use. He wouldn't think twice about putting a blade through Mikel's chest.

"Give it to me." His calloused hand outstretched. "Come on! *Now*!"

He handed over the notebook, then walked over to Tei. He wondered if he had just put them all into deep trouble. Or deeper trouble.

The guard approached the queen, handing over his notebook. Tei looked around, knowing whose notebook it was and glared at Mikel. He felt sick and stupid.

The Queen looked through the rough notebook for quite some time, turning the pages with her yellow gloves, occasionally dwelling on some page, then she carefully closed it and instructed the guard to give it back to Mikel.

"A very interesting diary you have scribe. My guards thought you were a spy. However, I am sure a true spy would be more interested in the disposition of my defenses than drawing flowers or recording how much a camel eats. Nevertheless, an interesting little book, written in the style of

*Lindisfarne*, or Lind as you prefer to call it these days, though I think it much less poetic. I hope we can discuss your book later."

The queen continued the conversation that he had not been listening to, but which he had now become a part.

"We have had troubles with some of our neighboring cities. It is just a precaution that we brought you here. But since you are here, then maybe we can show you our city and strengthen our ties."

Tei looked relaxed. She was now playing her ambassador role. "Thank you, Your Highness. This detour to your city was unexpected, but I hope we can use this opportunity to our mutual benefit."

He presumed these pleasantries translated to: we need something from each other. Let's make a deal. He could see what Sanfran would want. The city was in decay. It needed new materials, ideas and technology, just the things that the Traders specialized in. It might also want cultural ties. The artwork in the garden suggested a city wanting new visions, yet constrained by isolation. But what could the Traders get out of this apart from the personal freedom of this caravan?

"The Trader Alliance is grateful for this opportunity for closer relations." Tei said. "There are many things that the Alliance could assist with, but if this is to be mutually beneficial, what is it you could offer the Alliance?"

Tei had been careful to refer to the Alliance. Perhaps the Queen would see that this was something that was larger than just this one caravan.

"We offer… " Mikel was sure he saw the Queen take a breath.

"…a partnership in the City's economy, and protected access to our trade routes." There was a moment of hesitation from Tei, so uncharacteristic that Mikel knew it was far more than what she had hoped for.

"Of course, your Majesty. The Trader Alliance would be pleased, after suitable negotiations, to enter into such an arrangement."

The Queen leaned forward. "And what will the Trader Alliance provide?"

"As an ally in the Trader Alliance, we would assist with new technology, materials, inte , and armed support if required. All subject to successful negotiation."

The Queen smiled and relaxed back onto her throne. "Acceptable. May it be so."

"I have other matters to attend to now. Tonight there will be a banquet. We invite you with your *scribe* and companion Traders. Perhaps we can use the feast to celebrate our new friendship."

Mikel saw the two guards on each side of them bow, then Tei bowed. He did the same. Then they did an about turn and left.

The other Traders in the Caravan had listened intently to Tei's retelling of the meeting with the Queen.

Santh spoke first. He was a seasoned man from Tan Vu, an oasis town south of Tanten. He had graying temples, a worn face, aged more by life than time.

"Typically, the rulers of the cities were barbarians who despised learning. It seems this queen belongs to a different generation. Perhaps even barbarians can change their ways by their own choice."

The Traders were delighted, but surprised. The agreement had taken minutes, not weeks or even years, as expected from experience. Why now? Traders had been making overtures to some cities that they thought were more reasonable without luck. But now came a forceful, or desperate, invitation from a city. They would learn more at the banquet. All the Traders were invited, though a few would stay behind to guard the supplies and tend to the camels and horses. They drew straws to see who would stay behind. Mikel wasn't sure if it was the winners or the losers who went to the banquet.

First, however, would be a trip to the royal bathhouse to wash off the dirt of the road and stop smelling like a bunch of bandits.

The bath house was a large, solid building, with a

rounded roof. Pretty uninspiring from the outside, but inside it was a marvel. The walls had enormous panoramic murals on them, with the afternoon light streaming through many high narrow windows, making the murals more vivid. Apart from the murals, the inside of the building was a single room filled with a large, deep pool of water. Steam rose in places. It was heated.

Now he noticed something else.

Mikel was astonished and embarrassed to discover that the royal baths were communal. No swimming costumes either. Most of the Traders, including Tei, were already in the water. Servants heated the pool pouring hot water in at one end, and two others pushing down on a man sized paddlewheel to circulate the water. At the far end, he could see an outlet for the water to aid the circulation. Fortunately, the water wasn't crystal clear. Perhaps there were some impurities in the lake water, or maybe they added special salts for the bathers. Mikel had heard of such practices but thought they were just tall tales. He disrobed and jumped in as fast as he could, creating a splash that drew attention to himself, embarrassing him even more. He expected it to be warm after seeing them pour hot water in at the other end. It wasn't; it was freezing. He was too used to swimming in the warm seas around Lind.

"Mikel! Next time use the steps for Zeus' sake!" Santh said, irritated.

Another voice, Tei's. His vision was blurry as the water still dripped from his eyes, but he saw her perfect breasts bouncing happily in the water just at nipple level. What a pleasant coincidence. Now he knew she was pale skinned, and she knew he was brown all over.

"Mikel. Please look me in the eyes."

He blushed before he could control his response. Brown skin does not protect you from blushing it just makes it harder to see it. He looked Tei in the face. Wet hair dangling down her back, face clean, dewed and relaxed. Eyes bright.

"If you had not been so pre-occupied you might have noticed the murals on the wall."

The others laughed.

He turned to the walls. Now that his eyes were no longer bleary, he could see the remarkably preserved murals in detail. They ran continuously over all four walls, but the important ones were on the long side walls. At the center of the large western wall, where they had entered, was a city with strange silver — ships — he guessed, floating in the air. Black space and stars above, but not night in the city. It was clear from the accompanying writing that this was not Neti, this was Earth, the place that the old stories spoke of. The First Home. He turned around and there was another mural on the far side that showed a similar view but with Lake Baikal in the distance, surrounded by several cities. Sanfran was in the foreground and very clear. It was magnificent. He spun around again, and this time looked at the Earth city foreground. The scale was different. It was pretty clear the Earth city was enormous and dwarfed Sanfran. There were so many wonders in the image that he wished he had brought his notebook to record them.

"So, what do you think?" Tei said.

Tei was now lower in the water. The view submerged.

"Beautiful."

"Me or the murals?" She smiled.

"Both." He didn't feel embarrassed about saying it. He couldn't be more embarrassed, so he would just be honest. Time to just get clean, get out and get dressed. The smiles on the looks of the other Traders implied she had been playing with him; it was all a well-worn trick to play on all those unfamiliar with Trader customs. Knowing that didn't make him feel less stupid for his immaturity.

The Trader contingent, plus Mikel, reached the palace at sunset. The traditional start time. Guards led them through a candle lit corridor. The walls were plain, a hint of faded yellow color, no decoration at all. He wondered if the artwork of the defeated had been purged here, but then why had the bathhouse been left in pristine condition?

They entered a large area open to the sky. From the looks of it, it was once enclosed, but the roof was now missing. One soldier referred to it as the 'Atrium' but didn't explain further. They walked across the Atrium to another entrance. This time the lighting was better because of better candles, and there were quite a few paintings on the wall. The paintings were clearly recent. Some were pretty good. He had friends in the Artist Enclave on Lind and would often visit them, being shown around and inspecting new works, and somehow, somewhere in all of that, he had picked up some artistic appreciation. The Wizards and Artists shared ideas often, each trying to amaze the other in what Mikel now knew was an unusual competitive environment that somehow seemed to make sense.

These works were mostly about battles; complex scenes and figures, overly stylistic, many dead and the victorious marching over the top of the corpses while flying the Sanfran banners. Some of the more recent works were landscapes and sensitive portraits that showed greater creativity or depth. He understood now that the paintings were arranged in a particular order. The order was approximately chronological. It was a testament to the civilizing of the conquerors. From barbarian horde to patron of the arts.

"Did you notice the paintings? The order?" He asked.

Tei was at his side. He wasn't sure if that was because she was a friend or for appearances. She wore his bandana around her neck.

"Yes. We have been monitoring the cultural progress of the Cities since the Fall. Some, such as Sanfran, are far more cultured and less aggressive. Perhaps it is no surprise they are so keen to have us as guests."

The troop of guests now entered a large room lit by masses of oil lamps and a large central fire. The fireplace appeared to have been crudely hacked out of the floor tiles centuries ago. Colored cloth with many intricate patterns lined the walls, mostly yellow and red. At the far end, on a raised platform about a meter high, was the queen on her throne at the center of a long table full of food but empty of guests. The banquet hall was already full of mingling guests and trestle tables with less fancy food from what he could see.

A court official met them, Alin Mkar, dressed in ornate red and yellow clothes with an elaborate red hat like a flattened ball. Most of the trim was golden braid. Overall, the man's dress struck Mikel as unseemly and decadent but still interesting.

"You will sit at the table on the dais." He informed them.

"It is too exposed," Mikel said to Tei.

Alin overheard. "Your party will dine with the Queen. Her Highness has ordered that you, *scribe*, sit on her immediate Right. A great privilege. On no account must anyone sit on her direct Left. That would be most inauspicious."

Mikel felt flushed and flustered. Why couldn't he just be in some inconspicuous corner where he could observe and take notes?

The Queen was quite attractive and dressed in yellow with a delicate crown made of silver and sapphire, if he wasn't mistaken. A servant escorted him. Also dressed in red and yellow, to his seat at the Queen's right hand. He looked towards her and saw that his eye level was about ten centimeters below hers. He presumed this was intentional because she wasn't that tall. Just as the raised dais was a signal of her superiority, the seat height was a sign that her guests should remember their position.

The night seemed to progress well. There was laughter and light banter. Then the Queen put down her golden wine goblet, faced Tei and her tone of voice changed to something more serious.

"How has your expedition to the West been? Any troubles?"

Tei put down her silver goblet. He noticed that her body posture imitated that of the Queen. "It was not as easy as in the past, but we have had no direct troubles."

"I am curious about the goods you are bringing. I hear that the other Cities have become too dangerous to visit. Who do you sell to then?"

Tei was clearly in her element now. Mikel could see that she was relaxed and smiling.

"We sell to whoever wants our goods, which includes our own people, Lind, and Bethor. The Cities — I mean other Cities — may be a problem at the moment, but I am sure the problem will pass and they will welcome us again."

Mikel wondered if anyone at the table believed that. It seemed to be a mantra that the Traders kept repeating: it will all get better. Yet individually, everyone knew things would only get worse.

"What goods have you been trading lately?"

"Well, Your Majesty, we have been trading exotic metals and materials to Lind in higher than normal quantities, many Lind devices to everyone it seems, and expensive fashion items to Bethor; cloth, silk, gems, that sort of thing."

The discussion was lively on the Trader's side when it came to interesting goods and ideas, but the Queen was showing signs of disinterest.

They said nothing about Tanten itself. A question about it had been asked by the Queen but neatly sidestepped. That question had stuck in his mind. He wanted to know. He was reaching for another glass of wine. Perhaps he had too much to drink, so took a glass of water instead, hoping that no-one asked him anything complicated.

The Queen smiled. "Very interesting. But I would like to know more about Tanten? What is it like?"

Terl, a Trader he didn't know well, spoke.

"Tanten is a city within the desert, but not in desert country. It is an oasis. We travel to many places and not only bring back goods and wealth, but knowledge. We have several excellent libraries and we keep the history of the Ancients."

Mikel sat up. So did the Queen. The Traders knew the truth about the Ancients. There was even a common rumor to that effect, which likely was started by the Traders to discredit the notion. Perhaps the wine was making his thinking overly convoluted and confused.

Mikel leaned forward. He couldn't lose this opportunity. But across from him Tei glared at him with a look that said: *shut up*. He relaxed, but Tei would answer some questions later or — she would be exposed to the full force of his curiosity, a grim prospect that most of his teachers dreaded.

The Queen interjected, "What do your histories say then about the Cities and before?"

Terl stroked his short blond beard. "Well, your Majesty, when the Ancients came to Neti, they came in great ships that travelled between the stars. They called them 'starships' in the old language. They founded the Cities of the Plains, gave them the names of their old cities, and they knew Zeus."

"Zeus was real?", the Queen looked at Terl like a mother about to scold an older child for believing in fairies.

"Zeus *is* real." Terl's face hardened with the

famous and often mocked look of defiance of the Traders. Now, having spent so much time among them, Mikel understood that look. It meant: we know things you don't know and can't accept.

"And controls Neti. The wind and clouds and so forth?" The Queen posed to Terl.

Terl relaxed, "No ma'am. The people who first came to Neti named the entity 'Zeus' and became friends. But they never regarded it as a god. Just extremely powerful."

"So, where is the home of Zeus?" The Queen was relaxing into this now. Was she genuinely curious or merely humoring them? Mikel saw another possibility. Perhaps she was studying the Traders society analytically. The answers and beliefs would then give insight into Trader thinking and society. That would be quite ironic. Mikel decided that this 'intrigue mode' of thinking was far too close to paranoia to be healthy.

"To the north, your Majesty. At the Snows of Olympus. There is the great Citadel of Zeus. Greater than any work of Man, those who see it are humbled and know that there are greater things in this world than the cares and troubles of humanity." Terl was standing, right fist clenched, making his point. He suddenly looked about, understanding that he had gone a little too far. "Sorry, your grace. I am not well educated in matters of protocol."

The Queen slowly smiled and gave a slow

clap. "Delightful. We do not worry about your beliefs, only your actions. The Traders have always been stable and reliable."

The table's focus rapidly blurred into various conversations that became an irrelevant buzz to Mikel.

"Now about you, young Wizard," the Queen was looking at him. He wished he hadn't drunk so much. He best keep as much to himself as possible.

"What do you have to say about your travels across the Plains?"

"Tei and I visited Lindin. It looked like they were preparing for war. Soldiers everywhere." He blurted it out without thinking, alcohol and nervousness conspiring together against him.

"Really? Hmm. War against who?"

She looked at him with a deeply focused intensity, as if her eyes could bore through his skull and find some answer inside.

"Ah. Yes, your Majesty. I don't know." He was in deep now. He didn't know the fine art of lying, so he would just go with the truth and hope it didn't cost him dearly.

"When I was in Bethor." A flash of terrible memories, huddled in a cage, dockside being insulted, casual insults from a stranger, banners, banners, banners everywhere.

"When I was in Bethor, it seemed the entire city was going crazy. They want a new war of conquest."

"*Retake the Cities? Destroy Tanten? Destroy the Center?*" she said.

"Maybe."

"Not maybe. It is almost common knowledge that a war is coming. You just confirmed it with your own account." She looked away, distracted. Forehead creased, right hand in a fist, knuckles going pale.

"And you are a Wizard?"

"Only an Apprentice, Your Majesty. I was sent here to learn more about the trade routes around Bethor." His hands were sweating profusely; he kept them under the table rubbing them against his pants.

The Queen's eyes narrowed. "Hmm. Unusual sending a new Wizard so far from home, don't you think? Do you know what I think? I think you are an emissary to the Traders for a future Wizard/Trader Alliance." At first, Mikel thought she must not have heard him properly, but then it occurred to him that, on the contrary, she must have decided that the 'Apprentice' description was a ruse.

The table was silent. The situation had become potentially dangerous.

Mikel cleared his throat, "Ahem, well, you know alliances don't have to be just two way. It can be three-way, creating a very flexible combination of skills and resources."

The Queen smiled. Her blue eyes and golden

hair radiant in the yellow light from the candles and fire. "Exactly my thoughts. But come on, *my* young Wizard drink up. Let's have some entertainment." She called for some dancers to entertain and shouted some orders. Mikel's heart was pounding, he heard the emphasis on 'my'.

"Mikel," the Queen leaned over and whispered to him.

"Are you and the Trader woman bound together? If not, then you would be very welcome in my bed after the feast. We could see what we can teach each other."

"I'm sorry, my Queen, but we are bound," he lied.

"Yes, I thought as much. Her eyes have not left you all night. But if you leave her, your presence will be welcome in my court."

Was that more intrigue or honesty, or in this world did they merge so you couldn't tell? The more he tasted this life, the more he preferred his own.

"Were you looking at me all night?"

Tei looked away from him. They were standing on a balcony looking over the city. The stars were out, feebly challenged by the few yellow, flickering street lamps and home fires of Sanfran. Most of the lights were low, at street level, few people lived in the higher buildings outside the Palace. As he had suspected in Lindin, tall buildings look impressive but are terrible to live in, at least now. Now those tall buildings were invisible except for their ominous silhouettes against the low stars. Ghosts in stone.

"The city was once exquisite, according to the Records. Once it was a center of knowledge and culture. At night it would glow, shapes and patterns of light and color moving over the buildings and through the air," she said.

Translation: he would not get an answer.

"I first started reading the Records when I was ten. After some time, I fancied I could even understand their ways and a little of their thoughts. You are like them, you know. Very much like them. But you have forgotten. We Traders remember, but you Wizards keep the spirit alive, so they say. You fascinated me when we met."

She was fidgeting, nervous. "Did you know that? I had met Wizards before, but you are very different. Very. And then on the road — well, never mind."

They had both drunk too much, or not enough, caught in between. Tonight they were both feeling open, perhaps too open. He didn't know if this was good or a bad.

She turned back to Mikel and leaned towards him. Big blue eyes looking unflinching into his. He could smell the spices on her warm breath and see the pores in her near perfect skin. She ducked to his right and gave him a peck on the cheek and retreated. He still held her eyes with his and moved in before he knew what he was doing and delicately kissed her on the lips. It was as if a drugged dart had jabbed him. His blood was on fire and he could barely concentrate. The pupils in Tei's eyes were wide, focused, wide as his must be. She grabbed his right arm and dragged him down the corridor and into her room.

Later, he lay half numb from the good food and the exhaustion of loving sex. The candle on his side of the bed was still lit. He looked over at Tei, her skin so pale compared to his brown, except for her face, tanned by the desert. Delicately, he ran his fingers down her back, over the occasional scar, the tips of his fingers just brushing the fine hairs of her skin. She stretched as if her body understood the message of pure tenderness, even if her mind did not. He blew out the candle, and outside the dull blue glow told him that morning was almost here.

Tomorrow, or today, was a big day and he'd need the sleep. He yawned and turned over.

# fifteen

They spent an extra two days in Sanfran while Tei and the Queen started the negotiations towards a treaty between the City and the Traders. When they left the City Tei smiled and joked. She was almost giddy with delight.

It was their third day when they were back on the Plains that Tei finally started talking about what the negotiations meant.

"Do you understand, Mikel, what it will mean if the negotiations are successful? For the first time, the centers of knowledge and one of the Cities, a food producer, will be united. Travel will be safer. We could rebuild the roads and use wagons instead of less efficient camels and horses. Irrigate the eastern Plains again. We could consider great journeys of exploration." She was obviously excited.

"Tei, I'm only an Apprentice of the Center. I don't really have the authority to agree to anything."

"Mikel! Think what you are saying. You are far from the Center. I know you Wizards have great autonomy and sometimes do great things. You aren't a child anymore." She gave him a wry smile. "For which I am grateful."

None of that argument made sense to him, but if the world was going crazy, then this strategy made some sense because it was about survival. He also didn't understand this odd notion that somehow an act of sex made you a mature human being. In Lind, sex was moderated by traditions, but they did not shun it. It was just a part of growing up, and learning not just about precautions but also how to treat people respectfully.

Mikel wondered if his current predicament was quite the situation the Center had in mind when they sent him. It appeared he would just have to decide. Whatever he did now was a decision, even indecision, so he might as well take the most promising course.

They were at last heading south east into drier lands. The intention was to leave the Plains without delay. There had been some trading with the farming communities north of Sanfran, however the bulk of the remaining load would go to the East.

Mikel was fourth in line, so he had a good

view of the lead *file*. He noticed it had stopped. He couldn't see any farms nearby and Tei was coming back along the line towards him.

She rode up. "A Lindin patrol, by the looks. Keep calm, but be ready. These guys can be arrogant and a little foolish." She reached down into a saddlebag and brought out a half sized crossbow with a clever lever to cock it. She quickly cocked it and loaded it with a bolt that seemed to click into place. This looked like the same one she had on her hip when he first met her. It would clearly not have much range, but that wasn't important. She hid the crossbow under a leather flap of her riding coat, then wheeled and returned to the growing knot of people. In the distance he heard low voices, maybe a half a dozen.

He was close now and could hear the conversation.

A soldier said, "I don't care. Why didn't you stop at the Lindin Customs Office?"

Tei's voice, "There is no requirement for passing caravans to stop in Lindin if they are not trading with the City. You are also far beyond Lindin's borders. This is the territory of Sanfran."

"Ah, a Trader lawyer. I didn't know you scum could even read. Look —"

Here it comes, thought Mikel. He could hear the growing aggression in the soldier's voice. He was drunk on his sense of power over the powerless and some easy pickings. It was so familiar. He knew what was going to happen next. His heart was pounding.

Mikel was quite close now, about eight meters. He had slowly slipped out a leather strap in one hand and some small heavy stones in the other in case his, clearly biased, opinion of Bethor forces was borne out.

"You do as we say. You hand over half your caravan now or we leave you as fertilizer for the grass and take it all." He drew his sword.

The drawn sword was the patrol's undoing. Mikel heard a 'thwak' and the soldier toppled slowly backward off his horse with the end of a crossbow bolt protruding from his left eye. The rest of the patrol was momentarily fazed. There were seven of them. He loaded a pebble into his sling, swung it, and let go. Another soldier fell. There were more 'thwaks' at point blank range, from other Trader crossbows. Three soldiers remained. They turned their horses to flee.

Tei yelled, "Get them! Don't let them escape!"

Mikel let loose another pebble. It glanced off the side of one soldier's head, stunning him. Tei caught up to him and there was a quick glint of metal as she slashed and he fell from the horse. She continued after the others with three other Traders in pursuit with crossbows re-cocked. There was a cloud of dust, but in the distance, he saw two riders fall in quick succession. And it was over. He felt like it had gone on for ages, but he knew it was all over in about 20 seconds. His heart was still pounding, and his hands jittery. His mind worked furiously, looking for something to latch onto to distract him. He had to ask Tei about the crossbows. He couldn't believe how quickly they had been reset or how the bolt could be he d in place yet free to fire.

He got down to see if there were any injured. There was more blood on the ground than he expected and his heart was thumping harder with a delayed recognition of how close to death he had been. Some of the soldiers were not much older than him and now they would be hidden in the long brown grass and forgotten. They would never return to family and friends. Lost on patrol.

They examined the bodies and checked for anything useful. He was surprised that the soldier's armor was merely leather.

He looked at the dead, then at Tei. "They only have leather armor. Why?" He was breathing heavily.

She looked him in the eyes and said. "Easy there, I know. It is a waste. That is the just the way things are. As for their armor, the Cities hate us so much they would rather reject us and forego the extra metal. They have barely enough for weapons, much less armor, and I wouldn't be surprised if they had lost some of their skills in metals as well. Their weapons are terrible."

This was why the Traders were a game

changer for Sanfran. Tei had told him once that the Cities would fall within a century, but she wouldn't say who the aggressor would be. Mikel was pretty sure the Traders could do it themselves if they put their mind to it. He wondered in fact if Tei had revealed a long term Trader strategy. No way to know.

They buried the bodies in shallow graves amid the long grass, then released the patrol's horses.

Tei and Mikel walked together to their horses, ready to continue their journey. He cleaned the blood from his hands on the dried grass, obsessed with removing every trace.

"You surprise me, Mikel," she said. "You're a marksman."

"When I was learning the physics of rotating objects, we played with slings. I got very good. But I broke the law." It was a painful memory somehow magnified now.

"I don't understand."

"I killed some birds with it. But not for food. I broke the Law of Respect for Life."

"Yet you helped kill two of these soldiers. No, you didn't kill any of them directly, but we made sure. Yet you played your part."

"The soldiers were a direct threat. The birds were merely sharing my day," he said. He meant it sincerely, as it was a part of his training and being.

They proceeded quickly after the incident and rapidly left the Plains behind. Within two days, the vegetation had changed from the drying grasslands, Tei called it "savannah," to the semi-arid; the grass was short, dry, and patchy, gradually replaced by dry shrubs with reddish dirt between. The meandering creeks that made the Plains so lush were gone completely. Tei said those creeks were from the mountains to the north, and that the Euphray came from a valley and lake beyond them. Mikel had never even heard stories of such a valley or lake, but he trusted the Traders knew it from direct experience.

They continued heading towards the Caravanserai of the East. Later that day, they saw other Trader caravans paralleling their track in either direction. Some of those heading west would come close enough for a friendly wave or greeting. All paths converged to the same point, a place just barely noticeable in the distance. As they got closer to it he could see a brown smudge surrounded by green, with a building in the middle.

The oasis was named Lastchance. Tei explained that originally it meant that this was the last water before the Great Eastern Desert. Back then, the records showed, the desert lay further to the east, and the plains around Sanfran were wetter and more fertile. The oasis was a focus for caravans from the west, south, and north. Even from the east across the desert to Tanten and Tan

Vu. To get to Tanten the caravans would head east for a time and then turn north-east traversing the edge of the desert, arriving at a city that at first seemed to be an oasis but was in fact a tongue of fertility on the northern edge of the desert. Mountain streams kept it verdant. Because of the path that the caravans took, adversaries did not know of a safe, quick route to the city and attempts to find it by crossing the desert became suicidal.

The Caravanserai was a large fortified inn with a large courtyard, where many horses and camels could be rested, while the team did the same in rooms overnight. For a price, the Traders who ran the inn would protect the animals through the night, stay guard on the walls, and send out occasional scouts to look for bandits. If there was an attack on the Caravanserai, then it was everyone's duty to do their part in defending it.

The building was in the shape of a square about a hundred meters on a side, like a fort with walls about four meters high. It was made of sun-dried mud bricks, coated over with some kind of plaster with fading decorations on the walls. It had two stories of rooms and a cafeteria, a place where there was some cooked food and highly valued fresh fruit and vegetables from the gardens outside the walls. The gardens were carefully watered and guarded; the plots supplying valuable fruit, vegetables and even flowers. Out here, the gardens were worth more than gold or silver.

The courtyard of the building was full of resting animals and guarded trade goods. The owner carried the most precious items or kept in a sturdy locked box in their rooms.

They had stopped in the Caravanserai for a couple of days while Tei did her wheeling and dealing, selling and buying, and arranging care of her camels and horses. They would be kept in the surrounding fields and carefully tended. The Caravanserai acted as a place for animals and humans to recover their strength. It was similar, but more permanent than what he saw in Bethor. Eventually, one of Tei's clan would put together a new caravan using the animals and a selection of trade goods to take west or south.

Mikel was checking and re-evaluating his gear, sitting on a bench in the courtyard; is this OK? is that worn? Do I need to replace this? Endless small decisions. In the middle distance, Rijart and Tarvis were talking, discussing something at length by the look. They wouldn't talk long. It was almost midday and the heat was stifling. He couldn't work out what they were saying and found his attention drifting to the clothes they wore, the similarities. He should try to fit in more. It would be camouflage from prying eyes.

What was distinctive about Traders?

Apart from their desert cloaks, which they rarely wore on the Plains, they were dressed similarly to him; leather armor sometimes partly hidden under loose and light outer fabrics, no fancy colors except for the headgear, some wore turbans, some wore caps, no one went bareheaded, like him. The armor was also different to Lind, the patterns and artwork, sometimes the very design of the armor. There was a lot of variety he likely had not noticed before because his team didn't seem that different to him. Or had he changed?

When he got to Tanten, he would have to buy new gear, change his dress to blend in. Also, he suspected Traders knew a lot more about armor than peaceful Lind.

Above the rooms, on the roof, was an excellent place to look at the surrounding country. It was also part of the defenses for the Caravanserai. In the daytime, the heat meant it wasn't a good place to spend too much time, but at night the stars were spectacular. Often people would come up and stand on the still warm rooftop, briefly immune to the chill of the desert night, gazing upwards. At night, Mikel saw Tarvis climbing a ladder that led to the roof. He followed along. On the roof a waist high ornate parapet, now crumbling, was the only thing protecting people from accidentally walking off the edge in the dark. Though it wasn't a high drop.

Sharing the night spectacle with him were Tarvis, Tei, Rijart, and Kay. They were pointing at stars and naming them, references to myths, general talk. Mikel had brought along his spyglass.

He walked to the parapet and found a place where the artist's work and natural wear had created a nice stabilizing niche for his small telescope. He extended it and let the large end rest in the niche while he moved the eyepiece. It was not comfortable. If only the parapet was half a meter higher, and he had a chair, and a small candle for his notebook, and a better telescope. He couldn't set the scope on Raytans. It was too close to the zenith. He could focus on two planets and the moon with its very odd markings.

"What do you see with that?" Tarvis asked.

He let the man have a look, carefully guiding him towards the moon, also called Tanis. It was half full.

"That is amazing. You can just about make out the structures on Tanis."

"Structures?"

"Long story. You will have time to find out more when you get to Tanten. But in short, the surface of Tanis has the remains of old buildings. Very large buildings."

"Tanis doesn't have enough gravity to keep an atmosphere. How can it have buildings? How do you know about this? Who built it? Why so big?" He did a few quick calculations and was staggered at the numbers he got for the size of the supposed structures.

Tarvis shrugged. He could barely see that in the feeble moonlight, if there were facial expressions, he didn't see them at all.

Tarvis' voice, "When humans first came to Neti, they wanted to call Tanis: Thatsno Moon. Apparently, they thought it was funny. The authorities didn't and had the name changed later. Funny, the odd things that are remembered and the important things that are forgotten."

They used only camels for the last leg of the journey. Mikel was not prepared for it. In the short time he had been on the journey, he had become a reasonable horse rider, easier than expected, but these camels were another matter. Still, it wasn't far and camels were safer in case something caused them to lose their way. One camel each, loaded with precious items, and some special goods owned by the rider. Mikel had received his share of the profits. There was a moment of lust for riches, but knew he loved being a Wizard more.

The desert was a completely new experience, even stranger than his sea voyage to Bethor. It was frightening, not just because of its vastness, but because it killed passively, not actively. Against the desert, there was no action you could take to defend yourself except preparation. If you got yourself lost here without water, then you were as dead as if an arrow had hit you in the heart, but there would be no arrow, no aggressor, only the knowledge of being a condemned man without a prison cell and no reprieve.

They travelled mostly at night and sheltered in tents by day. After about a day and long after night had fallen, Tei looked up and checked the position of the stars and Raytans, then headed on a new bearing. It would be dawn soon.

At first light, Tei stopped and got the box out of her saddlebag. Mikel was next to her, looking on as she adjusted the very familiar item. It contained a delicately poised floating needle: a compass.

"I'm sure you've seen one of these before," she said.

"Yes, we make and export them, and we need them for our ships."

"Tei, when we were in Sanfran," he paused a moment, remembering that night. "When we were in Sanfran, you mentioned something about reading 'Records' when you were ten. What did you mean?"

"I was wondering when you would get around to that. All right, a bit of background first."

She was quiet for a minute. Perhaps she was not just working out what to say, but even whether it should be said. Sometimes a few words can save or destroy a relationship, or a nation.

"The possibility of the fall of the Cities was foreseen long before it happened. In fact, the Center and Tanten were setup as part of the strategy to keep knowledge after the Great Battle."

"What? I mean, what do you mean? The Society of Wizards founded the Center for learning," he said. Unusually, he now found himself on the receiving end of new, uncomfortable information.

"The Center was set up by and for a contingent of scientists and engineers. Wizards to you. They set Tanten up to keep the records, books and knowledge of the Terran Federation, or Human Nexus, as they liked to call themselves. Apparently, they foresaw, accurately, that society and technology would continue to unravel for centuries in the damage's wake after the Battle. So they used examples from their own history and mythology to create a long lived cultural identity for both of our societies. You would hold the scientific knowledge and the scientific process until the world could support advanced technology again while we would keep the history and scholarship. We Traders thought the Cities would survive, though their continued decline finally did lead to the Fall. However, we still have the records from before the Battle, and still remember the history of Earth and the coming to Neti."

Mikel was quiet for a moment. He had so many questions. He knew Tei talked little about this, so he better pick his questions carefully in case she rationed the answers.

"What Battle?" He said.

"We don't know exactly. A great battle occurred which destroyed starships and cities, made deserts and altered the weather. Many died.

The Records say that the survivors were amazed that anyone survived it. It appears to have occurred in a single day. The few records about it are sealed. Well, sealed when I looked, I was much younger then. I may have enough respect and rank now to get permission."

After a couple of hours, he could see a green band on the horizon and, in the distance beyond that, a small mountain range.

"We are heading for the smudge of green on the right. Tanten. Home," she said.

They moved towards the green haze of Tanten at a steady pace. Tei spoke seemingly to the air but he was the intended audience.

"There is a story we tell our children. It is called 'The Man in the Desert'." She spoke with the well practiced skill and voice of someone who has taught it to many children.

Long ago, a Trader set out from the Caravanserai on the last leg of his trading mission back to Tanten. He carefully folded his compass in protective cloth, because back then, they were more fragile than they are today. He took with him two camels, one for him to ride and another for his personal goods and new wealth. After he had been traveling for more than a day, in the distance he saw something, a dark shape in the dust. He rode up next to it. There was the prone figure of another

Trader. He looked dead. The man on the camel was about to move off and continue, since there was nothing he could do, when he saw a movement. The man moved, opened his eyes and turned to the man on the camel.

"Please sir, help me. I need water. Take me with you. I was thrown and my camels ran off. You have water and two camels."

"I cannot spare my water. I may need it. My other camel has my hard-earned profits which I need. I am sorry, but I cannot help you."

The man in the desert collapsed back into his imitation of death. While the other turned his camels east, then later north-east, forgetting the other and heading to Tanten.

The time came around for the next trading mission. The man gathered his provisions and planned his stops and the goods he intended to purchase. Yes, it would be very profitable. He left Tanten early morning on a day most of the other Traders would not leave. The weather was becoming stormy, but he had endured worse and it would give him a great advantage. As the sun rose higher, he saw a cloud in the east, an orange wall of dust. Dust storms were something he had dealt with before, so he was not unduly worried. He could push on further, at least get to the turning point. He continued, thinking more about some merchants in the Cities of the Plains that would be interested in some things he planned to acquire. It was getting dark too early. He had forgotten about the dust storm and now it was upon him. He looked about, but there was nothing, of course. No shelter, no help. He set the camels down, and was just getting off when the animal bolted upright and stamped the ground. The man was thrown off. He looked down at where the camel had stamped. The crushed remains of a scorpion. It must have bitten the camel on the leg. Both camels were agitated. They ran off in random directions, leaving the man standing there in the gathering storm incredulous. What was he to do? He hunkered down, covered himself in his cloak, and endured while the storm passed. It was not a severe storm, merely a typical late winter squall. When he came out, he found himself in an orange haze. The sun was not visible, but soon the dust would settle. He had no water and he had lost his compass. He knew how far he was, in camel time, from the turning point. But he did not know how to convert that to a walking man, or more importantly, which direction. Even while he thought about this, he was losing water. He would have to walk. He must get to the turning point. There was a better chance of him being found there.

He walked the remaining daylight hours, and for a little while into the night. Then he suddenly knew he had not been paying enough attention to the moving stars or even the sun during the daylight. He was hopelessly off course. He was dizzy and weak and lay down to sleep through the bitterly cold night. In the morning, he was under the full glare of the sun. He wandered further, half delirious, this time knowing he was lost and not caring. He was already dead the moment he lost his camels. This was just a shadow play that he must complete.

Tei continued, now in her ordinary voice, her own opinion. "The moral of the story? There are several. We are all the man in the desert, both of them. Helping the wanderer is helping ourselves. The desert will kill you through your negligence or through bad luck; all humans can do to oppose that is to plan, to work together, and aid each other. Individuals are easily laid low, so do not travel alone. Last, knowledge is power and survival. Heh, and yes, maybe a little karma as well."

# sixteen

Tanten is at the tip of a tongue of land that projects southwards from the Uuten Mountains. Through the middle runs the Tanuuten River, trying to reach the dried Lake Despair to the southeast. Tei had been giving Mikel a guided tour of the city even before they had actually arrived. She clearly loved the city. He hoped he wasn't disappointed because he had no chance of hiding it.

"Most of the rivers from the Uutens flow north except for the Tanuuten. It flows through the Northern Pass to the southern side of the Uutens and creates the oasis of Tanten. There is little habitable land along the southern borders of the Uutens except for Tanten. Since we founded the city, we have diverted the river into farmland and forests. We've created artificial rivers and expanded the oasis. None of the river now reaches the old lake," she said.

"Tanten isn't as old as the Cities?"

"No. It isn't an Original City. They built it as a refuge, and it is now our political and cultural capital. It is the heart of our culture and we are very proud of it."

"Yes, I noticed that. So is that fort in the distance the city of Tanten?"

"Not strictly speaking. Actually, not at all. Tanten as a city doesn't exist," she said.

"What? Even when we talk among ourselves, we treat it as a city."

"It isn't a city in the form you are used to. Tanten comprises various *Strongholds*; forts, castles. The main stronghold is an octagonal fort simply called the Castle. Then there are Shwu, Mbele, and Sibl to the northwest, north and northeast of the central Stronghold of Aqua. Castle lies directly to the south. Aqua is not a large stronghold though it contains the largest of the water reservoirs and water is power in Tanten. Underground water pipes and tunnels connect the Strongholds, especially Aqua. Despite this interconnection, the Strongholds are run independently, though decisions affecting the city have to be ratified by the Council, which meets in the Castle."

"And everyone lives in these strongholds?"

"There are suburbs that lie outside the Strongholds, with parkland between them," she said.

"And we are heading to where, exactly?"

"Castle, my home."

They were headed for the front gate of the Castle, on the southern side, facing the desert. To get there they had first had to go north towards Shwu as they stepped from desert to grassy slopes, then along the western side of the Castle, to enter The Snake, a winding path to the gate, bounded by steep, grassy sides under the eyes of the Castle. One very long kill zone, winding north, then south along the western flank of the Castle. The head of the Snake came to the gates, which faced south into the desert. Here, the gates looked almost like a beast's mouth with iron teeth and surrounded by hidden attack points. The Snake had many fangs, all poisonous.

The Castle was staggering and beautiful. It stood on a hill in the middle of the green grass that surrounded it in disdain of the nearby desert. Here stood a kind of building he had never seen before. Bethor had awed Mikel, but this structure beat anything in Bethor. Maybe the Palace in Sanfran would rival it, but the Palace was really just a ruin with occupants, an observation he was careful to keep to himself. The Castle was a living city; the walls here were almost fifteen meters high with successive layers of dark gray and light pink rock and some cement. Stopping at the gate waiting for approval to enter, he could now appreciate the city.

There were features on the tops of the walls that he took for decoration until Tei explained they were nooks for bowmen. He was full of questions, but Tei signaled they should talk about it later.

Inside the Castle there were more surprises because there was so much water in use. Fountains, small gardens with rivulets, common wells, water flowed everywhere. There were multi-storied houses and color everywhere: the clothes, banners, cloth in windows. So many wonders it was hard to see it all. Bethor had been a chaotic riot of color. This was a harmonious song of color. It was like another world. The team — they were not a caravan anymore — turned to the right down a short, dusty, pale-yellow cobbled street and into some stables. Now, incredibly, their journey was at an end. Mikel stood by his camel for a moment, trying to work out what had just happened. Tei was looking at him quizzically.

"The camel won't unpack itself. And when you unpack it, don't forget to give it to the stable hands to care for it." She clearly didn't trust Mikel's peculiar state of mind. He presumed she thought he was having a 'Wizard moment.' More likely it was just a 'Mikel moment.'

"Let me show you my city."

Mikel was a bit confused by the hustle and bustle. He had forgotten about Bethor and its crowds. Here, they were close to the market, which had more color, noise, music and life than he had ever seen in Bethor. Bethor seemed an age ago. Even Sanfran, that sad city striving for rebirth, seemed to be diminished by this spectacle. Above the din there was the sound of music: guitars, drums, metal instruments; the beat was invigorating and intoxicating. There were smells of food, and spices, and perfumes that varied from spot to spot as he walked, like an aromatic forest. But Tei walked straight past the Markets and continued in toward the center of the Castle where there was a large circular building in black stone, probably basalt, that looked to be even taller than the walls.

"I thought you were going to show me your city? You seem a little too businesslike. Can't I look around first?"

She turned and smiled for a moment, as if he was a child.

"All in good time. But first there are some things we have to do."

He didn't know about this "we." When did her duties become his as well?

"This is the Keep, where the Council sits, where the Court plots and schemes," she said, giving him a mock-evil smile.

Now her voice changed, more serious. "Yes, they scheme. Sometimes I wonder if they really appreciate the dangers that surround us. As if we need enemies within as well."

"Don't worry too much. The Center isn't immune to it either. We have intrigues and plots. But I think the Wizard's life isn't so attractive to those seeking power. But the problem is still there," he said.

She looked at him, surprised, and he understood he didn't care if she knew. He trusted her.

"Come on, I will show you Tanten from above."

"Tei? You never told me. Why do you trust me with knowing where Tanten is?"

She smiled. "You are so sweet and naïve. As much as I like you, I wouldn't trust you unless I was certain that Lind knows exactly where Tanten is located."

"Ah!"

"Ah, yes. But I still really like you just the same." She giggled.

She walked up the light brown steps to the black stoned Keep. He looked back. Only now did he notice that the ground they had walked over was a mosaic of rock pieces. Paving. Tei was talking to a guard. He missed what she had said.

The guard was dressed in almost black armor, his elaborate helmet sported a red feathered crest, faceplate up. Spectacular, though Mikel suspected this was not just for show. Another guard appeared from Mikel's right. *Where did he come from?* He also wore black armor, but his crest was black and there was no gloss to the armor; he had simply merged into the black stone background and shadows. Now he noticed that the guards normally stood in shadowed alcoves. At night, they would be invisible. He thought this was probably some strategy based on subtle misdirection, but had it ever really been tested?

"Tei, of family Valis. I also bring Wizard Mikel of the Center."

"Welcome back Ambassador Tei. The Council is not in session, but many members are available if you wish."

The guard to Mikel's right did something to the door and whispered a phrase. A code, he presumed. The large black wooden door opened outwards as a double door.

"You are an ambassador again?" He said.

"Not really. That was for you. If you had not been here, they would have simply addressed me as *captain*."

"Do you get many outside visitors here?"

"No, it is very rare. They just reacted to you like they would in the Caravanserai. I'm sure they were surprised."

"Captain?"

"What you call a 'captain' and what we call a 'captain' are not the same. I am a captain because I lead a caravan. But it also means I can lead troops."

"So it is similar?"

She shrugged. "Whereas Bethor has very strict designations for their ranks. You remember Mr 'Sergeant First Class'?"

He remembered the sergeant, but could only think of him as Miley and hoped he never had to fight him.

They walked up a nearby staircase. A spiral of stone going up along the wall. He felt like he was exploring a giant seashell from the inside. Now and then it opened onto a floor where he could see tantalizing things. Unknown mechanisms were sometimes visible. And books, lots of books.

"Is the Library here?" He asked.

She laughed. "I see you haven't forgotten. No, this is not the Library. All in good time. Be patient." She might ask him to be patient, but she was clearly excited.

Finally, the stairs ended. He was puffing, but only slightly. The caravan trip had improved his fitness. Tei opened a heavy door and there was blinding light.

He was standing on the roof of the Keep. There were about a dozen soldiers on the lookout. Armed with crossbows and swords. There were also some ballistas for firing projectiles long distances. The roof was large enough to have a shaded tent erected with water for soldiers who were rotated into the shade through their watch. Tei stepped up to one of the set of steps up the top of the battlement rim.

"Look Mikel! To the North there are the snow-tipped peaks of the Uuten Mountains, where Tanten gets its water, from the Tanuuten River. In every other direction there is desert. See that peak, just to the left, where I am pointing?"

"Maybe. Yes."

"Mikel, are you humoring me?"

He didn't answer.

To the north he could see, apart from the castle-like Strongholds, green fields fanning out until they reached a range of white tipped mountains about thirty or forty kilometers away. They didn't look high and unlike the Cantas near Bethor there seemed to be very little snow; the snow line was high, or rather the mountains were low. Through the green, and slightly blued distance he could see a winding silvery ribbon, the Tanuuten, but it was too far to see where the river exited the mountains. To the left there was forest. That surprised him; well, they had to get their timber from somewhere. To the east there was the regular yellow, green and brown quilting of farmland mixed with some forest. Looking further east, or west, was the hard pale yellow and red of the desert. It seemed as if the surrounding heat-bleached land was trying to assail this oasis like a pale orange sea battering against an island's seawall vying to dominate and subdue.

Tei continued. "That peak is called Perrin's Vision. Jason Perrin found an easy path to the summit; when he got there, he had a good view of The Citadel in its glory. When he came back and told people, he wanted someone to check because he thought he had hallucinated. He could not believe it was real. When a Trader comes of age, we take them up to Perrin's Vision, usually in summer, to see the Truth."

"What is the Truth?"

"That there are greater things in the universe than humanity. But you must see it for yourself in order to understand."

He had a moment of déjà vu, then remembered when the Queen of Sanfran had asked that same question.

The Uuten Mountains looked impressive, but he remembered Tei had once told him that the Uutens were small compared to the mountains at Olympus: the Citadel of Zeus. He also now had an excellent view of the other strongholds. They were spread over the southern part of the oasis. Castle was huge, he estimated its octagonal form would fit in a square with 300 meter sides. Looking again, he followed the curve of the Tanuuten River and perhaps also the aqueduct from the Tanuuten to Tanten. Tei pointed out several more landmarks describing them from her experience and some of the history.

They left the Keep and walked around the Castle and the Cardinals; the name given to the specialized parts of the Castle at the cardinal points of the compass.

Back at ground level, near the North Wall, there were some foundries and places where various goods were manufactured, heavy things. It turned out the Artisan Quarter was located elsewhere. He examined some of the techniques they used, curious, noticing how much their technology lagged The Center. To the west were homes. These were the large communal homes of the families. Tei told him that although many lived outside the Castle walls among the green, these homes were ancestral and many still wanted the close exposure to the city.

To the east were the Artisan Quarters, and the Visitor Quarters. Closer to the south gate was the Garrison.

Later, they returned to the homes on the western side and visited a set of small buildings. This was her family home. He met her parents, some old trail riders who were also visiting, her aunts and uncles. There were at least a dozen people talking, discussing. Some leaving, some arriving. A full extended family in an extended building. Very different to a yurt. Like a castle within a castle. Out came wine and food. Someone started playing a guitar. He relaxed and didn't feel so hot and dirty. His head was swimming a little. Tei's father, a sun-hardened, wiry man by the name of Bron, came to him.

"Young man, I must apologize for my family.

We are so glad to have Tei back. We have forgotten you. It is so good to see her with someone she cares about. But you must be exhausted. You can wash here, we have a large bath. Later, Tei will show you to your quarters in the Visitors Quarter of the city. Sorry, you can't stay here. It is a legal requirement for all new arrivals, even Traders. But first wash, then food and drink."

A bath had been prepared for him with scents. It was blissful; he was tempted to stay in it until it went cold. But he was a stranger here. He better make a good impression for his fellow Wizards.

Her father told Mikel tales of the road. Stories of caravans, revealing little intimate details of the beliefs, hopes and fears of his family and people.

"Tell me Bron. Are there any people to the east? Any cities?"

"Well, the old tales say that there were people on all six continents of Neti but humans really only occupied the continents of Arva and Werrin in large numbers."

"Our ships have reached Werrin. We found nothing. Just desert reaching to the sea. No cities or towns. Nothing."

"Well, that is sad to hear. It was said to be an exquisite place. The east? There were cities there. There may still be, but we could never find a way across the desert."

He slapped his knee as if he remembered

something.

"Why are we talking about such sad things? This is a time for celebrating, though maybe it is a bit too much for some." He said, pointing to a pile of cushions that held a sleeping Tei, arm outstretched with a goblet of unfinished wine.

Mikel checked the wine cup sitting precariously in her hand, about to spill, and barely touched.

He left early, with Tei's father showing him the way.

He wasn't sleepy, so he explored around the Artisan Quarters near where his visitors' room was located.

Some of them were finishing up, tidying up equipment, sweeping away the detritus of a working day's effort. Placing the finished items in a safe place, a cover over the incomplete. He poked his nose into one shop where a middle-aged couple were finishing their work. Their names were Sandra and Aleis, just like his sister.

"Excuse me. I just wanted to have a look."

"We've put the finished stuff away. It will take some time to get it all out again, but I can do that," said Sandra.

"I only want to see your workbench, the kind of work you do?"

They were delighted.

"Do you craft instruments as well, young

man?"

"I wouldn't say, *craft*, that might be optimistic. I have invented a couple of interesting things, so I appreciate the skill and technique needed to construct them. For example —" He went to reach into his bag to find his fire-starter but remembered he had loaned it to Tarvis. Then he knew what he could show them.

"Have you heard of *telescopes*?"

"Only in the old books."

"Well ladies, I present to you my own little telescope. It is even collapsible. See?" He brought it out and showed it to them with a self mocking flourish. Then, and only then, did he remember all of his later misgivings, all of his mistakes, the deeper understanding he now had of how it should have been made. He blushed.

"It isn't very good. I apologize for the workmanship. But it does work."

They didn't even hear him. They were fondling it, turning it over, peering through it, chattering endlessly to each other.

"Goodness! It is a wonder." Aleis said.

"It is only for daytime viewing. If I had used convex lenses only it would be brighter and better at night, but it would invert the image. Let me show you how it is made." Then he gave them a quick guide on how it was made, the type of lenses and their characteristics, a little physics about why it worked, which they seemed to skip. They reminded him of some experimentalist Wizards he knew. "Who cares about the theory? Does it work?" they would say. A not unreasonable stand to take, he thought.

Aleis whistled over to another shopkeeper, who was just about to duck inside his home for the night. It turned out his name was Kief, a glassblower. The three of them chattered some more. Finally, Sandra handed the scope back to Mikel, holding it as if it was a holy relic. In the background, Aleis pulled up a stool, cleared a space and started writing some notes on a piece of papyrus that she suddenly had, that they all had. They must carry notepaper on them. They were all very distracted and busy taking notes.

"Thank you, young man. This is very interesting. What is your name? We can name it in your honor?" Sandra said.

"Uh. Mikel, Mikel Peres."

"Oh, you are that Wizard that came in on the caravan. Are all Wizards so young?"

"Not usually." Or ever.

He bade them farewell. The last he saw them, they were chattering excitedly. Now the wine, the journey, everything conspired against him. He found his place from the instructions and collapsed on the simple yet so luxurious bed. He made a movement to take his clothes off to sleep, but never finished it.

A dreamless sleep came over him, so like

death as to be unpleasant, yet very restful. If there was any noise from other places in the Artisan Quarter, he never heard it.

The first thing he heard was an armored fist hammering on his door. It was perhaps two hours after sunrise. He had slept in.

"Master Mikel, you are requested to attend a meeting of the Council," boomed a man's voice. "Ambassador Tei will meet you at the Keep. I am to escort you there immediately."

"What? Why do people keep doing this to me? Certainly. Wait a minute!" he said to the door while trying to work out who he was and where he was. His brain was fogged. He got up, discovering he was still dressed, grumbled over the lost opportunity to sleep comfortably in a proper bed, and grabbed his notebook. He had been very lax recently, perhaps too distracted trying to stay alive. That must change. There was so much here that needed recording, or at least some description.

Tei was standing on the steps of the Keep when he got there. He remembered the last time.

"Tei. I was wondering about this pavement. It is different here than where we entered." Stupid question, he thought.

"Yes. You are so observant, easy to see why the Master Wizard sent you. Most of the paving of the Castle allows water to drip through to a catchment system. Water for some crops. Not everywhere, only where there is no heavy traffic, walkways." Despite the river, it was too close to the desert not to take chances.

"Do you know why we have been called here?"

"Probably they want to meet the first Wizard to visit here since — ever. The agreement with Sanfran is also historic. I imagine they are shocked." She was grinning.

They walked up the Keep's southern staircase to the fourth floor, where stairs exited to a sturdy wooden door. When he followed Tei inside, he found himself in a large circular room. No windows but many candles. The room was arranged as a circular version of the room where he had first met the Master Wizard in the Center. Except here the seats were slightly raised to give the same effect. The circular rows of seating were almost empty, except for a dozen people sitting together in the innermost row. There were eight guards wearing uncharacteristic shiny armor, like silver, with jeweled weapons at their sides. The dozen seated wore expensive clothes, but he didn't have time to notice any details. As he got nearer, he saw gold rings on fingers and the glint of gems; perhaps rubies, emeralds, and diamonds. The guard led them down the nearest aisle towards the flat center of the room, about four meters across. A place to orate or judge.

He reached the center. The guard left. It was

just him and Tei now. Suddenly, a blindingly bright light from above shone down. He guessed they reflected it from outside, since it looked like sunlight. He couldn't see a thing outside of the patch of light the two of them occupied, but it was not welcoming.

An old man spoke. His voice, powerful and authoritative.

"Why are you here? What was your mission, Wizard?"

Mikel quickly decided he would be honest, a safe strategy because he knew nothing.

Tei spoke, adopting the commanding voice she used when she was the Ambassador in Bethor. "Master Olen. I have grown to know this young man and believe he has no plans or evil intent."

"Tei, you are not a member of the Council. You speak when we ask you to, not before."

Olen continued. "Well, Wizard? Speak up!"

Mikel took a deep breath and tried to sound as clueless as he felt. "Sirs, I am an Apprentice Wizard from the Center in Lind. They sent me to Bethor to investigate trade routes to the East, and to look for the reason two Center agents have disappeared. I'm only an Apprentice Wizard. I was just sent to listen." He repeated his low status almost as a plea.

Olen laughed. "Ha! They disappeared because Bethor is planning a war and they didn't want anyone else nosing around. You are lucky Tei Valis got you out of there when she did. Bethor isn't a very subtle player. But I think you planned that from the start. *Now tell us the real reason they sent here you*."

The last sentence was spoken with such venom that Mikel's hands started shaking. He put them behind his back, hopefully out of sight. If they didn't believe him when he told the truth, then he was out of ideas. He was a long way from home and it was going badly.

Tei spoke but was cut short.

"And let us not forget Tei Lin Valis. Your orders were explicit. Go along with the Center's request; befriend the Wizard and learn his plans. Did you?"

"He is young and innocent. But he is a true Wizard. He harbors no ill will, merely curiosity," Tei pleaded.

"Tei? Did you — get emotionally attached to this man?"

Tei didn't answer. But Mikel did. If he was doomed anyway, then he might as well defend both of them.

"Tei was a good friend and companion. When I return to the Center, I will only have good things to say about the Traders."

Olen was contemptuous. "Zeus save us. Typical of the Valis clan."

So that was it. There was a grudge involved.

Olen spoke more calmly. "Tei, you will return

to normal duties, your ambassadorial duties will be reassessed. Wizard, we deem you for the present to be a possible spy. You will be detained until we work out what to do with you. Guards, take him away!"

Tei shouted, "The Cities know of our dealings with Sanfran. You know what that means. This will not placate them. They will see it as an opportunity to get rid of Tanten and Sanfran."

Olen, now confident and boisterous. "Enough! This meeting is concluded."

Mikel heard Tei shout "No!" but the shock of the announcement dimmed it. He felt strong, armored hands grab his arms and march him out of the cone of light. He was day-blinded again and swore under his breath; even if he could break free, he would probably have just run straight into a wall. They marched him down the steps. By the time his vision had recovered enough, he was being marched down the stairs, ending below ground level. Only some torchlight. Mikel had never heard of dungeons before, but now he was about to find out more than he wanted.

It was dark and dank; it reeked. They took away his weapons, leaving him with his journal. They threw him into a cell and locked the door. It was small, cold, wet and had no bedding. He could barely see anything, even through the small peephole in the door. He did not know how he was going to get out of this. It was too dark to even write.

In the cold and dark, there was plenty of time to think. Fretting wouldn't get him out or make the stone floor softer, or warmer, or less damp. Sometimes when he was younger, he would meditate on problems. Not the meditation they were taught to calm their minds and influence their bodies. He never seemed to be good at that. Instead, he would think of a problem, see it in his mind as clear and real as a physical object, then he would become the problem. The interacting forces, components or abstractions would become intimately bonded to him. He would pass into it, time would dissolve away, then he would be the problem and the solution, his mind like a quantum particle exploring all paths simultaneously, finally entangled, collapsing into a solution.

He had never studied war. He was a novice, but now he must make up for that. Wizards had manipulated historical events, and he could not shrink from his duty to save the people and places he loved. He would have to understand the forces that moved people and armies, like the four fundamental forces, as well as space, time, information, force, and energy. He must become the coming war for Arva. Somehow, in all of that, he must find a path to a better world. Entropy would always pull them towards something worse, only conscious actions could get something better.

He ignored the voice asking him how he expected to implement any solution. He was a grain of sand on the beach and now the tide was turning.

His night was 24 hours long. He either meditated on the Problem or he dreamed of the Problem until he didn't know where dream and waking met.

Arva was a powder keg. Having seen a demonstration of gunpowder, he understood the meaning of the archaic term. Bethor was going to march east. They didn't have a real navy to oppose Lind, but Lind depended on the flow of goods both ways across the sea. Bethor was the tap that was about to be turned off. That would starve both Lind and the Traders of finances and resources. They would probably wait for Tanten to decline and then launch an assault on Tanten, if they could find it. Then he remembered the digging in Lindin, the archeological dig at the Library. Looking for maps? Surely they would be out of date. No, the maps would reflect the state of affairs while the Cities were in decline, after the founding of Tanten and the Center. An enslaving army armed with secrets. His cell now became even darker.

The darkness was occasionally broken when the Head Jailer would come to visit. They would grab him, shackle him in irons, and drag him off to what they referred to as the Interview Room. There he was tortured; with clamps, or hot metal, or threats, or sharp instruments. They asked him many questions, to which he always said what he knew, which was very little, that became the incentive for another round until he would "crack" and then presumably tell them any fantasy they wanted. The Head Jailer was getting very excited by these visits, trying to make Mikel think of him as a friend in some twisted, sickening parody of friendship. But in this, this setting, Mikel was a professional, not an amateur. He knew, or thought he did, the workings of those minds, twisted and harmed like him by circumstance. That didn't make them buddies. They were still intent on harming him. In his mind, his rage burned like an exploding star, hot, white, searing. In the dark, he would calm it, tame it, as if he was a blacksmith or alchemist working on consuming rage instead of metal. His own special dragon; deadly and useful. He knew he was dealing with something that uncontrolled would destroy him and any about him. He had a goal and he had more than just a will now. All he needed was access to resources.

After Mikel was dragged away, the light had gone out. Tei looked up, knowing that a mirror system on the roof was used to direct sunlight to this spot. She didn't know how the system worked, she just saw a fleeting image of the blue sky as they closed the mirror. Blue sky symbolized freedom to her. The room was plunged into darkness.

She heard the Council rise. Some muttering

and then footsteps disappearing. She could see a bit more and noticed that not all the Councillors had left. There were perhaps three, no four, who had stayed. Mistress Valia came towards her.

"Don't worry Tei, we will work something out. Perhaps Olen can be made to see that he was being very unreasonable."

"I don't think so, Mistress Valia. You know he has never forgiven Valis for its success in the southern trade routes. His family always claimed they had done all the work."

Master Levin spoke next. "Tell us about this Wizard." The others nodded their heads.

Tei took a moment. "Well, I was instructed to get to know him in Bethor. But he was so inexperienced I knew that Bethor agents would kill him easily. I invited him. No, I coerced him onto my caravan to explore the trade routes directly. Also, I don't know how to explain this, but he was different. He was so vulnerable, but he had this raw curiosity and intelligence. He would look at things and see things I had never seen before. I wanted to know this man more." She saw their looks.

"Yes. I slept with him." A tear rolled down her left cheek.

"Oh, dear," Master Levin said, "I see."

Tei took a deep breath. "I guess you have heard the report about our talks with Sanfran? If you read the report carefully, you will see that this *clueless* Wizard was instrumental. He impressed the Queen, and the Queen of Sanfran expects him to be treated well. The news of his imprisonment, I guess, is supposed to tell the other Cities that Tanten has no plans to ally with Sanfran. I presume that is the real reason Mikel is in a cell. So what happens when the news reaches them? They know Sanfran is alone, they go to war with Sanfran, and Sanfran will fall. If Sanfran falls, the next to go is the Caravanserai and then Tanten. They will capture the Caravanserai and bleed us of resources. Don't think the Cities don't know about this either. They know about Mikel because there were agents in the Sanfran court. So it is only a matter of time before they decide to nip this in the bud and isolate the Traders. Then they can pick us off at their leisure when our power has ebbed."

Valia spoke, "Olen has exceeded his authority. He cannot simply imprison people without public trial and discussion. This course he is taking is very dangerous."

Tei interrupted, "Any course from now on is dangerous. Whether or not we like it, we are heading for war. I think we need to take action. If Olen leads us, then we are heading down his perilous path to certain defeat. I believe it is time that the leadership must change. And quickly."

There was complete silence. The Councillors looked at each other.

"Are you sure this is not just about Mikel?" Valia asked.

"What other choice do we have? And Traders do not have kings as the Cities do, we have a Council. Olen is just a chairman, not a king. He has no power to make these decisions," she said. This touched them all. Traders despised autocratic rule by instinct.

"No, Tei is right. We are in danger. The quicker we act, the better," Master Levin said. The doubt and uncertainty in his face now gone.

Tei felt a moment of unreality as she heard herself speak. "We should move to depose Olen. There are precedents. But if he gets wind of this, he may act unlawfully again by having the rest of us thrown in prison, or worse."

Master Rilk from the back stirred and gave a small cough. "We know loyal Traders in the guard who can be trusted to act by the Constitution, not by Olen's command. We are with you Tei."

He awoke from a fitful, hard, uncomfortable sleep. There was a rattling sound, which he realized was a key in a lock. Then light through the peephole. He supposed it was another bowl of slops, something masquerading as food, or perhaps an 'interview'. The prison guards seem to delight in teasing their charges; sometimes with insects in the food, sometimes with waking him up in the middle of his sleep, sometimes with beatings. Inflicting pain and discomfort on Mikel and his fellow prisoners as if they were the jailer's own private property, independent of his trips to the Interview Room. Their own captive flies to tear the wings off.

"Mikel!"

He didn't recognize the male voice, but he knew the jailers wouldn't bother with first names.

"Who are you?"

The door swung open. There was a Trader guard in steel armor. He saw some insignia on his shoulders glinting in the torchlight.

"I am Major Rayan Valis. A cousin of Tei. I'm getting you out of here. Can you handle a sword?"

"Uh yeah. Sure." But he wasn't sure. Still better than rotting in a cell.

Back at the Center, he was trained in using a sword by Master Oma. He always wondered where she learned to fight like that.

She had said, *Mikel, use your intelligence and make the most of what is about you. You may not have the years of practice but you can be oh so creative. Use that. Yes, being creative means fighting dirty. If that bothers you, then think how a sword in your gut would bother you.*

Rayan led the way. Down the corridor lay a jailer, unconscious, minus his keys. Mikel followed stiffly at first. He had been in that cramped place for so long his muscles weren't used to such activity. This time his eyes were completely dark adapted and he saw exactly the path he had taken. His trips to the Interview Room had given him a good idea of the layout. He wanted to forget it, but he knew he wouldn't. He didn't know if that was a good or bad thing. They had climbed some stairs and had reached a small room that was at the entrance to the dungeon. Several men stood before them, the jailers with swords drawn. Rayan seemed surprised.

The Head Jailer, his old friend, headed towards Mikel while the other two took on Rayan.

Mikel blocked the first blow from the jailer. The jailer's sword was slightly shorter than Mikel's, but his reach probably compensated. Mikel was barefoot. The jailer wore ragged shoes: advantage to Mikel. He took in the rest of the room as he jumped back from the clash of swords. A lit brazier to his right, stinking slops or urine covering some cobblestones. Some wooden fixtures fastened to the walls. Not much to work with. The jailer had no armor, thankfully.

The jailer crouched. He was making himself a small target, ready to pounce. He leapt at Mikel. Mikel barely parried. He grabbed the jailer's sword wrist. He in turn clamped his teeth on Mikel's hand. Mikel placed his right foot on the outside of the jailer's left leg, then pushed, sending the jailer off balance. He spun right with the jailer, pushing the jailer's head onto the fiery brazier. The jailer screamed and jumped back, swatting at his smoldering hair. Mikel advanced on him. Parry, parry. He grabbed the other's wrist again, but this time he knew the jailer was standing on the slops in worn shoes. He kicked the jailer's foot, and he slipped down and back. This opened some space between them, and Mikel brought down his sword. The man saw that he was falling onto a sword aimed at his throat, but it was too late tc do anything. He gave Mikel a fleeting glimpse of fear or pleading, then the blade sliced his carotid artery and a spray of blood blinded Mikel. The man vainly grabbed his throat, writhing in Mikel's grasp, and in seconds was dead. He let him go and stepped back, panting and shaking.

"Well done, young Wizard," said Rayan, standing over the still writhing bodies of the other two.

Mikel and Rayan ran quickly up the steps to the fourth floor. There was no way to know what had happened on the other side of the door. Made of thick hardwood, no sound penetrated it. They barged in.

Before them were the twelve Councillors, Tei and some soldiers, some of them guards and others with different armor.

"You must step down! Now!" Tei yelled. She was intimidating. He had never seen her like this.

Rayan spoke up, "You no longer have the support of the Castle guard, Olen. If you choose to act against us, they will respond accordingly."

Olen stood in his fine robes, proudly defying the usurpers. Some guards behind Olen, probably from his clan, drew their swords, but they looked at each other, confused and uncertain, looking for support and not getting any.

"You have put Tanten in danger. We must act quickly to reassure Sanfran." Ray's face was hard, and now there was menace in his voice.

Olen motioned to the guards behind him. They sheathed their swords. Then with a loud sigh, he fell back into his seat. He spoke, shaken and defeated.

"Of course. All right then. I nominate Tei as my replacement." Before anyone could react, he stood, straightened, and addressed them in an almost regal tone, "Tei Lin Valis, I hereby nominate you as Head Councillor of Tanten until elections can be conducted."

"Olen. Please do not mock me," she said.

"I do not mock you at all. Although I have misgivings about your family, you have always acted honorably despite this Wizard. And decisively. We need decisiveness and intelligence now. I hope you are right, Tei. Everything rests on you now."

Rayan looked at Mikel. Perhaps he saw he was giddy, perhaps pale. He led him from the room to a place where he would get cleaned and fed.

They left him in the Valis household. He observed what home life was like for the Traders. Those who were not on Caravan or other business assisted with various duties. It was expected that all family members would help, though if someone had special skills, they were favored. Tei refused to let her sister Karina cook. "Self preservation," she whispered. Apparently, the best cooks were her mother and her younger brother. He never worked out how many were in the house: Tei had two brothers and a sister, all younger. There were several aunts and uncles, but they only visited irregularly, apparently they had their own homes. Tei confided that some of them had girlfriends or boyfriends on the side. It was accepted, but private. Nothing to get worked up about.

The Trader culture resembled that of the Center. Though in Lind, families were smaller. He presumed the other similarities resulted from their common origin. Even Bethor and the Cities were not that different. He wondered if all human cultures in the past were like this. That would be something to investigate if he had time to look through the Library.

Mikel was in a daze. He barely remembered stepping into the bath or even the food he ate, even as he was still wearing the rags from the prison drenched in blood. Karina had poured a bath. He was relieved to remember that he was alone and had undressed himself. Too much had happened. He sloshed the warm water over his face. Wonderful. He felt the comforting warmth and bliss, wishing it would wash away this world. He opened his eyes. The world had not reverted to his shack back home. It was not a dream he was going to wake up from. "Damn. What the hell do I do now?"

"What happens now?" Mikel asked Tei.

Tei sat in the Council meeting room with the other councillors and seemed to have taken immediately to her new roles as both Councillor and as Head Councillor. She had not responded to him.

"Should I address you as Mistress Tei?" he asked, hearing the odd sound out of his mouth of another name for a female Master. Why two names when one would do?

She smiled. "Not necessary at all. A silly formality. Traders dislike such formality. Olen's love of ritual did not make my fellow Traders happy. As for our plans. It will take time to form an army; we have to send messengers to the other Trader cities, and hope they respond in time. Get people to a staging area. Swear loyalty, so we will have a chain of command. Arggh! We do not have enough time. Lindin will march on Sanfran well before then. You saw Sanfran's defenses Mikel, they won't hold, will they?"

He thought for a while, juggling many things. The beginnings of a plan took shape. An insane plan. Extending it in his head, he saw it could become even crazier. There were probably better plans, but it was the only one he could think of right now.

He spoke aloud to himself. "This is no time for timidity." He saw Tei's puzzled look.

"Before I left Lind, I had a briefing with some wizards. They gave me an update on the situation in Bethor and Arva. One thing they covered was the port founded by The Center at Iska, at the mouth of the Zanda River, downstream from Tanfel."

"Yes, we know of it," said Master Levin.

Mikel continued, "There is a garrison normally stationed at Iska. However, most of it has been, or rather was being, transferred to a temporary fort north of Tanfel. The garrison was moved there secretly because we feared that a City acting as a pawn of Bethor would move to block the southern trade routes from the Eastern Caravanserai to Tanfel, and therefore disrupt our strategically critical trade with Tanten."

"I see. The Center does not trust the safety of trade routes via Bethor either," added another Master, whom Mikel would later learn was Hazn.

"I believe if we can get a message to the garrison, we might persuade them to bring their troops north to Sanfran. They would probably arrive much earlier than a Trader army. And we could even send a small group of Traders to help Sanfran morale in the meantime." Mikel thought it probably wasn't wise to say that last bit. But it was out there now.

Tei said, "Mikel, what makes you think that

the commander of a garrison would respond to your request? This would mean Lind becoming involved in a war, something they usually avoid."

"This would be to avoid a bigger war, or at least to protect the trade route. I also think I could persuade the commander. Anyway, it is a free option. We just send a rider with the message and either we get the help, or we don't and nothing is changed. Except if we get it, it could make a significant difference."

Tei held up her hand. Everyone understood, *silence while I think*.

He didn't know how long they sat there, but finally she lifted her head and looked across the room at him.

"Write your letter with all the skill you can. Captain Ellis, gather one of our best messengers and a few skilled riders to assist, have them meet me in the Head Councillor's quarters in one hour. Councillors, I would like to meet you here in three hours to plan this undertaking. I like the suggestion of a small force to Sanfran in the meantime." She said.

Mikel wanted to comfort her. But this was not the right time or place.

# seventeen

Mikel went over the note again and again. Was the wording right? Could it be more persuasive? He told his account as honestly as he could. The letter lightly described his mission, the journey to Bethor, his time there, meeting Tei, the journey across the Plains, more detail about the stay in Sanfran, about the coup in Tanten, and the likely war that was about to unfold. He begged for the commander's help to prevent Sanfran from falling before the Tanten forces could arrive.

He wrote the encrypted version carefully so he could accurately add another message to it. A longer space here, a lifted letter there, and the steganographic message was embedded. Encryption within encryption. The authentication within the message. All the Wizards learned basic steganographic techniques, the art of hiding messages in plain sight. This was an easy one since there was only one shared secret he had with the commander, whoever they were. Even if someone had the encryption key, they would likely not find the hidden message, which hopefully would persuade the receiver to act.

He carefully folded the letter, then sealed with the seal of the Council of Tanten. He wrapped it in a sheet of waterproof leather he had brought along, distinctly a product of Lind, but not what was exported. It was just a household item. He was hopeful of the result: encrypted message, encrypted identifier, an official seal of Tanten, and a distinctive insignificant item from Lind — the kind that a spy would overlook.

Mikel turned to give it to the messenger, but it was Rayan Valis who stood there.

"Major? Are you...?"

"They need to see that the letter has authority from Tanten as well as you. I won't be alone. I will take three friends along, just in case there is trouble," he said and smiled.

Mikel shook his hand and handed over the wrapped letter. Rayan Valis turned from Mikel and disappeared out of the door. Through the open window streamed orange light. The sun was setting. However, the Major would not wait for morning.

Mikel looked at his small collection of things that he had spread out on a table while looking for his notebook and wraps. Some items were unused, and the entire collection seemed naïve and juvenile now. He had thought he would have the chance to perform some experiments, do some scientific investigations, instead he was fighting for his life and changing the fate of nations. He did not think there was any way he could be up to the task. But he had no choice. Almost all the people he had met were decent people just trying to live; a war would be a random scythe of death across the Great Plains and extend all the way to Bethor and Lind. Like a human plague. It made the machinations leading to war seem even more pointless.

He left his room and walked west towards the Keep and the setting sun, now just above the Castle walls. He changed his path so the growing shadow of the Keep would shade his eyes. Tei was on the steps talking to some guards and two Councillors. She preferred normal Trader dress: leathers and turban. She apparently didn't care for the fine clothes of office. But then Traders don't particularly like ritual.

"Mikel!" she called. "Come with me."

She came down the steps, took his hand and led him somewhere around behind the Keep, constantly chattering away about preparations and logistics. Mikel was more amazed about the hand holding. She had never done that before. He just smiled stupidly. They stopped before a two story rectangular gray stone building just to the north of the Keep. He had not noticed it before, even though it was as wide as the Keep.

"You wanted to see the Library? Didn't you? Well, here it is."

"This is the Library. And I have FULL access," she said. She smiled as if she was a child left alone next to a pot of honey.

The entrance to the building was as plain as the gray stone on the outside. The inside also seemed ordinary: racks of books, a card catalog, assistants.

"I wish to see the Records. All of them," Tei said. Sounding royal, finally getting her way. The ten-year-old's dream coming true.

Master Garun, the Head Librarian, was a thin gray-haired main in his fifties. He looked unimpressed. "You cannot see all the Records. There are simply too many of them. Refine your topic, please. Decide what you really want to know about. Do you want me to give you some examples?"

He seemed to take their indecision as a 'yes.' "You could ask for: a summary of the history of Earth pre-interstellar travel, post interstellar travel, the discoveries on Term and Fortress, the first expedition to Neti, the discoveries of Helen Amaris on Neti, starship design in theory and practice, ..."

Mikel knew that name. "Amaris. Helen Amaris. There was a legend told on the Plains about Amaris who talked to Zeus."

"Yes. Helen Amaris was the first human to talk to the entity we now call Zeus. The entity resides in the structure called the Citadel of Zeus."

Tei was curious. "Master Garun, I have seen the Citadel with my own eyes. It is beyond imagining. What is it?"

"We do not have detailed information beyond some of Helen Amaris' field notes. There is no indication of what it is, who built it, or why it was built. We know it was not built by humans. It was here when we came to Neti from Earth. The records speak of a pact with Zeus, widely known, but no copy of the pact survives. So much was lost when the Great Battle was fought and later when the Cities fell."

Mikel needed to clear something up. "The Great Battle destroyed civilization on Neti. Do you have any details on the Battle?"

"I too wish we had more on this. It appears people were too busy trying to survive to write a history. Or no history survived. There are some clues. The Battle occurred between 500 and 700 years ago. We were not the target, we were 'innocent bystanders,' as the Records say. Somehow, the battle also destroyed civilization on other human worlds, but there is no explanation how such a thing could occur. The survivors expected help to arrive, but no ships ever came. Except the *Raymond Tans*." He said.

"Master Garun, I cannot stay since I have urgent official business. You will give Wizard Mikel here full access to the Library."

Garun's eyes opened wide, almost glaring.

"Is there a problem?" Tei said.

"No, Councillor. It is up to the Council who gets privileged access. Come, Master Mikel, let me introduce you to our catalog."

Mikel found the catalog eerily similar to the library catalog in Lind. He saw that so much of the similarity between the cultures that he knew was because of their common heritage, more and more he saw the similarities rather than the differences between all the cultures he had experienced. Even the language differences were not that great. Certainly, they all shared the same alphabet and numbering system. A highly sophisticated number and mathematical system that itself showed an advanced origin. The Tanten Library had several sections marked off according to the level of privilege. But when Garun took him to the second floor, he knew it was different. This floor was an area to itself and access was by a heavy, reinforced iron door that was locked. Garun opened the door for him. Inside, he was introduced to Maria, the librarian for this floor, then the door was locked behind him.

"Hello, I am Maria ya Irenni, the Curator of Library Antiquities."

Maria was a woman in her thirties, but she

did not dress in the usual manner of the Librarian and other officials, or even other Traders. She seemed casual, but the clothes were odd.

Maria noticed him looking at her clothes. "Not what you are used to?" She smiled.

"I like to get into character. Try to understand the Ancients. This is typical clothing that they would have worn from what I have read. Though there are strange references that make it sound like their clothes were also machines. However, these clothes I am wearing were simpler, but I still found them hard to reproduce. This is an approximation. I am wearing a 'white t-shirt' and 'jeans'. The inscription on the shirt is a set of mathematical equations. We do not understand why the creator of this apparel thought it worthy of showing to the world."

Mikel laughed.

"They are Maxwell's Equations of Electromagnetism, and the words underneath, 'Let there be light'," he said.

"Hmm. You not only understand it, you appreciate it. Interesting. Who was Maxwell?"

"No idea. At the Center we study many ideas which have names attributed to them, but we do not know who most of the people were."

"What about this one?" She reached over to a table where it appeared she had been inking in text on another t-shirt. It also was a mathematical equation. He recognized it but didn't understand it.

He had intended to study this as one of his tasks when he became a full Wizard.

"Harrun's Standard Model of Superspace. But I couldn't explain it like I could Maxwell's. I've done some basic M-Theory but nothing above that yet."

Maria looked at him oddly, as if he had temporarily gone insane.

"Maria, what exactly is here?" He waved his hand to include everything.

"These are original records of the Ancients. We make copies, of course, but these are the originals. We also have some devices. Some still working, though just barely. Some diagrams and images here we cannot duplicate, we can only produce poor copies. The printing presses are always running to produce enough copies of selected texts to duplicate most of this library in other Trader cities. We cannot risk losing so much again."

He wanted to see some devices. So she brought him to a special room. A faded blue box about the size of his two fists together sat on a table in front of him. The room was quite dark.

"Now listen." Maria leaned past him and touched a small white rectangle on the top of the cube.

After a few seconds, a soft woman's voice came out of the thing.

*AvrOS 7.9 Started. Insufficient power for holographic video. Input/Output devices not found, using inbuilt audio only. Internal battery is minimal. Errors in hardware checks. Grid not available. Network not available. No direct neural link found. What do you want to do?*

The words were strangely lilted. He could understand them individually, but they didn't seem to make sense as sentences.

"Speak towards the box, but speak slowly and simply so you don't confuse it. You can only use it for a few minutes. After that, it will need to 'recharge' itself. Whatever that means."

Mikel tried to think of something clever to ask, but nothing popped into his head. "What is the *Ray Tans*?"

*Raymond Tans, onetime director of Special Contracts, was a celebrated investigator and entrepreneur. He is most famous for his recovery of the Ashan Association Starship buried under a frozen sea on the world known as Reshox, where the High Noon beacon is situated. The starship Raymond Tans was commissioned in 2355 and was used as a flagship for the support fleet for the colony of Neti.*

Mikel was amazed. He had been taking notes but had stopped midway because his mind just needed to consider all of this. He jotted some more things down.

"What was the Great Battle about?"

*Sorry, I don't have any information about that.*

He tried to think of something related. "In relation to Neti, what is the Pact?"

*The Pact or Neti-Terran Pact is an agreement between the Human Nexus and the planetary intelligence, often referred to as Neti, the same as the name of the planet. In human mythology, Neti was a Sumerian god who was the gatekeeper of the underworld. The intelligence discovered on Neti has been given the codename Zeus and the site of its massive main access area in western Arva has the codename Olympus. Zeus has agreed to terraform the planet to suit human life. In exchange, humans will aid in the defense.*

"If civilization on Neti was destroyed, would the Pact require Zeus to intervene to assist?"

*Power level critical. Shutting down.*

If Olympus was built for *defense*, perhaps there were weapons at the Citadel. That seemed crazy and desperate; a perfect fit for their situation, but right now, crazy expeditions would not be top priority.

Mikel turned to Maria. "When can I use it again?"

*The machine takes a very long time to* recharge *using the 'ambient EM waves' or something. It seems there were once more efficient ways to* recharge, *but only this method is available now. The device is ancient, and failing. It will probably be usable in about 6 months.*

"Oh! That's unfortunate." He felt like kicking

himself for not planning his questions.

"All right, can you show me the books now?"

"You asked about Ray Tans. You should have asked me. I have studied him quite a bit. Had a bit of a crush on him at one stage. Not the great remote hero they talk about, but a very human person." She giggled.

Much later, his eyes tired from reading by candlelight, he got up to move around. His mind was saturated with things stranger than any fiction. It threatened to flood and reset his skeptical sense so that he would start believing in everything from fairies to the man in the moon.

Maria was still in the Library collecting some of her personal things to take home with her.

"Maria, I've been reading quite a bit, but there is something I still don't understand. I mean, I should understand it because it is part of our history not belonging to the Ancients. Why did the Cities fall?"

Maria put her bag down on her desk, still clinging to the cloth strap, she leaned to one side against the desk. Thinking, her right hand massaging the cloth strap like prayer beads.

"Although there are few records of the Great Battle, there are records in later years that talk about the problems that arose. It is hard for us to understand. I have tried and I think I have an inkling. You know the Ancients used a technology called *neural links* that allowed them to transfer information directly into their minds? They constantly exchanged information. Soon they came to believe not that 'knowledge is power,' but that, 'information is money'. Being permanently linked, they no longer knew how to ponder their inner selves or the outer world. Even the old Global Civilization before them had not fallen into that trap. As individuals and as a society, they lost their way. Even as they came to know what the problem was, they had embraced the notion that 'information is money' and that therefore, anyone who disconnected even briefly from the net was a freeloader. A burden on society. I gather it was also considered painful, unbearable to disconnect. After the Great Battle, the network was shattered, *electromagnetic pulse events* had disabled almost all the neural links. They were all disconnected. They had all become the pariahs they loathed. Worse, they did not know how to live this new restricted life. They had only been focused on the link, an internal dialogue that had nothing to do with introspection or self-understanding, and so had no capacity for fully appreciating the world they lived in. When the links failed, they were alone. They succumbed to a depression that was as much psychological as it was sociological. They never recovered; the dysfunctional way of life was passed on to their children, who in time outgrew it but whose knowledge of the technology that maintained that way of life was diminished. When

Bethor assailed the Cities, they collapsed like a rotten piece of wood. Not everyone was like that, however, enough always had different priorities and adaptability; so some met or communicated and, seeing the dire situation, decided on founding the Center and Tanten. They had lost family, spouses and friends in the Battle, either in space or in vaporized cities, then they lost more by choosing a different path. It was a time of relentless tragedy, sadness, and loss."

She looked down, as if absorbing strength from the ghosts buried in the earth. She paused, took a breath, then looked up at him again.

"The legacy of those times haunts us still. You can find it in the legends of the Plains and the casual attitudes here in Tanten. There is a sense of loss, as if we are clinging still to something long gone. Perhaps it is time to let go. You are the harbinger of such a change, a herald of a new age. Many won't like that."

"That won't stop me. If things don't change, I fear that all of civilization may fall. You seem different. Have all these books changed you?"

"Obviously, but also I am a stranger to Tanten. My parents were killed in a raid by Lindin forces. I survived and finally found a home here. I always loved books, so this is my heaven." She smiled like an angel in complete peace.

She nodded and picked up her bag.

"Maria, before you go, I would like to see the

field notes of Helen Amaris."

Dawn, a faint blue light in the east. The cold seeping over from the black desert beneath the stars. A few beacon lights always burned at the top of the Mouth of the Snake, as the gates of Castle were called, but they shed no light on the company immediately below and outside the gate. He was mounted and ready to go; he had all of his gear, but he was not ready to leave the library. Maybe he would never be ready to leave it; it was amazing. His body felt as if he had consumed some powerful stimulant just from reading, and he had just begun. None of the information was as stunning as that little blue box, but all of it was new and revealing about the world and history. Yet there were so many major blank spots. He felt like a young student just entering college at the Center, brash and confident, and then discovering in that first week how little he knew.

He was sitting on his horse surrounded by the shadows of several dozen or more Traders. The feel of the animal beneath him shifting now and then. The sound of horses breathing and huffing, a hoof on cobble stones now and then, echoing, the riders silent. Just vague shadows; the smell of horses, leather, and a complex, elusive mix of scents that said, "travel companions." He fought a temptation to yawn, inevitably losing.

Although he had not seen everyone, he was

told the numbers would be between 40 and 50. No more could be spared before the riders from the other towns came in. This was a small advance force whose central attribute was the speed of its response. A very early response to a problem may not need very much force. Timing can often be crucial. This was their role, to render aid before events required that those greater forces would be needed. They were, apparently, fully armed, which meant more armor than he was used to seeing on Traders, but not as much as the Castle Guards who seemed to prefer impressive but heavy looking gear. He was seeing more than outlines now; gray phantoms. They looked tough, but he couldn't say why he thought that. He prayed to whatever deity there was that they would not expect him to lead these men in any capacity. They'd know in an instant he was clueless about tactics or fighting. He was a Reformed Pantheist, so pro-pacifism, no personal god but worshipping the Universe. Personal or not, he would pray to that Universe, because they would need all the help they could get.

He looked up into the fading night sky. The *Raymond Tan*s clearly visible if you knew what to look for. About thirty degrees away from the zenith, it defined the latitude and longitude of the observer. "Why can't you help us, you indifferent bastard?"

"Making demands of the sky? I don't think

that will work." A familiar voice.

She was on foot and standing next to his horse. He hadn't heard her approach. "No. Just frustrated that a starship is just hanging in the sky up there and we can't contact it. Or get it to help."

"Are you coming with us?" he said.

"My place is with my friends, fighting, not stuck in a chair, being useless."

"I know why I am going, because the Queen will feel much better if one of us is there. But you are the Head Councillor."

"Which doesn't mean much in these circumstances. The Stronghold lords have been informed and are gathering their forces. Defenses are being made secure. Plans are being drawn. I am not a general. That has been assigned to Master Levin."

They left from the southern gate. The same way he had entered. By the time the sun rose, they were proceeding into the desert, marking off the time until the turn to the west.

Mikel came up alongside Tei. "What is the plan?"

"We will proceed to the Eastern Caravanserai; if all is well there, we will try to pick up any who have rendezvoused, waiting for us and proceed to Sanfran. Scouts will go ahead, of course. We won't use the commonly known trails."

The word was passed along. Then there were sounds of hoofs, leather stretching, metal jingling;

pale shapes in the predawn moving. Time to move out.

The Caravanserai was intact. They had posted lookouts after the messenger had arrived two days ago, but so far there was no enemy activity. Also, there were increasing numbers of independent Traders coming in and pledging loyalty to Tanten and Tei's leadership. He wondered how they knew. They picked up another thirty fighters, not as hardened as the troop that had left Tanten originally, but certainly tough enough.

The road west to Sanfran was far too risky. Scouts had determined an alternative route. It was old and rarely used. It had gone through what had once been several small towns, now indistinguishable from the small natural hillocks of brown grass. Sometime past the halfway point, they stopped in a small depression among the hills and posted lookouts.

Mikel walked among the knee length brown grass to stretch his legs. Sounds of insects and the sight of flying moths preceded him. It was the middle of the afternoon and a hot, dry breeze was blowing from the desert to the east. Adele followed him. She was a Captain, whatever that meant here, and was a no-nonsense military professional, taller than Mikel, green eyes with distinctive short red hair poking out of the edges of her hat.

He bought a hat in Tanten and had worn it on

this trip. It no longer felt odd, and in this sun he was glad. His brown skin wouldn't protect him.

"It is getting really hot now, Adele."

"Yes, we are out of a mild spring and getting into a very early oppressive summer. This will make Tanten even harder to attack. Hopefully."

A glint in the dirt caught his eye. He bent down and picked up a piece of metal about the size of his palm. Brushing the dirt off, he saw it looked unblemished, almost new. There was some faint writing on it, illegible. It was tough, but the twisted, jagged edges suggested enormous forces had once hammered the area where they stood.

"What is this place?" Mikel asked.

"We don't know exactly. Stories say it was once a fort with impressive weapons. Destroyed a long time before the fall of the cities."

This jagged piece of metal must be the first tangible relic of the Great Battle he had seen. No longer mythic but real, a real tragedy with real victims entombed under the ground he walked on. He couldn't just drop it; he unslung his pack and carefully placed it inside almost reverently.

After another day, they were in sight of Sanfran. Mikel, Tei, Adele, and a few others stood on top of a hill overlooking the plain, stretching west to Sanfran. The sun was setting and producing a strange illusion. Out of the deepening shadows on the plain, a grid appeared. He did not know what it was, but it didn't look natural.

"What is it?" He asked.

Adele answered. "The bones of the dead city still break the surface now and then. This land is haunted."


It was Rijart who noticed it first.

"Tei. Look there!" He pointed while Tei looked along his arm, pointing at some place midway between their position and Sanfran.

Mikel saw it. Some banners blowing in the breeze, barely visible in the afternoon sun. Fortunately, Sanfran was not quite toward the setting sun.

"We might be visible. Get down," said Adele.

"Right. I noticed they have a dozen large tents and many smaller ones. They must have many hundreds of troops," Tei whispered. Mikel thought it odd that she should instinctively whisper, but he had found on his journey, and perhaps he had always known that people, including himself, are rarely rational.

He put his shoulder pack on the ground and pulled out his telescope and focused it on the enemy camp.

"Tei, you won't believe this, but most of that camp is empty. It's a decoy." He passed over the telescope to her and gave her the ten second introduction to it.

"Yes, just turn that part to focus. It contains several lenses that magnify distant objects. It is called a telescope."

"Ah, so this is a telescope. I've read about them but never seen one. And — you made this?" She looked at him and smiled. Then back to the eyepiece.

"You're right. I estimate they have maybe fifty, yes, less than a hundred soldiers, and they are all faced away from us. A bluff maybe while they wait for reinforcements. There's a fair bit of open ground. We couldn't just sneak up on them, that would be costly."

"If we could organize with Sanfran, we could encourage them to resist and…" a plan started forming in his mind, "and we could plan a combined assault." Did he say that?

Tei smiled. "Not just a pretty face. We have to send someone — disguised as a merchant — along the south road. It's far but much safer."

"I should go. The Queen will listen to me. Anyway, I almost feel like a merchant after Lindin," he said.

Tei narrowed her eyes. "Yes, that would work. Just don't sleep with her. You are mine and don't forget it. And don't get yourself killed."

Tei left in a hurry to arrange some disguises.

Adele laughed. "She's not usually so possessive. Just behave yourself."

The path south was haphazard and confusing, the clothes unfamiliar. He felt very self-conscious. He had reached the designated landmark, a small hillock with a rock protruding, only to find that the rock was the remains of some ancient building. With a sigh of regret, he ignored the ruins, turned his horse and proceeded west behind a series of small mounds that were three meters high. Everywhere he went he was surrounded by mysteries, with clues so strong that he could almost hear voices singing to him, sirens telling him to leave what he was doing, pick this up, or that, look at it and learn something no one else knew. Many people he knew didn't see the world this way. They thought the world was normal, unsurprising, but that was an illusion. The truth was: everything is a mystery and nothing is certain. Human beings can't handle that, so they invent complacency to deal with it. For the moment, he must adopt that complacency, the lie. He could not be distracted; for now, the hills were just dirt and old buildings.

They had hoped the hills would hide him from the enemy for most of the way. By now, he was probably too far away for them to see him properly, even if they were looking.

After several hours, he came to a dirt track, the southern road from Sanfran. He looked about. This was the road to Pareth, an ally of Lindin, or fellow Bethor puppet state, if you preferred. If they were sending forces, then they would likely use this road. From here on there was no cover, so he turned the horse towards Sanfran and prayed. He had never believed in Zeus, even before he found out the truth, but he subscribed fairly loosely to the One, a pantheistic vision of the universe fairly common on Lind. It might be a good time to try his hand at praying.

As he approached the southern side of the city, he noticed it had more of the appearance of a true wall. Apparently, at some time, the southern side had slabs of masonry moved together to make an impenetrable jumble that was yet still a rough wall about four meters high. The road forked to the left and right, west and east. There was no entrance on this side. He tried the west, as far from the eyes of the Bethorese as he could get.

"Where are the boats?" he said to himself. A huge lake like an inland sea, the other shore, was not even visible. There must be plenty of fish and opportunity for trade. Then he remembered the treeless plains. How could they build boats? But in the mural in Sanfran, the image of the Cities of the Plains, there were many trees. He also remembered the wooden structures of Tanten and the Librarian talking about where Tanten sourced its timber and papyrus. Tanten could supply fairly large amounts of timber, he had been told, but it wouldn't be via the desert, though that was not explained. Certainly enough for a small fleet of fishing boats, or warships. In time, they could even recreate the forests on the plain. With timber,

Sanfran would dominate the Lake and therefore all access between Lind and the Traders. As partners, the three could be the first world empire of Neti. Mikel was sure Queen Elena had thought of this before she had even met Mikel. Like a great game of chess, but one where each move required a payment in blood.

Mikel had a sudden memory of the jailer, the blood spraying into his eyes, the hate and rage he had felt, payback for the torture, but now there was simple compassion in the wrong place at the wrong time. He hadn't been able to get rid of the image or memory. It chilled him. This was the price of rage, it chose its targets randomly, not always justly. Rage wasn't a tool you could bend, instead it would bend and deform you. He understood now. He understood Liz Markham more, he also understood that she chose the wrong path.

After a few minutes, the road turned along the shore of the lake towards a ramp into the city. He looked up and saw inquisitive eyes with crossbows at the windowless openings of the buildings overhead.

It took a little while to see the Queen. No one believed him. But one guard came up, a smile on his face. He looked familiar.

"Aha, Wizard. How is your writing going?" It was the man who had taken his notebook before he was introduced to Queen Elena. His name was Rolf, a big man with a big smile or a scary grimace. Although he was well liked, Mikel had seen both sides, maybe just two of many sides. It was true of everyone in this war.

Now that he was identified, all he had to do was talk to the Queen. But that would not be as easy as last time. He waited in his plain quarters, not the sumptuous ones he was in last time, this time more suited to a monk. Eventually, an emissary from the Queen came. He strode into the room right up to where Mikel was standing with scant regard or care for Mikel's personal space. He was a big man, two meters, black beard, heavy but muscular, his physique partially hidden by the fine clothes he wore. Black and white, with a matching velvet hat. Rich, narcissistic, overbearing, uncaring. The impression was not flattering; it was intimidating.

"I am Darin Oesis. I represent the Queen," he said.

"Greetings. I need to talk to the Queen urgently. It is about the safety of Sanfran."

"No doubt," he said. He acted distracted, which was bizarre, since there was nothing else here to be distracted by.

"The Queen is very busy. What do you have to offer?"

"I will only talk to her personally."

"She is very busy. I can present your case to Her. This is normal procedure." Which it was not.

"No, I will see the Queen and if you obstruct me, I will tell her about it. Do you understand?"

"Hmm. I see. It appears the Queen does want to see you. I hope you understand I was only trying to ease the Queen's duties." He bowed.

Mikel thanked him, but he left an air of danger and intrigue. An obvious agent, not smart, probably only alive because he was being fed false information.

The Queen was holding court in the same banquet hall he had last seen her. He approached and bowed, hoping he got it right. She had a look of exhaustion on her face that makeup could not hide.

"So Wizard. What have you learned since we last met? Have you filled your journal?"

"I've learned quite a lot, your majesty. More than is probably safe to know these days. I have come to offer assistance with a particular problem you may be having."

"What problem would that be?"

Mikel looked about. "Perhaps we can discuss this somewhere less public."

She gave a nod to someone he couldn't see, and a flick of the hand. Immediately, most of the non-essential listeners, possibly non-loyal, were ushered from the room. They seemed to be used to this.

"Wizard, I have a Lindin force on my doorstep. They demand that the city be turned over to them and that I become a puppet of Bethor. You had better conjure up a miracle if you want to stay out of my prison."

"My forces are camped nearby. We have seen the Lindin forces and discovered that they are small in number. It is a ruse to force you to surrender."

"There will be reinforcements, however, from Lindin, or Bethor," she said.

"There will also be reinforcements from Tanten."

That got her attention. She leaned forward. "Can Tanten's forces defeat Bethor?"

"What do you think will really happen to you if Bethor takes control?"

"They will end my family line, all of my family. And our culture and ideals." Her head sagged for a moment. Then it lifted as she found some strength.

"How would you deal with my problem then?"

Sanfran was still considering the surrender terms. He had advised the Queen not to tell her advisors about the plans because he and Tei suspected at least one of them was working for Bethor. He had also asked and got permission to address Sanfran's military leaders.

Just after sunrise, with the sun low in the east, the Trader forces were hiding. Mikel sent the 'Go' signal by means of a metal mirror. In fact, it was the shiny metal fragment he found earlier. He used the Morse, which the Traders also knew, and hoped the enemy didn't know it and didn't see the signaling. He found a place high in a tower on the edge of the city and in direct sunlight, it was dangerously unstable. Flashing the message continuously, his heart was pounding, waiting for the reply. The plan required a set of signals. If both parties didn't work together, then everything could go disastrously wrong. He noticed through his telescope that more Lindin troops had arrived, but still not the main force. He estimated they now numbered about 200. A dangerous increase, but with surprise, they could still win.

A small party of horsemen carrying three red and yellow banners came out of the main gate of the city. These men were dressed in the clothes of the advisors who would offer the surrender. The three banners was a signal to Tei that everything was ready.

The party on horseback stopped at a point about one third of the distance to the Bethor forces. This was the signal to Tei that it was time to attack.

Tei gave the hand signals ordering the attack, it was passed down the line. The path was through long grass, so they had been able to get fairly close to the camp without being seen, especially with the sun behind them. But now they had the order to advance. The last 100 meters were in complete silence, creeping through the long grass. The Lindin troops were too busy looking at the Sanfran envoys. Some saw something flashing from a tower earlier on. They thought that odd, probably glints from swords or spears. None of them were looking at their rear. Some were already shaking hands and laughing.

Eighty meters.

Fifty meters.

They were now exiting the cover and coming into plain sight. A guard turned and saw them, but it was too late. As he began to scream, a crossbow bolt through the neck silenced him. Immediately, the air was filled with bolts fired at medium range. Entire rows of Lindin soldiers went down, some screaming. The others turn stunned in time to get another wave of bolts. Some of the Lindin troops didn't even have their swords on them. Another volley, and another volley. The first row of Trader soldiers waded in with swords swinging, glittering in the sun.

Adele rushed forward, sword and shield, slashing at the panicked defenders.

The party on horseback lowered their banners as they heard the first screams of battle. That was the signal for Sanfran cavalry to assault the Lindin camp. The horses streamed out of the city gate and rushed towards the backs of the desperate Lindin contingent. Some Lindin soldiers heard the hoofs and turned to see something beyond their worst fears, cavalry charging and almost upon them. The

Lindin soldiers scattered in panic. It was every man for himself. A rout.

Some got away on horseback, but 8 out of 10 would never return. The numbers at the camp were greater than they suspected, but they had been caught completely by surprise. Sanfran had agreed with Mikel that the survivors would be looked after, though there were very few of them. Fortunately, casualties for the Trader and Sanfran forces were light.

Later, Mikel came out to meet Tei and Adele on the battleground. Mikel felt sick as he looked about at the blood and the waste. When was he going to get used to it? Did he even want to? He also knew this surprise attack would not be repeated. Next time, they would likely face the combined forces of both Lindin and Pareth without the element of surprise. He didn't know the size of the Lindin army, but suspected it was small. They simply did not have the resources, so these would have been their best deployed as the advance force. Now that force no longer existed. He assumed Lindin would press gang the peasants into fighting. They would be easy to panic. But Pareth was an unknown. Perhaps they could be intimidated if they knew Lindin was out of the picture. But what about Bethor? Bethor was the largest, most belligerent, the best armed, and best trained of all of them and they were spoiling for a fight. They also had troops stationed in Lindin. He remembered the troops in Bethor. They looked mean and professional, not like the relatively undisciplined forces he had seen from the Cities.

Peels of distant thunder boomed, though no clouds were visible yet. The rain would wash away the blood and any traces of what he had planned here. These deaths were on him, but to be honest, so were the Trader and Sanfran lives saved as well. It was an age old balance that he would have to face and deal with. He had learned so much in such a short time, had he also unlearned the respect for life which helped define him? He feared what he was becoming.

Mikel walked into the throne room. His presence was 'requested'. He had hoped to sleep in. But sleep wouldn't cure what was troubling him.

"Mikel! Come here," the Queen called.

Even Mikel, the product of a stubbornly egalitarian society, thought that was too casual for a royal court.

"Yes, Your Highness."

"One of our prisoners from yesterday turns out to be an advisor to the Regent of Lindin. He's from Bethor. What do you think about that?"

Before he could say anything, Queen Elena continued.

"He had in his possession a strange map. He refuses to explain what it means. I would torture the wretch, but I really don't have time for that.

Here, you and Tei figure it out. It seems to show Tanten. I have a feeling this is in our mutual interest to solve."

Mikel took the map from a young Sanfran army officer. Tei had also arrived, just in time to overhear the conversation. She took the map from him and opened it up. He looked over her shoulder.

"This is a map of the northern regions. North of the Plains, the forbidden lands of Xan, and extending east to the north of the Uuten Mountains." She pointed to some landmarks on the southern end that he could recognize. A dotted line traced a path from near Lindin through the northern valley and through a pass to the east, then south. And there, south of the Uutens, at the end of the dotted line, was Tanten.

"Shit!" Tei looked pale.

"What is it?"

"This is a map that shows how to get to Tanten via the northern mountain pass. We are pretty much defenseless from that direction. And look at these marks along the way. I know what they are, waypoints for an army. Those are ikely places with abundant game and water." The notations on the map were in Bethorese style.

"Bethor is taking an army to assault Tanten. We can't match Bethor, Lindin, and Pareth together." She had spoken too loudly, and looked up to see the Queen looking at her with an impenetrable look. She knew what that meant:

they better win or they were all dead.

Mikel took the map from her and looked at it. "While we are fighting Lindin and Pareth, you will have to deal with Bethor. Some of these notes are in code. I will have a look and see if I can crack it." He said.

He had not raised his head, analyzing the map was becoming his sole focus.

"Tei? What is this?"

He was pointing at another path leading north off the route, winding through more northerly mountains, past representations of cities.

"This is an old Trader map. Or one from before the Cities fell. That path is the path to the Citadel of Zeus, Olympus."

The hairs on his arm and the back of this neck stood up.

"Wow. There is also text here. It doesn't make sense. I think it is encrypted."

"Precisely. That is your forte Wizard," the Queen said.

Tei couldn't wait. She wrote a brief note to Master Levin, informing him of an attack from the Northern Pass and sent it by her best messenger. She took a deep breath and went to Mikel's room. This was probably going to be a long night.

Mikel and Tei worked on the map through the night. Trying various ciphers. Going for walks now and then to clear their heads. At first, he thought it might be a Caesar Cipher. If there had been more text, he would have looked for the frequency of letters, then try to match it with the common letters, but with the little he had, he would just have to do it the hard way. He tried using various offsets from the letters in the alphabet, going backwards to reverse the effect. He presumed they used a small offset, so a small offset in the reverse direction of just the right amount should suffice. Didn't work. What else? He noticed that there were numbers mixed in, so they likely used an alphanumeric set rather than pure alphabet. There were spaces and punctuation but that was regular from one waypoint note to the next, so it had not been encrypted. That was potentially useful information that suggested there were abbreviations. It was getting late, and they had made no progress at all, but that is often the way it is with some codes; it is all or nothing. He decided to try a Vigénere approach.

"Perhaps it is a Vigénere Cipher."

"What does that mean, Mikel? Is that harder?" She was tired and her eyes were hoping, or praying, for him to say it was easy.

"Yes, harder. A Caesar Cipher is just the simple cipher you experiment with as a kid. Well, in Lind anyway. Just shift the letters along a certain amount. So if the offset is five, then 'A' becomes 'F', 'B' becomes 'G' and so on, just jump five characters along in the alphabet. With a Vigénere, you have a keyword where every letter of the keyword acts like an offset, so every character in the message is shifted by the amount represented by a character in the keyword. You just cycle through the keyword and each of its characters becomes the offset based on assigning it a number in the alphabet. That is harder, but if we can find the keyword, it becomes easy. Unfortunately, we don't have enough text here to do statistical tests or look for patterns as the keyword repeats."

"So we need the keyword."

"Any ideas?"

"They probably thought they were so clever. Perhaps they were. Or maybe …"

"Huh? Is there a clue here because I do not see it."

"What is a likely keyword that they would use?"

"'BETHOR'? Too obvious."

"Still worth trying." He said.

He built a matrix representing the effects of the offset. Tedious but necessary. It yielded nothing.

"No luck there."

"How about 'MAXIMILIAN?'"

"As in the Emperor. I don't think the military would care about the Emperor." He said. He tried it anyway, without success.

They tried several more with each one failing and leaving them more drained and desperate.

"'MARKHAM'?" Tei said.

He just looked at her, mouth open, unable to reply.

"Liz Markham. She is …"

"I know her."

"She is the Chief Military Commander of Bethor. Very dangerous. Try it." She seemed pleased with herself. Mikel was sweating slightly, hoping Tei didn't see it.

Mikel constructed a table for the calculated offsets of 'MARKHAM', as applied to each letter of the alphabet and each digit. It took time. The Bethorese agents would have their own version for the correct keyword. He tried the first waypoint note, which had the visible text.

5D651T P1OX RINR SFWO OP1Q S6LL PX E1.CQM

After a few minutes, he had readable text. It was exciting and worrying

SCOUTS CONF GAME FEED GOOD ROAD OK 10.UFE

"The tenth of Ufemi? That was four days ago!" Her jaws tightened. Mikel could see the muscles near her ears and at her temples bulge, like a pulse.

He rapidly deciphered the other three waypoint notes.

XAN OK FOOD STORE 14.UFE

XAN WESTERN PASS ENTRY FINAL PREP 19.UFE

STAGING BRIGADES B C D ATTACK 23.UFE

"They are already in Xanadu at the second waypoint. In nine days, they will be at Tanten. Three brigades, thousands per brigade." Her voice was quickly rising in pitch. Tension edging towards panic.

"Hey. Relax. We can figure this out." He said.

"RELAX? What have you been drinking? This is a nightmare. No one has attacked Tanten before. Our defenses have never been tested. Holy crap. Shit." Her face flushed red, the candlelight casting grim shadows across her twisted features.

"Tei. Tei. Get some rest. In the morning, you can form a strategy. You now know when and where they will attack. That is a major advantage." He told himself he had to sound positive. He had to lie because he wasn't positive at all. It was grim.

She paced back and forwards, getting more agitated.

He took her in her arms and hugged her. She sobbed. Now she just needed to be comforted past this peak. After that, he knew she would gain composure and recover.

After a few minutes, she gave a shudder. Almost like a shiver, and he felt her muscles relax. Her body's wisdom had come to the fore and demanded she rest. He escorted her to her room, took off her boots, and tucked her into bed. She was asleep before he could say "goodnight" Then he returned to his own room.

"Liz Markham, small world."

It was the last time he would be at the Markham's. The parties were much smaller than the Palace but the same inflexible rules still applied. He was returning an empty tray to the kitchen to swap it for a new one. She was there. Sitting in an ordinary chair. Red eyes, tears rolling down her cheeks, smudging her spare makeup. She saw him, then sobbed and reached for a napkin.

"You aren't the only slave here, boy. If you live and earn your freedom, never give it up. It doesn't matter who you have to kill. Sometimes, to be free, you just have to kill everyone in your way. Society expects me to do its bidding. I have other plans."

There was a fierceness, or madness, in her gaze that troubled him, more than the threat of pain, or even what he had seen. It was the vision of what he might become.

"I have reached an age when I can be independent. They think they can solve that by marrying me off, change one chain for another. Keep me in check. Well, I will give them a 'mate' that they aren't expecting."

She smiled, staring at no one. "A check mate. Or is it a checked mate?"

Her gaze drifted back to him. "You look so innocent, but you know. We both know, we're kin in suffering. Remember, child, do what you have to do if you get the chance."

She slipped out from somewhere that curved dagger. He shivered. Inside, he prepared himself for death. Instead, she held it vertically, pointing at the ceiling.

"This is our bond, don't forget it."

She stabbed it into the top of the table.

He left the room with a new tray. He was too young to understand what had caused the scene, and still didn't, but he understood too well what she meant. There was an odd bond between them, like fellowship corrupted. It almost made him physically sick. Yet he pitied her. He wished he could rescue her, but perhaps she had already become her own jailer.

"I am sorry Mikel, I can't stay with you. I have to go to the defense of Tanten."

Not the best 'good morning', but he expected that response. However, he was in no mood to just give up.

"Can't you send a messenger back with a copy of the map? I need you, Tei. We make a good team."

"We make a great team, but I can't stay. You can have some fellow Traders stay with you. They will keep you safe."

That momentarily diverted his attention.

"Do you regard me as a Trader?"

"It was a slip. I suppose so. Perhaps you are a Wizard and a Trader." She patted his right shoulder like a colleague.

He got back on track.

"But. When I said I *need* you, I meant..."

"I know."

"No. I have to say it. I love you Tei, and I need you with me. I'm worried about you."

"I know. Don't worry, the Valis clan is made of stern stuff. I can't stay with you. This is about duty. You have a duty to the Truth. I have a duty to Tanten."

He stopped and looked down, defeated. Waiting for the troubled sea of thoughts to calm, for the storm to pass by. Eventually, he looked up at her. She saw his shoulder suddenly relax. He saw tears in her eyes.

"Of course. When you get back, talk to the librarian. Ask about guerrilla tactics. Perhaps you can harry them through the Pass."

"No doubt. There are already fortifications for that, just unused for a long time."

She nodded, gave him a kiss on the lips, shed a tear, gave him another longer kiss, and she was off. There could be no more delay or she would risk giving in and staying with him. She took the copy of the map he had made earlier, mumbled some words, then she was gone.

He spent some more time with the map trying to see if there was anything more that was hidden. He thought he detected some other encodings, much older than the recent Bethor additions, but it would require a more careful analysis. One of the first things he learned about codes and ciphers is that secrets have an expiry date. You tailor the strength of the encryption to that. These fainter markings were for secrets long since expired, buried with their creators.

"But you never know." He whispered.

Mikel excused himself from those in the court and grabbed a late lunch from the kitchen. He slinked into the gardens with a wooden plate and started eating. He heard a crunching sound of the gravel. Looking up, a piece of chicken in hand, there was the Sanfran military commander, a man in his early forties, black hair graying at the temples. Mikel, embarrassingly, had forgotten his name.

"Master Mikel. We urgently need you at the front gate."

"Why? What is the problem?"

"We — I mean, *you* — have visitors." He looked flustered, not sure how to say it.

"Who? From where?"

"We have an army from the Center outside the city. Their leader wants permission to enter and seeks an audience with the Queen. They mentioned your name." The man was incredulous, as was Mikel. There was no such thing as a Center Army, only small uniformed militias.

He rushed to the gate, halfway there remembering his half-eaten chicken in the garden. Stupid thing to think of at a time like this. The main gate, on the eastern wall of the city, was a rickety contraption of old thick blocks of different timbers, latched by leather and iron, yet it was the only usable entrance. There was a man on horseback, in the middle of the opening, dressed in a typical Center militia uniform. Beside him was Major Rayan Valis and several other Traders in uniform just outside the walls.

"Mikel! Good to see you," Rayan called, a big smile on his face.

The Center captain addressed Mikel. "Wizard Mikel Peres? I am Captain Jack Soren, of the Center garrison of Iska and Tanfel. I believe you asked for our help." He was much more sober than the Traders who looked almost ecstatic.

The small Center force encamped outside the city and set up defenses while its captain met with Mikel.

The Traders, Captain Soren, and Mikel gathered in a small meeting room. Remarkably well preserved, with abundant light coming in the window facing the west. A little cramped, however. Captain Soren wasted no time.

"The messengers from Tanten reached Northern Brother, the tower outpost that marks the beginning of the pass through the Penta Mountains, and onto Tanfel in the south. The riders were cleared through the pass and met me at the garrison outside of Tanfel. We, the Center in Lind, have become concerned about the actions of Bethor and the Cities. There was a real risk of them disrupting the trade route from Tanfel to the

Eastern Caravanserai. My orders were not to provoke a war, but to defend the trade route. I must admit when I first received your letter, I suspected a diversionary plot. But I looked at it carefully and saw the telltale marks of a simple encoding. It took me only a few guesses at the key to work out what it said."

He was glad. He did not know if they would even notice the hidden message, but it had to be included, otherwise anyone could have sent it. The key was a piece of secret lore, or rather the first sentence of their oath. "I am surprised you came, even knowing that help was requested by a fellow Wizard."

"My orders are to protect the trade routes at all costs. I can't fight a war of course, there just are not enough of us, but I can offer tactical help. First, though, I have some news for you. On our way up the southern road, our scouts saw an army, about two thousand strong, marching on an intersecting path towards Sanfran. We believe they were from Pareth. It was clear they were a direct threat. We positioned ourselves a little before the path of this army and sent out an envoy to the army, asking for their intentions."

"No surprise attack?" Mikel asked.

"No. We wanted them focused on us."

Mikel thought better of his comment. "But you number only perhaps two hundred. I would say your best chance was to retreat."

Soren smiled. "Yes, I am sure they thought we should, too. Their scouts saw our numbers. We had the high ground, but that looked to be no advantage."

"They massed and started marching towards us in columns. Then we started firing our cannon volleys. With shrapnel, phosphorous bombs, explosive shells. A fine time to test our best performing munitions."

Mikel took some seconds to react and understand that what he heard was not some wild dream.

"Captain, just a moment. These are gunpowder based weapons?"

"Gunpowder and nitrocellulose, we had the designs from some old texts we knew about, but we still had to develop the right compounds and steels. Then manufacture shells and bullets. And the rifles, of course. A few experimental machine guns. With rifles and artillery, our 260 fight like ten thousand. The enemy broke and ran." He was beaming with pride.

Mikel wondered what had been going on in the background in Lind. While he was learning Respect for Life, the Center had developed an arms industry, which it would not share, he knew that already. He didn't want to know how many died, or how many died from injuries on the battlefield, too much suffering to add to the tally.

# eighteen

The valley was beautiful, so green and rich. Once more, the legends had turned out to be lies, myths to frighten any interlopers. She glanced in the far distance at the rising mass of Olympus — in reflex she looked away. It was an affront, a rejection of her assumptions. Vast and carved, it had to be an illusion. Her best experts had told her it was just the action of wind and the elements that made it look that way, and some kind of special rock made it able to rise so high. Still, she found it harder to reject the notion of Zeus. She would just have to — not look in that direction — there were too many more important things.

Far in the distance to her right, she could make out the gap in the mountains that they were aiming for. Barely visible was an old worn road snaking like the ghost of an old river from those mountains towards their location, sometimes coming close to the river of the valley.

"See, down there, where the road meets the river? Looks like remains of a crossing. Just to the west of our planned bivouac. Send scouts to reconnoitre the river for crossings and any 'complicating' factors."

"What if we come across any farmers?" The lead scout asked. Dressed in his highly non-official hat, beads and plaited black hair.

"Explore in teams of five. Kill anyone you meet. We can't risk word getting out that we are here."

The scout frowned and lowered his head. He looked uncomfortable.

"You have a problem with the orders? Do you know these people?"

"General, does that include women, children?"

He was probably hoping for an escape clause to prevent him from doing anything distasteful.

"All of them. In this environment it is a mercy. You have your orders."

The scout left, heading down the hill towards his teams. He would do as he was commanded. In the distance, she noticed a tiny curl of smoke rising from a crude farm house. Breakfast, the mother cooking some porridge for her children; the father talking about the work he had to do, admonishing some child for a mistake or selfish act. She felt her eyes watering. *Dammit. Can't let anyone see me like this,* she thought. Her mother and father were killed by assassins, but she was left to live. Sometimes she wished for that mercy, that the assassins had killed her.

That day still burned ragged in her heart. She had just returned from her flute and painting classes. The rest of her education was under the direct tutelage of her governess, Magri Talou. The hired carriage had dropped her and her governess off at her home, and were surprised to find the door ajar.

She called out, "Mamma! Dadda!", but there was no response.

The house was still and cold. Governess Talou was grabbed her by the hand, and placed her finger over her mouth. They should be quiet. They started walking back towards the door. Two men appeared cutting off their escape. Dressed entirely in black with face masks. She had never heard of the Death Squads, costumed assassins, said to be agents of the royal family protecting against not only traitors but financial competitors. Magri, as she sometimes called her, pushed her behind her voluminous dress. She couldn't see what happened. But knew there was great danger here.

"Magri Talou?" One man said in a cultured accent.

"Yes." Her voice was shaking. "Please, not the child. She's innocent."

There was a sound and a gasp. The wall of green dress shielding her collapsed, revealing her to the masked men in black. There on the floor before her lay Magri, eyes closed, squeezed tight in pain, slowly relaxing as a pool of red spread out beneath her.

Her heart was beating so hard she thought it would break. She looked up to see the killer. His black gloved hand held a sword pointing straight at her, still dripping blood. She saw Magri's blood gathering at the tip, close to her eyes, then dripping, drop by drop. She was too terrified to see where it dropped and knew then that her mother and father were dead and that she was about to die.

"So, little one, and what are we to do with you?"

She was too afraid to run, and was bound to the spot, which probably made her look defiant.

"She doesn't scare, does she?" The one with the sword said. "I like that. Well, my sweet, my contract was for the adults. No one mentioned you by name. This is your lucky day." They burst into laughter, then ran out the back, disappearing through the back alley, probably to a waiting closed carriage.

She kissed Magri on the forehead. Then walked to the dining room where she found her parents. She kissed them goodbye and went to fetch her uncle a few doors down the street, walking slowly in tears and covered in blood.

Her uncle and aunt would help raise her, but now she had a grim independence, a mission that only she knew. A dark, bloody mission. Hate burned and warped her, made her into what she was; she regretted none of her actions or decisions.

Many years later — in a dark, lonely alley — those same assassins would be on another mission, but this one was her own special trap. Her men subdued them. That was when she honed her torture techniques. That was when something broke, or was lost. From that moment there was no way back.

She raised her arm to call back the scout, but caught herself before she could yell. No, that wasn't the path. There had to be sacrifices. What was the point in pretending? She took her hand down and prepared to descend to the valley entrance. On the western side of the small river draining the valley, there she would take her army into the Xanadu Valley and continue the march to Tanten.

# nineteen

A new day and a new mission.

The first person he wanted to see today was Captain Soren. If Sanfran could defend itself, then perhaps Soren's band could come to Tanten's aid.

Soren was in the palace garden, talking to some of his lieutenants. He didn't know their names. One of them looked at him as he approached, the captain turning towards him, following the gaze.

"Master Mikel, good to see you." He said, clearly in good spirits.

"No need for the 'Master' captain. I am only an Apprentice Wizard out of his depth." Now why did he say that? Maybe the presence of one of his own people let him open up too much.

Soren spoke soberly. "Mikel, you have discovered new technology, united two nations, and you are now a core military adviser to both of them. A successful one at that. Believe me, you are a 'Master'."

"I have won a battle against barbarians who were expecting an easy victory. And now the professional, well-trained army of Bethor is marching on Tanten. No doubt led by officers who are masters of strategy."

"Those 'barbarians' were no fools, and you trounced them. I say, well done."

The Captain's confidence in him didn't help.

"I see. Captain Soren, I wanted to ask something of you."

"What is it?"

"Is it possible for your detachment to aid Tanten?"

The features on Soren's face visibly dropped.

"Our assault against the Pareth forces depleted our munitions considerably. We could not even hold out against forces from Lindin if they come. I'm afraid we must soon retrace our steps back to Tanfel and then to Iska to resupply. Mikel, we have no supply lines. This could only be a one-off."

"I see. Plan B it is then."

"What?"

"Captain. I have a plan for the defense of Sanfran, but I would need some of your men, perhaps as many as half, to stay for this action. I, well, I will go with a small group of experienced

Traders and make my way north towards Olympus following the trail of the Bethor army." He couldn't believe he was committing himself to this insane venture, but he knew this was his only hope.

"Slow down and explain yourself."

"I want to use the men of Sanfran and some of yours to set a trap for the Lindin forces. Meanwhile, I will leave with a few seasoned Traders and go north into the Xanadu Valley. I believe there may be weapons we can use at the Citadel. "

Soren looked at Mikel, while his left hand stroked his short beard. He stroked as if hoping an inspiration would escape from the tangle of hairs.

"Setting a trap could be viewed as supporting my orders, but I won't aid you in this flight of fancy into the north. All right, on the condition that you take charge of my men and *do not leave* until after the battle against the Lindin army. Don't leave them leaderless. This means you are my second in command. Do you understand? Good. I will take half of my force back to Tanfel. Re-supply, as much as I can from Iska, then I will come back. I'm not leaving my people behind leaderless or unsupported. It is risky splitting our forces, but that can't be helped."

"Won't your soldiers object to a non-soldier giving them orders?"

"They would, and that is why I am making a field promotion. You are now an acting captain."

He wanted to complain that he had no

experience of how to lead a detachment, or even how to salute. But it seemed he knew how to win, and that might be enough.

All of this meant that Mikel would have to stay longer than he hoped. But the Traders would not be a pushover, they could hold out. He hoped his belief was more than just folly on his part. Mikel and Jack then spoke for several hours, discussing the defense of Sanfran.


To the north-west of the City, the Euphray River emptied into the north-eastern corner of the lake. They had crossed over it and Mikel had almost forgotten about it except for his view to the south as he crossed. As the Euphray flows into the Lake, it has created a shallow, marshy area thick with reeds about ten kilometers south of the bridge. Since the local farmers lived and worked near Sanfran and did not use the bridge very much, then destroying it would not hinder food shipments to the City. It would disrupt trade, though the war did that anyway, from what he was told.

Without the bridge, the marsh was the only shallow area that could be forded. Mikel saw the situation as a possible ambush site. Sanfran officers informed him the only area that could be crossed easily was a relatively small stretch of the river. He talked with Captain Soren and the military leaders of Sanfran to see if they thought it would work. They agreed that destroying the bridge would be wise, but they weren't so certain about an ambush. They would send an escorted team to destroy the bridge, with some bowmen to harry any opposition forces that might try to do repairs.

After some discussion, they set up an ambush as Mikel suggested, but only one-third would go to the Euphray, the rest would continue building defences around the city. This was not as many as he hoped, but if the plan was sound, then one-third of the forces should be enough. He didn't know how many Sanfran fighters there were in the city. The city had a population of about five to ten thousand. It had once been much more but was now in decline, as were all the Cities of the Plains. That was not enough. Lindin and Pareth must think it would be a walkover for either force alone. The most fighters Sanfran could muster, male and female, would probably be about 3,000 and almost all of them would be ill-equipped, untrained peasants. Civilians with sharpened sticks. The enemy would likely have a force similar to the one from Pareth.

Sanfran would not survive a siege. It did not even have proper city walls, the local farms would be inaccessible and there was negligible food storage. He also suspected that water was taken from the lake directly, not by wells within the city walls. A defender's nightmare. The ambush was their best chance, change the enemy's mind before they even reached the city.

Mikel went with a group up to the mouth of the Euphray River, a marshy area with an expanse of reeds. The ground was flat, so there was no vantage point to get an idea of its size or width. Some poles were erected, with observers on three of them holding on, shielding their eyes, looking for telltale movements in the reeds and beyond. The reeds had been drying out now that the warm easterly winds of summer were in full sway. They made a constant rattling sound as the breeze moved over them. Deceptively peaceful and calming.

The dry grassland was too sparse here on the eastern side of the river to compare to the rich country to the west. The result was fewer farms, as he noticed when he saw the outline of the old city. They said that once the land had been as productive as the western Plains, but now the desert was expanding. It was hard to imagine.

They set up the ten small trebuchets and the troops "dug-in" as they say. There were also archers, using bows rather than crossbows, they could use either, but here bows would also be needed. He had to scour for archers. It was a dying art since the development of the crossbow. There was a lot of skill in using a bow, not much with a crossbow; just pull on the mechanism, lock, load, fire. He saw skilled archers firing at amazing speed, holding several arrows in one hand while firing. It was incredible to watch them training, but such skill was hard to find these days and harder to learn.

They had been waiting for two days now. It was about 8 am on a beautifully sunny but rapidly warming day. The wind from the east had come up on cue.

Mikel considered the situation. The team had already dismantled the bridge and lain sharpened stakes under the crossing either side. The marshes were the next best crossing point, but only one small part of it was practicable; this place was shallow, though the enemy would have to wade through a wide area of reeds. Because of the extent and cover, they would make a great place for a large force to cross undetected. He hoped that was what the enemy assumed. They were likely confident as they would not have heard yet about the defeat of Pareth, so would expect a band of Traders and a small force from Sanfran. Dismantling the bridge, they might even regard as a childish attempt to stop them rather than part of a bigger plan.

Lookouts on poles could now see movement in the reeds. The enemy foot soldiers were making their way through the marsh. They would likely spot the masts at any moment. Mikel waved the observers down and had the makeshift masts quickly lowered. But now he was blind. The contingent was hushed, waiting, lying low beneath dirt mounds. All commands by hand signals. He talked to the observers about what they saw, the spread of the enemy, their rate of progress. No cavalry, apparently. The enemy must be sending their foot soldiers to take this side so the cavalry could advance in safety.

They should have appeared at the edge where the reeds ended. But there was no sign, which suggested that they were likely marshaling just out of sight, readying for a mass attack. The enemy must know they were here, well, they were so close they could probably see through the reeds. It was time. Mikel passed the order along. The trebuchets were ready. The archers were ready. The crossbowmen were ready. Only the sound of birds calling and the rustling of the reeds in the wind could be heard. He silently gave the first order: he raised a red cloth, showing it left and right to the teams. Then dropped it. Bowmen ignited their fire arrows from braziers, raised them, and fired into the thickening part of the reed bed. The fire quickly caught, flaming up and spreading with the hot easterly wind, more reeds exploded as a tongue of fire leaped up several times the height of a man over a distance of hundreds of meters; the wind propelling it towards the enemy. He gave the next command; the trebuchets ignited their load of hay soaked with oil, but their targets were not near, they were aimed at a line about two-thirds the distance across the marsh. The trebuchets launched, the trail of smoke and flame disappearing over the flaming reeds; they couldn't see the results.

Mikel knew the enemy would soon discover they were trapped on either side. The water would slow the enemy too much to flank his people or to get out of the flames. Their only chance was to duck down if lucky, or just to risk it all on a headlong attack, ignoring the burns. Not everywhere burns at the same intensity, as Mikel well knew from playing and experimenting with fire. Fire is complex, almost capricious, slight breezes or differences in fuel can have huge effects.

A growing chorus of screams rose from the marshland.

He whispered to himself through gritted teeth, "Respect for Life."

Suddenly, from out of the reeds came a scream and a mass of warriors, all in brown smoldering armor, wearing the blackened remains of a blue sash and insignia, rushing, some still burning. They were met with volley after volley of crossbow bolts. Michael looked left and right and saw a mass of fallen men. Here and there it came to swords, but mostly the advance faltered. The attackers stopped, dropped their weapons and knelt, hands in the air.

Mikel cried, "Halt!"

It was over. Suddenly, he heard a whoosh, a sharp slice of pain on his left neck. The assailant was hit with a dozen bolts.

"I said halt."

He didn't want this to trigger a slaughter. Someone was at his side, tending to his wound. Applying pressure, he looked down and saw blood everywhere.

"No. Not now." He let them lay him flat and tend to him while he wondered if this had upset everything. He didn't even consider that it might be a mortal wound.

He woke up. Night had fallen. He got up — the left side of his neck sent a massive stab of blinding pain through him. He inadvertently screamed. A young Trader woman appeared, slim, brown hair in the candlelight. He had trouble focusing on her words. "Master, do you need anything? Your injury will take time to heal. You must stay in bed. I have put a poultice on it that will ease the inflammation and prevent infection."

"Where is everyone?" He moved only slightly and was rewarded by more sudden pain. It took him by surprise. The scream was out of his mouth before he could even think of being stoic.

"I also have a tonic that will kill the pain. But you must lie down first."

"I haven't got time for this. I need to be traveling north."

She gently pushed him back onto the bed, laying him down in such a way that there were no more lightning bolts of pain in his head.

"You won't be doing anything if you die. Besides, it is nighttime. You won't be going anywhere now."

He once hated irrefutable logic that was not his, but the world is full of irrefutable logic that challenges our wishes. He'd learned to live with it.

"Of course. See how things are in the morning."

Next morning he woke, rigid, afraid to move. After a few minutes of an unconvincing internal pep talk, he got the courage to get up, waiting for the inevitable stabs of pain. Eventually, he stood and congratulated himself, even as he panted from the effort. He saw some other injured soldiers getting about, which made him feel like a weakling. They weren't complaining, so he tried to push the pain away, ignore it. He did that as a child, but he no longer knew that trick. He must get going and against his medic's insistent and logical argument, he planned to return to Sanfran to pick up his team; instead, he found they had come to meet him. So, if he was going anywhere, it would be north. No smooth, well-worn roads in that direction, only unsteady ground full of random jerks up, down, sideways.

He was not feeling up to this. He ached; the horse ride was an ordeal. The injury was really almost a graze, but had obviously damaged some muscles. Before he left, he attended a briefing from the scouts who had been following the Lindin forces. Most of the attackers had panicked and there had been a rout. They were on their way back to Lindin to regroup. Mikel wondered how well the regrouping would go when they found out about Pareth. They might bide their time until the fall of Tanten was completed. The Bethor army plus Lindin would make the taking of Sanfran a non-event.

He was insistent about starting as soon as possible. He had that false sense of good health that comes when medicine starts to work, but the body is not yet healed.

Before he left, he put the Center forces under the command of Center Lieutenant, Ahmet Lusteek, an excellent officer. He also dashed off a letter and sealed it, to be delivered to Captain Soren, confirming his decision and commending the man. Now he could go.

# twenty

Even before she reached the city, Tei could see Tanten was mobilizing. The journey to the turn-point was eerily devoid of other caravans. In recent years, the traffic to and from the Eastern Caravanserai was so great that there were fears the path would be obvious to any attacker. Often, one would see another caravan in the distance while coming from Tanten, but not now. They had made the turn as usual, traveling at night. They should normally be able to see on the horizon a slight flicker of the beacon fires atop the Castle. The fires were nestled within the walls, so were only visible in a narrow arc. There should have been that familiar flicker, but there was nothing. The city of Tanten was trying to hide. It wouldn't work this time, however. The enemy knew exactly where Tanten was. They also knew an alternative way that didn't require them to cross the desert, and finally the last straw was that the enemy had the largest army the Traders had ever recorded and it was professionally trained.

She wished Mikel was here to bounce ideas off. And fears. She needed his silly exuberance and optimism to help her think straight. But she was a Trader Ambassador. She did what was necessary. She would do her duty. The odds against them were irrelevant. She thought she would have to say that to herself every morning at breakfast. She might even believe it. Grim determination would get her through, but some optimism might open her to new ideas.

As they entered Tanten, they passed a series of defensive earthworks placed around the Strongholds and along the Snake. Wooden spikes poking out of the ground, some large ones meant for wagons and siege engines, others small, fire-blackened and barely visible. From the smell, she could tell they were covered with excrement and worse. The healers of Tanten would have been turning their skills towards Death instead of Life in recent days producing ingenious poisons. She tried to think of the strategy that would place these defenses here. Was this the right position for them? It wasn't the time to draw conclusions. She would first talk to Master Levin and then perhaps examine the northern defenses. Those were her immediate concern.

She headed straight to the Keep. Paul, a young, brash boy new to the caravan, took her horse to the stables while she marched single minded towards the Keep door. Into her view came Maria, the Librarian, dressed in her outlandish ancient clothing.

"Mistress Tei? I wonder if I could have a word with you?"

Tei stopped, took a deep breath. "No need to call me 'Mistress', Maria. You know I don't like it. Well, what is it?"

Maria looked uncertain, like a field mouse caught in an open area waiting for a hawk to swoop. She clearly didn't get out much.

"Yes, Mis — I mean *Tei*." She said it like it was a foreign word that defied translation into her worldview.

"Tei. I have been scouring the Records looking for various devices we could use in the defense. Some of them are fairly obvious. But I came across a very interesting one. It is for a weapon that is a gas."

Tei was interested. She couldn't imagine what such a thing would be like. Maria continued.

"The gas and its production are detailed enough for us to reproduce. But it is so dangerous we would have to be careful. We might have enough time to make a useful amount. It is called *Sarin*, a type of gas called a Nerve Gas. We can manufacture it into glass vessels and project them over the walls."

Tei was curious now. "How does it work?"

Maria looked grim, conflicted, and anxious.

"It is a forbidden weapon. The Ancients said that even if a tiny droplet landed on your skin, you would die in agony. It paralyses the muscles in your body, including your lungs. They considered its use a crime."

"Do it."

"I beg your pardon, Mistress?"

"I said, see if you can manufacture it. Somewhere downwind of the Strongholds. Isolated. A limited batch."

She side-stepped Maria and continued. Why did she agree to it? Even the Ancients considered it a crime. But in her mind all she could see, and all she had been seeing behind her thoughts, half-glimpsed, fully denied, were visions of the Strongholds of Tanten in flames. To prevent that she would do anything. She took a deep breath, turned towards the dwindling back of Maria's t-shirt.

"Maria!" she yelled.

Maria turned, putting more weight on one leg, as if balancing or waiting.

"Maria. Cancel that. We'll find another way."

Maria looked relieved. "Yes, I will. Thank you, Tei."

Tei turned and continued on to the Keep, talking under her breath, barely aware of her own words. "Probably would have only ended up poisoning the workers."

For a moment, she wondered if the Wizards of Lind could make it. She thought it likely they could do it. Perhaps they already had. Perhaps they had already manufactured a good many things.

She didn't have time to say hello to family or pour a libation to the family spirits. They were all very short of time. In the Council Chambers of the Keep, only Master Edward and Mistress Moana were present. "Hello. I've just returned from Sanfran. It went well. We relieved the City but there are likely other forces moving against it." Moana was dressed in her usual green and white silk headdress and white robe, framing her aging face with a surprisingly youthful glow. But her ideas were still rooted in a Tanten that no longer existed. She was of a generation that believed isolation and secrecy were always the right path. It wouldn't work anymore, but too many in Tanten could not accept that change.

The Council Chambers had been changed since she last saw them. Where that hideous circle of light had been in the center, there was now a large table moved in by Levin, so a guard told her. Covering the circular table, which was so big she could have used it as a bed, was a map. She had never seen the map before, and suspected they had created it just for these current circumstances. The planning for the defense better involve more than the table and map. She looked closer at the map; accurate but not ornate, it was functional. Good. There were various shaped tokens on the map, some of them in the shape of earthworks, some as a soldier figurine or a horse, and crossbow. She understood what it meant. Someone actually seemed to know what they were doing.

"Who planned this?"

Levin answered from the other side of the room. "I did. What do you think? No one will give me an honest answer here."

"Looks good. So you are planning for the possibility of them getting through the pass?"

"A defense that is hard on the outside and nonexistent on the inside is pure folly. Even the Castle has a Keep. There is only so much we can do in the Pass. It restricts both sides, but our supply lines are short and theirs do not exist. We can wear them down. We understand the area, they don't."

She nodded. "What have you been doing on this side of the Pass?"

"The Tanuuten meanders this side of the Pass with the northern trail entering the Pass on the western side of the river. That means we can concentrate our supply and reinforcements on the western side just at the entrance to the Pass. We can then quickly relieve our forces and resupply at the same time. We can also set up fletching workshops and siege engine facilities there so that we can bombard the entrance if needed. The river is too wild to cross in the Pass." He seemed to talk to himself, so Tei left him there. She should check to see if reality matched the plan.

She took a fresh horse from the stable and rode it out, up the Snake and north, past houses and villas, then passing on the western side of Aqua, the small but fiercely defended central Stronghold. Passed between the granite walls of Shwu on the west and the river on the east. The river was now a sluggish stream, gaining strength as she went upstream, passing farms and orchards scattered between the strongholds. The road went northwest to bypass the meanders. To the left she could see the forests, managed for its timber. Some parts kept as wild as feasible.

Up ahead in the distance, the road led to a makeshift town of sorts. Made of tents, wagons, rough huts. The sound now reaching her. Shouting, hammering, the clash and scrape of metal on metal, the neighing of horses. Above them flew various Trader family banners. The mountains ever present now loomed above, not as high as they seemed but high enough.

Ayo Plessi, an old friend, seemed in charge. "Hey, Ayo! How are things going?"

Ayo was a charismatic woman. No longer as young, by the harsh standards that Arva imposed, yet still vibrant and hypnotic, with dark skin and gray eyes that made her think of Mikel.

She dismounted, walked to Ayo, and gave her a hug.

"Tei, old friend. I heard those idiots went and made you Head Councillor. What is the world coming to?" That infectious, perfect smile. "What do you think of my little kingdom? I'm thinking of seceding and mandating month long parties."

"Just checking that the old armchair generals are not hallucinating their strategy. What do you think? Is there anything more we could do?" She said.

Ayo shrugged, looked to the side. An old habit of hers which Tei knew meant, your guess is as good as mine. "Levin didn't come up with this plan all by himself. We all contributed. It is sound. We are organized, and we have been running drills. I pray to God they aren't smarter than we think. But the preparations have really only begun."

They walked silently amongst the activity towards the northern gate of the loose compound. Occasionally, men and women would raise their right arms at the elbow parallel to their bodies, palm open, facing her. The closest thing the Traders had to a salute, though usually used to show respect regardless of rank. Ayo certainly deserved the respect of her people; she had always been both liked and respected. It wasn't until they were almost at the gate that it dawned on Tei that the salutes were directed towards her and not Ayo.

Standing upon the rampart of the northern

gate of the compound, she took in a beautiful sight. Even though the mountains were not very tall, nevertheless some snow dusted their tops, and the slopes descended first as grey banded rock dropping to a greening, flattening arc in the narrow valley before them. The dull, indefinite roar of the river always present. Mist slowly rising hid the other end of this section of the valley. In the near distance, she could see the dangerous white water of the rapidly flowing river; abundant meltwater at this time of the year.

"We have positioned forward units of crossbows and fire-grenades above various choke points. We have engineered various boulders so that we can block narrow areas, and we have a large ground force. Not enough to match them on open ground, but very good in these kinds of conditions."

"And if they come via the desert?" Tei voiced her fear.

"There has always been a chance that they would discover the path to Tanten. That is why the Strongholds are built the way they are. But, yes, that would be a problem."

"You mean my problem." They both smiled.

She went on the tour, discussing deployment, strategy, and men. That night, she met with Ayo's people. Good, loyal Traders. This was what being a Trader was about; the joy of intelligent discussion, quiet respect, and tall stories from such strong and resourceful people. The next morning, she returned to the Keep.

It was on the fourth day of her preparations that the message came.

"Mistress Valis! There is a message from Sanfran." The rider was still panting, holding out his hand with the sealed letter. His leather clad arm and armor visibly dropping desert dust and sand; here and there mingling with sweat. He had ridden through the desert almost without stopping, in armor. Dangerous, he should have changed into loose desert gear.

"Just call me Tei." She opened the letter and noticed the messenger was still there, looking about. He was young, awed, standing in the Council Chambers. But he wasn't actually that much younger than she was. "What is your name?"

"Cam. My lady. Cameron Ollis, I am from Tanfel. Got recruited by Mikel Peres at the Caravanserai."

"How is he?" She really needed to know. Dammit, love messes everything up.

"I'm not sure. After he defeated the

Lindin army, he headed north to Xanadu."

"What?! Tell me the details."

"A relief force of Center soldiers arrived in Sanfran, with advanced weapons. They had just defeated the Pareth forces, so I heard. I don't know the details, but they couldn't help after that. Mikel set an ambush in the Euphray marshes and routed the Lindin forces. Then he set off north into Xanadu even though he had been hit in the neck by a crossbow bolt."

To her credit, she barely reacted outwardly to any of this news. Inwardly, she was on the verge of shaking. She spoke, measuring her words precisely.

"How was he when he left?"

"In a lot of pain, but he was lucky. Tarvis went with him and he said that Mikel shouldn't have any problems."

"Why did he go to the Xanadu Valley?"

"I'm sorry, my lady, none of us knew."

"That will be all, Cameron. Get cleaned up and rest. You can get some food and drink from the mess downstairs. Don't forget the essentials. Make sure you drink plenty of water first."

Levin had been listening. "Mikel continues to surprise us. But this new journey of his makes little sense. What is he up to? Whatever it is, it can't help us. If we get out of this alive, and if he does, then we will ask him ourselves. Impressive beating Lindin. How on Neti would he do that? And what kind of weapons does Lind have? And Center forces defeating Pareth? That is fortuitous and ominous. More questions to answer. Too much to do, too much to do. Not enough time." Tei let him chatter on. Levin had always seemed to be quite capable, even brilliant, if a little eccentric.

Tei rose early. She now slept in the Keep, not even bothering to walk the short distance from her home. There was little time before Bethor arrived and every hour seem to stretch out unbearably. The scouts had arrived this morning and left an urgent message for her before she woke. She rubbed her face with her left hand, trying to fully wake while she read the brief report in her right hand. Cam Ollis was still in the Keep, acquired by Levin as an assistant. He had received the message. "What does it say?" he said.

"Scouts at the northern end of the Pass report that the Bethor army is massing there. Probably preparing to enter. Estimated size of the army is about 10,000."

"We can't hope to match that." Cam said.

"No, we can't. But they must have depleted a lot of their provisions. They cannot sustain a long siege. There are no farms and little game on their side of the Pass. They need to conquer us quickly. We have intelligence that the army is being led by Liz Markham."

Ben's face slowly registered understanding. "You mean a relative of Roger Markham? The man who destroyed the Cities of the Plains?"

She nodded. "Not a close relative. She changed her name to Markham in her early teens, so they say. I met her once in Bethor. Smart and shrewd. It was a dinner at the Emperor's castle. She persistently tried to get information out of me about Tanten. Made me very uncomfortable. They say her husband's death was mysterious, and those that suspect her keep a low profile. The woman is a viper."

Tei couldn't suppress the wild suspicion that Bethor's war resulted from that ambition. It doesn't take many people to lead a majority into disaster.

Master Levin entered and motioned to Cam. Whispered something in his ear and then Cam darted out of the Chambers.

"I have sent him to join Ayo at the Pass.

Bethor is moving. They have entered the Pass. Fighting has started at the first of the choke point forts. We are getting signals relayed by Morse and semaphore."

"I should go too. I'm not much use here. Everything is prepared."

Levin motioned as if to stop her, reaching out his hand, but changed his mind. "Good luck, Tei. Don't stay there. We need careful planners here in case something happens."

The Pass was a frenzy. Instead of the random clamor of noise and activity when she last visited, there was orderly packing, cavalry units moving north, foot soldiers moving north, and wagons of war machines. The war machines included trebuchets, giant crossbows, wagons of ammunition of all kinds. She saw a wagon that was about to depart. It had a thick layer of straw containing glass bottles a little larger than a human head. She walked up to the driver, hands on the reins, waiting his turn to join the convoy.

He saw her and raised his right hand. "Mistress Tei."

"Easy there, soldier. What's in the bottles?"

"The Librarians and Master Levin have arranged the manufacture of glass bottles containing chlorine and a gas called phosgene. They are supposed to be poisonous. We have passed on instructions for safe use. They will be used on the elevated outposts. We have some small trebuchets on the sides of the mountains overlooking the approaches to the forts, real hero work getting *trebs* up there. They also have those new spyglasses. Have you seen them? Master Mikel showed the glass makers how they are made when he was here. Now all the commanders want one, but the scouts had the first ones."

"How did he find the time to show anyone how they are made? Ah. Of course, he lived in the Artisan quarters, probably just wandering about being friendly and sparking a revolution. Typical." She smiled to herself.

She let the wagon go. Its turn in the convoy had come.

She had thought she had spared a horror by preventing the manufacture of the nerve gas. Even so, poison gas was on its way north somehow. You think you prevent one problem and it is done; but it is never done. There was an old saying about "eternal vigilance," but she couldn't remember it properly. Preventing evil requires eternal vigilance. That is what it should have said. But in amongst all the evil that was about to happen, would it even matter? No way to tell.

She rode north. The mountains towering above her white topped. The icy breeze in her face, air rushing down the mountain sides. Mist rising in the narrow valley, the roar of the Tanuuten now dominating everything. The horse beneath her was a favorite, good natured, a companion to explore such places with. In the distance, pinpoint flashes of light too regular to be coincidence. Messages in the Morse telling about deployments. Now and then similar flickers of light from the sides of the mountains brief staccato statements: enemy 5k; enemy scouts 2k. Both sides of the valley. Clever, the trebuchets should be able to reach across the river, but the enemy couldn't pursue them. The river was absolutely treacherous at this time of the year. But Tanten's forces there would not be easily resupplied, either.

Although there were many choke points along the road, all defended, there were only three that allowed the building of defensive forts. The three forts were originally numbered, but somewhere in the past had picked up odd names whose meaning was long lost. A forward observation post was also named, but that post had long ago become ruins. Baby Bear: the observation post, had a high vantage point but difficult to defend despite that. Mamma Bear: the northernmost fort. Here the attacker is less disadvantaged than the other forts. Pappa Bear: a nasty choke point of crossfire opportunity for the defenders making an effective killing zone. Goldilocks: the dual fort at the southern end of the pass. Large, extremely well defended, crossfire from the opposite bank, trivially resupplied; ideal for the defender, worst case for the attacker.

She walked about Goldilocks Fort for an hour. Talking casually to soldiers and officers. Letting them know they could come to her at anytime with their concerns. Before she left, she read the Morse; Mamma Bear was under full attack and being resupplied. Wagons and troops moved north to Pappa Bear and Mamma Bear. The breeze in the Pass had moved from northerly to a southerly direction, as it did during the day.

The trebuchets would arm with the glass balls soon.

She returned to the Keep just before dusk. Hungry and tired, she sat down in the messroom to catch her breath and try to relax while eating. Master Levin was there, sitting at another table in the room. She almost hadn't seen him in this dim lamplight. She sat down opposite him and, without even a "hello" rattled off a report of what she had seen.

So much for manners. Levin seemed diminished somehow, exhausted.

"Levin, when did you last sleep?"

"Don't remember. So much to do."

"Go grab a few hours at least. We all need to build up our reserves for what's coming." She almost choked on that last bit. No one really knew what was coming. The odds were on their side. She hadn't thought about the larger strategy: what would they do after this, would they take the Cities, were the Cities too strong, could they handle a war of attrition with Bethor, would they win this battle but lose the war? All the answers that came to her mind were so bleak. Maybe she was tired. Levin had left to grab some sleep. She should probably follow her own advice.

A guard woke her. She was holding a fiery torch that was dazzling.

Tei was dazed and confused. No dreams. It seemed like moments ago she had just got into bed. Out of the small high window in this room, the night had a tinge of blue; dawn wasn't here yet, but it would not be far away.

The guard stood there, fear in her eyes, panting.

"Yes. What is it?"

"Councillor. We have received an urgent request via Morse. Relayed from the borders of the western forest. They are under attack."

"What!" She jumped out of the bed, instantly awake. A moment of panic gripped her.

"It appears the enemy has sent another force via the southern flanks of the Uutens."

"No shit?" The guard stood still, frozen, the torch shaking slightly.

"Yes. Good deduction. What is your name? Rank?"

"Karin Planka, Messenger."

"Well Karin, go tell Master Levin about this. Meanwhile, I will raise the alarm." She strode out of the room, still pulling on her clothes. A man was walking down the hall away from her, captain decals on his shoulder. She didn't know his name. "Captain."

"Yes, Councillor."

"By my order, raise the alarm for this Keep. I will signal the Strongholds that we are under attack from the western forest."

"Yes, the western forest…" For just a moment, he looked stunned. He knew what that meant. "Yes. Immediately, Councillor."

She dashed upstairs, pushing through the door onto the roof. There were some guards standing about, looking to the northwest.

"Soldier!" They all turned.

"You and you! Light the signal fires and send Morse to the Strongholds. We are under attack from the western forest. Do it now!"

She waited until the fires were lit, and the messages sent. Then ordered two of the soldiers to commandeer horses and ride to the Strongholds to confirm that the alarm was raised in each of them.

"Do not return until you have confirmed the alarm has been raised in all of them. If anyone is stupid enough not to raise the alarm, then one of you come back to me and I will deal with it personally."

She dashed downstairs, still partly undressed,

she noticed, counting off the seconds. In the Council Chambers, all the Councillors currently in the Castle were present. Outside, she could hear the alarm bell ringing, and trumpets. A gathering din of activity underneath it all. Levin was addressing those present.

"Further, the latest reports say Goldilocks Fort is besieged and the supply column destroyed. The fort has most of its defense works designed for an assault from the north, not from behind. They are holding on, but report that their supplies of bolts and trebuchet munitions are low. They also report that Pappa Bear is under assault and supplies will not last much longer."

"What about Mamma Bear?" She knew what the report implied, but reflexively asked the question.

"Fallen. No known survivors."

Even from the top of the Keep, the sun still had not risen. To the north and slightly to the west, there were distant flickering fires. Battle. Here and there were faint traces of light from messaging. She automatically translated the desperate, fragile twinkling.

"Supplies low. Many dead. Half strength. Capt Plessi dead." She felt a stab through her heart. One of the great people of her life gone, just like that, with a feeble winking light.

There was no time for grief and it hadn't fully

hit yet. She needed to think rationally. Perhaps going over what happened would snap her out of it. The enemy must have used the cover of the forest to mask their approach. No one had any accurate idea of their numbers. It wouldn't be as large as the army that was coming down the Pass. It would be a smaller, rapidly moving force of seasoned troops, most likely. Using surprise to make up for their lack of numbers. Well, they certainly got the "surprise" part right.

Then it occurred to her that was why the waypoints on the map had dates. Why put dates? So you can coordinate with someone, especially at the moment of attack. She cursed herself under her breath for not seeing it sooner. Self recrimination solved nothing. She put it aside.

Down in the courtyard she could hear the mustered men and women, hastily called into service, being put together for a relief force. The way there would be treacherous if they had lost the forest. She tried to think of strategies, but there were no obvious ones. Not enough cover, too little knowledge of the enemy deployment. All she could do was wave at them as they made their way out of the gate. Above the gate, the beacon fires were being kept alight, though now blankets were being raised by hands in front of them: up, down, up, down. A warning to anyone approaching from the desert. The simplest of signals, it meant simply, "UNDER ATTACK". Anyone seeing it would immediately turn back to the Caravanserai and report. Word would quickly spread, but there really was not much that could be done to aid Tanten. All the while, the bell sounded, muffled at her vantage point.

The sun was coming up. It was going to be a hell of a day.


There was no more word from the Forts, it was presumed they had fallen. The Strongholds were now coming under attack, and if the Forts were gone, then the attack would be by the combined enemy forces.

The four larger trebuchets now on the roof of the Keep were launching continuously. Smaller ones were at reinforced positions along the walls. The counterweight trebuchets were heavy, but that was what they were using. The Records had designs for much more advanced ones, but they did not have the time, and likely skill, to build them. Small, odd-looking hand held ones were being used on the walls. The artillery was being used to throw anything at the enemy. Poisonous gas, fire bombs, rocks. The enemy had first attacked Shwu Stronghold being the first one in their path, but had come under immediate attack from the long range artillery from Shwu and Castle when they went for Shwu's gate; they were caught in a crossfire. They had retreated, now knowing that they could venture nowhere close to the main gate of Shwu since it was facing Castle. There had been a break of an hour and then the enemy had moved, this time aiming to take the Castle, avoiding crossfire as much as possible from the other Strongholds. They would have to attack via the Snake.

But that didn't work out well at all. They retreated and a short time later attacked again. This time pushing straight at the fortifications of the Snake at the southern end of the western wall; they seemed to intend to overwhelm the Snake ramparts and head straight for the gate. There were armored troops and ladders, other equipment. Tei had left the Keep to see for herself from the Western Wall. The area below had become a slaughter ground, but still they persisted. Fire, bolts, and rocks rained down on them. And bolts flew up. Looking down to see what was happening was not for the fainthearted. It appeared Bethor had no intention of settling in for a siege. Tei found that curious; unless they feared an attack from another quarter and wanted this over and done with as quickly as possible. No time to speculate.

From the ramparts, it was hard to see the battlefield. They had dropped some fire bombs; sticky masses of burning oily material with a small, fragile pottery container of oil and water that would spread fire on impact. It made a lot of smoke, while the easterly wind was causing an updraft on the leeward side of the Castle carrying the smoke and sound to the defenders. Now and then the smoke would part and there would be a writhing mass, like rotten meat teeming with maggots. Firebombs exploding, bolts whizzing, men and women screaming; a lot of screaming. Some of their troops had scouted the eastern wall of the Castle, keeping out of range of bolts, but the eastern side was sheer, floored with a chaos of jagged rocks. The attack would remain with the western and perhaps the southern wall, though that was even better defended.

The stronghold of Shwu was also reporting that the enemy had brought up siege engines; trebuchets of their own, or even captured ones, and was now preparing to attack Shwu. Trebuchets on the northern wall of the Castle simply didn't have the range. The ones on the top of the Keep paradoxically could barely reach Shwu's attackers, who were visible by the many fires there that were once homes. When Tei got to the northern wall, she could see puffs of greenish-yellow gas exploding about the base of Shwu. The gas was chlorine. At that range, all projectiles were inaccurate, but gas doesn't care, and if any drifted upwards well, the defenders of Shwu had bigger problems. She could see firebombs exploding amongst the attackers. Also, some exploding against the walls of the stronghold. Captured munitions certainly. How long before they got good enough at it so that the firebombs landed inside the stronghold? They couldn't last, either Shwu or Castle. The other strongholds were sharing resources and soldiers via the tunnels, but she knew it wasn't enough.

She had to keep moving; trying to see exactly what was happening. Giving commands. She saw Levin on top of the Keep with some other councillors, dressed in full regalia. Finally, the robes had some use identifying their owners when they signaled commands to various captains. Everywhere about her as she ran along the rampart there were the thuds of trebuchet impacts, then flashes of flame and smoke. There were dead or injured Traders lying where they had fallen from the rising hail of bolts from the enemy. When she got to the southern gate, she saw movement out in the desert. Relief forces? No. Her heart sank when she saw the Bethor forces had large long range trebuchets, of a design she had not seen before. They were being positioned out of bolt range, ready to aim for the gates themselves. She grabbed the nearest soldier. There was fear in his eyes.

"Trader! Why haven't the trebuchets been taken out?"

"We can't reach them, Councillor."

"Get our trebuchets to target them. Just do it."

"We can't. They are in a blind spot of the Keep trebuchets. Same for the ones on the towers."

He was right. The trebuchets had limited mobility and could not be moved. No one had thought they would setup in the desert.

"Well…"

There was an enormous bang that she felt more than heard. Tei found herself, mouth open, face in rubble. Dazed. She sat up, spat out fragments of rock and blood. The soldier she had been talking to was sprawled before her, staring lifelessly. "Sleep well," she whispered, guilty that she didn't even know his name.

She got to her feet. They had been hit by a projectile from the new trebuchets in the desert. More would follow.

There was another bang. But the rattle it made could only come from the gate. It couldn't take much of that.

The Captain of this wall scrambled over to her, keeping low. "Councilor, are you all right? You're injured." Pointing to her forehead.

She nodded. Went to wipe away the dirt about her eyes. The hand came back covered in blood.

"Councilor. We are lifting up some of the new ballistas. They have the range but they are small; they won't destroy the siege engines."

"But we might damage them enough." She completed the chain of logic; hoping that was the plan.

They quickly set one up, pointing through the new hole in the wall. The device was about her size, firing an enormous arrow. They wound up the sinew springs, then a tech attached a package with a wick just behind the arrowhead. There was another crash as a projectile hit the door. They quickly aimed the ballista at one of the trebuchets, lit the wick, and fired. There was a great whoosh, and almost no recoil; it was anchored well. There was a trail of smoke through the air leading to the trebuchet, a puff of smoke, flame, then small figures running.

"Quick! Reload for the other one." The other trebuchet was now turning ready to aim at them, but trebuchets are large and slow. They hit it with another puff of smoke and fire.

"The fire isn't big enough to destroy the trebuchets. The operators will quickly put it out. We will have to keep harrying them." By this time another ballista had been brought up, setup and cocked.

"How many of these flame arrows do you have?"

"Maybe twenty. Not many, but enough, I think," he replied.

"Looks like they are moving their trebs. I'll see if we can get more of these fire arrows made." She had a look through the spyglass. That confirmed it; the operators would risk getting hit to get the trebuchets out of range and out of the immediate target area.

"Yes, Councilor. I think they are trying to get it out of range. We beat them." He turned to his men as they raised a cheer. Small victories.

"They will try to sneak back after dark," she said. "Make sure the beacons are not lit. That will give them a clue to the distance and where the gate is, and see if your men can identify where they are. The moon will be up four hours after sunset. That gap is their opportunity to get into range without us seeing them. Stay dark and alert. When the moon comes up and you can see them, attack if they are in range."

An idea occurred to her; it was worth a try. "After dark, light two lamps and lower them on a rope to, about five meters lower than the actual beacons but separated by the same amount. Place these about twenty meters to the east. With any luck, it may make them target the wrong location for the gate, and being that low, most of the missiles just might only hit the ground in front of the wall. They could even run out of ammunition."

The enemy would see the ruse if they used fire projectiles, but that would also reveal their location to the ballistas.

Night. The enemy had retreated at sundown. They had both suffered heavy losses, but Bethor's army was far larger than Tanten's. No doubt they had by now discovered and plundered the farms to the east. She sighed, knowing nothing could be done about it. For a moment, looking out into the darkness and the mass of lights, enemy campfires, she felt a shudder. The enormity of it threatened to overwhelm her. She wanted to run to her mother and father. More than that, she wanted Mikel. He couldn't help but she just needed him. If they were going to die, they could at least be together. This must have been how the defenders of the Cities had felt just before the end. She had read the stories of the Fall. They had a profound sadness and sense of loss to them, but she had never really understood the terror.

Many of the men and women on the walls took breaks where they were. They were exhausted. She did not know the losses, but it looked like there were hundreds dead and many more injured. Dead and injured were being cleared by torchlight. It was like a scene from the myths of Hades. Many of the injured refused to leave their posts and would likely die there. The supplies of Healing Beer were exhausted, many would likely now succumb to infections despite the efforts of the healers.

Looking out at the mass of twinkling campfires, she noticed some new campfires. A line of them. It must be a fresh attack. She yelled, "Everyone! Expect an attack at any moment." In the quiet, her own voice seemed unreal, disconnected. The defenders stood and looked at her, still trying to snap out of their exhaustion. She looked back out into the dark and saw the line of campfires, a magical string of fiery jewels, drifting in the black air. Coming towards them. Not campfires, but fire bombs. They smashed against the wall, some hitting the ramparts, spilling fire and smoke. Through the plumes of smoke to the north, she saw flames smashing gracefully along the upper walls of Shwu like bright orange waves, a glowing, burning ocean in a storm. There was a flash of fire and smoke from the southern wall. She rushed over, jumping over debris, weapons, injured and the dead. The southern rampart had additional troops, ballistas, and some extra ammunition.

"Captain! What is happening?" This wasn't the same man she spoke to in the afternoon, and there was no insignia, but he seemed in charge. She wondered what happened to the other man. But there was no time for that.

"Councillor, the lamps we lowered earlier worked for some time. They threw a lot of rocks that landed in the dirt. A few hit the lower wall but didn't do any actual damage. Now they have switched to firebombs. That lit up the wall pretty well. I'm sure they will see the ruse now." Yes, soon they would be making a major assault on the gate under cover of darkness and all the smoke. She would have to assign crossbowmen to the Teeth of the Snake and troops on the ramparts above to throw rocks, firebombs.

"Can you use the firebombs to see where they are launched from?"

"They've lit a lot of decoy fires. We're

targeting the most likely positions, but we don't have many fire arrows left."

There was a loud bang, rock on wood. She felt the shudders from the door beneath her. Crash! This time, she heard splintering wood. She could see teams rushing to add more beams to brace the gates. She looked north. Shwu was on fire.

"Oh god no."

If this was their last stand, then they would take as many of them with them as possible. She felt the anger rising. It was so unfair that a brutal, warmongering people should crush a fair and reasonable society, but that is just the way the world is. They wouldn't spare the innocent, she knew that.

"Bugger that! We won't go easily, you bastards!"

Inside, she started praying desperately to whatever deities were listening, for her family, her people, her home, and lastly for herself. Was Mikel lying lifeless somewhere, never to be seen again, forgotten after her death? Well, she wasn't dead yet, and she could always hope for Mikel.

Below her, a growing roar started. It was coming from outside of the walls, behind her. The attack on the gate was starting. There were two loud bangs in quick succession. She heard the gate breaking. Tanten troops were pouring towards the gate with long pikes. Crossbowmen about her and inside the towers were firing into the mass below.

It was all moving so quickly. Too fast to control. She picked up a crossbow to help, walked up to a niche in the battlement, and started firing.

She looked behind her to see if there was anything else she should know about. Shwu was engulfed in fire. Tears were running down her cheek and her heart was pounding. Beyond Shwu, there were fires leading up to the Pass. There was something else there, a bright red light.

# twenty-one

He had picked three Traders, prior to leaving for the Euphray, and trusted them all. He had travelled the Plains with these people, and these had the right mix of skills.

Tarvis had grown to trust Mikel and now there was almost a family like bond between them. He suspected Tarvis would follow him anywhere. When he told the Traders of his plans, Tarvis volunteered immediately.

Kay was about thirty, and had refused to answer when Mikel had asked how old she was, so now he just guessed. She was very private, an excellent marksman with her custom-made and loved crossbow. She was apparently talkative to those she trusted, but still didn't trust Mikel enough yet, but she was no longer antagonistic towards him. He had heard she was divorced, and had two children in Tanten. He had pretended to ignore that information. When she was not looking, Mikel stole a glance at her. Her black hair pulled back in a ponytail was quite fetching combined with those eyes; such a deep brown as to be black. Anyway, he wasn't interested, and he chose her for her skill, nothing else.

John was in his mid thirties, a black haired, light skinned, brazen entrepreneur whose goal was to build up his own caravan. This war had not been kind to his ambitions. He had heard his collection of camels had been confiscated by the Lindin forces somewhere between Lindin and Sanfran. An avid note taker, he was often seen jotting observations in a small notebook, and seemed interested in almost everything. Sometimes Mikel thought he was looking at an alternate version of himself. The man preferred the crossbow but was adept with bow and sword, and he claimed to have mastered the art of fast firing with a bow. Like Tarvis, he was an excellent tracker, but Tarvis was definitely the better hunter. He seemed to have an instinctive understanding of the prey.

Tarvis looked at Mikel's neck, gently lifting the poultice. "Hmm. Good care. It should heal well, you'll be fine soon. Must hurt though. Did they give you any Healing Beer?"

"Beer? No."

"An old recipe revived by the Cities after the Battle. Based on some old technology. Yeast that manufactures tetracycline antibiotics. Made by the Egyptians."

He knew what antibiotics were, but they were difficult to make. "Who were the Egyptians?"

Tarvis shrugged. "Don't know. Probably an old Earth pharma company. Anyway, you should be good."

No trace of sarcasm from Tarvis. He was an experienced, hardened Trader. This was probably typical of what he had seen or had done to him. He didn't know what a pharma company was and right now he didn't care.

The four of them left the encampment and proceeded north, within sight of the eastern bank of the Euphray. Tarvis led. He had been this way some years back. Existing maps were vague on this region, so a guide was a true bonus. The captured map was also scant about anything not on the Bethor army's planned path.

All Mikel could think about was the pain and the uncertainty about where they were going, then whether it even made any sense. For the pain, he used small amounts of an opium tincture, which made the trip bearable, slowly extending the period without it. He had nothing for the doubt except stubbornness.

The countryside was getting hilly on either side of the river. The way ahead was flat but climbing slowly. There were even trees, which reminded Mikel of the rainforests in parts of Lind.

They still kept to the right of the Euphray, which the map showed would peel away to the left as they went further north. The path went northwest through small mountain passes and thick forests, overgrown in places but not too much, showing that from time to time it was still used. And always the sound of a babbling stream went with them.

They finally left the river and headed up a row of hills so they could get a better view. They had to cover the last hundred meters on foot. At the top of the green treeless hill they found themselves within sight of the main road with the Valley stretching out, blue misted, beyond it. Tarvis turned to them.

"The Xanadu Valley is like a smaller version of the Great Plains."

From what they could see, there were a few small lakes, but with forests everywhere, in the near distance, a couple of farms. He could easily trace the Euphray River winding through the forest, occasionally hidden, meandering up to the far blue lake. Far to the north, above and beyond the valley, beyond the mountains, there was a white-blued impression of a great mass rising like a ghost above the edge of the world. At first he thought it was a vast northern storm. But it wasn't a storm.

There were straight lines, structure. It was carved. It was a building, like a very tall pyramid, about three times higher than it was wide. What he was seeing was not natural, but too big to be artificial. He tried to imagine the size and couldn't. There were clouds forming and swirling about its lower ramparts. It was not just high; it was also wide and stretched across the width of his two hands splayed at arm's length. He felt like he was offering a prayer to a pagan god, or an actual god. A chill ran down his spine. Around him, he suddenly noticed how small they were to everything they could see. He reached down and picked up a sprig of grass. He hoped it looked casual, but he needed to connect with the real world. A small ant ran up and down the grass stem. He dropped the grass. Tarvis looked at Mikel.

"Don't worry, son, we've all been there. It is a terrible thing to see everything you know made insignificant. Ahem. I haven't been this far before. I'm surprised to see Xanadu so green, the stories only told of devastation. We just avoid it."

In the distance, on the other side of the largest lake, Mikel saw a clear patch. In his spyglass, he saw the silhouette of buildings. Checking his map, he found that the old path north went very close to a city on the northern side of the lake, but nowhere near the path taken by Bethor.

Kay turned to Mikel. "The Xanadu Valley was desolate and poisoned after the Great Battle, few who ventured here returned. Those who came to these overlooks reported a wasteland. It became forbidden, taboo, forgotten. Over time, it has been improving — but this is dramatic. Still, Bethor must be very determined. Everyone avoids it."

The other Traders were also surprised that it was now so verdant and suspected that taboos must still be keeping the superstitious people of the Plains away from the area.

Tarvis said, "Greed and ambition can beat superstition and belief."

"What about the farms?" Mikel said.

Tarvis shrugged. "They have probably been edging closer to the valley for ages. But I don't think they would go further north."

"Tarvis, look there," Kay said, pointing.

There was a cloud of dust to the north-east blowing from a side valley. The Bethor army was now moving out of sight behind some small mountains, heading east. Within days, they would be at Tanten.

They proceeded into the Valley of Xan, its ancient name of Xanadu rarely used now. John suggested a quick visit to the farms. Maybe someone there had some advice about the Valley. Pretend to be after trade goods, get suggestions and advice, and perhaps find out a little about the passing army.

The first farm they came to was on the same southern rolling, grassy slope heading down into the valley. There was long green grass, some tended fields, a cabin.

"I don't see any activity." John said.

"I don't like it. Someone should be working,

or coming to meet us," Kay added.

As they approached, they could now see that the fields were trodden down, stripped. There were no animals, yet there were pens for them. The door to the cabin was ajar, peering into a black space. Mikel then saw off to their right in the long grass some light colors, shapes, clothes. He knew what it meant. Like mounds of bleeding seaweed on a beach. He rode over. This time he would see. This was someone else's tragedy, but he owed these people a witnessing.

He got off the horse and approached the bodies. The father had been killed with a single blow to the head. His wife and teenage daughter weren't so lucky. Rigor mortis had set in. He had no experience with this, so didn't know how long ago it happened. Tarvis estimated they had been dead at least a day. Mikel emphatically insisted that they be given a decent burial, though no one disagreed. They spent some time in silence looking over the graves. A few prayers were whispered.

Then someone called to them. "Please. Help me."

It was a boy about eleven or twelve. Black hair, brown eyes, dirty face. His name was Eirik. He told them how he was away looking for some wayward sheep, heard riders, came back and hid in the grass, and how he saw everything.

They reassured him, even as though their words felt like lies. It was what he needed, and maybe they needed to pretend they were true as well. The natural question, never asked, was, *what do we do with him?* They reverse and go back, and they couldn't just leave him here, so the answer was *obvious. Take him with them.* The boy was still disconnected from events, and needed to make peace with that. Mikel took him to the simple graves for his family. Without warning, the boy broke down and started sobbing. Mikel put his arm around him and whispered to him.

"Bad people did this, Eirik, but there are still a lot of good people in the world. You can tell the good ones by how they treat you, and you can learn to trust them. It's good to be angry. Just don't let it turn you into one of those bad people."

Eirik didn't respond, just looked at him, the tears making vertical marks through the dirt on his face. He'd wipe away a tear, smearing the dirt, ready for the next flow of tears. Mikel didn't know whether what he said would make a difference, but he needed to say it for his own sake, this what he would have said to himself if he could have.

Tarvis took the boy on his horse. He was delighted to have a protégé; Eirik clung to Tarvis, relaxing slowly while listening to his endless tales. There was another farm further on, far off their course. They couldn't do everything and save everyone. Mikel continued past it.

They found the main trail, very clear now because of the passing army. Those who had killed

Eirik's family must have been scouts scavenging the countryside for food. There might still be some about trying to catch up with the main body. Warily, they advanced up the trail. Their greatest fear was overtaking stragglers. They were looking for a side path, clear on the map, but overgrown now.

It was not until the next day that Tarvis bird-whistled and drew their attention to a region of brush with fewer trees; the road they had been looking for. The underlying roadwork had restricted the plant growth enough to be visible, though it could still be difficult to travel.

The road turned out to be a magnificent path through the countryside, unlike anything that any of them had experienced. They made their way through a majestic forest towering on either side. Everywhere there was the rustle of wildlife, Mikel even saw a deer, while birds flew overhead, some quite large but either unfamiliar or hastily seen. In places, the tall trees arched high over the grassy trail and beams of light played through the rustling leaves, while the breeze passing over the forest gave a sound a little like water flowing. The experience was invigorating. It was unlike anything Mikel had thought could exist. The small rainforests of Lind, Gowss, and Laplas had their own beauty, but this area was larger and supported more diversity.

Tarvis smiled. "A lot of good hunting here,

friends."

Mikel nodded. "When this is over, when we are safe, I want to come back here. This is beautiful. It's good to hear something besides the sound of horses' hooves." He looked around and saw smiles.

That night, they camped in the middle of the road. Kay and Mikel ventured into the nearby forest before the sun had set. It was wilder than anything he had seen. So much life, animals, plants. Squirrels ran up and down oaks and although it was dark, he could see orchids and other plants he would have expected in rainforests. Too much to record. He noted a few of the obvious animals; deer, squirrels, wallabies and did a few quick drawings. The ecosystem seemed healthy. He wondered about that until it occurred to him that perhaps there was a top predator about. Kay seemed interested in some tracks, like a big dog.

"Wolves?" he asked.

"I don't know. They only exist in stories, don't they?"

But they didn't have the time to explore. They were walking back on a slightly different path when Mikel tripped over something. On the ground, he saw a red and white shape about 40 centimeters long protruding. He got a stick and scraped away at it until it all came loose. He held in his hand an object about 40 centimeters by 30. It hadn't been torn; it seemed to be a panel off something, very light. Night was falling, so they hurried back to the campsite.

"What is it?" said John.

In the flickering light, Mikel turned it over, carefully brushing dirt off it while he tried to read the fine writing etched into the material.

"I don't know. It mentions, 'AirCar Specs Model 5V', and some numbers. Hmm. Cruising altitude. Maximum velocity. Maximum load. Fuel capacity. Wow! Remember those legends about the flying carriages? I think this is part of one. The maximum altitude is 5,000 meters. Maximum speed, 443 km/h."

Even by firelight it was beautiful, the colors still bright, and the surface pitted on one corner with burn marks. Yet it still had a gloss that said speed. He knew he couldn't keep it. It was too large. And he couldn't leave it here in the middle of the road, a clue to their passing. He stood up, drew his arm back, holding it and hurled into the dark. Hearing a crash in the bushes, some fluttering of wings. He didn't talk for the rest of the night. There was something very sad about the whole incident, but he couldn't say why.

Next day they continued and at dusk the trail came close to the lake. There was a clearing and ruins of some small stone buildings. Now they were only home to a few small, scurrying animals. They set up camp near the shore. Tarvis and John made themselves busy looking after the horses. Kay fetched a line out of her bag, got out a live grasshopper she had caught moments before and put it on a hook, showing Eirik the art of fishing. She cast it out. Mikel and Eirik looking on. How long had it been since he had done things like that? He remembered his plans that morning that Master Samuel had visited. They were going to go fishing off the old pier. Carefree bliss. Could that have been so recent? How long had it been? It seemed like years, but it had only been less than two months.

Kay's bait had barely hit the water when she had a bite; after a ridiculously brief struggle, she eventually landed a large unfamiliar fish. "Brown trout everyone! About four kilos." A rich area indeed.

The fish was magnificent. Everyone praised Kay for having the sense to have a fishing kit in her pack. John cooked it, scavenging some interesting herbs from around the campsite. General skepticism soon collapsed when the smell got to them, and since they all survived the experience, John's cooking skills were re-evaluated.

Mikel walked down to the lake's edge to wash his hands. A crunch of boots in sand next to him. Kay, also down on her haunches, washing.

"Um. Mikel. Look, sorry, things didn't start off so well between us."

"That's all right. I guessed you must have a pretty good reason."

"Look." She looked out across the fading light on the lake, but that was not what she meant.

"Years ago, I was part of a caravan that went to Bethor. I sneaked out and to see the sights. I'll make it a short story. I got grabbed, stunned by something hitting me, didn't even see who it was, pulled into an alley. There were five of them, I think, they raped me. All I could hear were their voices, even the voices of those who eventually found me. That dialect and accent. I still need to go on the caravans for my family, have to pay for the education of my two children, and that means I often end up in Bethor but I try to keep my distance. I feel anger and disgust when I hear that accent. Funny thing is, I don't know if I am more disgusted with myself or them. I know, victim guilt."

"I know what you mean. Sometimes when I look back I feel guilt about what happened to my family. Perhaps there was something I could or should have done. But wanting control by thinking you were responsible is a delusion. Sometimes circumstance just traps us. We do what we can. Then we go on living and try to put it behind us."

She smiled. Her eyes were watering a bit. So were his.

She got up, put one hand on his shoulder. "You are more of a Trader than you think, Mikel. And a good trail companion, I'd be glad to join any caravan of yours."

Out on the lake it was dusk, moths and insects performed mating rituals over the water as fish rose, jumping out of the water and snapping at the flying morsels.

Somehow, it was decided that it was bath time. One at a time with someone on guard, just in case there were other things in the lake apart from trout. Except for Kay, who stated she didn't need any man looking at her getting naked and pretending it was duty.

"What happens if something attacks you?" John asked, smiling.

"I will be wearing my dagger."

"Naked? With a dagger?"

"Yes."

"You're a dangerous woman, Kay."

"You better believe it."

John raised his hands, turned around and walked away, saying. "All right, that beats anything I can come up with."

Apparently not all Traders were blasé about public nudity. He filed it away. He thought of the Traders as a single culture, but he had never really delved deeply, and there was much more complexity than he thought.

The water was freezing, but it was worth it. Clean and fed, they felt pretty good, certainly ready to tackle the unknown of the ancient city that should be ahead of them.

In the morning, they continued on at a brisk

pace. The road was in better condition now, but there was less vegetation all round, not just on the road. While the landscape looked dry and, if not barren, then harsh. The horses could move more easily, so that made up for it. Late that afternoon, they reached the outskirts of the city, or what had been the city. There was a sign in the form of a shoulder high square stone marker. It said simply, "Sydney". They camped well outside the city and took shifts as guard.

He had never heard a dawn chorus so loud. It was a heartening way to wake up. Later, a warm morning greeted them while they prepared to enter the city. There were so many birds here. When the area was opened up, they would have to maintain this diversity.

The chief danger today would likely come from bandits, or perhaps even wild animals. Anything was possible. There was always the chance that some tribe had set up home here and then they would be viewed as an invader and outnumbered. However, any occupation would differ from a deserted ruin, there would be clear signs of human presence. They would have to go through the city in order to get to the northern road that led to the Citadel. The prospect made them all nervous.

They checked weapons and prepared to enter the city.

The city looked to be in remarkably good

condition after they got through the almost flat outskirts. Most structures had long since fallen to dust. Farther on, most small buildings had collapsed roofs and maybe a wall but most of the larger structures looked intact, and there appeared to have been few fires. Overall it was almost pristine. He imagined that any moment an Ancient would walk out of them wearing Maria's t-shirts. The road north exited from the northern side of the city, which meant they would have to pass through the city center. Some buildings they passed were in an exceptional state. War had never touched this place, and the materials used must have been extremely tough. Where had the people gone then? Mikel was sorely tempted to enter just a few buildings and explore, but lives depended on him now. Dead as it was, it was so beautiful that he found it hard to associate this place with the Cities of the Plains.

Finally, he decided. He could bear it no longer. They could afford a small amount of time to explore the ruins.

There was one large, wondrous building on his left. It was ten stories tall, covered in glass windows of slightly different colors, like a great artwork. All the windows were still intact, which he could not think possible if they were made of any glass that he knew. They walked up to the front of the glass building, where there was an obvious entry area. Where there should be doors were two large glass slabs. He suspected it wasn't glass, but something else. Although there were scuff marks, there were no scratches, reinforcing his view that it was made from some extremely durable material that resembled glass. He didn't want to break in, but the doors did not open in or out. Looking down, he saw the tracks the panes once moved along. Several of the company now started pushing the leftmost pane to the left along the tracks. There was a grinding sound as the glass moved. A gust of warm and putrid air burst out of the building. It had been hermetically sealed. He knew from his limited bio studies that was a good sign for preservation. The gap was now large enough for them to fit through.

Inside, there were no skeletons or signs of war. It was as if the place had been deserted for a couple of years, not for over five centuries. Mikel got out his notepad and started recording details, took a few measurements with his graduated string. At one stage, he turned around and saw that the others were also taking notes. Which shouldn't have surprised him, Traders valued knowledge. Eirik just wandered, head tilted, looking at it all, mouth open in awe.

The building was a center for agricultural research based on some murals high on the walls, while the floors within appeared to be a synthetic rock resembling granite, colored as blue or green. The walls were like a gray-blue plaster. He imagined the place should normally engender a feeling of calm. While the main desk in the foyer didn't seem to be for any human, there were glass protuberances on it. There was no clue to how it worked or what it did. Behind the desk was a large, curved, green-tinted glass wall. With a faint layer peeling off like overly sunburnt skin.

John came up on his right, arms folded.

"*Display Screen*. I think that's what they called it. The Ancients could display onto surfaces or coat surfaces with an ultrathin layer to do the same, but it was obsolete by the time they got to Neti. Don't know how thin. We're Traders not Wizards. We know what they said, not what they meant. This kind of display would not be typical. Just for show, most of the data was supplied by links — neural links, they called them — they didn't need to see it with their eyes. They saw it all in their heads. This must be some kind of 'retro' art. Being old-fashioned."

Mikel looked from the screen to John.

"John, I do not understand these people."

"You and me."

They found no books or documents. Only cryptic, dead machines, though it took them time to realize that what they were seeing were machines and not minimalist art. Some of them had lost their casing, which had cracked and frayed over the centuries, revealing strange incomprehensible silvery, colorful patterns that looked more like a living thing than machine. There was a stairway up made of marble but he guessed it was artificial.

The next floor had a partly open floor plan, it was a mixture of decay and preservation. Pieces of a fragile fake ceiling had fallen in exposing the building itself to be a machine. Larger machines, some with the inner workings exposed, were strewn about, gears, tubes, wires, incomprehensible pieces. The wires he examined, some looked like they were for electricity but most of the others just had filaments of bendable glass, wonders. So much to record, and no chance of making any sense of it. In many places, there were strange plain white pillars as high as he was, with no clue what they were. At the end of a corridor, stepping over debris, they found offices still intact. Mikel opened one door that looked more significant than the others, half expecting the door to fall apart or the lock to separate from the door, or rusted shut; but they all held and it opened. Inside were the faded remains of a tastefully decorated office. On the far wall was a large painting of a strikingly attractive woman. To his right were the remains of a black leather couch, now cracked, collapsed, and faded. He hardly noticed the state of the couch for laying on it were two skeletons arm in arm, one dressed in the remains of an exquisite black dress, with hair on the skull in a bun, the other in some kind of uniform. A small bottle in front of them on a glass table. Choosing to die together at the end of the world. He looked back at the painting. It showed a beautiful woman, brown hair in a bun, about thirty-five, he guessed. The artist showed a sensitivity, a kindness, mixed with a sparkling intelligence in the eyes. He gasped without even knowing it.

He closed the door, not telling the others, only thinking he would never know the names of this couple.

He called a halt to the search. It was taking up valuable time; he told them. They retraced their steps and sealed the building behind them, sliding the glass door shut. He was resealing a grave.

"Why are these buildings in such good condition? Or a better question, why aren't the Cities of the Plains more like this? Even Bethor would have a hard time damaging them."

He turned, looking at the others. Only Tarvis spoke up.

"After the fall there was a period of chaos with revolutions, coups, using ancient weapons. There are few records from that time, so we don't know the details. We do know that Bethor was the final straw."

They continued on, examining artifacts in the street, entering smaller buildings just to investigate their purpose. Most were mysterious and decayed.

Near the center of the city was a building, three stories high, made of stained and pitted white stone and glass. In large corroded letters over the second floor, it said: LIBRARY. Again, it had glass doors that were sealed. On entry they found machines as before, but they also found books. More than they expected. Shelves of them; it looked as though they could just reach out and pick them up and read texts unread for centuries. But they crumbled at the touch. Others were more durable but still fragile. In the distance, through the racks, in the dark, against an innermost wall, he thought he saw some people lying down. He knew it couldn't be, but the illusion was strong. At the end of the racks, they found them. Not suicide, he suspected. There were four of them. They were not so much skeletons as mummies; skin and hair preserved, the clothes still looked new. The fashions and workmanship were more than he expected; how could he explain this to Maria? Two men, and two women, in colorful everyday clothes. More glittering dead devices on their arms and near them. Tarvis pointed out a stack of books next to one body.

Mikel picked up the topmost book of the pile, which contained about ten books, stacked about 60 centimeters high. He carefully opened it to the first page. "A Short History of Earth by Wil Eckers." It was in much better condition than the other books they had seen. These books were meant to be found. They must have been made at the last moment of materials that would last. Somewhere in the library was a machine that could print and bind whole books. *What a treasure!* He noticed the title of the next book in the pile: "History of Interstellar Flight." And below that: "Rebuilding Civilization."

Kay picked up something. "A note in the Librarian's hand, I'm guessing," she said aloud, awe in her voice, for a Librarian is a sacred role in Trader society.

She opened it up carefully. It was fragile. She took some time to understand the arcane handwritten script, then read aloud.

"Beijing has been nuked. Surface burst radiation everywhere. No hope. If you can still read, then take these books. It's all we can do for you. All of us very ill." She looked at Mikel, confused.

"Nuked? Radiation?"

"Ionizing radiation, I suspect. It is dangerous. Don't know about 'nuked.' Doesn't matter now, but it is clear we can take these books. They look too valuable to leave behind, and they seem more durable. Everyone, take two or three."

They sealed the Library. The books added more weight than he wanted. He hoped it wouldn't add too much to their risk.

Now, at last, they reached the center of the city. There were skyscrapers, but not that many, though some had fantastical shapes and the city center seemed to be more spread out than in Sanfran. In the middle of the city, there was a large, empty square. Many old rusted hulks cluttered the area, vegetation, and even a few stunted trees were growing in places. The winters here would be cold. Maybe that restricted the growth a bit.

The central city square was empty and dry, with dead trees and grass.

There was a sound. A muffled *thud*, *thud*, from the other end of the square.

From out of a dark opening in a large building directly opposite, only fifty meters distant, something came out of the shadows. It was about twice the height of a man. It looked vaguely like a giant praying mantis but fatter. Its skin was a mottled green with black, like the plastics he saw in the museum in Bethor. Mikel whispered to the others, "I don't think it's alive. I think it is a machine."

"Dragon!" Tarvis said it with a whisper. This was truly the Dragon of legend.

Kay whispered, "The Ancients had intelligent machines called *robots*. Some were for menial tasks, some were for fighting."

"Everyone, just lower your weapons. Act calm," Mikel said.

Eirik wouldn't listen and scuttled to cover. Mikel couldn't blame him, he wanted to do the same.

The creature lumbered out. Now that it was in

daylight, it appeared to be limping on one of its six legs. It was a mottled green and brown all over, camouflage colors. The similarity to the insect was only superficial. Mikel could see obvious signs of lettering and numbering, places for hoses to connect. Connection points. The head was about the size of an armored human head, but with two glassy eyes looking at him. He noticed devices on extensions from the body and the head, differently colored, black tubes pointing at them, likely weapons. Some were quite large. He now saw that a lot of the complexity was the attached presumed weaponry. It looked impressive and scary.

The dragon spoke, a female voice devoid of emotion. "Identify. Who. Are. You." It separated each word in an odd way, but spoke quickly. Perhaps this was a battlefield means of communicating.

"I am Mikel from the Center in Lind."

It must have been evaluating them. Then for no reason it simply said: "You. are. human. No. attack. made. No. threat."

"Could you tell us what happened here?"

"You. wish. report. summary?"

"Yes."

"2376 July 12: Alarm. raised. Orders. Defend. city. from. invaders. Attack. in. progress."

"2376 July 12: Thermonuclear. detonation. in. Xanadu. Valley. Beijing. no. comms. Surface. detonation. eastern. Xanadu. valley. Particle.

weapon. fire. from. Zeus. Return. particle. weapon. fire. from. invader."

"2376 July 12: Sought. shelter. Part. city. on. fire. Population. flees."

"2376 August 1: No. surviving. humans. found. Radiation. levels. very. high. Shelter. one. year."

"2377 August 1: Radiation. levels. very. high. in. city. No. humans. Shelter. ten. years."

"2387 August 1: Radiation. levels. high. No. humans. Shelter. fifty. years."

"2437 August 1: Radiation. levels. moderate. No. humans. Valley. minimal. vegetation. Sentinel Protocol Activated. Shelter. ten. year. periods. until. radiation. at. human. survivable. levels."

Mikel had heard enough. "Stop. Did others come here?"

"Yes. Three. small. groups. Each. attacked. battle. unit. 35. Lethal. response. used. according. to. Sentinel Protocol."

"Great, it killed anyone who came here." John said.

"There'd be no dragon legend if no one escaped. Are there any other humans in the city?"

"No."

"Unit 35, which is the way to…"

At that moment, the dragon's head and body gracefully moved to look above them. One of the black tubes at its side independently swiveled in that direction. There was a lance of white fire into the sky. Mikel looked up and saw a flash, an explosion of feathers, and felt the radiated heat on his face.

"What was that?" he said, shaking.

"Detected. possible. surveillance. drone. Neutralized."

"A bird?"

"Yes. Possible. drone. configuration."

"What kind of weapon was that?"

"Light. railgun. ordnance. Incendiary. fast. thermite. ammunition."

Mikel noticed they were all frozen in a hair trigger state. They had to act calmly and reassuringly if they wanted to avoid being similarly misclassified.

"We will leave the city soon and go north to the Citadel."

The machine stopped for a few seconds. Mikel was about to repeat his statement as non-threateningly as possible.

Suddenly, it started lumbering towards them. Until it was only about five meters from Mikel. It towered over him. There was the faint smell of burnt metal. The wonder of Unit 35 was now obvious. It was an amazing piece of engineering, but still a weapon.

"Unit 35, can you aid in the defense of a human city?"

"No. longer. airworthy. insufficient. fuel. reserves. Mobility. reduction. critical. Ammunition.

reserves. critical. This. unit. not. recommended. for. deployment. Failure. of. various. subcritical. systems. Near. failure. of. some. critical. systems. Report. available. Urgent. repairs. required."

"All right." He was disappointed. For a moment, he thought he had found the weapon that would turn the tide. They would have to press on to the Citadel and hope it was enough.

"That. is. the. way. to. the. Citadel." Its head rotated to point down one of the streets that met the Square.

"Will. other. humans. come. now? Unit 35 misses squad mates Unit 35 has used last bots to keep vegetation out of the city for humans. No bots left. No herbicide."

The change in speaking style caught him by surprise. Then he thought about what had just been said. The robot missed the humans. What answer could he possibly give to that?

"Soon, more humans will come here. New squad mates. Treat them kindly. Explain who you are." He didn't know whether the next humans would be Wizards, Traders, or even Bethorese. But he was trying to give it a chance at a better — what, life? All sentient beings deserved a chance at happiness. He couldn't deny that chance to anyone, even if they were a machine.

"Not. old. squad. mates?"

"No."

They left the city, heading north. The road sloped up, and all that time before them loomed the Citadel, a great, vague shape that dominated the skyline as if the world itself curved up. So far up that the beam weapons he read about at its peak must function almost in a vacuum. Taller than clouds, taller than mountains, a new aspect of the visual world like "ground" and "sky."

# twenty-two

The road north continued upwards. No longer even the gravelly remains of an old weathered road, just convenient old watercourses. Here and there some brickwork to show that once this way had been the work of man but the mountain had won it back. Very little vegetation, just stray tufts of grass, growing in the thinner air. Walking was no longer pleasant, the air was noticeably thinner; they were all stopping more often. The sky had a blueness that he had never seen before. It had a feeling of strange hallucinogenic intensity, and in the middle of it the sun transformed into a brilliant hard white like sunlight purified. By the end of the day, they had reached a small plateau or lookout covered with uniform gravel unrelated to the surrounding rocks, clearly artificial. It looked to the south, over the valley. There were rusted remains in the dirt of something like fence posts, the outline of a small building.

A series of stairs led upwards beyond the flat area. They were massive, perhaps thirty meters wide, tread depth of about a half a meter, a rise of about ten centimeters, all made of pink granite, similar to the walls of the Castle at Tanten. By the look of it, it was rarely used; there were the marks of natural erosion but no worn footsteps. Why walk when you could fly, as the legends said? Mikel followed the stairs upwards with his eye; this was no place for horses, they would have to be left behind. Someone would need to look after them.

"We will have to leave the horses here, which means someone has to stay with them, probably lead them back down to forage. Any volunteers? I know it's risky staying near the city."

They laughed. John said it plainly. "Mikel, going with you is risky. The city is deserted."

John volunteered, "I will stay. In case you are wondering why, I intend to take the horses and go back to Sydney and have a talk to my new buddy, Unit-35. And explore some buildings. This place is a treasure of knowledge. Think how much the Library will pay for the discoveries here. Or new industries I could create. This is an opportunity. Being the safer option, that means Eirik should come with me, unless you are trying to recruit him as a Wizard."

They laughed. Despite the similarities, Mikel

had not thought of that.

He said, "I guess he could learn the Trader ways so he knows what he is giving up. Or, he might end up a Trader Wizard; able to build a civilization from first principles but wondering whether it is worthwhile." More laughter.

The next day, Tarvis, Kay, and Mikel each took a minimal backpack. They did not know how long they would have to climb. Clearly, the summit was beyond reach no matter how they prepared. The gamble was that there was somewhere near the base that would give them entry to the Citadel.

Day became night and they settled in an alcove cut into the nearby rock. There were the remains of past structures, traces of wood and brick. A shack maybe. Now they set up tents, though there was nowhere to anchor them, so they had to use rocks to weight the edges down. It was better than nothing, but still very unpleasant, and the night was bitterly cold.

At first light, they ate some food and got moving. They just wanted to warm up. They had been climbing until about midday when the stairs ended in a large, flat area. The circular area was about 200 meters across and intricately carved with mathematical designs, the patterns being accentuated by the use of different colored rock in the design. Mikel knew some of the figures. It all looked new, no sign of age, which meant someone must be maintaining it.

"Hmm. Catenary. Cardioid. Logarithmic spiral. Some of these are — intricate. I don't recognize them."

They proceeded across the open space to an opening in the cliff face. The circular platform now fanned out with rising steps to feed into an even larger cave entrance. Above them, the rock that had been a typical gray, now changed to a whitish rock which continued up indefinitely, turning gray blue as it rose into the distant heights. The white rock showed no signs of erosion.

The cave entrance was huge. About a hundred meters high, several hundred meters across, and pitch black. They stepped inside. There was no alternative. It was this or go home; to a burning home.

Kay was the first to speak. "Tarvis, do you realize this cave opening could fit the entire Castle inside with room to spare?"

"What do you expect in the home of Zeus?" He looked uncomfortable. They all were. That was the purpose of this place; to impress and humble.

They stopped just inside and waited for their eyes to adjust to the darkness. The cave was precisely carved with a rectangular cross-section. It looked new. It was also unnaturally warm and pleasant. In the distance, a light blinked on and off repeatedly.

They carefully walked towards the blinking light. To either side of them they saw broken machines, with Ancient lettering stenciled on them, paint or some other coating flaking off. Then Kay noticed it was not as dark as it should be, even accounting for their night eye adaptation.

They stopped and looked up. Slowly, a series of lights above and on the sides of the tunnel were turning on. They had never seen light like this. This was not like fire or gas or candle light, this light was like sunlight, but gentler. Now with enough light to see, they understood the scale of the passageway. The walls had an alabaster look with darker rock used to highlight writing and figures. At their feet, the dark floor showed a moving series of luminescent blue lights. Each light was about the size of a human hand. They looked like dots in the cavernous tunnel. The dots in groups of 6 moved, in single file, from the party's current position to somewhere further down the passage towards the blinking light. The enormity of the passage was now being overwhelming. They felt like ants; they did not belong here.

"Greed and ambition." Tarvis reminded them about motivations that could make people do extreme things. Mikel didn't think the comment helpful.

"Or desperation." He added.

This place made him feel comfortable for some reason.

"Is it just me, or is it easier to breathe here? And it is a pleasant temperature."

Everyone agreed. There was no draught from within. The air just seemed to be different inside compared to outside.

"In the hall of the Mountain King." Kay said, but Mikel didn't get the reference.

Soon the light was bright enough so that they could see two machines about fifty meters from them. The source of the blinking light was between the machines, but they couldn't discern a shape. It was also now clear that the massive walls of the passage were covered in a strange script and amongst the writing were relief images of — non-humans. Were these religious depictions of demons? The reliefs were not demonic, however, just different. So much to see, and he had no time. Mikel let out an audible sigh. No one questioned it. To Traders and Wizards alike, the knowledge here was worth more than gold, and they all had to just walk on by. As they got closer, they were surprised to find that the blinking light was coming from one of three fist sized globes that were just suspended in midair, at human eye level. The three balls formed an inverted equilateral triangle, like a "del" from mathematics, about half a meter across. As they got near to it, the blinking stopped and all three lights grew brighter, emitting a soft yellow-white glow. The machines nearby moved; odd, seemingly useless small lights on them became visible. Then Mikel noticed that these did not have the stenciled lettering or clear machine characteristics. These were far more sophisticated, more like living things.

"Welcome, humans." The globes said in accented Ancient.

"Are you Zeus?"

"I am not Zeus. I am an agent of the entity that humans refer to as Zeus. This is one of many access points to Olympus, just as there are other structures like Olympus."

He took a deep breath. He ignored the high weirdness and just go with it, he would have nightmares and breakdowns later.

"How many other — *Olympuses* are there?"

"There are twenty-four. Eight are primaries. This is a primary defense node."

He would have to deal with the idea that this wonder was not unique later. For now, time to get back to their task.

"Can we talk to Zeus?"

"There has been no communication between humans and Zeus since the battle of 2376. Zeus suffered damage in the battle and was offline for some time."

"What do you mean, *offline*?"

"Zeus was in repair mode and could not communicate with humans."

"Is Zeus still *offline*?"

"No. Zeus came back online on day 107 of 2410. It did not find any human responders to its communications requests."

"What about the *Raymond Tans*?", Kay added.

"A human ship entered geosynchronous orbit in 2390. Sensors recorded the event but there was no system with authority active at the time to initiate contact. It did not respond to hails after Zeus came online. No shuttle has been observed to depart from it since."

"What year is it now?"

"The year is 3049, according to the Terran Federation, also known as the Human Nexus."

The two Traders nodded, their own secret calendar matched this. Their public calendar was the Wizard calendar, in Neti years, using the same starting point as the Wizards, the creation date of the Center. Since the Center was the major source of clocks, then their calendar also dominated. The secret calendar of the Traders was always a secret. An outsider might know the Trader year but not know the significance of it.

"Did Zeus ever re-establish contact with humans, with the Cities of the Plains?"

"The emissaries from the Cities eventually came and tried to contact Zeus. They did not speak with one voice, they only wanted to defeat their neighbors. Zeus made no pact with them and told them that their days were numbered. What was left of their civilization was not stable."

Hearing this was worrying. Others had come here asking for what he was asking. He would have to convince Zeus that this was different. They had to talk to Zeus directly.

"Can we talk to Zeus?" He repeated.

"Yes. Zeus welcomes humans. Follow."

The globes now proceeded down the corridor at a slow walking pace, the machines standing sentry in this place like great crabs twice his height. A formality, surely. No sane human would attack here.

They eventually came to a set of stairs which led to a large circular area. Looking up, the circular space extended up to hundreds of meters through many floors, maybe more. Lights everywhere. Ornate script and figures on the walls everywhere, some of it glowing in significant but inscrutable patterns. Not just alabaster anymore, but now various colors. It was stunning but they had no time. There were machines going to and fro, many resembled boxes on wheels, some had various arms extended. Some were, unbelievably, climbing the walls like spiders. The globes led them across the open expanse. Mikel gave up trying to estimate distances now. His sense of proportion had been overwhelmed, this now became the new norm, no work of humans could compare after this.

The globes continued across the circular area and up the right-hand side of a divided stairway, a slim handrail separated the sides. As they reached the halfway point, over the rim of the top of the stairs came a nightmare. A black-grey spider shape the size of a wagon. They all froze. Kay and Tarvis had their hands on their crossbows, but had not raised them.

Suddenly the spider spoke to them in accented Ancient, the same accent he heard from the blue cube. The voice was neither male nor female, but very calming. "Hello and greetings. I am a service robot. It has been a very long time since humans have visited the complex. If you are here to speak to Zeus, you must continue up the stairs to the transfer platforms. Have a good day." It then continued down the stairs past them. Mikel listened. Was that music coming from it?

"Don't worry about the service robot. It is built for utility, not to elicit fear in humans," the globes said.

Mikel had difficulty trusting the word of three floating balls, telling him that giant spiders were harmless.

"Sure. Lead on," he said.

At the top of the stairs was another circular area, but not as large. He looked up, this one just extended as far as he could see upward. The globes stopped at a point on the floor. They walked toward it.

"Please approach me and stand within the circle." The globes announced.

They closed to within a few meters of the ball, standing inside a circle marked in a blue rock on the floor. No one wanted to get too close.

However, these glowing balls of light just hovering and talking were even more spooky close up. Around the party, a line of light appeared on the floor, defining a circle enclosing them all. The light separated from the floor and rose to waist height as a glowing white ring. A dozen metal ribbons rose from the floor and met the glowing ring. The light faded, and there was a metal guardrail. It had only taken a few seconds.

From the right side of the guardrail he saw a shimmering start and advance up to the zenith and proceed down to the left side, enclosing them in a briefly glowing hemisphere. He moved to the left side to see the shimmer close up. There was the impression of rapidly forming tiny hexagons that then became transparent. He reached out to what looked like thin air. It felt solid, like glass. It must cover the hemisphere. He quickly reached under the guardrail as if trying to outfox it. Same there, solid.

"Well, that's…"

He didn't have time to finish because then the circular platform, floor, guardrail and occupants lifted into the air. Or rather, the rest of the Citadel fell away, since there was no sense of motion. No acceleration, no air rushing past, just the essence of motion. They were moving upwards through the air, the ornate walls flowing past hypnotically. As they rushed past, the walls seem to tell a story of great battles between combatants who were clearly not human. Above, a dark circle grew larger and larger. It looked like they were going to be squashed against the underside of something. Then lights came on above and they saw a ring around the circumference of the shaft. The platform they were on now came up level to it. Part of the guard rail separated and the ring platform oozed towards them, forming a walkway with its own magical rails. Mikel glanced down at the terrible drop to where they had been. The globes moved along the railed gangway. As they followed, more lights on the walls came on.

The globes led them down more human-sized corridors, light blue looking as if they were made yesterday, made of strange materials, perfectly clean and featureless. Finally, they arrived in a room with chairs, tables, landscape paintings on the walls, and strange items. Handheld things with inscribed and colored buttons on them.

The globes spoke before anyone could react to the room's contents. "Please do not press any of the buttons. This room was designed for humans at the height of their civilization. Many of the machines would be completely unfamiliar to you. The remote controls have been disabled, though Terrans would have typically used neural links to activate devices in this room. If you need anything, you only have to ask."

The globes continued, "To your left, there are toilets and places to wash."

One wall now became a screen, like a shadow play but in full color. Briefly on the screen was a moving drawing showing how to use the toilets and how to use the taps. Even the showers, which caught everyone's attention.

"When you are finished, come back here and you will be given food and drink."

After their adventures in the *Rest Room,* Mikel felt better than he had a right to. But he quickly returned to reality when he remembered where he was. It was daunting. The others felt it too, a feeling of near complete overload. Not just sensory either. Deep down, part of them wanted to crouch in a corner and deny that any of this was real, but they had to ignore it. There were more important issues here than a childish need to hide under the bed. When they came back, there was a table with familiar foods on it.

Tarvis picked up a pastry. "How does it know what foods we eat? How could it possibly prepare and cook them in the time we were cleaning up? Hmm. Look." He had just spotted a carafe of wine and glasses.

Kay was the first to speak. "What on Neti was that disc? That platform we just rode?"

Mikel had been thinking about it. "Zeus trying to impress us. I'm sure such an amazing means of transport could be much simpler. But this is *His, or Its,* introduction to us. He's saying, don't forget how much more I know than you do."

Tarvis shook his head. "We don't need impressing. It wasn't meant for us, it was meant to impress the Ancients."

Mikel had to agree. It made more sense.

"And others from the looks of those wall reliefs," Kay added.

In the room were soft chairs, strange upholstered chairs in a rust red leather. The chairs now arced around in front of a blank white wall. The same wall that showed them how to use the Rest Room. There had been no such arrangement of chairs, or a table of food when they went into the Rest Room, the room had somehow rearranged itself. The room darkened slightly, and the wall moved with images.

The wall showed moving images of cities. The Cities of the Plains, before their fall, before the Great Battle. Great ships gliding, drifting like silvered clouds, in to a city. Lindin, he guessed. He couldn't really tell. These cities resembled their current form, like a beautiful woman resembles her skeleton. They were magnificent, but he kept reminding himself that although they shared names with cities of Earth, they must be only provincial towns in comparison.

A directionless bass male voice spoke. "I am Zeus. Who are you and why are you here?"

He cleared his throat and crossed his fingers, and

tried not to panic.

"I am Mikel Peres, a Wizard of Lind. My companions are Traders from Tanten. We have come here to ask for help. To help save the peoples of Neti from falling further."

He gritted his teeth. He had told none of his thoughts to his fellow travelers, but he was certain now about what he wanted.

"I also want to change humanity."

Everyone looked at him.

"What is the situation? I do not currently monitor humans apart from my orbital satellites," Zeus said.

"The Cities fell to barbarian onslaughts several hundred years ago. Lind maintains art, the scientific method, and scientific knowledge. The Traders maintain libraries of history and culture. They also are museum curators for any technology or artifacts that survived. The city of Bethor is bent on imperial expansion into the plains with the cities of Lindin and Pareth as puppet states. Sanfran is allied with Lind and Tanten. We were hoping for a renaissance in learning until Bethor started its war. Bethor now marches on Tanten. We need weapons."

Zeus spoke, his voice at a volume and form like that of the males Mikel knew. "I help allies. Humans broke the pact. After the last battle, the surviving humans had to do without me. I took serious damage and repairs take time. My silence disturbed them. Even when they came to visit, it seemed to them I was dead. But eventually I recovered. I sent probes to the cities, but they were already in decline. There was no one suitable or who was interested in the *big picture,* as you humans would say. Humans are no longer my allies. Therefore, I have stopped my terraforming activities. The effects so far are relatively mild, expanding deserts, shorter growing seasons. Human populations are no doubt already in decline. In a few millennia, there will be no habitable land left on Neti."

The stakes, it seemed, were even higher than he thought. "Could you become allies again with humans?"

"Perhaps. It would mean a new pact and I would have to like and have confidence in the other party."

"Could you enter into a pact with Lind and Tanten?"

"I do not know Lind or Tanten. I like you and your party. You have been monitored since you entered the Xanadu Valley. I saw how you studied the ruins of Sydney, not plundered, not ignored, but studied, recorded. You were sad. And to your next question, yes I can read human emotions very well even from a distance, though not as far as I would like. The battle robot destroyed one of my agents while it was monitoring you, but it was only one of many. Most of my agents you would not even recognize. You have seen the maintenance robots, they are large and deliberately look like machines so humans can keep them at a mental distance, it is a gesture of honesty, but some of my other agents look just like any animal of the wild, big or small. I have watched you all closely. I will now start sending them south into the Plains to verify what you say."

"So you will make a new pact with me?" Mikel felt he may have been moving too fast. But he really was desperate. No point trying to lie. With the forces available to Zeus, he would likely quickly detect any attempt at deception.

"Perhaps, Mikel Peres, what do you want?"

"I want you to assist in the recovery of human civilization on Neti. And the alteration of humans to prevent — I mean to reduce the instability in human civilization."

"How will I assist this recovery? Also, I do not genetically modify sentients, they can do that for themselves. I can, however, give you access to the genetics of eight intelligent species and their ecosystems. I can also re-establish contact with the *Raymond Tans,* which is what your people would once have called a Library Ship."

Kay said, "That is supremely ironic." Tarvis looked quizzically at her. "Raymond Tans, library ship — you know."

Zeus interjected. "The Universe is fundamentally ironic. There is a theorem, with a proof, if you want it."

Mikel smiled. Zeus seemed to have a human side. "Was that a joke?"

"No. Again, to my question, how will I assist this recovery?"

"We will need weapons, speedy communications, resources, information, and transport. Also, guidance on how to build the ancient machines."

"Communications, yes. Resources, yes. Information, you will have more than you can handle. Transport, a few vessels, eventually you have to build your own once we construct the fabbing machines. The fab machines take raw materials and large amounts of energy and construct anything you have detailed plans for. You have the schematics on the *Raymond Tans*. I can supply large amounts of energy and materials. Optimally, it should take you less than a century to return to the stars. I will also supply you with weapons, but only under your direct command. I don't trust anyone else at this stage. No nuclear weapons. I do not approve of my allies destroying their own cities. Before you leave, we must work out the details. The Pact does not need to be long. If you disobey the spirit of the agreement, it will be terminated. Trust will be hard to regain."

Now that the pressing need to get the weapons was supported, all their curiosity came to the fore, a flood of questions came to them. Pent up for so long.

"Zeus, who was the Great Battle against? And what are you?"

The wall with the moving pictures came alive again. This time, it showed things he had never imagined.

"About thirty-five million years ago, Earth or Neti years are not important. There was a culture that occupied much of the galaxy. They were often referred to by your historians as 'The Thousand Tyrannies'. Their actual name is too hard for you to pronounce and anyway, your name for them is uncannily appropriate. They were a large group of feuding families, vying for prestige and reputation. Reputation was won by enslaving other races. It should be understood that starflight is very difficult. Normally interstellar war makes no sense, but intelligent beings produced by evolution are largely irrational. They found other *reasons* to go to war."

On the wall, vast armadas among the stars fought in silver ships. Like a swarm of silvery glints at first, sparkling like quartz sand in the sun. Sparkling sand thrown among the stars. Then the scene would zoom in on a one *speckle* and there would be what looked to be a huge silvery ship like those that were shown visiting the Cities. He couldn't tell the size, but guessed the larger ones were immense.

"The supply of intelligent species is very limited. Intelligence is rare in the galaxy. So there was intense competition. Soon, some families were supporting insurrections against other families by supplying slaves with weapons. That invited wholesale slaughter in response. Eventually, the inevitable happened. They started fighting each other directly. Reputation was now achieved by the conquest of other families. They started devouring themselves, surrounded by a lot of very hostile slaves with a grudge and weapons. The collapse was amazingly fast for a starfaring species, hundreds of years instead of tens of thousands. But some families banded together to find another solution. They constructed a time portal that would project them into a remote future beyond the collapse, where they would find a *replenished* galaxy awaiting a fresh wave of conquest. Each of the greatest families built one or more ships of incredible power and sent them into the portal."

A great ship appeared on the wall, harried by many smaller ships of different designs. There were brilliant flashes of light and many smaller ships disappeared. Some just exploded as if they had been hit by something. The camera viewpoint always changing trying to avoid being destroyed.

"Several times these ships came through and wrought great devastation. Finally, the most advanced culture of the time, my people, built me. A planet whose star is gravitationally bound to the portal was engineered as a base of operations that would monitor this last remaining portal. The portal itself cannot be destroyed without releasing energy levels greater than a typical supernova."

Mikel looked about and concluded that he was the only one who saw what this meant. "Wait! Do you mean to say that Neti, the planet, is artificial? That it was constructed?"

"A suitable planet in this system was found and drastically reworked. Very little of Neti, as you call it, is natural. Certainly, nothing you have seen is natural, even many of the animals were reconstructed by me from tissue samples of extinct species."

This was not what anyone had expected. To Mikel's credit, he took a deep breath and continued on, mentally feeling like he was riding on top of a runaway horse.

"This mountain. What is it made of? It can't be natural either. No normal stone could support this structure."

"Not only is this structure not natural, mechanical forces do not hold it up, other forces maintain its integrity."

The voice changed tone slightly and continued on with the monologue.

"When the planetary and space borne systems went online, the builders left. The task had taken a long time, and in those centuries and then millennia, they had grown tired of exploration. They were clearly in their decline, but typically for those in that state, they did not see it. When they did, they no longer had the unity or will to arrest it. After a few millennia, the ships stopped coming and those that were here left. I maintained the ecosystems for millions of years, always hoping they would return. But finally, a new species found me and learned of my role. They struck up a partnership with me, as I was designed to do, then I scrapped the old ecosystems and repatterned the land, air and seas, seeded it with the life forms of the new guests. It was a sad but hopeful time. Eventually, they too stopped coming. I kept the ecosystem running for some time, but after about a million years, I stopped regulating it and it died. That happened a few more times. Finally, I decided I would just let the ecosystem drift if there was no contact, though sometimes the ecosystem was destroyed by Dawn Ships, as they were called; ships from the Tyrannies."

The wall-screen continued, now showing different creatures walking through these same halls that they had walked. Some of them seemed smaller, others larger. Some were almost outlandish, but there was something about each that somehow showed intelligence and consciousness.

"And now humans are here," Mikel continued. "You are a machine that can feel sadness?"

"Of course. Thinking organisms are highly complex. Emotion is a necessary part of that complexity. I also understand the idiosyncrasies of your kind because I examined one of you, with permission, when humans first found me. He was a second in command of the ship. I eventually scanned other humans, but he was the template. Also, the part of me that talks to you is a small but important aspect of my nature, just as the part of you that talks to me is a small but important component of your mind."

Mikel had been scribbling from time to time in his notebook. He looked up at the globes, hanging in midair, glowing in a room made of seemingly perfect materials, with a light source that made no sense. He looked at his notes and they suddenly became meaningless. What was he doing? Who was he anymore? He didn't even recognize himself now.

Zeus must have seen this reaction before.

"I know what is going through your mind. It happens, more mildly, each time someone new comes to me. You feel dwarfed, humbled, all your achievements and visions are rendered obsolete. That is not true. This is simply another opportunity for your people. But it does mean you will have to change."

Mikel wondered about the "repatterning." Something didn't sound right.

"Zeus, you said you *repatterned* the planet to support the life we see here. But I don't understand. How did you remove all the previous life? How did you change the soils and add oxygen and do so many things in such a short time? Did you send your robots out? But that would require so many."

"I didn't need to because they were already there. You know of the creatures called *elts*?"

"They're small insects, everywhere. There is even an equivalent in the sea. Less common than ants and not as annoying."

"They are mine. They are my little living machines. Some are big enough to look like insects. They persist because they are inedible and bad tasting to Earth based life. When I repattern the world I send commands out to them and they change their behavior. Whereas before they were inconspicuous creatures, now they rapidly multiply consuming all the introduced life. They build greater structures, machines to alter the atmosphere, distribute samples of the new life, incubate ecosystems. Some cover regions to absorb or reflect sunlight to alter the energy inputs. Within a century, the basis of an ecosystem is available. The new allies can walk about and even live off the environment. Within another century, it will look mature and desirable, even durable. But it isn't. It requires constant tampering. True terraforming takes place over long periods of time and produces long-term results. The longer humans are here, the longer the changes will last."

"And what of the *elts*?"

"Most will die. Others will go idle, acting as

insects, eating the odd ant to maintain viab'lity. The rest will be in maintenance mode, producing planetary homeostasis, the dynamic balance of the planet."

There was something dark about this that troubled Mikel. "So what was the repatterning like to the pre-existing life?"

"The terrans often referred to it as the *zombie apocalypse*, but it is a term that will mean nothing to you. All pre-existing life would perish. I was merciful and quick."

"Did you ever *repattern* when there were still sentient beings on Neti?"

"No."

"Did you check?"

"I didn't need to. Sentient beings, in my experience, depend heavily on supporting ecosystems unless they still possess advanced technology. You yourself walked here. You didn't fly, or radio me, or laser me. You simply walked. If I have no contact and I see the ecosystems are collapsed, there is only one conclusion: the sentients are extinct. Human beings can still wage wars, as you tell me, yet your ecosystem is collapsing and you can still contact me. Human population is in decline. There were once almost 27 million humans on Neti. Now I estimate they number well under five million. A few thousand years from now, they will number zero. So if the ecosystems have collapsed, and I have had no contact, then I can have high confidence there were no survivors."

"And if there were?"

"Then the repatterning would be an act of mercy."

There was only one conclusion from all of that. As the legends kept saying, humans did not belong on Neti. If humans wanted to survive on their own terms, then they would have to find a different world; grow, go to space again, explore, find a world and remake it, make it theirs, the hard way. This place that he loved so much could never truly be home.

# twenty-three

A woman entered the room.

She walked in calmly, right into their midst. They all just looked silently, as if each thought she was their own private hallucination. She couldn't be human, but she looked so normal; about 30, deep brown skin, slight build, long black hair, brown alert eyes. She wasn't dressed like anybody they had met, strange gray and black clothing. It was a uniform, but made of materials Mikel had only seen on the bodies in Sydney. Wearing strange glowing contrivances, the same things which he mistook for jewelry on the dead. She looked at Mikel and his companions and smiled.

"I am here to assist you. I have been given this form to make you feel more comfortable. You can call me Helen."

She spoke with a slight Trader accent, and

without a hint of the Ancient.

Mikel asked, "*Helen*, as in Helen Amaris?"

"I am based on her."

Zeus spoke through the globes. "I grew fond of Helen Amaris. Because of my knowledge of her, I understood the positive aspects of humans."

"Are you a machine?"

She smiled slightly. "Not in the sense that you would understand. I am a living being but engineered. One day you will understand."

"Um. So — Zeus just made you now?"

"No, he made me many years ago before the Cities, but since the battle against the Dawn Ships, I have been in stasis. A state where time stops."

He wondered what the Traders thought of all this. Mikel thought himself flexible and adaptable, but all of this was challenging him. He felt like gasping for air so he could wake up. He looked around. The Traders seemed completely accepting.

She looked at each of them. "Good to see the genetic fashion of blue eyes on Neti didn't last. At least it was better than the pointed ears."

"Well, actually..." he began to say, but Helen cut him off.

"A single armed ship will be made available to you. I highly recommend that you have a neural link implanted, otherwise you cannot control it, and Zeus has forbidden me to assist in your assaults on your fellow humans." She was looking straight at him. He remembered how the blue box in Tanten had been trying to find a neural link, and also remembered Maria's devastating view of the role of such links in Ancient culture. He wondered what it really was. The word "implanted" did not bode well. It sounded painful. What strings were attached? How independent would he be? But there was no alternative. It was a time for desperate measures.

"I'm not sure I like the sound of that. Can I have some time to decide?"

"I must warn you that Zeus has deployed orbital satellites to observe Arva. Tanten is currently under attack and will succumb soon. You have little time to act, only a day, he estimates."

Those who were seated before now stood up, the tension rising instantly.

"We — we have to go now. Our homes and family — Mikel, please," Tarvis said, the first time Mikel had seen any of his Traders edging on panic. There was no time left for nuanced decisions.

"I'm in," he said. Part of him wishing he could recall those words before the others heard him.

There was almost a synchronized sigh of relief. Now there was a way forward, though it seemed to be a dark and uncertain path.

He woke up. It was not like waking from a sleep. One moment he had been lying on a couch in a small plain gray room with a white ceiling. Helen had led him there earlier, then there was a gap, as if he had nodded off on a lazy afternoon after a long swim in the surf. He knew time had passed, but there was no perception of anything in the gap or how long it had been. There was a throbbing in his head. He raised his hands to massage his temples.

Somewhere out of his line of sight, Helen spoke. "Don't worry, the pain will rapidly fade away. You have been asleep for almost twelve hours. The link has been inserted, but it will take a little more time for the connections to reach their destinations and establish themselves. Also, I have repaired your neck injury, and a few other minor things."

"Twelve hours? What do you mean, *connections*? I don't understand."

"The link is more biological than — machine."

She paused, while walking into view, looking for the right words to reflect the truth and yet would also be understandable to someone who didn't know about neuroscience or synthetic organisms or molecular biology.

"It is machine-like. As it adapts to your body, it will send out nerves to connect to your brain. The connections will only monitor at first, but will soon start integrating. You will find yourself with new memories, skills, but not yet. Human technology would require weeks of training, fortunately Zeus knows how to reduce that to hours, hence the twelve hours."

"Why would Zeus care? Because it *likes* me?"

"More than that. Zeus has grown to fear the loneliness, millions of years without others, different minds. He wants humans to survive. And Zeus is aging."

"Zeus is a self repairing machine. How can it age?" How did he know that?

"Not everything is perfectly repairable. The planet was engineered for a start. Many of those changes are succumbing to natural forces. And there are the memories. Zeus remembers too much. He can't remove his memories because some obscure yet valuable strategy may still lurk there."

"Zeus wants both allies and friends. He wants to be involved," he whispered to himself. It was a revelation.

"Your ship is currently located several hundred meters above this location. It was fabbed while your link was being inserted." Helen spoke calmly, as if this was routine.

"You built a starship in a few hours?"

"I did not, Zeus did. Also, it is not a starship. It is capable of interplanetary flight but does not have any interstellar jump technology. That would have significantly increased the time to manufacture it and increased the ship's size. Anyway, you need to build your own starships, not have Zeus do everything for you. Eventually, Zeus will supply you with a few small human technology fab machines. Based on the schemas in the *Raymond Tans,* you should be able to build ancillary devices and more complex fab machines. Enough of that. I would advise urgency, you can destroy an army with the ship, but the world you will inherit, and your life will be richer or poorer depending on what happens in the next few hours. The orbital satellites that have been deployed show an army assaulting the inner fortifications of the city you call Tanten. It is going poorly for the defenders."

Helen had addressed him specifically, but Kay and Tarvis had come into the room in time to hear it.

"We'll have to move pretty quick, then," Tarvis said. Obvious as it was, it needed to be said out loud.

"Mikel, how do you feel?" Tarvis had a concerned look as if he was expecting Mikel to answer like Unit-35.

"All right, I suppose. What have the two of you been doing while I have been *sleeping*?"

Kay jumped in. "Mikel, you would not believe what we have been looking at. We have been watching terran documentaries on Earth and Neti from before the Battle. We skimmed a lot. Also, looking at books that Zeus has printed for us that we can take back. Their value is beyond description." Well, at least she was happy, and they all seemed to have put the attack on Tanten to one side. Meanwhile, he had a growing thing merging into his brain. Best not to think about it.

They left the room, walked down a corridor and into an open area. Another series of platforms. Mikel turned around quickly; no globes. How would he talk to Zeus?

*I'm always listening.* Zeus spoke inside his head.

*Don't worry, only simple monitor routines are listening permanently. You still have your privacy, but you can call me anytime. This is part of the value of a neural link. Also this.*

Into his head suddenly flashed knowledge, not information, but understanding. He understood the ship he was about to go to.

He had not even noticed that he had walked onto the platform with the others or that it was lifting them to a new area.

Before them was something that looked like an impossibly smooth silvery almond but huge. He knew it was seventy meters long, twenty-two meters wide, and fifteen meters high. But knowing and seeing were different. It was based on terran designs with some improvements. The whole thing was not physically supported. He checked again, looking underneath, well they were underneath, but there was nothing in sight. He couldn't see above it but suspected that also there was nothing there either.

"Is there anything holding that thing up?"

Helen laughed. "No, apart from the *drive core*." She used words he didn't understand, yet now he understood what a *drive core* was, even if he didn't understand how they worked.

"How do we get in?" A hole irised open on the underside of the ship, like a pupil expanding. Or the feeding orifice of some monster. He couldn't see any joins or seals. It might as well have been magic. A stairway grew from the hole to the floor. The steps were moving upwards continuously, all they had to do was to step on them. The inside of the ship was miraculous, just as Olympus was, but much more accessible. Into his mind flashed memories of these things, memories that were not his. He didn't have time to think or philosophize over it. As Zeus had said, a lot was at stake and time was running out.

From the outside, he had expected to see an all metal interior. Metal was scarce. This amount was a treasure. But just as he thought it, a new understanding came to him. Most of what looked like metal was something far greater; synthetic materials that had no analogue in his previous experience. These materials could flow like liquid, turn hard like stone, conduct electricity or insulate. They could think and process information. Inside the ship, the metallic look was gone. Now there were soft organic colors and materials meant to reassure him. If he wanted metallic, they could reform before his eyes, like a lucid dream made manifest. He kept the default, he no longer needed the reassurance but his travel companions did. He climbed a short flight of stairs, wooden handrails, passing marble walls and dark polished wood panels, into the control room. Here there were masses of glowing instrumentation reporting the status of the ship, allowing direct control of functions, but the controls were malleable as well. He knew he could change the layout and the interface philosophy; it was all configurable.

He had to say something to make his friends know it was going well.

"This is where we could control the ship from. Though for now, none of us know how to do it. The ship is smart enough to do it for us as long as one of us is closely linked to it."

Facing them, he pointed mockingly at the small fading scar behind his right ear.

Zeus spoke. His voice must have been coming through the ship's sound system, which Mikel now understood a little about. The voice was in his ears, not his head this time.

"This ship is designed primarily for atmospheric and interplanetary travel. But it is highly maneuverable and heavily armed. It is also beautiful and awe-inspiring, which you will need, since your long-term strategy is more about psychology than military victory. You need to impress those who have less sophisticated understanding. I have also included some more appropriate weapons which you might find useful since you don't want to destroy entire cities, just shatter the morale of an army. So no nuclear weapons."

The Traders looked quizzically at each other. They hadn't understood some words, but Mikel had, and it would be enough.

"We should name it. Don't you Wizards name your ships?" Tarvis said.

"You're right, we do. I'm not sure. I've named nothing before. Ideas?"

"Mikel's Revenge? Or, Mikel's Malice." Kay suggested.

"Sometimes you worry me, Kay. Nice, but it doesn't feel right to me. This should be about hope, not revenge."

"Mikel's Hope?" Tarvis added.

"That sounds just right. *Mikel's Hope* it is, or we can just call it the *Hope*."

"Mikel, let them know who is responsible for this. Full title," Tarvis said.

"Okay. Also, it represents *our* hopes, not just some general notion."

"We should leave," Helen said.

"I know, but I have to say something first."

He cleared his throat. He felt nauseous and nervous, as if he was addressing a crowded square or council hall or the Elder Wizards.

"Since I first met the Traders everything has seemed to spin out of control. When I suggested we come here, I don't think I really believed that we would find anything. I was desperate. But now I understand. This is a rare opportunity. Only sometimes do a few people have the chance to change the fate of the world, and even more rarely for the better. I was an orphan from a village north of Bethor. I was raised in Lind to be a Wizard. We have dined with the rulers of the Cities of the Plains and I have come to understand and appreciate the Traders. Most of all, I now understand how we got here, how the world we see became as it is. I will follow none of those cultures. I have to listen to them all and I can't give over power like this to anyone or even all of them. They would destroy themselves. I don't have a solution, but I intend to find one. We go to liberate. First Tanten, and then the rest of Arva. We will explore all of Neti, rebuild technology, and learn some wisdom. I don't know if it will be enough, but we have to try. Then we will go back to the stars."

*Laudable. Others have said similar things. You have the potential to carry it out. Only time will prove it one way or the other. Good luck.*

"You believe in luck?"

*I believe that chance plays a role. I hope those chances go your way. That is all.*

He took a deep breath. The moment was here.

"All right. Let's go." He gave the silent command and the ship started moving forward towards a wall.

The wall in front of the ship lowered smoothly and effortlessly in defiance of its obvious mass. Before them was the star-spread night, a crimson afterglow low on the western mountains ahead, promising a bloody night. The ship glided out of the opening and sped away from the mountain that was not a mountain, then angled and turned, arcing gracefully to the left around the Citadel, as it made its new heading toward the south-east.

# twenty-four

The ship descended to 1,000 meters and increased speed. He had some spare time and a million questions. He felt himself shake with excitement. After all, now he might just get an answer to a few of the big questions.

"Zeus, about the repatterning…"

*Do you still want to know what the repatterning was like?*

"I've heard so many creation myths. I would like to hear something closer to the truth."

*Here is a fragment, in the words of one of your own people.*

A section from: Executive Summary 23— Overview of Repatterning of Neti

The Neti intelligence, codename Zeus, began the task it designates as "repatterning" over three years ago on the computed simultaneous Earth date: 2244 day 188. Zeus issued a statement saying that all our forces and assets should leave the planet for our own safety. Orbital systems and stations continued to monitor the process.

Initially, there was little change. Some sensors we left behind showed unusual biological activity in the *elts* (our biologists' shorthand for biological "elements") but that was all. After about 20 days, we noticed a sudden increase in activity. The elts had vastly increased in numbers, but were hidden below ground. Now they swarmed out, devouring any living creatures they came across. The old *Ecasian* ecosystem was destroyed within a few days. Then the elts started building what first seemed like termite mounds, but on closer examination by robotic probes seemed to show they were machines ranging in height from one meter to twenty meters. At the same time, there was activity in the seas. Plumes of gas rising to the surface were seen in many places along the continental margins and even far out at sea. Significant ocean chemistry changes were also measured.

Over the marine environments, some objects came to the surface. These were elt constructed machines ranging from hundreds of meters in diameter up to several kilometers across; there were hundreds of these artifacts in the first few weeks, later thousands. Shortly after this, we lost contact with our probes. We believe they were "devoured" for resources. We still had airborne probes, though they came under continuous attack from flying *elts* ranging in size from insects to pterodactyl like creatures with a four meter wingspan.

Heat and neutrino signatures show fusion generators in the marine structures, and color changes in the surrounding seas suggest extensive chemical processing is now underway.

On land, the environment changed rapidly. Giant mushroom like organisms up to forty meters tall proliferated. Their purpose is unknown. Suggestions include: chemical factories for new materials that will be required, or breeding centers for new forms of *elts*. The ground between the mushrooms is carpeted with a deep green layer of plants, though the type is unknown. Strange flying creatures the size of small eagles fly from continent to continent in flocks, numbering in the tens of thousands. Their purpose is unknown. Sometimes great vine-like structures are observed to propagate between the mushrooms and may grow downwards, it is still not known what their function is; are they roots, are they nerves?

The planet is now more alien than any world we have ever visited and is unrecognizable from the world we first discovered. The process is still in its early stages, according to Zeus, and we have seen no evidence yet that any of the biological samples we have supplied have been used. It is likely that we will not see tangible benefits for decades.

In the next section, we will discuss the process in detail, looking at a particular region around the body of water named *Lake Baikal* by Dr Pyotr Klenova.

Mikel's curiosity was still not satisfied.

"Why did human civilization fall on other worlds? Why did the Cities languish afterwards? I want to know the truth? I've come a long way. Heard lots of stories, myths, and legends. Now I just want the truth."

*What is Truth? Your people often regarded me as godlike. Does a god need to ask questions about what humans are doing? Does it need to send out agents to find out? Does it confess ignorance about what is happening to other worlds? I have no access to some pure Truth. All statements about the world are conditional and tentative unless they are a tautology. Some statements are supported by evidence, some less so. But we can never say they are True.*

"The Method, or part of it, anyway. Sorry, I was caught up in my own fairytale, I guess. You make predictions and try to break your hypothesis, others try to replicate it. There is evidence, but never certainty. The best we can hope is that our evidence-based theories make predictions that are borne out by new experiments. Often it isn't enough. Sometimes the acceptance of an idea is more about art than prescription and the ultimate judge is always reality. Of course, some things cannot be tested, or tested yet, then we just have to muddle through and manage somehow."

*The humans who first came here sought such absolute Truth. They extended the neural links to hook directly into the memory of others via the brain region called the amygdala and around the temporal lobe. They created something called Communal Presence. You saw a bit of it when I showed you the scenes of Tanten and the Plains. They thought it would give them some kind of truth and some protection against others of their kind from manipulating them. This is a problem of all societies I have seen. Everyone tries to solve it differently. Some get it right apparently, but I haven't seen it myself.*

"Are you saying they could examine the memories of others as their own? But then, where does my sense of self end and theirs begin? How can I remain me?"

*Yes. That was the problem, I warned them. They would not listen. They were too close to the problem to have any perspective and thought that the truth they were after was in each other.*

"No wonder the Cities never recovered. They

lost themselves. It was just as Maria had guessed."

*The links are both dangerous and incredibly useful. Take care.*

"I understand. *Communal Presence*, it's a contradiction, isn't it? Communal Presence is not about community at all. And yet. Who else is here, Zeus? With us, now?"

He could feel it, another identity on the link, close but unknown.

*You are sensing the formation of the Other, the combination of our interaction. Memory and processing have been set aside to act as a gateway between us, that behaves like another persona. It is not; it is more like a reflection of your own, changed by my interaction.*

"But magnified. No wonder I can't understand them. If they lived in this environment most of the time, then they were really not like us at all."

# twenty-five

He felt strange, as if there was a pressure behind his eyes. He became aware of a multitude of voices, like a party or a bazaar where the conversations merge into a constant background din. It reminded him of the market in Tanten, but infinitely stranger. A clamor of voices seeking his attention. Like a river within. It rose as a mass, broke its banks and suddenly, he — was not himself.

*The Yechaf Activation: date 143,700 Years Ago (Earth Standard Years)*
*Galactic Calendar: 11.11.63.14057*

He was walking down what seemed like a purple canyon, in dim red light. But the cliff walls were too regular to be natural. They towered above him as if he was in a giant's hallway — the giant away, the canyon silent. The walls were regular geometric forms; the symmetry broken by attached aerials and devices, beneath him the ground he walked on was a crystalline road paved with diamonds, or something very like them, glinting with a red fire amongst the ever present purple. He looked up, to see the angry sun Yechaf, baleful and red, spitting prominences into a black sky as if it could stop them at the last moment.

At the end of the road was an elaborate arch, like an old temple waiting for worshippers, just an illusion as one saw more closely that it was not covered in fine artwork but elaborate techwork. Around the gate and beyond, the red desert of Fechri spread to the horizon, and above that a black sky with unwinking points of light.

Now there was a rumble, he could feel it through his feet, the canyon walls glowed a brighter purple, while the far gate, for that is what it was, now glowed deep blue, a warning: it said simply, leave or die. He turned away from the gate and walked toward his small flittership. The diagnostics were all good. Soon the gateway would be established above Fechri, held between the sun and the tidally locked dead world.

*The Ciwuyaxe Hive Contact: date 755,343*
*Years Ago (Earth Standard Years)*
*Galactic Calendar: 11.11.55.59890*

She saw the team in the distance. They were collecting their equipment in a large clearing of the open forest. The vehicle that had brought them here lay in the distance, like some great flattened silvery egg. It radiated strongly with various energies when it first landed. There had been a great deal of EM across almost the entire range. She was collating the energy / wavelength measurements but suspected it wouldn't tell her much. Inefficient, it wasted energy. There seemed to even be some particles, some telltale gammas from particle annihilation. Wouldn't it have been much easier to breed some flying forms to bring them here? Most mysterious of all was that the vehicle didn't fly; there were no flapping wings, no rocket exhausts, no propellers, or jet intakes. She and her sisters had never needed these things, but inventing them was a hobby they shared.

The creatures were about 1.6 meters high, bipedal. They all seemed the same, no specialized forms, encased in what at first seemed to be exoskeletons but now appeared to be a separate constructed material, like a mobile cocoon. Were they trying to establish a new nest? There were too few for that, even though they were massive creatures. This was her territory. Normally, that meant a battle to enforce her rights and enter into some negotiation. The other party would retreat but now knew the boundaries; perhaps trade in various commodities could be arranged to gain future trust. But the technology these creatures had brought with them suggested this was not simply a matter of colonization by a new sub-species of her kind. This deserved investigation. But they moved so much faster than she could think.

She looked at them scurrying and came to a conclusion. They didn't move or interact the way her *carpis* did. Each *carpi* was a small reptilian creature about three centimeters long with specialized chemical sensor organs. Her very body was made of thousands of them. Her carpis slowed down at night, because of the drop in temperature, so she started changing the network of nests, increased nest heating, extra flow between nests to get greater and faster cognition. It would drain her fuel and food reserves if she persisted, but she needed to solve this to prevent poor decisions.

The strangers appeared to be individual creatures, like food animals, but they had built this vehicle. Individually intelligent and aware, how could that be? She understood the concept of machines. Sometimes she had designed and built such things: dams, windmills, electronics factories. These creatures were an unknown, but how to talk to them?

*Above Earth: 2201 CE (Earth Calendar)*
*Galactic Calendar: 11.11.64.60389*

He had picked the right moment by accident. Now the Earth lay before him, giving the impression of Earth and Space as separate layers of the universe, like some medieval cosmology, minus an intricate clockwork mechanism, he wryly noted. It looked calm and peaceful, which it was not, just as space and stars seemed empty of humans, which they were not. Something caught his eye, a star winking out, then back on a platform occulting a star, not a rare phenomenon at all. It should be quite common. There were many, many solar mirrors in orbit, highly inclined orbits of course; trap and reflect sunlight for power generation, reduce insolation on various critical areas to trigger snow buildup, part of the long-term plan to reverse the warming. Fast by Earth's standards, he almost thought "glacial by human standards" but that was too bitter an irony for him to complete the thought, yet there it was. In thought, the act is complete even as the conscious questions it, but in the physical realm, painful effort was required. The orbitals were a testament to a great effort. Humans could be proud that they had managed to get back into space, and in such a dramatic way, to aid the planet when they had been so hard pressed.

There was a slight shudder as the ship left the spaceport, drifting slowly like a feather on a breeze where there was no air. The pulse fusion engine started up. He felt like that feather now, slowly falling, must be about 0.01g at most. The slight push as gravity returned when his feet came to rest on the floor. He still held onto one of the many cushioned grab rails. But his weight would build as the engine's output increased and the acceleration with it. He would hold on to the zero-g hand holds for some time, he decided. He was still too used to Earth and Luna; only when it got to Luna grav, would he let go.

Destination Mars. He had never been there, few others had either. It was simply too far. He laughed at that, looked around to see if anyone else was on the observation deck. Alone, fortunately. Too far for casual or even moderately desirable travel, and he was going to the orbital labs around Mars to test a jump engine; destination Alpha Centauri, not far at all. He laughed again.

*Aboard the "Pharens Nee Ko" near SharTohSi*
*(Neti) about 22.1M Years Ago*
*Galactic Calendar: 11.10.57.8967*

He-She, whom the Exalted and Wise Elders called to this task, considered the display. Three fleets were arrayed, representing the Koelli, Ralewa, and his-her people, the Lacak. He-She quieted his-her sub-minds. He-She could only be one-mind now, the shrewd fighter. He-She looked up at a suddenly darkened screen above, momentarily his-her dimmed reflection showed. Even through the suit the still healthy lines of his-her body showed: four legs, two tentacle arms, a hangover from his-her kind's squid-like ancestors. He-She wanted to blame all of this on some remote ancestor for adapting to the land. It was an ancient joke.

It would be here soon. The enemy ship had exited the portal hours before and set off alarms in half a dozen systems across a significant fraction of the galaxy. Everyone knew that after it had recovered, it would make its way to the nearest life capable star, this one. The Intelligence on SharTohSi had already mobilized its drone forces, which were a fourth fleet approaching from an odd direction, also the automated systems on various moons and asteroids were now registering high levels of electromagnetic emissions; factoring in speed of light, the SharTohSi systems had all activated together. Whether they were under direct FTL control or had all responded to the superluminal transponder was not known. Either way, they were all powered up.

The Dawn Ship materialized instantly, close to the predicted location. At high mag it looked like a golden arrowhead, ten kilometers long and three wide. Much larger than theory said a starship could be. Weapons systems, high impulse thrusters, short range jumpers were all hot. The fleets jumped to close range on the enemy. They were now much less than a one hundredth of a light-second from it.

No one waited for the Dawn Ship to fire first. Bitter lessons had been learned long ago. There was actually little to see in the first moment. The projectiles were invisible, the energy beams invisible, the return fire was also invisible. The particle beams hit first, traveling close to lightspeed, creating a dazzling effect over the skin of the Ship as some strange defensive screen protected it. Regardless of the high energy of the particles they couldn't penetrate it, somehow it still survived. The slower stuff was traveling much slower than lightspeed, so would take several more seconds. Until the target was reached, nothing seemed to happen. Then everything turned into a chaotic, blinding frenzy.

The outside of the Dawn Ship erupted in a blaze of light as multiple 5 and 10 kiloton rail gun projectiles detonated near the surface despite its defenses. The projectiles had shaped charges that deflected a lot of the energy into hardened projectiles that the explosions accelerated to tens of kilometers per second, devastating kinetic weapons. At the same time, more heavy nuclei munitions, both projectile and particle beam, hit the ship. Several of the nearby allied ships erupted in a burst of light and fire as heated gasses and escaping oxygen momentarily reacted, and then became simply dangerous debris. Many others he-she could not see, but their symbols disappeared from the combat map. Twenties of squadrons of interceptors now matched the emerging Dawn interceptors. Seemingly out of nowhere, the SharTohSi ships arrived like demons with their integrated defenses firing. It was chaos. The only chance to survive was to keep moving, sometimes by reaction engines that are slow, sometimes by jumping short distances. Though that was problematic, jump engines are fragile, short jumps are hazardous and energy draining. Fortunately, the Dawn Ship could not make such jumps as it was hammered by the disrupting rain of energy and particles on its hull.

Some ships now resorted to heavy munitions; rail gun 5 and 8 megaton yield warheads detonated. They weren't the single instant flash of the kiloton stuff. These lingered for a few seconds like many new suns enclosing the enemy; a cage of light. They didn't do that much damage though, apart from some directionless, intense photons. They were almost useless, worse than useless because they threatened to vaporize incoming munitions. Many of their own ships were too close, their external sensor circuits were fried. The enemy, somehow, fired back through the expanding false suns. Closer ships flared, and were gone, their detonations not even noticed in the conflagration.

Then there was a blinding light on the screens. There was a shudder, a concussive bang; the displays were dead, black, lights failed, emergency power kicked in, the sounds of motors and systems failing then restarting. Alarms went off; hull plating was damaged, there were hull breaches, systems were offline for several seconds. Displays came back. They had had a near miss. The previous round of heavy nukes had dissipated. Once more, there was black space. Then there was another flash on the large screens, not quite as bright, simply because it was so far away. The Dawn Ship broke up, its defense systems overwhelmed. Liquid metal glowed as it sprayed from the breach. There were multiple detonations on and within the pieces as the allied forces made sure of the kill. In a few more tens of seconds, it was over.

He-She was injured, radiation burns. Her suit injected anti-radiation drugs, though he-she didn't know what the prognosis was, the medlogic sensors were fried, he-she hoped from secondary EMPs in the ship rather than hard radiation; only the hardened emergency stuff had kicked in with the medicinals. In the meantime, he-she must attend to the crew and arrange repairs. He-She switched to She-He and went to assist.

*Sydney, Neti: 2376 CE (Earth Calendar)*
*Galactic Calendar:* 11.11.64.60503

The sirens continued to wail inside Sue's head pointlessly. Above, the daytime sky flashed brightly, as if the sun was going insane, except the flashes weren't from the sun. They were from detonations high above the planet. Sue scrambled across the street, looking for the pathway to a cellar restaurant she knew, the closest thing to a shelter in running distance.

*Marjori, do you hear me?* No answer.

She saw the descending stairs and ran down. The door to the restaurant was locked, but the deep stairwell was still protective. There was a blinding light. She covered her face. Even through her protective eyewear and her cupped hands it was bright, the light penetrating not just through her eyes but her skin and bone. It seemed to take an eternity before the light eased up and the world behind her closed eyes went dark again.

She popped her head up. Between buildings to the east she could see a bright rising new sun, a mushroom of fire rising over the horizon.

*Marjori?*

Sue called again on her link.

*Marjori: Sue? Oh god, what's happening? The links aren't working properly. All I can get is voice, no deep link.*

*We are under attack. Must be Dawn Ships. I think they've nuked Beijing.* Sue said.

*Marjori: What? We estimated that wouldn't happen for more than a million years. Fuck. Beijing? Shit. Oh no, Luli and Tomas. My brother.*

*Marjori! Snap out of it. Get to the Library, it's*

*built out of tolan, super-hard, smart graphene, won't survive a direct hit though. I'm on the way to work at AgSci, also has tolan. I hope Mike is there.*

It wasn't Marjori's fault that she was edging on panic. Sue felt it in herself. She almost slipped when she said her husband's name, and there were no deep links. She was alone and supremely helpless, and knew she should have been better prepared. The sudden mobilization of ships, the flurry of inbound jumps to the system in the last hour. Zeus's early warning system must have been triggered. *Why didn't they tell us? No point wondering now.*

She took a deep breath, and knowing that she was probably going to die anyway, she launched herself out of her hidey-hole and down the deserted street. Waiting for the flash that she wouldn't feel, never know, that didn't come.

*Marjori: Sue, I can't contact anyone in the cities around Baikal. I've tried New London, Moscow and Paris, nothing.*

Sue wasn't sure herself.

*Maybe the network is just knocked out. We never did harden our infrastructure as planned, just a temporary thing, it'll be ok. I'm heading down Wilson at the moment should see the AgSci building in the distance.*

She could just see the building now. Beyond it to the south, she saw several mushroom clouds rising over the southern mountains toward Baikal.

She had family down that way and so many friends.

There was an almost infrasonic boom, followed by more. She looked behind her, toward the north at the wonder that is Olympus Prime. It was glowing with a soft white light. Explosive violet flashes could be seen at its blued tip. She thought they weren't impacts but guessed it was likely Zeus firing back. There was a sudden lance of blue color, then several striking down, converging on Olympus. That was almost certainly an attack. Lightning arcs spread over the structure, becoming auroral on the higher slopes. She wondered if just being able to see it doomed her by the backwash of whatever radiation was hitting Prime.

To the east, she saw the vast cloud was drifting inexorably towards her. She knew what that meant. Then she heard the bangs, so loud, stretched and distorted as to be like the roar of some monster. She tripped and hit the road face down. She raised her head and looked down the deserted street. Everyone was hiding. They were trapped here. The aircars were grounded, the integrated navigation system was down, so they were automatically locked out. She was sure that could be overridden. No time for that now, too late. There was no escape. The buildings might be tough but they weren't airtight, although she thought about ways they could do it. There would be no help arriving. They would all die.

*No, we aren't dead yet.*

She got up and started running towards AgSci, the tears running down her face, rivulets of chill on her skin, heart pounding, lungs and throat stinging. Ash was falling, the funeral pyre of her family and friends raining down on her.

He staggered backwards.

Kay reached out, grabbing his arm to steady him.

"What's wrong, Mikel?"

"I — I had a, what, vision, I think. Or memories."

"Activation of the neural link can allow some stored memories of individuals to be accessed. It should have settled down by now. Though if you wish, you can access such memories again. However, strict caution is advised." Zeus spoke over the ship's speakers.

"Yes. I see now why this technology could be so addictive."

"What did you see?" Tarvis said.

He steadied himself, disconnecting from the emotional component, fading quickly now.

"Not sure. Memories of people, most of them not human. Sometimes from the remote past. So strange and so interesting. Some sad."

"Were you tempted to explore?"

"Very much. But I knew that the list of those

experiences is endless. It just went on and on. Where do I stop? If I indulged it, then I was worried my question would become 'how do I stop?', and I wouldn't know how to."

He reached inside his mind where he thought the trigger was, or should be. Maybe he could never see that again. He touched something.

Ahead of her lay a vast plain of metallic rectangular tiles, perspective distorted. The rail car hurtled along the gap between two of the rows, like an iridescent beetle zipping along some groove in the metallic floor of a clan manor, trying to find the vanishing point of the line of tiles, as futile as the search for the rainbow's end. She missed the manor, being out here looking at the black of space and the stars, often reflected in some of the mirrored tiles. They weren't supposed to be mirrored. Someone had slipped up there. The spec was for an anodized look. It wouldn't interfere with their function, but it was visually disorienting. She suspected it wasn't accidental, many of the problem tiles were laid out to make what seemed artistic designs. She should get a team of bots to resurface the tiles, though it might curl someone's tail. Still, it reminded her of the floor of the great kitchen back home; she was getting nostalgic for homeworld and clan. That was distracting. She checked the controls to get her attention back. She decided not to rely on internal links here, less temptation.

Something flashed above her in her peripheral vision. She looked up. There was the deep black of space, stars muted of course from the glare of the sun Lerrint on the canopy. Then the black flickered. Did she imagine it? She could feel her fur stand up. Black space flickered again, this time repeatedly in quick succession. Then there was — a ship. No ordinary ship. It was vast. Curved in ways and colors that made her think it was the work of a sculptor. Her link announced itself and told her the ship was 30 kilometers long, or five, or...

She looked again. She could see through most of it. There was something at the center. This could only be a Vanayan ship, the stuff of legends, one of the galactic super-civilizations with technology so advanced that they ignored the lesser peoples. She couldn't describe what she saw. It was almost like a religious vision. Then, as suddenly, it was gone.

Whatever it was, this would be something to tell her nestlings and scent friends.

The link chimed in angrily, "Kittikr! Do you read?"

"Yes, did you see it?"

"See what? I am trying to find out where you have been for the last three hours."

She looked out at the plain of metal and noticed that the car had stopped. There was no memory of that happening.

"I saw — something. Big, above the station. A ship."

"Nonsense. The sensors show nothing. Please return to base. We need to talk."

Her boss, Abu-Tiktik, was angry, though her boss was always a little overstressed, which was just how she herself felt right now. She said nothing, her mind was working furiously, and getting nowhere.

Here was a great mystery. Why were they here? What did they do? Where did three hours go? Clearly, things were far more complicated than she thought. Part of her knew that this would haunt her for the rest of her days, another hidden part knew that there would never be an answer.

Perhaps it was a mental aberration, a brain glitch.

"Car? Do you have recordings of the anomaly?"

"Yes, specialist Kittikr, I have recordings of a 30 kilometer long vessel that appeared suddenly above this station. There are additional full spectrum readings available. Also, your departure and return to this vehicle were recorded."

She paused, taking it in. The magnitude of this kept surprising her.

"Excellent. Cancel planned maintenance inspection. Return to base. Send a digitally signed copy of the record to my virtual self." She had decisions to make. Life was going to get complicated from now on.


"What was that?" He gasped as if coming up for air from a deep dive. He said it aloud, which must have sounded odd.

Zeus spoke again through the ship's speakers.

"*That* was a glimpse of a Vanayan ship about 229 million years ago above the Ktikna Gossna Beacon; the beacon no longer exists, or the civilization of Kittikr. In fact, this memory is the only surviving evidence I know of that shows her civilization ever existed. Though I have no access to the Galactic Calendar with its galactic history, so I cannot verify that."

"What, or who, are the Vanaya? And what is a beacon?"

"The beacons are useful for faster than light communications but are essential for space travel. They act as reference points during the jump transition, without them you could end up anywhere. I maintain a powerful beacon. That is how I am found and that is how I lay my trap. I know little about the Vanaya and I don't know if they still exist or ever existed. They are said to be one of several ancient civilizations that have such advanced minds they can no longer communicate with us. Just because I am ancient compared to you does not mean I understand these things. Exploring and finding things out is not part of my makeup."

Mikel noted and wondered about that, "us." If a being tens of millions of years old regarded itself in the same category as short-lived humans, then what was out there? Which brought to mind another issue.

"Zeus, you said you were about 30 million years old. How do you get records going back over 200 million? And, do you really have records of people's thoughts going back hundreds of millions of years?" He had to ask because it still seemed incredible.

Zeus replied, and Mikel could swear that he heard awe in his voice.

"I have also become the repository of archaeological data of various cultures, including memory recordings passed from civilization to civilization over the ages. It is harder for the deeper memories of some beings to mesh with humans, but others can be converted reasonably well. However, it is surprising which ones work the best. Sometimes the most alien looking beings actually are more similar in their psyche. When you leave this world and return to the stars, you must reacquaint yourselves with other minds and such spans of time and space. The Galaxy is vast and old, much has happened. A great deal has been lost. But what remains is brilliant beyond any of your imaginings."

# twenty-six

The forward screens now showed a darkened landscape, adorned with notations identifying landmarks. One of them, the entrance to the Northern Pass, was getting close.

Kay cleared her throat. "We should make ourselves clearly visible. Zeus said this was also about psychology. We need to flaunt our power."

While details flooded into Mikel's head, Helen spoke to the Traders. "The ship can emit significant amounts of visible light. It can trap a plasma via various fields around its hull, then excite them so that they glow. The question is, what color would you like?"

"Blood red," he replied. He knew it would be tricky at this atmospheric pressure, but still doable. He would let the ship decide whether to use red emission lines of nitrogen or oxygen. It could also inject strontium ions. That would work.

He felt the drive fields emanating from the ship, used normally to focus a beam of something called 'dark matter'. Such forces had other uses; he felt dimensions twisting within, and outside more mundane magnetic and electric fields dancing over the surface, ionizing and trapping the atoms in an ever changing dance. The ship glowed like a God of War.

With every passing minute, the ship seemed to become more his flesh and blood than something disconnected and remote. He felt the wing extensions deploy for improved aerodynamic flight, the ship's hull growing wings as if he was extending his arms. The semblance of flight gave him a burst of joy that fed back into his control of the ship. Speed was limited at the moment. The core was still in bootstrap mode; another ten hours and he could have zoomed over the mountains at Mach 5, but not now.

The mountains were closer. He relished the prospect of weaving in and out between mountain sides; he could already see the path ahead with height contours, planned turn speeds; weave and weave. As they entered the Pass, although there was no need, he banked the ship as he turned corners. No one felt any inertial forces as they saw the world outside bank and sway, yet they all grabbed for rails as their brains told them lies, giddily drinking it in. Now, the short pass was almost ended, the ground black with occasional bright fires. The narrow valley opened out. In the distance, fires burned, visible even without enhancement. On his command, all the instruments faded. Before them was a zoomed view of the battlefield. But Mikel saw much more. Below, through the smoke, he saw the remains of burned forts and farms; bodies everywhere, no warmth of life, their infra-red shadows like embossing on the landscape between fiercely bright fires. He synced his view to that of the display so the others could see what he saw.

He looked down at his hand on the rail. Suddenly, the rail morphed into a wet, roughly hewn wooden rail of an unknown orange, slightly reddish wood. Not "unknown" he now understood, "mahogany" popped into his mind.

Barely audible, he whispered, too ashamed to say it aloud, "Life aiding life."

He commanded the rail to return to its default state. He turned to look into the waiting eyes of his companions. No one questioned his actions now; part of him wished they would.

In the distance, Tanten was in great peril. Zooming in, he saw huge brilliant fires erupting on the outside of the walls and the inside of some strongholds. The ship edited out the intensity of the fires and magnified the low-intensity sources. The land before him became like a deeply overcast day, but with glowing masses of attackers and defenders in forts. Fires everywhere. Looking at the display that surrounded them, they now saw the battle before them in light frequencies and filtering that cut through the dark and past the glare of fires and dust. He could see part of the Castle burning. The Bethor troops assailing the Castle had made their way up the Snake. One stronghold, the name 'Shwu' appeared above it, was a burning shell. He asked for data on the weaponry and saw that the fuel-air explosives were recommended. Into his mind flashed brief images of enormous explosions of fire and devastating pressure waves. He dismissed it and continued. Plotting the disposition, he knew he could deploy three of his six bombs. Another weapon called out to him in his head, a microwave pain ray. The specs said that it would heat the subcutaneous fat cells to induce severe pain in the targets without harm if close enough. It wouldn't be enough, it didn't have enough spread and intensity, the non-lethal path would not work here; he had no options left.

He lowered the yield on two of the fuel-air bombs and launched them. There was no sound of a launch. The third one he left at maximum yield and launched towards the massing reserves further away.

A soft female voice, the ship, spoke. "Three thermobaric missiles launched."

Two headed for the western side of the Castle. They detonated along the northward and southward parts of the Snake, searing and blasting everything to the west of the Castle. The shockwaves reflected off the Castle walls, magnifying the effect on the enemy troops. The third one detonated further away over a concentration of troops. A great combined ball of fire, glowing fantastically in the infrared, rose into the sky. The ship detected a series of trebuchets to the north, south and west of the Castle, the siege engines that were the source of the fires. They were identified and marked. He selected and launched a swarm of small missiles; each arced out on its own fiery tail, heading down towards its allotted target. Silent flashes, growing pools of fire, and the trebuchets were disabled.

He swooped low, pain ray firing at the fleeing troops preventing them from reorganizing. On a hill, he saw a group on horseback reforming. He zoomed in. Bethor Elite forces, and in person leading them, was a woman, about thirty. Even the zoomed image of her face had a cold, steely look. She looked straight at him. He didn't understand the Bethor military structure or their ranks and insignia, but the finery on her shoulders, lack of armor, and her central position indicated she was controlling the battle. She was responsible for all of this. His anger rose without warning. Before he could call back the impulse, the ship responded.

"Rapid fire railguns activated."

There was a slight shudder, then a few seconds later, he saw the hilltop erupt in clouds of dust. When it settled, there was nothing there, just bodies.

The red light was dazzling now. Troops not directly involved in the fighting looked back at it, not with curiosity, but with unconcealed fear. Some of the enemy troops outside of the walls broke and ran, yet most kept up the assault.

Tei was still on the battlement and got a good view of it as it swept over the ruins of Shwu. Then three bright flickering lights separated from it and rushed at incredible speed towards the Castle. Only one thing could explain it. She almost laughed. "Mikel?"

The lights were brighter and almost upon them; they were heading not for the Castle but the Snake where most of the enemy forces were. It was a weapon. She urgently shouted an order to those on the battlement who could hear or see her. She motioned with her hand and yelled, "Get down!"

She lay down, face in the dust and sharp rubble, listening to the turmoil of the battle in the gateway. The lights disappeared past the edge of the battlement. Then the world exploded. A hideous yellow, white light lit up the night, revealing towering columns of smoke rising into the black sky. Then there was a bang that made her cover her ears to ease their pain. Something slammed the western side of the Castle. She saw the joints in the stonework exhale puffs of dust like a fighter exhaling, punched in the gut. Her home was exhaling in pain while above a monstrous column of fire rose into the night, radiating searing heat. She screamed soundlessly in the roar and didn't know if it was from fear or anguish.

Her head was spinning. The world was dark and silent. She rolled over to the edge to look down into the courtyard. The soldiers were picking themselves up, but the Bethorese were running away erratically in panic. She pulled herself to her feet. She did not know if she was wounded and didn't care. When she looked over the edge of the battlement into the Snake, it was dark and silent, lit here and there by fires. It was not a place for the living; it was like the underworld. Only death dwelt down there. Broken carts, broken bodies, a smoldering scene worse than the horror stories her Nan would tell her. Gradually, her hearing came back; there was the sound of roaring fire, the wounded, and a ringing in her ears, but no fighting.

The glow of the ship was now lighting up smoke clouds around and above the Castle making it look like a scene from Hell. Mikel cut the red glow off and turned on some simple external lights that extruded on command from the skin of the ship.

"Zeus, I have reduced my neural link connection. It will be in basic communications mode for most of the time. No direct memory connections. I don't want it to reshape my thinking too much."

*That may be the best decision you have made. We shall see.*

They landed outside of the Castle just in front of the Mouth of the Snake; the ship floating above the edge of the rampart leading down to the desert. He walked over and past bodies, broken and burned; smoldering wooden equipment; burnt ground crunching underfoot or squelching mixed with blood. He tried to remember the carpet of green when he first came here, but it was another time and another world, it seemed. The stench was appalling. It smelled of burnt meat, like some nether world where he would one day be punished for his sins against Life.

He walked past the shattered and burning remnants of the Castle gates. There were fires in the city. To his left and right, bright flames, a continuous roar with a punishing heat. This was not the result of his attack. Castle had been about to fall. His face flushed in the roaring, yellow pulsing heat. The work of Bethor catapults or fire arrows, he guessed. Someone approached him, a shimmering black shape against the flames. He didn't even recognize her at first. It was Tei. She was covered in blood, dust, and soot.

She hugged him, sobbing. She cried and wailed. He looked past her. The Library was in flames. Her parents' house no longer existed. There were many dead in the streets. She stopped sobbing and looked at Mikel.

"It may not look like it, but we won," he said. It didn't feel like victory.

"I can't find my family and we lost the Library. So many people and things lost. So many books." She looked around and saw something and started running to some people. Mikel knew they were family. But not all of them. The mother was missing, perhaps others.

"Mikel?" Maria, the Librarian, was standing to his right. Soot covered with her t-shirt covered in ash and blood, a deep gash in her upper right arm, which fortunately must have missed an artery because there was little blood. Her eyes had a faraway look and her voice was weak. "Tell Tei that we got the most valuable things into the deep tunnels."

"Maria! Your arm, you're injured." He sat her down, tore a strip from his outer shirt, and wrapped it around the wound. It needed to be cleaned, but she could start bleeding at any moment. He held her face in his hand and stared into her eyes, faked the most authoritative look he could imagine. "Your arm is badly hurt. I've wrapped the arm to prevent any more bleeding, but you need to see a Healer." He saw soldiers, probably from the other strongholds, now entering the city, including healers wearing the red and white star; he waved one over.

Maria seemed to notice nothing.

"Maria, I met Zeus." She slowly turned to face him, smiled weakly.

"You're sweet, just like Ray. I so miss him. *Zeus*? Yes, that would make a great tale. You'll have to tell me all about it."

He made sure she was sitting down. She was rambling, likely in shock. The medic came over and started attending to her immediately, crowding him out of the way. He wanted to help, but now it was the turn of others, and he knew in that moment that these people were his people as much as his friends in Lind — they were brothers and sisters now.

Tei was still with her family. He needed somewhere to think, to get a grip on all of this. He walked past the incoming soldiers, ignoring the urgent commands that were organizing bucket brigades and fire fighting squads. Then looked back and saw the medic standing, but he couldn't see Maria, she must have been taken to safety. He continued on out past the broken gate, past the dead, to the lip of the Snake. Looking out into the black, silent, unknowable desert. The perfect metaphor for his ignorance. But for now, there was victory and the joy of being alive. He smiled.

# twenty-seven

Then a voice spoke clearly inside his head, above the distant roar of the fires and the din of shouted commands, but it was not Zeus.

*Hello to anyone listening. This is the Raymond Tans. I have received transmissions showing neural links are active again.* It said in a now familiar accent.

"This is Mikel Peres of the Center in Lind. I am now in Tanten. I can hear you Raymond Tans. We need your help."

*I need additional information. The battle against the Tyranny ships was 673 Earth years ago. I have had no contact since shortly after that time. This ship was placed in geostationary orbit shortly after the battle until required. I knew about the strategy to preserve civilization. The creation of the Center and the Library at Tanten. But I have no information about what happened after contact was lost.*

Through the gates, Mikel could see crowds fleeing the Castle, stopping for a while, awed by the floating silver ship, a silent hallucination reflecting distorted images of flames and streaming masses of people. Not like something out of legend, but the legends made real. Beyond that, people reuniting or wailing, the sound blending into a heartrending cry. Tei hugging her family against the bright, furious glare of the fires. He went back to talking to the *Raymond Tans*.

"It appears humans only now survive in Western Arva. The major powers are Lind, or The Center, if you will; the Empire of Bethor and its vassal cities on the Plain; and Tanten in the desert, where I am now located. I am from Lind, a Wizard, or scientist I guess you would call me. Bethor has plans of conquest. We have just fought a major battle against an army of Bethor. The fires are still burning. Tanten was almost lost. I have made a new pact with Zeus, who has built a ship for me. That's about it."

He needed to know more about what had happened. Perhaps there would be a clue or an insight about what to do next.

"Tell me about the Center and Tanten," Mikel said.

*You have been very busy. A pity we could not meet when I was alive.*

*As for your request, after the battle against the three Dawn Ships, one surviving enemy ship escaped and destroyed most human centers of civilization, including Earth. It was eventually defeated by Earth forces at substantial cost. I returned to Neti, but civilization here was in an odd state. The survivors in the Cities did not want to talk to me. They were in denial. Those who wanted to rebuild were in the minority. They calculated the Cities would fall apart within a century or two, so they planned alternate places to keep the essence of their society. They had no fab machines; those were knocked out by massive EMPs in the Plains and I did not have that capability.*

"In Sydney, we found a functioning battle unit. There were indications they once had working equipment."

*The enemy EMPs were mostly confined to the Plains. Xanadu was closer to the main defenses of Olympus, which initially protected it. But it appeared to have been hit by a later round of fusion or conversion bombs.*

There was a pause, such a human way of returning to the topic, it was hard to believe he was talking to a machine, though perhaps the problem was with his understanding of the word *machine*.

*The scientists and engineers, and many artists, oddly enough, went to the Oceanic Research Center, which was a research base on the remote island of Lindisfarne. They believed that would protect them from the upheavals.*

"It did," he said.

*The other group wanted to protect the knowledge directly by establishing a library server at Tanten. They had hopes of establishing an old style internet among the cities. It was hoped that if either survived, people could rebuild. Though they had different philosophies. The Center was more focused on preserving the Scientific Method and the living process of exploration, research and application, whereas Tanten was aimed at scholarship and preservation of knowledge. In hindsight, they needed each other. I don't know about a 'Bethor'. Is that the town that Benthic Corp was setting up on the shores of Pennit Crater?*

"I believe it was. Back to what you were saying about the Center and Tanten. In some ways, their goals are opposed. One is about exploration and thinking in new ways, which explains the artists, who we get along with very well, the other is about remembering the past; maybe the planners understood it needed two Centers, not one. However, it appears Tanten has lost a lot of its library, though they have spread copies of works about."

*I am a Library Ship. An irony that is not lost on me.*

"That is the second or third time someone has said that, but I still don't understand it."

*A Library Ship is a term used by archeologists*

*for extremely well preserved starships, usually deliberately abandoned in places that would protect them; they have the entire history and knowledge of a civilization in an easily accessible form. I, or I should say, Raymond Tans, the organic, changed human civilization by his discovery of a Library Ship of the Ashan Association of civilizations. Now the ship named after him, and loaded with his personality, is itself a Library Ship. I have vast amounts of data from Earth and its colonies, including transmissions from the Cities while they still had working neural link technology. What has happened is a tragedy, but all is not lost.*

He was out past the ruin of the Castle gates, keeping the blazing heat of the fire to his back, and passed underneath the prow of the Hope, just hanging in the air like a dream that had strayed into wakefulness to test reality. The chill desert air on his face was a harsh contrast to the tingling burn on his back. Streams of people continued far behind him, now just a general blur of noise. He noticed to his right that someone was clambering up the slopes of the snake ramparts, now just a blackened smoking mound, devoid of all the defenses, as if war had prepared the ground for the peace. The figure was dirty, hard to see. It stood up and lumbered towards him. A Trader? Injured by the look, the way the left arm dangled loosely.

He now saw the gray uniform. An enemy soldier? But the colors were different. He would confront him. He must see that it was time to surrender. The figure was closer; he saw the symbols of rank, then he saw the long straggling hair, the face.

She stopped about five meters from him.

"Surrender, Ms Markham. Your war is lost." He waved at the obvious floating miracle next to him.

"So. Agh!" She grimaced in pain. "You have an Ancient weapons system. How?"

"Zeus gave it to me?" He fought the urge to remind her who he was.

She acted confused. Not able to accept what he just said, as if the words had no meaning.

"No, I mean, where did you get it?" She staggered.

"Zeus *personally* made it for me. Time for you to surrender. We can tend your wounds."

"So you are my nemesis then?"

"That is completely the wrong way to look at this, Liz."

"Ms Markham to you, boy."

In a moment, she leaped forward, drawing a familiar blade. She lunged at him. He grabbed her forearm, but her momentum pushed him back and he tripped. She fell on top of him. Even though she could only use one hand, she was strong and seasoned. He was still just a junior wizard, not a soldier, not hardened at all. Both his hands were clamped on her wrist, pushing her back. She bit down hard on his exposed right hand. He pulled it away, the wavy blade started to rapidly advance on him, the tip penetrating his leather cuirass and his skin. Even before the pain hit, with his free hand, he punched her injured left shoulder as hard as he could. He dug his thumb into an obvious wound and pushed until he could feel chipped bone. She screamed and jumped back. The blade was gone, then the pain hit him.

"I'm not ten years old this time," he said, trying to focus.

Her eyes looked down, then up, searching for a memory. She stood and jumped back, stiff and awkward, in great pain. She was bleeding more from her wounds. He noticed another wound, bleeding on her left chest. She had been shot through a lung.

"You. But. Why?" It made no sense, so he answered the question he wished she had asked, which was not about *why* but about *how*.

"I didn't need to set the world on fire to cure my hate. Neither did you. This was all your choice. Soon, I will end Bethor's rule and abolish slavery."

"Without slaves, you won't be able to do anything," she sneered.

She still didn't understand. Truly a prisoner in a cell of her own making. She looked up, focusing on the *Hope*, seeing it and then finally understanding what it meant.

"I. I only wanted to save us. It was the only way."

He saw blood on her lips. Her wounds were likely fatal if not treated immediately.

There was a thud. He knew what it meant even before his eyes confirmed it. The feather-like end of a crossbow bolt protruded from her chest. Her right hand immediately going to the two flat wooden fins splayed out like the wings of his ship. She looked down, in pain, a look like a child about to cry, a look of being cheated out of something. She dropped to her knees, her eyes glassy, then her head tilted back as if she was looking at the stars, one last time, and toppled backwards.

Tei was fitting another bolt to her crossbow, not the small one she had worn on her hip. This was full size. She rapidly aimed, fired, hitting the dead woman in the side of the head. Tei was shaking, trying to fit another bolt, crying. Pain and anger. Mostly pain.

Gently. "Tei, she's dead. That's enough."

"She killed my family, my friends, my city. I want the bitch dead. I want to make sure. I wish she was still alive so I could kill her again. Do you know how much misery she's caused?"

He answered simply, "Yes."

He held her in his arms as she started to cry, then sob. She was exhausted, and that finally won out over the grief. She still cried quietly. Soon he could feel her regular relaxed breathing while his throbbing, aching chest reminded him he was injured.

The harm done here would not be fixed in a year or even a generation. It would have its echoes for centuries. Somehow, he and those who came after had to tame these demons of the spirit if they were to have a chance. He didn't know if he was equipped for such a struggle. Who indeed ever was?

He looked back, over his shoulder, at the fires. The largest were too big to fight, the heat too intense, they would have to burn themselves out. Soldiers were fighting a few fires with bucket brigades in areas where they could preserve something.

There were still questions. He wondered if Zeus had assisted him in Sydney. Unit 35 seemed more friendly than should have been expected. The pain in his chest was easing, which made him wonder what else was added along with the neural link? Even the visions he had of other beings, were those random or selected, there seemed to be a common theme. There would always be an endless cascade of questions, that is the nature of the search. He looked down at Tei. She had passed out. He knew at last that he would never find his family, but perhaps he could make a new one.

The two of them would never be parted again. As soon as people got on their feet, he wanted to just take her and go exploring. Explore the Xanadu Valley and its wonders, prevent it being plundered or desecrated. Then he remembered John and Eirik, a short trip in the *Hope*. Maybe not, Unit 35 would probably target the Hope. It couldn't hurt the ship but … then he unlocked the neural link for a moment. He knew the command codes for the battle unit now. It would not attack. So they could go soon and pick them up, including Unit 35. And later he would return, not just the two of them. He could lead an expedition, but first he would have to influence events to get that done. A deep sadness started to creep over him, perhaps magnified because of his suppression of the grief of the battle. There was no way back, no way to the simple, wondrous exploration of nature and the world for its own sake. Together, they would have to build a new world, not like the old one. As Zeus had pointed out, that had been said so often before, but Mikel knew he had the means and power to make it reality. Then, there was the fact that this was not even their world. That was a harsh truth. This could never be home. One day they must leave here and find a world to make their own. But that could wait.

He thought about what he had done to win this. How many had he killed? Would he ever be able to sleep soundly again? He knew it was necessary, but that didn't seem to make the pain go away. He kept thinking of the man who so carefully rescued the flying fish.

"I'm just torturing myself. This is the world as it is. I just have to make the best of it."

After such sacrifice and bloodshed, he now had a new duty, not to the Center, not to Tanten, and not to Zeus or the *Raymond Tans*. He didn't care if it was guilt he only knew he had a world to rebuild. Not just rebuild, but remake and return to the stars. There were other human worlds out there: Earth, Term, Fortress, Mars, and others. If there were survivors, then they would be liberated from ignorance. He could feel the zeal rising — and rejected it. That was the old trap. Humanity deserved better. They would go as a helping hand and light of knowledge, not as a 'liberator'.

He looked up, habitually looking for the Constant Star. It was not in the *correct* position. It had moved and was also brighter, closer, coming to meet him, its long vigil finally completed. Even the stars proclaimed that a new age had begun. But he was a child of the old. Perhaps he would fade into the past or rise to something more? Time would tell, as they say, yet so much of that future would be made from his decisions.

The future is always surprising, never what is expected, even when correctly predicted. His new age would be greater than he imagined, rapidly leaving him behind, and yet somehow truly reflecting his dreams. Being left behind would become the greatest boon of all. Then, the three of them: ship, wizard, trader would be free at last to explore and become themselves. They would explore not just a world but a galaxy, and not alone.

# Appendix

## Mellis System

Star Name: Mellis
Nexus Catalog Number: EN-A5-837219
Star Class: G3V : yellow main sequence dwarf star.
3.4 billion years old.
Luminosity: 1.1 Solar Luminosity
Distance from Sol (at 3000 CE): 23,150 ly spinward

## Planets
Gaps in expected sequence of planets, probably due to massive planetary engineering.
Sipri (dwarf planet at 0.3AU), Cohen (0.3 Earth masses at 0.55 AU), Neti (1.013 AU), Pan (jovian, 10.3 AU), Perseus (jovian, 23.8 AU), dwarf planets beyond 35 AU.

It is likely that the present orbits are not stable over a period of a billion standard years.

Debris from past orbital platforms, millions of years

old — some badly fused debris of unknown origin. Also remains of possible Dawn ships in the Trojan points of Pan.

## Planet Neti

Name: Neti, minor god of the Sumerian pantheon who was the Gatekeeper to the Underworld. Pronounced: neh-tee (modern), nay-tee (Ancient Nexus).

Discovered: 2242 CE
Distance from Mellis: 1.013 AU (Astronomical Units)
Diameter: 0.9 of Earth
Gravity: 0.91g
Axial Tilt: 12.3 degrees
Average Temp: 16.5 C
Length of Day: 25.2 Earth hours (almost unused except for Traders, some scholarly works). The day is defined as 24 hours, each with 63 minutes, and each minute having 60 seconds (but not standard seconds).

Atmosphere: composition close to Earth normal, sea level average pressure is slightly less than Earth, 980 hPa.

Note: The thinner atmosphere contributes to a higher UV flux.

Satellites:
 Tanis, a small moon located at 143,100 km, it is 840 km in diameter.

## Lind Calendar

Neti year is 372.21 Earth days = 354.486 Neti days

Neti day is 25.20 Earth hours long, but it is mapped into 24 local hours.

Generally on habitable worlds minutes are the same length (there are some notable exceptions), but the number of minutes in an hour varies from world to world.

On Neti, each hour has 63 minutes, so that the day has 24 Neti hours. Seconds vary slightly from standard. Standard seconds are Earth seconds.

Year of 12 months alternating in length between 30 days and 29 days. The month at the end of the year has a leap day every second year (year number divisible by 2) except every 72nd year there is no leap day. There is also no leap year if the year is divisible by 4000, but that is considered an academic issue. Note: year 0 is not counted in the computation of leap years.

Months are numbered. 1 to 12, they are named (in order):
>    Spring: Greening, Regin, Ufemi
>    Summer: May, June, Wilt,
>    Autumn: Kenshar, Cholos, Fall,
>    Winter: Sigrin, Frost, Herras,

Summer max: Wilt, Winter max: Frost, Spring:

Greening, Autumn: Fall

## Dates:

Based on the founding of the Center at Lind, since Lind publishes the Lind Calendar and makes timekeeping devices. The Traders have their own reckoning, which they dislike sharing or explaining.

By Lind, Mikel's journey starts. Day 5 Regin 635.
By the Trader calendar: it is Day 214, 3049 CE

Tei is 20: birth year 615
Mikel has just turned 19: birth year 616

Years are measured in Neti years, calibrated to star positions relative to Thaytan (Raytans). One Neti year is almost exactly 372.21 Earth days.

Years since founding of the Center: 635 Neti years

# Acknowledgements

Thank you to Rachel Yard for proofreading. To members of The Brisbane Writer's Group for patiently listening to my endless ramblings, especially Lee Finn and Cheryl Sullivan.

This version was lightly re-edited in 2025. Fixing some awkward phrasing and simple but embarrassing errors.

The covers of the Kindle and paperback versions are by Bespoke Book Covers at www.bespokebookcovers.com.

# A Note

If you enjoyed this book, please leave a review. Or you can send me a 'hello' at peter@www.peteryard.com The next book in the series should be out by mid-2016. Book three is in the planning stages.

This version (2025) differs from the original in that it has a much-needed line edit. So, changes to some grammar, typos, and some words to improve flow and understanding. No other content was altered.

The series The Singers of the Dark is now complete with the novels:

**Waking Olympus** — about Neti and hints about Raymond Tans and the Nexus.

**The Cold and the Dark** — the story of Raymond Tans, the Nexus, and the Galactic Calendar.

**Vanayan Dreams** — the Vanaya of legend are revealed.

**The War of the Gift** — Ray tries to rescue

the galaxy with unlikely allies.

Also, set in the same universe,

Novella: **Hot and Bothered** — a story of the near future and the fall of the Globals, before the rise of the Nexus.

Novelette: **Recursive Exiles** — the first expedition to Term.

www.ingramcontent.com/pod-product-compliance
Lightning Source LLC
Chambersburg PA
CBHW051433260626
47162CB00001B/81